WITHDRAWN

WHERE ARMADILLOS GO TO DIE

ALSO BY JAMES HIME

Scared Money
The Night of the Dance

WHERE ARMADILLOS GO TO DIE

JAMES HIME

MINOTAUR BOOKS ✹ NEW YORK

This is a work of fiction. All of the characters, organizations, and events portrayed in this novel are either products of the author's imagination or are used fictitiously.

www.minotaurbooks.com

Library of Congress Cataloging-in-Publication Data

Hime, James L.
  Where armadillos go to die / James Hime.—1st ed.
    p. cm.
  ISBN 978-0-312-53486-8
  1. Police—Texas—Fiction. 2. Missing persons—Investigation—Fiction. 3. City and town life—Texas—Fiction. 4. Brenham (Tex.)—Fiction. I. Title.
  PS3608.I47W47 2009
  813'.6—dc22

          2009028471

First Edition: December 2009

10 9 8 7 6 5 4 3 2 1

For Matt, Don, and Gene, and in tribute to Bill's ingenuity, and his grit.
Fortes fortuna adiuvat.

ACKNOWLEDGMENTS

I would like to thank my agent, David Hale Smith, and my editor, Kelley Ragland. You guys both could have given up long ago. Why you didn't, Heaven only knows.

Thanks also to Madeira James (Web site designer to the mystery writing stars), Hershel Parker (the Dean of Melville scholars), and Joseph Stecher (savvy real estate investor) for reading and commenting on early drafts.

Finally, as always, my most profound thanks to Paulette, Travis, and Joshua for their love and support and in particular for mercifully modulating, where my writing is concerned, the Hime family predisposition toward the view that nothing is sacred, and that the price inevitably to be paid for taking anything too seriously is to see it tendered for use by everyone else as a punch line.

WHERE ARMADILLOS GO TO DIE

1

THE DEAL THEY'D MADE WAS, NO RABBIT VICTUALS OF A FRIDAY NIGHT.

A weekend furlough from the healthy eating his wife had committed them to was no small thing to Jeremiah Spur, retired Texas Ranger and perennially struggling cattle rancher. At the close of a full week of punching cattle on his ranch northwest of Brenham, Texas, the last thing he wanted to face was a dinner of fresh produce, baked fish, and soy derivatives. Since his wife's return from that rehab clinic back east, Martha had taken to serving the two of them food that was such a departure from the simple southern fare he'd grown up on it seemed somehow inauthentic. As though she were pretending they were Buddhists or Swedes or something else they weren't.

Some of it was simply too much to ask. Eggplant. Baby spinach. He wasn't eating that stuff, he didn't much care how many cartoon sailors swore by it.

That one Friday night he was behind the wheel of his pickup, headed to their favorite catfish restaurant, thinking how, since he'd given up cigarettes and never took to drinking with enthusiasm, fried foods were near about the closest thing he had to a vice and he aimed to cling to them.

Martha, bless her heart, had insisted they go out to eat even though he could tell she was feeling puny. She had a peaked look about her and was engaged in considerable pronounced swallowing. When he'd quizzed her about wouldn't she rather stay in, though, she'd said she'd be fine, just felt a little lightheaded was all. Jeremiah was tempted to say, a lack of solid food could do that to a person.

On the radio came that new song by Kyle something-or-other, that kid who hailed from over near Bryan—College Station. He sounded a little like a young George Strait, and his music was about pickup trucks and heartbreak and getting drunk and all. This particular song—well, it tended to put Jeremiah in mind of Washington County itself.

There's a place that I love
It's like Heaven above
Especially if you are a guy
A wide spot in the road
You can lay down your load
Where armadillos go to die

All the cobbler's homemade
Ain't no pink lemonade
And don't ask for no corned beef on rye
Lone Star is the beer
We go huntin' for deer
Where armadillos go to die

They come on stubby legs
Roll up like plated eggs
They meet their Maker in a ball
At the end the brave 'dillo
Don't need him no pillow
As he takes his leave of you all

Lord give me the grace
'Fore we meet face to face
Without so much as a sigh
My fate in Your hands
To accept like a man
Where armadillos go to die

Jeremiah could not help but marvel at such talent. Made him wonder if the kid wrote the words and the music both.

He pulled his pickup into the parking lot at Bourré, a name that had always struck him as peculiar. There was nothing much Cajun about Brenham, a town of some fifteen thousand souls an hour and a half northwest of Houston. So why name a local restaurant after a Cajun card game?

Jeremiah looked at his bride of long ago. "You're sure you're up for this?"

She nodded and fetched up a weak smile.

"You don't look too good."

"Fiddlesticks. I'll be fine."

The retreating sun had left the parking lot baking. They headed through it into the eatery, where they were greeted by the proprietor, a somewhat stooped man in his sixties named Sylvester Bradshaw who had the sense of humor, native charm, and sweetness of a crocodile. Sylvester's smile was rarer than a jogger's.

Tonight Sylvester was busy directing hostile looks at a party of African American patrons who had taken a table in one corner and seemed to be enjoying themselves immensely. Among them were kin of Tyrone Daniels, a local celebrity whose youngest son was tearing 'em up on the college football scene as the quarterback for the Texas A&M Aggies.

A waitress guided the Spurs to their table. Jeremiah set to studying the menu, even though he had it practically committed to memory. "I'm so hungry I could order the entire right side of this dadgum thing. What are you havin'?"

"The fish here is so good, I'm going to have them grill mine."

"Waste of a fine fillet, you ask me."

"I wonder why Sylvester has to be such a sourpuss all the time?"

"He's just that way. Backwards about everybody and everything. He'd complain if you hung him with a new rope."

"I hear he's as crazy as a mouse in a milk can."

"Some people around here claim he's pretty smart."

"He wouldn't be the first person ever there was who answered to both intelligent and cock-a-doodle-doo. Take a look at his face—it's like he's trying to pass a peach pit."

Jeremiah set the menu aside and glanced around the place. Most of the customers were people he knew from around town, including a couple he had locked horns with over the years. George Barnett and Joe Bob Cole sat across the room and pretended not to see the Spurs. Jeremiah was the principal reason George was engaged in the private practice of law instead of still district attorney of Washington County. The blood between them wasn't especially good and never would be. Jeremiah did his best to ignore them reciprocally.

One table over from the Spurs sat two young men who weren't from these parts. They wore oxford cloth shirts and tassel loafers and dress slacks and sport coats and had their hair cut junior executive style. They might have been two Young Republicans on their way to a seminar on the flat tax. They looked in the direction of the kitchen so often it was as though they were road agents waiting in ambush of someone carrying a cash box through that swinging door.

The Spurs' waitress took their order just as the African American party quit their table and headed outside. Sylvester stared them on their way dyspeptically.

The Spurs were halfway through their meal when Jeremiah looked up and saw Sylvester swaggering in their direction. Jeremiah supposed it must be something about all these people coming to his place and paying him money to eat his food that put that slow swing in the man's gait, like a freeholder lording it over his sharecroppers.

Sylvester dropped a hand on Jeremiah's shoulder. "How are y'all this evenin'?"

Jeremiah set his fork to one side. "I been worse. You?"

"Fine as frog hair. Why, Martha, you've barely touched your fish. Somethin' wrong with it?"

She shook her head. "It's delicious as always. I just don't have much appetite."

"She started feeling poorly on the way over here. I was fixin' to turn around and go home, but she wouldn't hear of it. She knows how much I look forward to your fish of a Friday night."

Jeremiah could see the man swell up at this. "It's all about the catfish, ain't it?"

"I don't know how you do it, Sylvester. I used to hate catfish. Tasted muddy half the time, but yours? Always terrific."

Sylvester half turned, as though to make sure the young men seated at the next table could hear what was coming next. "We got this special process, see. Cleans up the taste of catfish, but that ain't the half of what it can do."

"People always said you was smart as a tree full of owls."

"I owe it all to the grace of God." Jeremiah didn't know the restaurateur that well, but he had a nose for false modesty. If it were rhythm, Sylvester would have been Chubby Checker. "We a little busy just now, or I'd show you my invention. Of course"—he winked at the two

Young Republicans, who were listening to his every word—"I'd need to make you swear secrecy first."

He patted Jeremiah on the shoulder and strutted back to the cash register.

Jeremiah glanced over at the table where sat George and Joe Bob. George looked to be trying to make some point, talking to Joe Bob and tapping the tabletop with a blunt index finger. Contrary to all practice and character, Joe Bob seemed to be paying less than full attention. Instead he was frowning at Sylvester as the restaurant owner worked his way across the room. As though summoning up the nerve to register some complaint about his meal, which sat unfinished before him.

Jeremiah looked back at Martha and could see his wife was fading fast. He signaled for the check and pushed back his chair and helped Martha out of hers.

They stopped at the cash register, and Jeremiah reached for his wallet. "You go ahead and get comfortable in the truck," he said to Martha.

She swallowed and nodded and pushed through the door.

Jeremiah handed a twenty to Sylvester, who counted out change. Sylvester leaned in. "You got a second?"

"I really ought to get Martha home—"

"I just want to show you my invention. Won't take but a minute."

Jeremiah hesitated. Sylvester seemed the kind of person who took rejection poorly. He nodded and followed Sylvester to the kitchen.

The back of the place was active. There was help everywhere, at the stove frying fish and potatoes, at a big table in the middle chopping vegetables and breading fish, at a sink in back. Jeremiah recognized one young man, a big ol' boy with his scalp shaved clean, as one of Sylvester's sons. They swapped nods.

Sylvester led the way to a countertop where sat a device consisting of a white plastic drum that was being continuously turned, rotisserie style, by the rollers on which it rested. "Yonder it is."

"What's it doin'?"

"Cleanin' up the fish."

Through the side of the drum Jeremiah could just make out fillets being tumbled in some kind of liquid. "What's in the solution?"

"Water and a little organic acid. Enough to drop the pH well into the acidic range."

"Not a lot of point in asking how it works, I reckon, if you're naught but a layman."

"The deep science wouldn't mean much to someone other than a microbiologist."

"That's what I figgered." Jeremiah supposed he was meant to be impressed by all this, but what he really was, was ill at ease that he had left his ailing wife to sit alone in a stifling parking lot while he came back here to puzzle over peculiar kitchen equipment. "Well," he said, "I got to git. 'Preciate the demonstration."

Jeremiah quit the place after he and Sylvester shook hands and wished one another a good evening.

2

SYLVESTER BRADSHAW SAT COUNTING THE CONTENTS OF HIS CASH BOX and grousing to himself about the very folks who had paid him that bounty.

This chore he attended to alone. He kept the lights low and worked his way to the bottom of the cash box with his left hand while he labored at a ten-key with his right. His office was little better than a closet off the kitchen into which had been shoved a desk and a chair and a file cabinet. On one wall hung a calendar that had been some food service company's idea of a holiday season marketing ploy. When August ended last week that had not been enough to provoke anyone to turn the page.

The restaurant had been closed a good hour, and the staff, which consisted for the most part of the owner's two sons and some sadly used Hispanics, had cleaned up and left Sylvester to his sums.

He had white hair that was thinning in front and a face that owed its hue to the rage that burned more or less constantly inside him. He didn't much care for this world or those who peopled it, and while one part of his mind did the math the other part thought of the night's traffic in the most demeaning terms he could summon.

At the top of his list were the blacks. In the good old days he wouldn't have served them at all, but what could he do? It was the law.

They arrived in groups of ten or twelve every Friday night, rolling into his parking lot in enormous SUVs with EPA mileage ratings of seventy-one feet per gallon and tire rims made from platinum that spun to the beat of the rap music issuing from inside. They boiled into his restaurant like a home invasion, attired in suits the color of mustard, salmon, seafoam, coral. They sported broad-brimmed hats like those of comic-book villains, jewelry swung from their necks, and behind them trailed children with their hair done up in complicated beads and braids.

This crowd owed its spending money to a local celebrity, a retired professional football player who lived in a house big enough to hold an entire federal agency set back from the highway north of town. Sylvester took umbrage at its very gates, great wrought-iron devices that brought to mind European royalty instead of a man who couldn't spell dog if you spotted him the *d* and the *o* and who had set several career receiving records before retiring from the NFL to become an infomercial sensation, peddling home products to gullible consumers on cable television.

There was nothing about this darker trade that Sylvester liked, not even their money. It didn't matter to him that they ordered enough food to feed the entire area code and ran up his largest weekly tab by far. They weren't his kind, and he preferred to trade with his kind only. He would scowl them in and out of his place in hopes they would take the hint, but no, they kept coming back.

It was the catfish that brought them back. Everyone raved about the catfish.

Lately one or two of them had taken to stopping on their way out the door and asking him about his invention, as though it were any business of theirs, and that was beyond annoying. It was disturbing, on some level. He was pretty sure the only way they could have heard about it to begin with was, somebody had talked out of school.

Sylvester ground his teeth. He reached for his coffee, but his hand stopped in midair at a sound that did not belong out here at this hour when aside from the eighteen-wheelers engine-braking on the bypass and the occasional barking of a yard dog all was silence. He tried to think what the sound might be. It was quick and sharp, a door being slammed, or something being dropped onto a hardwood floor.

He opened a desk drawer and produced his wheelgun. He checked that it was loaded and slipped the safety off and laid it down next to the adding machine. Sat listening.

The central air whispered in the ventilation ducts. A faucet dripped languidly. The freezer on the far side of the kitchen hummed, and the icemaker made a clicking noise. The nocturnal orchestra of the restaurant kitchen, working its way through an improvised score.

Out on the bypass the light changed and a couple of eighteen-wheelers revved up, their engines a throaty gurgle. They Dopplered off into the night.

He sipped his coffee. Out here alone at night his mind was apt to play him tricks.

He bent once more to his work. He took a check in hand and entered the amount into the machine and was about to set it aside when the signature caught his eye. George Barnett. The former district attorney who had taken up the private practice of law. Time was when he all but ran this county, and there were some who would tell you he still did.

Here was yet another customer that hailed from a different segment of the local caste system than did Sylvester, what with their country club memberships and their Rotarianism and their trips into Houston for evenings of fine dining and road show musicals.

They were as aloof as Episcopalian bishops, and they made Sylvester's ass twitch.

The likes of George Barnett thought themselves too good for Bourré, and he wouldn't have had dinner here tonight on a bet if it hadn't been for that dust-up last year with Big Lettuce. Sylvester smirked at how he'd called up that Jew food scientist out in the Salinas Valley and told him what his lab studies proved about their product, their bagged salads and their commodity stuff as well.

Talk about bacterial contamination. If folks only knew.

That phone call had degenerated into a shouting match, and the next thing Sylvester knew George was calling him, threatening to law him on behalf of his new client, the Cranky Green Giant. Libel and slander and who knew what all.

Sylvester had responded with copies of the actual lab reports.

Their next conversation had a different tone. Seems George's California client wanted to know if they could learn more about Sylvester's invention, which had been the point of Sylvester calling them in the first place.

"You sure got their attention," George had said.

"They damn well better pay attention. They baggin' and sellin' a first-class public health crisis, is what they're doin'."

"They'd love for you to come out there. Talk to them about your research. Explain your invention. They'll pay your way."

"They fired that Jew PhD who was so rude to me?"

"Sylvester, look—"

"He called me a hillbilly, George."

"In the heat of the moment—"

"Hell, there ain't even any hills around here. How can I be a hill-billy?"

"I'm sure I can arrange an apology—"

"You arrange a firin' and then we'll see."

That had been nearly a year ago, and George was still at it. No wonder, since in the meantime there had been a half dozen outbreaks of food-borne illness linked to produce. Kids on dialysis, old folks dead. After every single one, George had called.

Was Sylvester sure he couldn't see his way clear to take a meeting in California?

Whatever Sylvester Bradshaw lacked in taste, savoir faire, and artistic sensibility he made up for in stubbornness. He was to stubbornness what General Patton was to tank warfare. Just ask his kids. They were always after him to do this with his invention, or that, or the other thing.

But it was the fruit of his own personal work and brains and sacrifice, and he wasn't going to do anything with it until he was good and ready, he didn't care if it harelipped his kids or George Barnett or the God of Produce himself.

George's check had a bigger number on it than usual, on account of tonight he showed up in the dubious company of his sidekick Joe Bob Cole, a massive man, former deputy sheriff, who worked over at the ice cream plant. Joe Bob had greasy black hair that hung in a face pitted with acne scars. He and Sylvester's two sons were notoriously crosswise, owing to their shared affinity for hard liquor and a tendency to want to settle every dispute, be it trivial or profound, with the thrown punch.

Surprised Sylvester some to find Joe Bob in his place, looking puffed up and sullen, but Joe Bob was known to carry water for George and so maybe had agreed to set his differences with Sylvester's family aside in order to join his patron for a meal.

He laid George's check on the stack with the others and finished his tabulation. He bound the money with a rubber band and turned to his left. On the floor sat a safe. He twisted the dial and swung the door open and set the money inside.

Beneath the cash rested a file folder. In that folder was the most valuable information in the world, scribbled down in his very own hand on sheets of lined paper. Secret information. Like the formula to Coca-Cola.

Information about what made his invention work, known only to him and his sons, who would never divulge it, if they ever hoped to rise above their circumstances.

He closed the door and gave the knob a sharp twist, and then he heard it again.

This time it sounded like a car door being slammed, but at this hour there was no legitimate reason for that.

He took his wheelgun in hand. He eased through the kitchen to the front of the place, where he stopped to let his eyes adjust to the gloom. Tables and chairs materialized from the darkness.

Over in that corner is where the two young men sat tonight, couldn't have looked more out of place if they had been wearing headgear common to the gods of Norse mythology. They ate their fish and french fries slowly and craned their necks every time the kitchen door opened and tried to look inside.

Sylvester made them for venture capitalists the moment they stepped in his restaurant, and this surmise they confirmed by leaving him their business cards on their way out and telling him they'd like to come by and visit with him about his invention.

He'd dropped the cards into a drawer with all the others.

Word was definitely getting around. Had been for some months now.

He stood listening. What little illumination there was fell through the window from a lone light on a pole in the parking lot. Dim though it was, it was sufficient.

There was someone there.

The figure of a man standing at the edge of the window.

Backlit as he was by the kitchen, Sylvester knew the man could see him. "Who's there?" he cried. His voice sounded thin and high-pitched.

The figure moved toward the door, casting his own faint shadow across the red-and-white checkered tables one by one. The shadow table-hopped slowly toward the front door and vanished.

The doorknob rattled, and the door swung inward.

Hadn't nobody thought to lock up?

The man stepped into the room, and Sylvester raised the pistol in a two-hand grip and cocked it. He was at the point of pulling the trigger when he stopped. He lowered the wheelgun and let the hammer down with his thumb.

"What in the world—"

A blow to the head from behind dropped Sylvester in a heap on the floor.

3

WHEN JEREMIAH FINALLY MADE IT TO HIS PICKUP HE FOUND HIS WIFE ON the passenger side, sitting with one hand on the door frame as if holding herself in. As if the feel of the door frame against her fingertips were the only thing keeping her from imploding.

Jeremiah's concern for her was such that he tested the speed limit on the way home. Directly he was turning off Highway 36 onto the county road and roaring up it in a great eruption of caliche dust. Martha sat as before, with her eyes closed and one hand resting on the door frame.

He pulled around back of their little ranch house and skidded to a halt. He leapt from the cab and hustled around to Martha's side. Helped her down and led her by the arm to the back gate, where they were greeted by Jake, their black Lab. The dog leapt about and sniffed Jeremiah's pants cuffs while he guided his wife through the back door.

Once inside the bedroom she sat on the bed and kicked off her pumps.

"You need any help?"

She held up one hand and shook her head.

"I'll be back to check on you directly."

Jeremiah proceeded into the kitchen, where he set coffee to dripping. He leaned against the counter with his arms crossed over his chest and listened to the coffeemaker.

He considered the man mirrored in the kitchen window. Blue-eyed, khaki clad, hair more salt than pepper by the day. Solid of jaw. Skin coppered from pursuing his livelihood under the Texas sun.

His career in law enforcement, his nearly thirty years of keeping the peace first in the highway patrol and then as a Texas Ranger, seemed that of another man anymore. About all he had left to show for it was a drawer full of keepsakes and a pension check.

His life had shrunk to a couple hundred dusty acres on which he kept cattle, three horses, a small vegetable patch that was mostly his wife's doing, and a stock tank from which he would pull the occasional fish.

Retirement was, in his view, overrated.

He hauled himself upright and returned to the bedroom, where he found Martha already tucked in with eyes closed. The light still burned in the ceiling.

He sat on the edge of the bed and brushed the gray curls out of his wife's face. She had been a beauty in her day, and traces of that beauty yet remained. Ever since she quit drinking a playful light had returned to her eyes. "You gon' be okay?"

"Feels like squirrels are chasing around in my stomach," she said with eyes closed.

He leaned down and kissed her forehead. "You get some sleep. See if you don't feel better come mornin'."

He hit the light switch and gently pulled the door to.

Back in the kitchen he helped himself to a cup of black and fetched a ranching magazine off the countertop. He took a seat in the family room and commenced to read.

His reading was interrupted by the sound of a door closing. He rose and walked to the bedroom and eased the door open a fraction. The bed was empty and the sheets thrown back. A strip of light shone under the bathroom door.

Jeremiah crossed the room and stood at the door listening. "Martha?"

No response.

He knocked softly.

"Gimme a minute." Her voice sounded strained.

To stand at the door listening felt like voyeurism. He took a seat at the foot of the bed with his hands resting palm down on his thighs and considered the possibilities. After what seemed a long time he heard the toilet flush and water running in the sink. The strip of light at floor level winked out, and the door swung open. Martha shuffled out with her shoulders slumped. She looked all but shapeless, as though formed from plastic extruded into a lumpy and asymmetric mold.

Jeremiah helped her back to bed. "You gon' be okay?"

She sighed. "Having been through that episode, I'd like to think so."

But her distress continued on, and when it became evident that she couldn't stop and further owned up to losing a disturbing quantity of blood Jeremiah helped her into her clothes and then walked her to his truck, where he seated her on the passenger side.

He climbed in behind the wheel and keyed the engine to life.

They drove through the night to the county hospital at speeds greater than what made good sense in a high-carriage vehicle.

4

AT THAT PRECISE MOMENT, SHERIFF'S DEPUTY BOBBY CROWNER WAS MANning a speed trap over on the bypass. His cruiser sat tucked in behind a stand of mesquite with easy access to the northbound lanes. He had his radar gun trained to the south, aimed at the crest of a hill that gave him further cover. He felt like a hunter in a deer blind, waiting for a buck with a Boone and Crockett rack to come trotting into view.

"Bobby? You there?"

He leaned forward and took up the mike and thumbed the button. "Can't think where else I'd be, Darlene." The way he pronounced it, "can't" rhymed with "ain't."

"You been thinkin' about what we talked about?"

Bobby's hand dropped to his side, and he looked off into the darkness. He couldn't believe she was bringing this up over the county twoway. He thumbed the mike. "It's a open network, Darlene. Lots of ears out there."

"Just the other deputies."

"And folks with scanners."

"You been thinkin' about it, or not?"

"Ain't gonna do it, Darlene."

"Come on, Bobby. You know the sheriff better than the rest of us."

"I don't know the man so well as to broach no subject of that nature."

"If I were him I'd like to know I was being talked about in such terms."

"I don't see there's a thing to be done if a man is being talked about behind his back 'cept leave it be and hope people lose interest." He released the button and sat listening. He could hear an engine in the distance, coming his way at a gallop. He thumbed the button once more. "Look, I got to go."

He replaced the mike and turned slightly to his left and adjusted the radar gun. The hill at which it was pointed was backlit by a rapidly accruing brightness.

The big SUV topped the rise, and the radar gun read 93 in red numerals on the back.

Bobby pulled the radar gun down and cranked the engine. He switched on flashers and headlights just in time to catch the white Hummer in his high beams as it raced past. He fired out of his hiding place like a bullet on wheels.

He pulled behind the Hummer and started to close the distance. The Hummer's brake lights flashed, and then a funny thing happened.

The Hummer started pulling away.

Bobby floored the Impala, pushing his two hundred horses to their limit. The speedometer needle shot to the right, and with his off hand he slid his window up so he could hear himself think. Once the cab was tight he took the two-way mike in hand.

He thumbed the button. "Darlene, this is Bobby."

"Come ahead on, Deputy Crowner."

"I am in pursuit of a white Hummer out here on the bypass. I need you to run some tags for me."

He read her the license plate number and replaced the handset. He already had a pretty fair notion what she'd turn up.

They were doing better than a hundred down a road that was blessedly empty save for the Hummer and him. Up ahead the Hummer took curves with an abandon that struck Bobby as a species of madness.

Around them all was darkness except what their high beams and the lightbar on Bobby's cruiser lit up, and traveling at that speed it was simply a fluke that it caught his eye for an instant, something white sailing out of a back window just as they rounded the last curve before the bypass cloverleafed back into the main highway. He made a mental note to add that to his report.

Littering would set this jackass back yet another couple hundred bucks.

The two-way squawked. "Yo, Bobby. Your Hummer is registered to Tyrone Daniels Enterprises."

"TD his own self."

"Probably one of the kids or hangers-on."

"He's got 'em both in abundance."

"He still runnin'?"

"Like a spotted-ass ape."

"You want backup? 'Nando is hanging out near the county line."

"Yeah. Send him this way, if you would."

Bobby took the wheel with both hands again. Big turn coming up.

The Hummer took the exit from the bypass going full tilt, and as Bobby watched the laws of the universe reasserted themselves. First the big white vehicle went up on two wheels, and then it lost its purchase on the tarmac entirely and was wheels over roof and then upright and then over on its back again in a roll that only ended when it slammed upside-down into a stand of scrub oaks.

Bobby pulled over to the side of the road and sat watching. No one emerged from the vehicle. He reached for the mike.

"Darlene, this peckerwood just spun out over at the cloverleaf. He's ass over elbows on the side of the road. You best better send out a couple ambulances."

"That's a roger."

Bobby hit the button in the armrest, and the window slid down. He sat watching for signs of life. Hard to see with it as dark as it was. Even at this remove the smell of marijuana smoke reached him.

He backed the cruiser up and spun the wheel to the left. He parked perpendicular to the highway with his headlights shining toward the wreckage. The air bags had deployed and obscured the occupants from better than a partial view.

In the distance sirens could be heard. The cavalry was en route.

He stepped out of his vehicle and approached the wreckage, hand resting on the butt of his sidearm.

5

KAREN BRADSHAW STEPPED OUT OF HER CAR INTO THE EMPTY PARKING lot and listened to the sirens crying in the distance. She couldn't help but wonder if they had anything to do with what brought her to her father's restaurant at this hour of the morning.

She had been dead to the world when the ringing of the phone fetched her back to consciousness. Her first thought was of trouble at the hospital, but then she saw her parents' phone number on the display. She snatched up the handset. "Hello."

"I'm sorry to call so late, baby."

Her mother was country in ways too numerous to count, but among them was this insistence on calling her "baby" even though she was in her early thirties and had a Doctor of Pharmacy. "What is it, Mama?"

"It's your dad."

"Is he ill?"

"He never come home from the restaurant. I just now realized it. I woke up alone and thought maybe he was asleep in his easy chair like he'll sometimes do. But I went in yonder and he ain't there. His car ain't here, neither."

"Maybe he fell asleep down at the restaurant."

"I called down there, but there wasn't no answer."

She knew better than to ask after her brothers, whether her mom had bothered to call them. It was Friday night, after all. They'd be passed out drunk in that converted hunting cabin they shared. "I'll get dressed and head over there."

"I hate to ask you to do that, but I don't know what else to do."

Now she stood in the parking lot and listened to the sirens calling and looked about. No sign of her father's ancient Lincoln Continental Mark V, a car so big and venerable it ought to ferry the King of Bacchus in the Mardi Gras parade. She walked to the front door and gave it a try. Locked up tight.

She peered through the windows at the front room with its assortment of tables and chairs that looked to have been salvaged from garage sales. Nothing seemed amiss. She wouldn't have seen the need to go inside even if she had a key, which she didn't. Sylvester had never entrusted her with one, since she had declined, as politely and respectfully as she knew how, his every effort to get her involved in the restaurant.

She had a career of her own, and it didn't matter to her if it was a family business. She was way past slinging fish and fries to the locals.

She walked around the building to the back. No Mark V. Just the faint reek of the Dumpsters and the low-to-the-ground movement of animal life. Her health care training brought to mind unbidden the myriad diseases rats host, and she shuddered and turned back to the front of the joint.

This is what comes of being the Good Kid. The one that can be counted on to be at home sleeping a sober sleep when the family crisis pops up at some ungodly hour. You get the call that sends you prowling the dark spaces where the rodents feed.

Maybe her dad had fallen asleep at the wheel and landed in a ditch between here and home.

She got back in her Honda and cranked the engine. She exited the parking lot headed south, following the bypass to where it intersected with 36 south of town.

Here was yet another reason to regret that love and marriage had eluded her. Would that when she got these calls in the middle of the night she had someone who loved her and cared for her enough to share this misery. In her twenties she had been single-minded about the business of her career and hadn't had the time or the patience for relationships. Men that age were all the wrong kind of work anyway.

Now that she was fully engaged in the workaday world, though, it seemed that all the eligible bachelors had disappeared into some vast emptiness, some cross between the Bermuda Triangle and the Federal Witness Protection Program, that no one had had the courtesy to warn her about in advance.

The sort of male she attracted was invariably one bearing a wedding ring, either on his finger or in his pocket, a ring that was still on active duty. Tying him to some woman who "didn't understand him," who withheld her love and affection.

If she'd agree to meet for dinner or a beer after work, he'd be only too happy to pour out his suffering heart to her.

She turned off the highway in Chappell Hill and followed a series of roads that became progressively narrower and less well paved until she pulled up in the yard of her parents' home. The place had once been a cotton farm, but her dad quit working the land when he started the restaurant a few years back. The original house had been added to over the years by her father and brothers, following theories from their own personal architectural school of the haphazard.

She emerged from the car and bent to scratch the heads of the dogs that came to greet her despite the hour. There was a light on in the front room, and by the time she gained the porch her mother was standing behind the screen door, backlit in a flowered houserobe.

"Hey, Mama."

"He wasn't there?"

"His car was gone. I decided I'd drive his route home to see if he'd had car trouble or something. No luck."

Karen followed her mother into the family room and picked up the telephone. She punched in a number.

"Washington County General Hospital. How may I direct your call?"

"Hey, Nancy. It's Karen."

"What are you doin', callin' up here this time of night?"

"Dad didn't come home after work."

"I'll put you through to the ER."

The emergency room nurse allowed they'd admitted a few folks that evening and were on standby for a few others thanks to a Hummer that had spun out north of town, but Sylvester Bradshaw was not among the sufferers present there tonight.

Karen hung up the phone and sat on the couch.

Her mother took an armchair. "You think we should call the sheriff?"

Karen shook her head. "Let's wait until morning. For all we know, he went to spend the night at the boys'."

"That's not somethin' he'd do, leastwise, not without callin' me first."

Karen agreed, but she didn't say so. She glanced at the clock on the hearth. A little past three. To be about at this hour—well, it was not typical of her father and his ways. Early to bed, early to rise, be in your favorite pew every Sunday morning for services, say grace before each and every meal. That was more his speed.

"Let's not assume the worst, okay? If he doesn't show up or call by dawn, I'll go back to the restaurant and have a look around. Then we can decide what to do."

They headed to bed.

As she slid between the sheets in her old bedroom, Karen wished she could be as calm as she had made herself sound.

6

JEREMIAH AND MARTHA FOLLOWED A YOUNG NURSE THROUGH THE TREAT-
ment area, Jeremiah supporting his wife like a lifeguard might support
an exhausted swimmer he'd rescued from the surf. The nurse led them
to an examining table that depended for its privacy on a curtain hanging by rings from rails affixed to the ceiling. Fluorescent lights hummed
overhead. Martha turned loose of Jeremiah and reclined on the table
while the nurse paid the curtain out its full length.

"The doctor should be here directly."

The time waiting they passed in tired and uneventful silence except
for the couple of occasions on which the distress in Martha's intestinal
tract sent her to the facilities with her husband's assistance.

From elsewhere in the room, they could hear others. An old man
complaining in a weakened voice. A mother speaking soothingly to a
child. An argument conducted in furious whispers. It was as though the
curtain that impeded their sight had served to sharpen their sense of
hearing, as happens with the blind.

Martha lay with her eyes closed, looking tired, old, and washed out.
Jeremiah sat in a chair by the examining table with his elbows on his
knees, turning his Stetson in his hands and trying to be tough-minded.
Lucinda Williams sang "Jackson" in his head, and he wanted a cigarette, but unfortunately he had had the good sense and discipline to
give the dadgum things up.

At length the doctor arrived with a different nurse at his side, a young
African American female who was all sympathetic efficiency and who
started taking the patient's vital signs.

The doctor was a short man, dark of skin, with the look of those
who hail from India and thereabouts. He spoke with a slight British accent and held himself as though standing for inspection.

He shook Jeremiah's hand and said his own name, which, from the looks of his name tag, appeared to have been formed by dumping the contents of a Scrabble game on a table and selecting fifteen or so letters at random.

"What seems to be the matter, then?" the doctor said.

Jeremiah swung his hat in Martha's direction. "My wife here has the diarrhea somethin' fierce. There's been a sight of blood."

Martha opened her eyes and groaned and laid her hand palm up on her forehead.

Jeremiah leaned in. "How you feelin', honey?"

She made no reply.

The doctor said, "Maybe you should take a seat in the waiting area."

Jeremiah patted his wife's arm and straightened up. "Fair enough."

The waiting room contained a half dozen folks, most of whom were asleep. A wall clock read 3:25.

Suspended on a platform in one corner was a television set. A movie was playing on a snowy screen. A man and a woman appeared to be on the verge of perpetrating a kiss before the viewing public. Jeremiah hoped there was nothing worse to follow.

One young man sat off to the side, reading a financial newspaper and sipping coffee from a foam cup. He had dark hair slicked back and wore wire-rimmed eyeglasses, and his britches were held up by a pair of red braces. His shirtsleeves were rolled halfway up his forearms. One loafer rested on the table in front of him.

"'Scuse me," Jeremiah said.

The young man lowered his newspaper. "Yes?"

"Where'd you find the coffee?"

"Around the corner there, but don't get your hopes up. They're not brewing Starbucks here."

When Jeremiah returned to the waiting room he sat a couple seats over from the young man. He sipped the coffee and grimaced. "You weren't kiddin'. I've drunk some bad coffee in my day, but this here would make a mule walk backwards."

"Told you." The young man held up a section of newspaper. "You interested?"

"No, thanks. I'll just sit here and enjoy my cup of hot mud."

"No interest in the capital markets, huh?"

"There's a story in there about the cattle market?"

"Not cattle. Cap-i-tal. As in money. Wall Street."

"Not interested enough so's you could tell it. You from New York?"

"What makes you think that?"

"I dunno. You got that look about you, I reckon. Like in that movie from a while back. Where the feller claimed greed is good."

"I look greedy?"

"You look like a Wall Street type, is all."

"We live down in Houston, my wife and our daughter and myself."

"How come you to be hanging out here in the middle of the night?"

"We were in town visiting my in-laws and tending to some business when my little girl got sick. Absolutely unstoppable case of bloody diarrhea."

"My wife's got the same symptoms."

"I'm sorry to hear that, but at the same time it's almost a relief."

"How come?"

"If there's some kind of stomach bug that's sending people to the emergency room in droves, it should make it that much easier to diagnose and treat." The young man leaned over and stuck out his hand. "Robert Bruni."

"Jeremiah Spur."

"You're from around here, then."

"Got a ranch, up near Burleson."

"How's the cattle business?"

"It ain't really a business. More like a way of goin' broke in slow motion."

"Why do you do it then?"

"It's what I was brought up to do. You can't escape your antecedents."

"Must be boring as hell. How do you stand it?"

"Fear of imminent bankruptcy keeps you interested. What line of work are you in?"

"I'm an attorney."

"I take it back. You do look greedy."

"Hey. At least I don't have the blood of innocent animals on my hands."

"You with a firm or what?"

"I went the big firm route out of law school. Didn't take long for me to get tired of the politics, and so I quit and hung out my own shingle."

"So what business do you have around here, if your law practice is down yonder?"

"I have a client or two in the area."

"Anybody I might know?"

"I'm not really supposed to discuss it. The Code of Professional Responsibility. You know how it is."

That struck Jeremiah as peculiar. He'd known plenty of lawyers who were only too willing to talk about their big deal clients. But he let it pass. None of his business anyway. "Fair enough. What kind of law do you do?"

"Whatever comes my way. A little trial work, a little corporate. I write a heckuva mean will."

"How old's your daughter?"

"She's four next month. What about you? Got any kids?"

"We had a daughter, too. Lost her to cancer, though."

The lawyer sat looking at Jeremiah.

"It was a while back," Jeremiah said.

The young man shrugged and went back to his paper.

Jeremiah was still nursing his coffee when the door opened and in came what appeared to be the entire Washington County Sheriff's Department, five deputies in total. They had in custody three young black men dressed in running suits sporting diamond studs and gold chains and with their hands cuffed behind their backs. Two of the prisoners had superficial facial wounds, and the third was walking with a limp.

All the deputies Jeremiah knew by name, but what commanded his attention was the tallest of their three prisoners. *This doesn't look good.*

The admitting nurse led them back into the deeper reaches of the emergency room.

Robert looked up from his paper. "What do you suppose that's all about?"

Jeremiah got to his feet. "If that doctor with the eye-chart name comes lookin' for me, tell him I'm in back with Bobby and them."

"Bobby and them?"

"Deputy Crowner and the others."

"This *is* a small town if you know the names of all the cops."

"It ain't that." He didn't stop to explain.

Jeremiah followed the voices until he came to an area set off by movable partitions. Outside it stood Bobby, talking on a cell phone. Behind the partition one of the young men was complaining that the handcuffs were hurting his wrists.

Bobby held up one finger as Jeremiah approached. "We're there now," he was saying to the other party. "When we're done here, we'll take 'em in and book 'em."

He listened and then said, "That's why I thought you oughta know, Sheriff. He'll get his phone call, but the question is whether someone oughta call over to his daddy's house and let 'em know. As a courtesy. Then there's the matter of the coach."

More listening. "Yes, sir. That's what I know. . . . Okay. That's a roger."

Bobby put the phone away. He stuck out a hand. "Hey, Cap'n Spur. How come you to be here in the middle of the night?"

"Martha's come down with somethin'. Was that Little Ty you all marched in here?"

"Him and a couple of his ne'er-do-well buddies."

"They been in a fight, or what?"

"Naw. I clocked 'em doin' better than ninety out on the bypass, and when I tried to pull 'em over Little Ty stuck his foot in the carburetor. He was drivin' one of Big Ty's Hummers, and when he took the exit off the bypass he rolled it. You ought to see what's left of that thing."

"So you're runnin' 'em in for speedin' and evadin' arrest. Which is a state jail felony, since he used a motor vehicle."

"And possession. They was smokin' dope. And for litterin'. They pitched somethin' out the window near that big curve before the interchange."

"You checked to see if Little Ty's driver's license has expired?"

"That's a good—"

"What that was, was a joke. Don't you think a litterin' citation might be pilin' it on just a bit?"

The deputy shrugged. "Somebody's got to relieve the taxpayers from the burden of payin' for all this fun. Might as well be Brenham's own rich retired superjock."

Back behind the partition voices were being raised.

"Yeah, well. That ain't nothin'. My ol' man gon' have my ass on a soda cracker when he sees that Hummer."

"It all fixable. Only takes money."

"Money we ain't got."

"Bullshit. All that bank yo' daddy got from the toaster people?"

"You don't know what the fuck you talkin' about. My daddy say, it somehow manage to go out faster than it come in."

One of the deputies told them to shut up, and they were silent once more.

Jeremiah nodded in that direction. "I expect he's right. When Big Ty hears about this he's gonna be measurin' Little Ty for a set of matched bruises and a busted lip."

"They're gonna want to keep it out of the papers, for sure."

"Them and Coach Ballard both. The Aggies kick off tonight at six o'clock, and if number eleven is sitting in a jail cell instead of taking the snap from center—well, that's a damned favorable way for Little Ty to lose his status as a Heisman contender. Coach and Big Ty and all the rest are gonna want Little Ty out of the juzgado right quick."

"How you figger that will sit with Dewey?"

"Dewey ain't their problem. It's our fire-breathin', headline-huntin' DA that they're gonna have to get past."

Bobby commenced to cracking his knuckles. "Ever since Sonya took that job? She's been on what you might call a tear."

"Word is she's got her eye on runnin' for something that will need substantial amounts of what folks call name ID. As in statewide name ID."

"Well, if she puts Texas A&M's starting quarterback and national championship hopes behind bars or manages to get him suspended, she'll have more name ID among that crowd than she can say grace over. They'll take that name ID right into the voting booth and do everything they can to elect the other guy with it."

"Might make her no never mind if she could lock up the tea-sipper vote," Jeremiah said, employing the dismissive phrase Aggie fans typically use when referring to the University of Texas Longhorns faithful.

"Don't you just hate it when somethin' no account like politics interferes with somethin' important like college football?"

Behind Jeremiah a voice said, "Mr. Spur?"

He turned around. The admitting nurse stood there in her white uniform with her left hand cupped in her right. "The doctor would like to speak with you, sir."

Jeremiah shook Bobby's hand. "Good luck with that mess in yonder."

Jeremiah found the doctor in conversation with his new lawyer friend. "Ah, there you are, my good man."

"How's our patient coming along, Doc?"

"She's a bit more stable. She has lost quite a lot of fluids, so we have her rehydrating intravenously. We've also started her on a course of antibiotics, just to be safe. I think we would be well advised to keep her overnight. Just like little Shelly." He nodded toward Robert.

"They both come down with the same thing, you reckon?"

"They suffer from the same symptoms, but I must confess, I find the identity of their malady a bit elusive. Perhaps once we have had a chance to run a few tests. In the event, we're about to transfer them to patient rooms. We'll let you know when we're done. Oh, and as luck would have it, your wife's personal physician just arrived."

Jeremiah said, "Doc Anderson?"

The doctor nodded. "He's with her now."

Jeremiah glanced at the wall clock. "Ain't it kinda early for him to be makin' his rounds?"

The doctor just shrugged. He shook their hands and quit their presence. They sat back down.

Robert said, "Looks like it's gonna be a long night."

"Gonna be? Hell. Already been."

"Yeah." The lawyer leaned back and closed his eyes.

Jeremiah took a seat and closed his eyes.

He thought briefly about what Little Ty had said about his family's money situation being tight but decided it couldn't possibly mean anything. Hell, everyone knew Big Ty had made so much money off his infomercials that the *banks* borrowed from *him*.

Them boys was still high, I'll bet. When they're high like that, there's no tellin' what they're apt to say.

He was asleep before the next thought could form itself in his head.

7

IT WAS STILL FULL DARK WHEN A LONE PICKUP HEADING NORTH ON 36 turned off the highway just across the Burleson County line onto an unpaved road running east. It proceeded to a gate, and there it stopped.

The driver took a bolt cutter from the floorboard. He got out of the pickup and walked around to the gate, which was held fast by a length of chain and a padlock. He cut a link in the chain, and it fell to the ground with a rattle.

He pushed the gate open and held it fast with a large rock.

The pickup rumbled over the cattle guard. A dirt road led to a small house that sat vaguely skylighted at the top of a hill. The driver veered off the road and went bouncing across the pasture. His headlights picked up jackrabbits that froze for a moment and then were gone in a couple of frantic leaps.

He crested a rise and headed down into a swale toward his objective, a smallish stock tank, just a few water acres, which sat out of sight of the highway.

He parked the pickup next to the tank and got out, and as he did so the moon emerged from behind a cloud. He let down the tailgate and climbed into the bed, where sat a number of small plastic coolers, the kind with a handle on top. He selected a cooler at random. He half turned and then slung the cooler into the air.

The cooler followed an arc that ended with a splash in the middle of the stock tank, where it sat floating for a few moments before disappearing beneath the surface. The water rings created on impact caught up the light from the moon.

When he had thus disposed of all such items, he was down to the last thing, something too heavy to chuck one-handed into the tank. This he dragged from the bed of the pickup and carried in both arms to the edge of the water. He heaved it as far as he could, and it landed with a great splash and disappeared instantly from sight.

The driver got back into his pickup and drove back through the gate. He got out and closed the gate behind him and draped the chain in place to hold it there, leaving the cut link as the only evidence of his trespass.

As he headed south on 36, the sky to the east was beginning to lighten.

Just then, on the other side of town, a sedan, one of the new hybrids, was also on the move. It left the county hospital parking lot headed south toward Chappell Hill. There it followed the same path Karen Bradshaw had followed a few hours earlier, and indeed it pulled right into the driveway at her parents' house.

The hybrid followed the driveway to the back, where it parked next to the barn. It was powered by its electric motor, all but silent. It didn't even fetch the dogs that slept beneath the porch.

The driver got out and hurried to the barn door, where he worked a combination lock until it fell away. He slid the door open and disappeared inside.

He came back out in a few minutes, holding a plastic ziplock bag. Inside the bag were several syringes, each with a protective plastic cap covering the needle.

He tucked the bag under his arm long enough to lock the barn door once again.

Then he got back in his vehicle and drove back the way he came.

8

LATER THAT MORNING THE SHERIFF OF WASHINGTON COUNTY WAS SITTING
in a booth by the front window at the Farm-to-Market Café sipping coffee and reading an offense report. When he had finished going through it for a second time he squared it up on the table before him and checked his watch.

Kickoff was just nine hours away. The North Texas Mean Green weren't expected to stay on the same field with the Aggies. 'Course, that was before the Ags' star quarterback got himself thrown in Dewey Sharpe's jail.

Lord, but ain't this a fine how do you do?

The sheriff looked at the town square and nursed his coffee and sat tapping the offense report with his index finger.

In the center of the square sat the newly constructed courthouse, a precast concrete structure devoid of all art and history. It seemed designed for the specific purpose of avoiding the fate of its predecessor, destroyed in an act of domestic terrorism a couple years back. The streets facing the courthouse were lined with small shops. Stores featuring antiques, apparel, fabric. A barbershop, a florist.

At this hour there was but one other establishment open, and it was doing a brisk trade in more young people driving more vehicles of Bavarian origin than Dewey would have thought possible here in Brenham. They appeared seemingly from nowhere to patronize this establishment with its low lighting, its cool jazz, its European-style seating on the sidewalk, its overpriced caffeinated beverages that went by Italian names.

The proprietress of the Café appeared at his table and refreshed his coffee and stood looking out the window with him.

"There oughta be a law," Dewey said.

Rose Emory shrugged. "I don't know. It's kind of nice how the place fetches all these young people to town early of a Saturday morning. Livens up the scene."

"You're not worried about the competition?"

"I'll worry about the competition when they start selling grande cups of chili that's as good as mine."

"Well, I don't care for it. The town square is no place for this fancy-pants joint."

"Can't stand in the way of progress, Sheriff. I would have thought you of all people would understand that."

"What's that supposed to mean?"

But by the time he could get the question out she had moved on to another table.

Has Rose heard 'em talkin' about me, too?

He hated to think she had, because if Rose had heard the rumors then like as not everyone in town had. Which meant every time someone saw him they were thinking—

God. Don't let them all be thinkin' that.

If only his wife hadn't shot her mouth off to her book club.

Dewey first realized that he might have become a topic of conversation around town week before last when he was out at the country club downing white whiskey and playing gin rummy with his old high school golf team buddies.

Figured that it would be Les who'd bring it up. "So, how are things at home, Woody? I mean, Dewey?" Les's eyes cut about, and his bulbous lips slipped into a grin that said he was up to some mischief. Barry and Stan examined their cards and chortled.

Dewey laid his cards facedown. "Okay. What's so fricking funny?"

Barry said, "Our wives came home from their book club the other night with some pretty durned interesting information is all."

Stan said, "Yeah. Seems like your wife is a walking advertorial for a miracle of modern medicine. Went on and on about it."

Les said, "Hard for an immoderately happy woman to contain herself, I reckon. Emphasis on 'hard.'"

Laughter made its rounds. Except for Dewey. He sat fuming.

For he knew it could only mean one thing. He picked his cards up and played on, hoping that, if ignored, the subject would disappear.

The troubles had started six months ago, when Dewey's doctor put him on blood pressure medication, which in turn began to interfere with his reproductive hydraulics.

He returned to his doctor with this new complaint and was rewarded with a prescription that fixed his problem and then some but that carried with it a certain stigma if you hailed from a culture that celebrated Lone Star beer–drinking, Red Man tobacco–chewing, Smith and Wesson gun–toting, John Wayne–idolizing manhood as much as Texas does.

And if this stigma attached itself to your ordinary civilians, it was triply applicable to a man who expected to be addressed as "Sheriff."

Whatever hopes he entertained about the subject being dropped disappeared about the third time he was addressed as the "mighty Swordsman" and the "High Sheriff of Deaf Stiff County," a play on Deaf Smith County way out in West Texas.

Where, Dewey was meant to understand, real men don't need drugs to get the job done.

Dewey had leaned in, the better to keep his remarks from being overheard.

"Listen, you peckerwoods—"

"I believe you would be the peckerwood, Dew."

More laughter.

"What you all don't understand is, it's a performance enhancer. It's to the bedroom what steroids is to the batter's box."

"Batter *up*."

Dewey said, "What I'm sayin' is, you can go for like a couple hours."

Stan said, "Yeah, well, my wife would be, like, go ahead and get started and call me when you're an hour and forty-five minutes into it."

By this time the laughter had become general throughout the locker room as others had picked up on the conversation at the card table. Dewey staged a strategic retreat to the urinals, but the damage was done and his afternoon ruined.

Since then Dewey's life had been a kind of hell. He found hidden meanings in every sideways look and chance remark. Seemingly innocent comments came freighted with sinister overtones.

Or maybe it was just his imagination.

Problem was, there was no way to know. He couldn't really go about town asking people what they had heard about him. The best he could do was ignore it and hope that with time it would stop coming up.

He looked out the window and watched as the district attorney emerged from the coffee shop on the corner and headed his way, their signature insulated paper cup in one hand and her briefcase in the other.

Sonya Nichols came through the front door and crossed the room and slid into the booth opposite Dewey. "Good morning, Sheriff."

"Mornin'."

She was young and good-looking and particularly well turned out for a country Saturday morning, with makeup carefully applied and brunette hair pulled back in a ponytail and dark blue skirt and matching jacket over a white blouse. She had a quick mind, no tolerance for idiocy in any form, and was in general about as subtle as a chain saw. Dewey could show you the scars.

He shuddered to think what she would make of these rumors that were going around. He couldn't help but wonder if they'd reached her ears.

"That the offense report?"

Dewey pushed it across the table. "Seems like if we was gonna meet here, you'd buy your coffee from Rose, instead of at that other joint."

"Rose doesn't have a cappuccino machine," Sonya said without taking her eyes from the paper.

"Wonder where they got the name."

"What name?"

"Of that fancy damn coffee chain."

"They named it after a sailor on the *Pequod*."

"Do what now?"

"The Pequod. Ahab's ship in *Moby-Dick*."

Why's she talking about Moby-Dick *for no apparent reason? Seems a little too close to that other subject to be a mere coincidence.*

"How come you to know that?"

"Because I am the product of a classical education from an actual university, whereas you, Sheriff, have an accounting degree from Texas A&M. Littering?" She looked up for the first time and reached for her paper cup.

"Don't mess with Texas."

"Sloganizing aside, it seems a bit excessive." She consulted her watch. "We've got time to check out the Hummer. Let's go."

Dewey dropped a couple bucks on the table and picked up the offense report and followed the DA out the door. He caught up with her on the courthouse lawn. "Texas A&M *is* a university, I'll have you know."

"Where a dedicated student can get an advanced degree in animal husbandry. With an emphasis on poultry."

"If you eat, you're involved in agriculture."

"Come to Dewey Sharpe's Bumper Sticker World, where we can fit you with a slogan for any occasion."

"You shouldn't be so dismissive of A&M, Sonya. It has proud traditions, both military and athletic."

She stopped and turned in his direction. "No. The answer, Dewey, is no."

"What do you mean, no?"

"What I mean is, we are not treating this case one bit differently, just because the driver of the vehicle happened to be the Big 12 conference leader in total offense last year. People who violate the law have to pay the consequences, I don't care how many season-ticket holders' hearts are broken in the bargain."

Sonya took off again, and he hustled to keep up.

They rounded a corner and came upon the Hummer, which a tow truck had deposited in a parking lot. The windshield was spiderwebbed and the glass in the side windows blown out. One side was partly caved in, and there was massive denting.

Sonya used a tissue to open the driver's side door. The air bags lay pooled and deflated, like oversized tongues.

She closed the front door and moved to the back. "You can still smell the weed those guys were—Hello. What's this?"

She bent down. Straightened back up. "Does that look like blood to you?"

Dewey bent over to examine a stain on the carpet. "Maybe. But how surprising is that? The offense report said the occupants suffered some cuts from flying glass."

"It said Ty Jr. and Mario had superficial cuts. They were riding in the front seat. The one in back had a banged-up knee and that was it."

Dewey flipped open the offense report and scanned its contents. "Dadgum."

"Call the DPS and have them send over a mobile crime lab, okay?"

"Don't you think that's kinda overdoing it?"

"Look, the littering charge was cute and all, but why don't we just see if there was any real criminality going on last night? We'll find some pot in the car at a minimum. More evidence for the controlled substance charge."

Dewey could have given her a few reasons why they didn't need even as much as they already had on Little Ty, but he didn't think it would have been a good use of breath. They turned away from the wreckage in time to see a long black limo sliding to a stop in front of the courthouse.

"Show time," Sonya said, and headed that way.

Dewey stopped to answer his cell phone, which was playing the "Aggie War Hymn." Occurred to him, maybe he should rethink his ringtone until this case was done.

He held it to his ear. "This is Sheriff Sharpe."

"Sheriff, it's Barbara. We just fielded a call from the daughter of that man what owns the restaurant out on the bypass. Bourré. You know the one?"

"Best damn catfish in the world."

"She's over there now. Seems her pa has gone missin'."

"I'm goin' into a meetin'. Call her and tell her I'll be there in an hour or so."

"She seemed mighty anxious, Sheriff."

"Either he'll still be missin' in an hour or he won't."

He pocketed the phone and hurried to the curb, where Sonya was talking to four of the biggest men he had ever seen in his life.

9

IN HER DREAM SHE WAS LITTLE ONCE MORE AND SEATED AT THE DINNER table with her father and brothers, and he was talking to them, just the boys, not her, about the fishing trip he was planning, to a lake up near the Oklahoma state line. She knew that she was excluded from this as she was excluded from all such plans because she was a girl and in her father's eyes this meant she simply did not belong in such pursuits.

Her accomplishments in school and athletics, no matter how significant, never seemed to matter to her father as much as the boys' did. She never heard him bragging about her the way he did about them.

Then again, she was spared much of the abuse he dealt them.

Her father was of that breed of southern men who thought their children were to be commanded and controlled, instead of raised with love and patience. He turned not to Dr. Spock for his guidance as a parent but more to the spirit of Henry Wingo, the abusive father in *The Prince of Tides*.

She lay in her old bed listening to the sound of bacon frying in the kitchen, and that's all the sound there was. She knew this meant her father had not come home or else there would have also been the sound of him working his wife over about whatever came to mind. In a way he no doubt would have thought amusing but in reality was just another form of cruelty.

She rolled out of bed and pulled on her clothes and found a brush in a bureau drawer and hit her hair a couple licks. By the time she emerged into the kitchen her mother had breakfast laid out.

"Mornin', Mama."

"Hey, baby. You sleep alright?"

"Strange dreams. No word from Daddy?"

Her mother shook her head. She seemed on the verge of tears.

Karen gave her a hug. "I'll make short work of breakfast and then run back over to Bourré."

"I waited on you before calling the boys."

"Let me handle that, okay? I want to go to the restaurant and have a look around first."

"It's not like him—"

"I know, Mama. I know."

It was a little past nine when she pulled into the parking lot and rolled to a stop. She walked to the front door and slotted a key into the lock. She entered the front room. Nothing seemed amiss.

She walked into the kitchen. The door to her father's office was shut. She pulled it open and took a step backward as a chill ran through her.

She wheeled around and scanned the kitchen.

It was gone. The device was gone.

She pulled out her cell phone and dialed 911.

10

JEREMIAH WAS ASLEEP IN A CHAIR WHEN THE DOCTOR ENTERED. MARTHA had been asleep, too, but when the bed shifted she awoke and looked into the man's familiar blue eyes.

He patted her hand lightly lest he disturb the IV tube inserted there. "How are you doin', young lady?"

Dr. Frank Anderson III, or "Tres" as he was known to everyone, had been the Spur family physician since Martha and Jeremiah had settled in Brenham. He was in his midseventies and had a hank of white hair that fell across his forehead and a bedside manner that had done nothing but grow more kind and attentive through the years.

The sound of Tres's voice had fetched Jeremiah from his slumber, and he worked the arms of his chair with his elbows that he might sit erect.

"Just like a doctor to come wake up a person when she's trying to get her beauty sleep," Martha said. "But in answer to your question, I feel like I'm recovering from having been force-fed a can of Drano."

"Feeling well and truly cleaned out, eh?"

"I think I may have shed a pound or ten."

"I hadn't expected to find you quite so chipper after the night you had. The good news is, while you're not out of the woods yet, I do believe we can just about see that last line of trees."

Jeremiah leaned forward with his elbows on his knees. "Any word from the lab?"

The doctor turned his way. "Just finished talkin' to 'em." He turned back to Martha. "When's the last time you had a hamburger?"

"Oh, my goodness. I couldn't say. Why do you ask? Are you conducting a survey on behalf of the Chick-fil-A cows or something?"

"She ain't much of a red meat eater."

"No hamburgers this week, then?"

"Tell the cows I'll sit for a lie detector if they want."

"Well, you got *E. coli* from somewhere, Sarah."

"It's Martha, Doc."

"Of course. Sorry." The doctor looked acutely embarrassed. "We've known each other, what? Thirty years? You'd think I'd get your name right."

Jeremiah got to his feet and stretched. He placed his hands in the small of his back and pressed. He felt the need for a hot shower and a change of clothes. "*E. coli*, huh?"

Doc looked over the rims of his glasses at the Ranger. "It is a bacterium, various strains of which are commonly found in the lower intestines of warm-blooded animals, including humans. You have multiple strains of *E. coli* in you right now, for instance."

"Good thing I like you so much or I'd be forced to give you a thrashin'."

"Don't take it personally. These bacteria were passed on to us by the world within the first couple of days after birth. They live in our gut and do some useful work."

"Like giving me a raging case of the trots?"

Tres turned back toward Martha. "Ah, but that was not your native *E. coli*. That was a strain known to scientists as O157:H7. It happens to live most times in the lower intestines of cattle. Scientists first identified this bug as a source of food-borne illness in the early eighties, but it really came to prominence in the early nineties when there was a massive outbreak linked to undercooked hamburgers served by Jack-in-the-Box. Hundreds of people got sick in several states. Several kids actually died. That's because, in severe cases, the infection can destroy the victim's red blood cells and cause kidney failure. This is what the little Bruni girl is suffering from now."

"Good Lord."

"She's on dialysis. It's going to be touch-and-go for a few days."

"The hamburger has to be undercooked for it to be a problem, then?"

"Raising the temperature of food to at least one hundred sixty-five degrees kills the bacterium. This is why you cannot buy a medium rare burger in a restaurant anymore. Hamburger tends to be a particular problem because the bacterium is released from the animals' bowels during the slaughtering process, and gets ground into the meat, where it can replicate itself every twenty minutes under the right circumstances."

Martha said, "It's enough to make you want to become a vegetarian."

Jeremiah said, "It would take a sight more than that in my case."

The doctor shook his head. "Even so, you'd still be at risk. These days many outbreaks of *E. coli* are caused by fresh produce."

"How can that be, if the bug comes from cattle?"

"No one can say for sure, but most of the produce we eat in this country comes from fields that are situated hard by feedlots or land where cattle are pastured. It's simply a matter of the bacterium being transmitted from a cow pile to a spinach plant, and that can happen any number of ways. There's been research of late that proves the American bullfrog can harbor *E. coli*, and the frog lives in the ditches from which the water is taken to irrigate produce fields."

"So if a frog was to cross a feedlot on his way home and carry the bug into the ditch from which the water got pulled—"

"There you go. And the thing about produce is, it's mostly served raw."

"But we wash ours."

"That's no guarantee. If the bug is in the irrigation water, it can be taken up inside the plant through its root system."

"You sure know a lot about this, Doc."

The man smiled. "We can get into why that is some other time, maybe." He said to Martha, "So if you haven't had a hamburger lately—"

"I do love my spinach salads."

"Uh-huh." He turned back to Jeremiah. "The state health department has a man on his way from Austin. He'd like to have a look in your all's refrigerator."

"Sounds like a hall pass to me."

The phone on Martha's bedside table rang. Tres reached over and took the receiver in hand. "This is the Spur room. . . . Yes, he is." He held the receiver out for Jeremiah to take.

"This is Spur."

A woman's voice said, "This is the operator, Mr. Spur. Do you expect you'll be around the hospital this evenin'?"

"Hang on a second." He put his hand over the receiver and looked at Tres. "When you reckon Martha can vamoose on outta here?"

"I'd say she ought to stay one more night."

Jeremiah said into the receiver, "'Pears that way."

"The head of our pharmacy department just called. She'd like a few minutes of your time."

"On account of how come?"

"She didn't say."

"Well, what's her name?"

"Karen Bradshaw."

"Her daddy the one owns Bourré?"

"Yes, sir. She'll be by sometime this afternoon."

"Fair enough."

He hung up the phone and checked his watch. "Guess I better get on home."

The doctor stood up. "I'll walk you out."

"Want to check on the little girl on my way, too."

"She's in ICU."

Jeremiah looked down at his wife. "You gon' be okay for a couple hours?"

"If I felt any better, I'd want you to take me dancing."

Jeremiah winced and looked at the physician. "Ain't there nothin' y'all got that will cure her of that?"

"Nothing short of a sex change operation."

Martha gave Jeremiah a list of items she wanted him to fetch back on his return, and when he had jotted them all down, he leaned over and kissed his wife on the cheek. "See you in a bit."

He and the doctor left the room together. They walked down the hall toward the elevators, the kuh-lunking of Jeremiah's boots echoing off the walls. The morning meals and medicine had been distributed, and the halls were mostly empty. Nurses sat reviewing charts or talking on the telephone at desks near the building core. Here and there a wheelchair or a gurney lined up against the wall pending need.

Jeremiah said, "Wonder what it is the pharmacy head wants with me."

"Karen Bradshaw?"

"Yep. Switchboard said she needs a few minutes of my time this afternoon."

"No tellin'. You know her daddy?"

"Was in his establishment last night, as a matter of fact. He's ornery as hell, but he cooks up a mean catfish fillet."

"There's a measure of people in this town, think he's not worth the powder it would take to blow him to hell. I'll have to admit, though, I'm sort of fond of him myself. Ever heard him pick a banjo?"

"Can't say as I have."

"I think it's him that's the banjo player. Maybe it's somebody else. I get people mixed up sometimes." They came upon the elevators, and Doc punched the UP button. They stood listening to the cables groan and rattle.

The elevator deposited them on the fourth floor, and the nurse at the desk waved them through to the ICU waiting area. There they found a beautiful young woman sitting alone on a couch, leaning forward with her forearms resting on her knees. She had long dark hair touched with highlights, and she was working a tissue in both hands. She looked up as they entered. Her eyes were red from crying.

"Hey, Mrs. Bruni," said Tres. He took a seat next to her, and Jeremiah sat in a chair on the other side of a coffee table. "This is the man I was telling you about. His wife has the same thing your little girl has. I'm sorry. I've forgotten her name."

The woman said, "Shelly."

"That's right. Senior moment. Sorry."

Mrs. Bruni and Jeremiah shook hands, and then she returned to worrying her tissue.

"Your husband and I kept one another company in the ER last night." She nodded and touched the tissue to her eye.

Doc Anderson laid a hand on her forearm. "How's the little girl?"

The woman tossed her hair. "She's asleep. I probably should get back in there. I just needed a few minutes alone. Couldn't stand to be around that machine anymore."

"Your husband is with her, then?"

She shook her head. "He's been called away. Client emergency." She caught the look on Jeremiah's face. "That's the way it goes, sometimes, when you're a sole practitioner. Still. Makes me wish he hadn't left that big firm." She touched the tissue to her eyes once more and then sat looking at it, as if it owed her an answer for her troubles.

"Is there anything we can do to help?"

She shook her head. Looked at Jeremiah. "How's your wife doing?"

"She seems to be on the mend."

"That's good. Hopefully that's where Shell will be soon."

They passed a few more minutes in conversation, and then Jeremiah and Tres said their good-byes and excused themselves. In the elevator on the way down, Jeremiah said, "What machine is it she couldn't stand bein' around?"

"Dialysis machine."

"Oh, yeah. You said. Shithouse mouse."

"They're in for a rocky ride."

"We'll keep 'em in our prayers." Jeremiah didn't set much store by praying, but it was what people in these parts said.

As he and the doctor parted company, Jeremiah said, "You keep a close eye on my bride for me, you hear?" He meant it as a joke, but the response he got surprised him.

"Who?" said the doctor, looking momentarily confused.

"My bride. Martha. Your patient. You ain't forgot her already, have you?"

"Oh, no, no. Sorry. Just a little preoccupied is all."

They shook hands, and Jeremiah walked out into a parking lot that was already baking in the late summer sunshine, wondering if maybe Doc Anderson's age was beginning to show some. Forgetting the little Bruni girl's name. Acting like he didn't know who Jeremiah was referring to when he mentioned his bride. Other signs of forgetfulness. The man seemed distracted and not completely himself.

He shrugged it off and hustled to his pickup.

After the old Ranger disappeared, Doc Anderson stood for a few moments in contemplation of the look the man had given him before he left for the parking lot.

He must suspect me of losing my edge. Getting on in years to the point where I might not be able to cut the mustard.

He smiled to himself and walked briskly to Martha Spur's room.

He pushed the door open gently and looked inside. The patient lay on her back with her eyes closed. The doctor could hear her breathing softly in her sleep.

He eased inside and pushed the door to behind him. He crossed the room as quietly as he could and stopped at the bedside table, where sat a water pitcher and a cup.

From an inside pocket of his lab coat he produced a ziplock bag containing a number of syringes. He selected a syringe and replaced the bag inside his coat. He pulled the protective plastic cap from the needle.

He inserted the needle into the mouth of the pitcher and depressed the plunger, watching the sleeping woman the while. She began to stir just as he finished emptying the syringe into the pitcher. Quickly he capped the needle and tucked it away.

He was standing at her bedside, smiling his most benign doctor smile, when she opened her eyes and smiled back at him.

"I appreciate the attention, Doc," she said, "but don't you have other patients you need to attend to?"

"None whom I care more about."

"That's nice," she said as she yawned.

He reached for the pitcher and poured a cup of water and handed it to her. "You need to make sure you stay hydrated."

She sat up in bed and started drinking. She handed him back the empty cup.

"Good girl." He smiled and began to fill the cup again.

11

KAREN CUT THE CONNECTION. SO THE SHERIFF WOULD BE A WHILE GETTING here. that was the bad news.

The good news was that in the course of checking in at the hospital she had stumbled over the fact that Martha Spur had been admitted early that morning. Were she a character in a cartoon, a lightbulb would have lit up over her head.

Jeremiah Spur must know a thing or two about missing persons cases.

Now came the call she least wanted to make.

She sighed and took up her cell phone and hit a speed-dial number.

Mark said, "Hello?" He answered the phone much as their father did, less salutation than challenge. *You better have a good reason for calling me.*

"It's Karen. I'm at Bourré. You and Luke had better get over here."

"We ain't due there for another hour."

"Daddy's missing. Someone has ransacked his office. The safe is gone."

"Damn. You checked with Mama to see what she knows?"

"She called me in the middle of the night to tell me he never made it home. I came down here and found that he and his car both were gone. Went looking for him but didn't have any luck."

"We on our way."

She killed the connection and sat looking at the parking lot. She tried to imagine what had become of her father even as she worked to keep from being consumed by her augmenting fear. His office had been left a shambles. Files emptied out, drawers hanging open, trash can overturned. Floor a wreck where someone had wrenched up the safe.

The office appeared to have been searched only, though, not fought in. There wasn't any blood anywhere that she could see.

Before long, Luke's pickup came swinging into the parking lot and slid to a stop next to her Honda. Her brothers emerged, huge men who had the demeanor and posture and shaved heads and verbal gifts of soccer hooligans, except that instead of cockney accents they sounded like *Dukes of Hazzard* extras.

If they spoke at all. After a lifetime of being ridiculed, criticized, challenged, and derided by their father at their every utterance, they had grown progressively more sullen and silent.

Yet despite everything he had done to break their spirits they remained fiercely loyal to their old man, like prisoners who fall in love with their jailer.

They came stomping through the front door and nodded at her and went straight to the back.

"Be careful not to touch anything," she called after them.

They reemerged and joined her in the corner, where they pulled up chairs and sat.

"I've called the sheriff's department, and he should be out here within the hour. I've checked with the hospital, and Daddy's not there. Did you all work last night?"

"We stayed to clean up. When we left, he was still in his office doin' his sums."

Karen said, "If it was a robbery—which it seems to have been, since the safe is missing—why wouldn't they just take the money and leave him be?"

"Maybe he knew the person and they didn't want to leave no witnesses behind."

"I hate to think that," she said, looking out the window.

A car turned into the parking lot and rolled to a stop next to her brother's pickup. Karen said, "What's he doing here?"

"Seemed to us, he might have some advice would come in handy."

"Plus, him and Daddy been spending a lot of time together here lately."

As Karen Bradshaw watched, the family lawyer, Robert Bruni, emerged from the car.

12

THE CURBSIDE INTRODUCTIONS WERE QUICKLY DONE, AND AT SONYA'S suggestion they hastened inside the courthouse. A Saturday morning meeting between Brenham's most famous celebrity and his retainers on the one hand and the representatives of local law enforcement on the other was sure to incite speculation. That was in no one's best interests.

They gathered in a conference room on opposite sides of the table. Big Ty took the seat across from Sonya. His size more than earned him the adjective by which he was known to all. He stood six-five and still moved with the quick muscular grace that had turned many a defensive back into a nationally televised embarrassment.

His was the face that had launched twenty million toaster ovens, with an easy grin and infectious enthusiasm for an appliance that did nothing more exalted than leave things warmer and crispier than it found them. Sonya could not look at him without thinking of the print ads in which he appeared in an apron with the words GIVE BIG TY'S A TRY! printed above his image.

He wore a white knit shirt and slacks and loafers with no socks. On the left breast of his shirt rode in maroon the *T, A,* and *M* of the local land grant college for which his currently incarcerated son played football.

All the others were attired in suits.

To Big Ty's right sat a man in his late twenties who slid a business card across the table. It announced him as Isaac Daniels, Executive Vice President of Tyrone Daniels Enterprises. He had a friendly face and half-closed eyes and the relaxed look of somebody who was comfortable in everyone's company.

The man to Big Ty's left offered up the business card of a lawyer. Ken Washington was almost Big Ty's equal in size, and they had in fact been teammates. Ken had played on the other side of the ball, but his career had been cut short by a demolished ACL. He had earned a law degree and settled into a big firm practice down in Houston. He wore a gray pinstriped suit and a blue shirt with a white collar and a gold collar pin, and he had shaved his head completely.

The fourth member of their party offered no business card, nor was one necessary. He was the lone white man, with a jowly face familiar even to Sonya from a thousand tight shots, pacing a sideline in headphones and holding a plastic card the size of the menu at a Mexican food joint. Coach Tom Ballard had been hired on a couple of years back to rescue the Texas A&M Aggies from their abiding mediocrity, and his first move had been to recruit Little Ty Daniels after his senior year at Brenham High and install the option read offense specifically to exploit Little Ty's size, speed, throwing ability, and natural game-breaking instincts. Here sat a man with the bags under his eyes of someone who year in and year out entrusted his career to the performance before network television cameras of football players who had barely reached the age of majority.

Sonya figured she was looking at half a short ton of very worried meat-on-the-hoof. Make that half a metric ton if you added in the sheriff who sat to her left, what with his fight-song-playing cell phone and his Aggie senior ring.

What was the old saying?

In Texas, there are only two sports—football and spring football.

But there was a good deal more at stake here than mere *W*'s and *L*'s. There were the greatest prizes in football-dom, the national championship, the New York Athletic Club trophy, not to mention bragging rights, recruiting success, endorsement deals.

"I believe this is your meeting, Mr. Washington," Sonya said. She folded her hands on the table.

The lawyer pointed at the document in front of Dewey. "That it?"

In response, the sheriff slid it forward.

The lawyer squared it before him and produced a pair of tiny reading spectacles. The rest of the room sat waiting. There was not a sound to be heard other than that of a page occasionally being turned.

When Washington was done, he took off his reading glasses. "How 'bout we cop to the litterin' charge and you all dismiss the rest?"

Sonya leaned forward. "I'm surprised you're able to see any humor in this, Mr. Washington. Because, frankly, your client could be looking at going from a maroon and white uniform to one that's jailhouse orange."

Big Ty shifted in his seat and glanced at the lawyer but didn't speak.

Washington said, "Let's talk about that. It says here your deputy smelled marijuana when he approached the vehicle. But unless I'm missing something"—the lawyer took up the offense report once more and leafed through it—"he found no other evidence. No physical evidence, such as an actual marijuana cigarette. We supposed to convict these young people on account of what this man *smelled*?"

"He's prepared to testify—"

"Uh-huh. I bet he is. And we prepared to deny it."

"Our theory is that the evidence got thrown out of the vehicle during the chase."

"I done said we'll plead to the litterin'."

"We're ordering up a mobile crime scene unit from Austin. If those young men had a controlled substance in that vehicle, there will no doubt be trace evidence."

"Ain't but a Class B misdemeanor if they find less than two ounces. You think they can vacuum up more than that?"

"We'll see where the investigation takes us, Mr. Washington. Besides, there's still the evading charge. That's serious crime."

The football coach said, "We prefer to think of it as a youthful indiscretion. One which will make young Ty a better and wiser and more responsible citizen."

"Not to mention," Big Ty said, "his Hummer privileges done been revoked for good. His transportation from now on gon' be the sorriest excuse for a hoopdee I can lay my hands on."

Sonya sat back. "I don't think you fully understand the scope of what this young man did. He led a deputy sheriff on a hell-for-leather chase at speeds upwards of a hundred and ten miles an hour. He could have gotten himself and his friends killed. Not to mention putting Deputy Crowner's life in jeopardy. Now why would someone take such a risk?"

The lawyer said, "It seems to me—"

"It seems to *me* there must have been something pretty serious going on in that Hummer for him to run like that. What did they throw out the window, after all? Could it have been a Baggie containing a good deal more than two ounces of weed?"

"Reckon we'll never know."

"Says who?"

What followed was an awkward silence broken only when Isaac Daniels leaned forward and held his hand out to the lawyer. "Mind if I take a look?"

The lawyer passed along the offense report and rested his elbows on the arms of his chair and steepled his fingers before him. He frowned. "I wonder," he said, "if the DA and I might have a few minutes alone."

Big Ty and his son and the coach got to their feet, and Dewey followed suit. Instead of walking out of the room, though, Big Ty leaned over and placed both hands on the table and looked directly at Sonya. "Before we go," he said, "I got one question for this young lady here." He leaned in and stared at Sonya.

She planted her elbows on the table and leaned forward. "I don't actually like being referred to as a lady."

Ken Washington laid a hand on Big Ty's arm. "Now, Ty, I'm not sure this is the time or place—"

"My question," the big man said, "is this: Do you know for sure, if you died today, that you would go to heaven?"

In all her years of law practice, in all her years *as an adult*, Sonya had never been asked quite such a question. She hesitated. Tried to decide if the man was joking or not.

"Well. Do you?"

No. He wasn't joking.

Problem was, there were so many things wrong with the question, Sonya didn't know where to begin. Her instinct was to say something light and self-deprecating. "Let's just say I'm working on it as best I know how."

"You don't get there by works, young lady, but by faith in the Blood of the Lamb."

Isaac touched his father on the arm. "Come on, Pops. Let's go."

"Seems your client has got religion on us," Sonya said.

Washington shrugged. "Last year his mama's ticker blew, carried her off to the sweet bye-and-bye. That's what started Big Ty down the path of righteousness."

"I suppose losing a mother would do that."

"His spiritual journey has been further propelled by a string of business reversals."

"What do you mean, business reversals? Isn't he lousy with it from all those toaster ovens he's sold?"

"He's made some. But then there's what's become of it. Ever heard of Big Ty's Red Zone Wings?"

"No."

"How about Big Ty Goes Long, the video game?"

"Again, no."

"Big Ty's Margarita Maker? Big Ty's Tae-kwon-do Hut? Big Ty's line of men's hair products?"

"What's your point?"

"My point is, you haven't ever heard of any of this shit and neither has anybody else. Even though Big Ty has spent millions of his own dollars developing and promoting all these brands. Therein lies the problem, see. As in, once the toaster oven took off, Big Ty thought he had that ol' Midas touch. At a time when his newfound wealth was causing the hucksters and scam artists to come slithering up out of the sewer gates into Ty's office with a dozen dog-ass schemes not a one of which was worth what my daddy would have called a tinker's dam."

"So the antidote to bad management can now be found in the Old Rugged Cross?"

The lawyer smiled. "You know your way around a hymnal, huh?"

"I did once."

"The real solution to the Daniels family problem lies more along the lines of brand revitalization."

"The kind of brand revitalization that comes with a much coveted trophy—"

"And a high draft pick. Now, we can do this one of two ways."

"Yeah? What are they?"

"Got an election year comin' up."

"What? Is a cable television talk show about to break out?"

"I hear tell you might be lookin' at some kind of run at a statewide office. Say, attorney general? On the way to something even bigger?"

Sonya shrugged. "Not that it's any business of yours, but I've had a few calls from people. The mayor down in Houston. County judge up in Travis. Couple of congressmen in the Valley."

"Your problem is, you know too many of the right kind of people."

"What's that supposed to mean?"

"You got to make it through the primary before you get anywhere—and it's gonna take more than the likes of those white boys to get you through the gate."

"The congressmen are Latino."

"You think that makes it better somehow?"

"Why are we even discussing this?"

"Now maybe you think, you tack a prominent black athlete's hide up on the wall, that shows you all tough on crime and what have you. But you got to know, you ruin a young man's life with nothin' more substantial than what you got here, that ain't gonna sit well with roughly eleven point nine percent of the electorate."

"Look, I have a job to do, irrespective of—"

"On the other hand, you show a little leniency, accept the good faith assurances of the young man and his family that there will be no *re*-peat of this reckless behavior, recognize that the barrel-rolling of a sixty-five-thousand-dollar automobile at a high rate of speed is enough to scare a young man straight—well, this sort of prosecutorial discretion will not be forgotten when the rubber meets the asphalt down in the Fifth Ward, up in Oak Cliff, over in East Austin."

"You're saying cut Little Ty loose as an act of political expediency."

"It's not a question of, is it politically smart. It is a question of, why you want to make trouble for yourself over nothin' more than this."

"What if there *is* more? Those young men ran for a reason, and it wasn't just to avoid being written up for speeding."

"Where's your proof?"

"We're working on that."

Washington rested his forearms on the table and leaned in. "Then how 'bout we make this deal. You come up with something more than trace evidence of marijuana and a speeding charge, something you can make stick, and we will walk right back in here and face the hip-hop. In the meantime, tuck that offense report away in a drawer, cut my man loose so he can get some rest before the game tonight, and your dispensation will not be forgotten when you come lookin' for somethin' from my people. Otherwise—"

"Otherwise, what?"

The lawyer leaned back. "You follow baseball, Ms. Nichols?"

Sonya shook her head. "Not enough action. All that standing around, waiting for something to happen. You should think of me as more of a basketball person."

The lawyer shrugged. "Too bad. There's a kid, hails from these parts. Relief pitcher. Plays for Minnesota. Makin' quite a name for himself, thanks to a wicked split-finger and the second chance he got. You see, back in his college days, ten years or so ago, he rolled his car over on the bypass, same as Little Ty. Girl that was with him? She broke her neck. Now the dude, his blood alcohol level was considerably in excess of the legal limit, but that part of the story never made it out into the public."

"News to me. Guess it must have happened before I joined on here."

"The DA back then deemed it wise to exercise his prosecutorial discretion in such a fashion that the young man's life wasn't ruined."

Sonya shrugged. "Different DA, different exercise of discretion."

"Folks ain't apt to view the matter quite that benignly, if you will. You see, that young pitcher who was allowed to walk away from that situation? He was white."

"I had a feeling you were going to say something like that."

"This is just the kind of racially discriminatory application of different standards of justice that is sure to cause Jesse and Al and them to come swarmin' over this county like the crows in that Hitchcock flick."

"You'd be only too happy to see that happen, I suppose."

"Told you there was a hard way we could go."

"So the theory of the case is, what? Little Ty is the victim of a racist system that lets whites go but comes down with both feet on blacks in similar situations? And I'm the evil personification of that system?"

"Hey, if the jackboot fits."

Sonya leaned in. "There's not but one problem with that theory."

Ken leaned in reciprocally, as if joining her in some conspiracy. "And that would be?"

"How can I be a racist, if I dated a black man for better than two years?"

Ken grinned broadly. He looked up at the ceiling briefly and sat back and folded his arms across his chest. "So that's how you go about getting elected statewide these days? Drawing attention to an intimate multiyear relationship with a black man? How you think that's gonna play with the Christian conservatives and the Confederate flag wavers over in East Texas? Gonna be mighty costly in terms of the redneck vote. Not to mention the Hispanics."

Sonya's smile froze on her face.

Ken steepled his fingers once more. "Checkmate, counselor."

Sonya sat back and folded her hands on the table before her. She thought a few moments about her shrinking menu of options. Funny how race complicated everything it touched. "Tell you what. We'll release Ty Daniels Jr. into the custody of his father, and wait to file the offense report until our investigation is complete."

"Thus keepin' it away from the newspaper types."

Sonya held up a hand. "I'm not finished. We will be doing a thorough forensics workup of the Hummer and also a search of the chase route, yard by yard. If we find evidence of any criminality that rises to the level of a state jail felony—"

"Meaning more than trace evidence of pot—"

"Or anything, we will arrest Little Ty and his friends for that and on the evading charge, I don't care how many civil rights hustlers you truck in here."

"And in the absence of any such evidence?"

"We'll take the position that a totaled Hummer and the increased parental supervision that we expect to attend this incident are a sufficient price to pay for the poor judgment your client showed in running from Deputy Crowner, and we'll let him off with a speeding ticket. And the littering, of course."

"Of course."

They got to their feet and shook hands.

Sonya walked to the end of the room and picked up a telephone handset and dialed a number. "Sheriff," she said into the phone, "could you please join me back in the conference room?"

13

OUTSIDE THE CONFERENCE ROOM THEY FORMED A HUDDLE.

"Why don't we wait in my office?" said Dewey.

Nods made their rounds, and they set off down the hall, with Isaac bringing up the rear, engrossed in the offense report.

Dewey's office was a big sunlit number. One wall was floor-to-ceiling windows, and against the wall opposite stood bookshelves. Between them, a paper-strewn desk. Dewey sat in the desk chair.

Big Ty and the coach dropped into the guest chairs and looked around. Isaac leaned against the door frame, reading.

Big Ty studied the bookshelves. "You quite the football fan, then, huh."

It was true. Dewey had turned his bookshelves into a shrine to Aggie football. He had on display autographed helmets and balls, framed photographs taken of him with coaches and players from yesteryear, ticket stubs encased forever in Lucite. A needlepoint sampler of the school logo his mother had given him one Christmas.

Dewey said, "Been following the Ags since I was a kid. Pretty excited about how this season is shaping up."

Big Ty said, "With Little Ty under center, we'll kill every cat in the alley."

"You think he'll stick around for his senior year?"

"Depends on how high he might go in the draft."

Coach Ballard said, "You ever watched a game from the sidelines, Sheriff?"

"Can't say as I have."

"I got an extra pass for tonight's game."

From over by the door, Isaac stopped reading. "Pops?"

Big Ty half turned. "Yeah?"

"I need to make a phone call."

"Alright."

Isaac made his way to the first floor. He walked out of the building and around the corner to a spot that was hidden from the upper-floor windows.

He took his BlackBerry from its holster and searched the address book for a name. He clicked the track wheel. The phone was answered on the first ring.

"Clyde Thomas."

"You know who this is?"

"I do if caller ID ain't lyin' its ass off."

"You still interested in doin' some work for the family?"

"Only on days that end in a y."

"Last night Little Ty got clocked doin' a hunnerd miles an hour out on the bypass. In the ensuing chase, he spun out at the interchange on 36. Rolled his Hummer."

"He alright?"

"He is until my pops gets ahold of his sorry ass. Cop that was chasin' 'em claims they was smokin' reefer. But they didn't, like, find no evidence at the scene. What the cop's report does say is, he saw somethin' go flyin' out the vehicle at that last big curve before you get to the cloverleaf."

"You thinkin' it was the weed."

"I'm thinkin' you need to get over there and look for whatever it was before Washington County's finest can organize their dumb asses to do it."

"Well, am I lookin' for weed or ain't I?"

"You lookin' for whatever don't look right by the side of the road. Drugs wouldn't look right. Same's true of any number of items."

"I'm on it."

"And whatever it is you find out there, I don't even want to know about it. Just disappear it for me, know what I'm sayin?"

"I hear you."

"Call me when you done. And keep this on the down low, man."

Isaac cut the connection and walked around the west side of the building to the south side, where the Hummer was parked under a live oak tree. He stood looking at it, all the dents and busted glass and chrome hanging loose. Shook his head.

"Shit, little brother. How many times I got to tell you, all you need do is play football and not worry about gettin' all tangled up in this?"

Ironic, how he'd give anything to be like Little Ty, and vice versa. Isaac wasn't as tall as his daddy or his brother either one, didn't have that speed, that quickness, that pure athletic thing. Nor the love of sports, neither. He'd played some hoops in school, but his heart was never in it, mostly because he wasn't worth a damn. He took to the books, though, and after he finished college he got his MBA and went to work in the family business, looking to extend the brand outside of home appliances.

He started off like a house afire. Unfortunately, after a few early successes, some aprons and spatulas and shit like that where there was a direct kitchen connection, he had branched out and his luck had turned turtle and since then he'd been like Charlie Brown playing the slots in a Mexican casino, feeding the beast until his brain felt numb.

He couldn't launch a successful product for love nor money. Made him start to lose confidence in himself, commence to doubt his own judgment.

Nothing harder on a man than that.

Isaac took his BlackBerry in hand and dialed up voice mail. He listened to the message his brother had left him in the middle of the night once again.

"Yo, Ike. Don't tell me you done turned in, man. My homeboy come through, and I got the proof right here. Wait till you see it, brother."

Isaac hit the 7 key and sent the recording to data heaven. Last thing he needed was potentially incriminating voice mail messages lurking on some server somewhere.

He thought about his man Clyde Thomas, hustling out to that curve in the road where that jackleg cop had seen something go sailing out the Hummer. Clyde had been police himself once, right here in Washington County, until he resigned a while back. That's also when he quit seeing the lady DA, as in romantically.

Isaac grunted at the turn of phrase, seeing her. Yeah, he was seeing her, alright. Seeing all the way up and down that tender white body. Isaac wouldn't mind seeing some of that himself. He'd like to screw her till her ears rang, is what he'd like to do. He shook his head and told himself to focus. If there was any of that old spark left between the two of them, it might could come in handy if this situation here got any stickier. Clyde had charmed her once. Could be he could do it again.

Clyde's law enforcement career and his interracial love life had taken the pipe simultaneously for reasons that had never been entirely explained, leaving the man broke, lonely, and trying to make a go of it as a private investigator here in a town where there didn't seem to be a whole lot of call for that, aside from some hymnals maybe going missing down at the Free Will Baptist Church. You could put all the scandal there was in this dinky burg in a sandwich bag and still have room for a BLT.

Since the Daniels family was that absolutely super-rare thing, both black and rich, Clyde had been around to Isaac's office any number of times, trying to find out, was there something useful he could do for Isaac or his people, something that would supplement his meager cash flow. Isaac had given the man a few gigs, driving assignments that had been dressed up as security work.

Now the time had come for something with a little substance to it, and Isaac hoped Clyde didn't screw it up. Hoped the man known generally among the children as "the Judge" would find whatever it was that was lying over yonder off 36 before the authorities did.

Isaac wasn't completely sure what it might be that rested out there in the roadside weeds, but he was willing to lay odds, it wasn't no dime bag.

He took his BlackBerry in hand once more and keyed the address book. Typed in a name. Phone was answered right off.

"Mr. Daniels, how are you today?"

Caller ID had dimed him again. Made him wonder how many address books there were around that had his name in it. "Yo. Call me Isaac. I wanted to call and, like, tell you of our renewed interest in talkin' to your client."

Hesitation. Isaac could imagine what was going through the man's head.

"I'll pass it along. Supposed to see them this morning, as a matter of fact."

"We'd like a quicker answer this time. We ain't got forever, you know."

"When did you want to meet?"

"How 'bout Monday?"

"Monday's a holiday."

"What? Was you plannin' to spend the day watchin' the telethon?"

"I'll get back to you."

He killed the connection and tucked his device away and headed back to the courthouse. Time to rejoin the good ol' boys all coveyed up in the sheriff's office, watch his old man and the coach work on that cracker sheriff.

They needed to get on with it, though, quit this fucking around, spring Junior and get his ass over to the stadium. Gonna be game time here directly.

Sonya and Dewey stood looking out the window as Little Ty and his friends crossed the courthouse lawn in the company of the older men.

Sonya said, "We're clear on this, right?"

Dewey shrugged. "You want a search of the scene of the spinout and back along the route where Bobby saw something being thrown from the vehicle."

"Those young men were running for a reason, Sheriff. Find out why."

Dewey left the conference room, headed outside to where he had parked his cruiser. He needed to get to the catfish restaurant and find out what that was all about. He'd order up the roadside search by cell phone while he was on his way.

When he was done, the deputies who drew the duty would be only too clear about the fact that Dewey's heart wouldn't be broken if they came up empty-handed.

14

WHAT ISAAC DANIELS DID NOT KNOW WAS THAT CLYDE THOMAS HAD begun to expand his product and service offerings based on the reasoning of, if he didn't, the path he was on led directly to the poorhouse.

This is how come, on that particular Saturday morning, he was just leaving the office of one Quincy Postelwaite, who operated Brenham's premier grocery store. After weeks of persistent salesmanship, Clyde had convinced the grocer to install video cameras on a test basis. Clyde's fundamental pitch was the same one he'd been making to other local merchants here of late.

"It's all about controlling your shrinkage, you know what I'm sayin'? As in, how many candy bars and packages of carrots and cans of soup get liberated free for nothin' out your store on a daily basis in somebody's pocket or purse."

"It's a problem," Quincy had said. Postelwaite had white hair and pronounced eyeteeth, and he wore thick glasses with black plastic frames. Brought to mind Rocky the Squirrel from the Bullwinkle cartoon series.

"Damn right, it's a problem. What's it costin' you a year?"

"Between two and three percent of my top line, near as I can figure."

"Uh-huh. And groceries is a thin margin business, ain't that right? What's that shrinkage amount to? Half your EBITDA?"

"EBITDA" is business jargon for free cash flow. What Mr. Postelwaite could take home to Mrs. Postelwaite that she wouldn't leave his ass or ride it without mercy. A woman who awoke one morning to the melancholy realization that in her desperation not to be alone she had hauled off and married a negligible small-town grocer who in appearance favored a cartoon squirrel.

"Something like that," Postelwaite had replied.

Clyde figured the man knew his shrinkage down to the penny, but that he was going to be careful how much information he shared with this tall black man with his head shaved bald, a man who was all but a total stranger.

"So, if we can cut down on your shrink more than my video surveillance system is gon' cost you, then we both make money, ain't that right?"

"Hard to argue with that logic. But look. I can't bring charges against everyone who pilfers from me. It's just not practical."

"Point is, you won't have to. Fact they bein' watched will be enough to make folks think twice before they palm a Snickers bar. Most of 'em will bitch out in the end."

"Excuse me?"

"Bitch out. Lose their nerve, man. But, hey. Don't take my word for it. Let's run a pilot test, so you can prove it to yourself."

And with that they had a deal. Clyde had subcontracted out the actual installation to some tech guys, and the cameras had been up and running in the store the last ten days. He had personally been over here every day to check on things. Yesterday, he'd posted the THIS AREA UNDER VIDEO SURVEILLANCE signs.

The only thing he worried about was what they called customer pushback. Could be, not everybody cared to be videotaped while they were shopping. It was apt to raise privacy issues with some folks.

On his way out the store, he stopped by the checkout counter where stood a heavyset woman whose name tag read JANICE and who was passing the time studying a magazine devoted to the love lives, chemical dependencies, and other misadventures of movie stars and European jet-setters. Janice had the look of a lifelong ordained sister in the Sacred Order of the Minimum Wage.

"Mornin'."

Janice favored him with a look of maximum disinterest. As though her station placed her above the salutations of strange men.

"I'm Mr. Postelwaite's security consultant, Clyde Thomas. Was my firm that installed the new video surveillance system."

"Nice to meet you," she said unconvincingly.

"Anybody said anything about the cameras?"

"Like what?"

"Like not wanting to be caught on tape while they shop. That sorta thing."

"Not to me, they haven't. The way you all positioned the cameras, I don't think most people have even noticed."

"Uh-huh. Well, we got signs up now. You may start hearing about it."

"We'll see, I reckon."

It was at this point that his cell phone chirped and Isaac Daniels's name and phone number appeared on the display.

Directly he was in his black Impala SS, headed around the bypass to that bend in the road where he was to search the right-of-way for something that might cause trouble for the local gridiron hero.

As he drove, he wondered why exactly he was still here in Brenham, all this time after he had lost the job that had brought him down here in the first place. On reflection he concluded that he had been kept here largely by the fear that if he quit this place, then he would never live anywhere without wondering shortly upon his arrival how soon he would quit that place as well. He realized that he needed to stick it out, learn how to be happy where he was, instead of opting for what he'd heard some folks refer to as a geographic cure.

Now, finally, after all these months of struggle, it looked like it was going to start paying off, maybe. First he managed to get his video surveillance equipment in an actual place of business in this white man's town, for a test run.

On top of that, now comes this call from Isaac. Real work, at long last, from the House of Daniels, instead of the glorified chauffeur jobs they'd thrown his way.

Was enough to make a man wonder if the seven lean years were behind him, like in the Book of Genesis. Not that it had been anything close to seven years, mind you. More like one. But a bad year in Brenham, Texas, was like a dog year. Equaled seven human years, to Clyde's way of thinking.

He pulled his Impala to the shoulder and set the hazard lights to flashing. He stepped carefully out the vehicle, for his presence on the side of the road had done nothing to slow the rush of traffic that came bombing toward him in the two northbound lanes, not a soul among them going less than ten miles an hour over the speed limit.

In Texas, speeding is a form of self-expression, like playing a musical instrument or creating a calligraphy scroll or knitting a sweater.

Clyde walked into the tall grass that bordered the road. Seemed to him like the highway department used to do a better job of Bush-Hogging this mess, keeping it from growing knee high. Wasn't going to make his search any easier. Was gonna be like looking for a golf ball in a cornfield.

Besides, he wasn't completely sure what he was meant to find. A Baggie of dope most likely.

The sun was up, and it was beginning to get warm. Dark circles formed under Clyde's armpits as he trudged this way and that, head bent, scanning the ground. He looked like a man sleepwalking through some dream of prison confinement.

Everything he saw seemed the most common and innocuous litter. Beer cans, fast food wrappers, page or two out of a newspaper, piece of what looked like bloody gauze, a diaper and a soiled one at that, of this there could be no doubt.

No Baggie. No dope.

Out on the highway, the eighteen-wheelers roared past, and their wake turbulence went rippling through the grass, causing it to heel and twist and then right itself to await a burst from the next passing truck.

All this walking around and staring at the ground made Clyde feel a little weird physically, so he looked up, the better to restore his internal gyroscope.

He was starting to feel conspicuous.

He returned to his search, thinking how this was typical of what it meant to be a PI in rural Texas. Not one thing glamorous about it. No rolls in the hay with mysterious blondes who might turn out in the final scene to be the killer. Just a bunch of damn drudgery that paid fifty bucks an hour. His life could never be made into a script that would catch Will Smith's eye, not even for a feature-length comedy.

It was just too damn dull.

He stood with hands on hips and looked about. Wondered if maybe he should look farther up the road.

Out on the highway a vehicle slowed and pulled in behind his car. It was a pickup. Jeremiah Spur emerged from behind the wheel. Clyde knew Jeremiah from a couple of cases they'd worked back in the day when Clyde was on active duty. He liked the man well enough, although some of his ways were distinctly old timey.

Jeremiah raised a hand in salutation. "You havin' car trouble?"

"No. How come?"

"Recognized your wheel rocket and thought maybe you was broke down."

"I'm on a job."

The man stopped and stood squinting at the landscape. "Wouldn't have nothin' to do with Little Ty, would it?"

Clyde tried to keep the surprise off his face. "What makes you think it does?"

"Ran into Bobby Crowner and a few of the boys last night up at Emergency, when they brought the kid in along with a couple of his buddies. Bobby and I fell to visitin', and he told me that they had been speedin' and when he went to pull 'em over they ran on him and in the process somethin' got chucked out the window at about this location."

"I don't know nothin' about that."

"Well."

"Besides, I'm fixin' to be done with this line of work."

"Yeah?"

"I done vertically integrated into video surveillance and in-store security. Providing the honest businessman the means to keep track of his stock and inventory. Improve his bottom line. You know what I'm sayin'?"

"Don't that seem a little high-tech for these parts?"

"I got a pilot test under way already. Down at Postelwaite's. I figure if I can sign him up, the rest of the marketin' be, like, just order-takin'."

"Yeah, well." The old Ranger looked him squarely in the eye. "You might give some thought to the fact that if the sheriff's boys come out here and find you trollin' for evidence, they might tag you with obstruction of justice."

"I don't even know what you talkin' about, man."

"Suit yourself." He turned and started back toward his pickup.

"Hey."

Jeremiah turned back.

"Why was you up in ER in the middle of the night?"

"Martha got sick from somethin' she ate."

"Sorry to hear that, man."

"Thanks." He turned his back once more and made for his vehicle.

"Tell her I said get well soon."

The man raised a hand in acknowledgment. He got in his truck and pulled around Clyde's car and disappeared from sight.

After another few minutes of wandering about, Clyde was on the verge of resigning his commission in the Right-of-Way Militia when something he had seen earlier caught his eye. He bent to give it a closer inspection. He produced a ballpoint pen from his pocket and poked at it.

"Son of a bitch."

Just then the sound of a door being slammed caught his attention. He glanced up to see two deputies in brown Washington County uniforms coming his way.

Repulsive though it was, he had no other choice.

He reached down and took the bloody gauze and its disgusting contents in hand and palmed it. He shoved the thing into his hip pocket and turned to face his former colleagues.

15

DEWEY PARKED HIS CRUISER NEXT TO A LATE-MODEL SAAB AND HAULED himself out of the vehicle. Through the front windows he could see four people seated about a table, watching his arrival. He hitched up his gunbelt and squared his Stetson on his head.

Like most of the local citizenry, Dewey made it to Bourré a couple times a month for his catfish and hush puppies fix. His wife had developed scruples against fried foods thanks to daytime television, so she generally stuck to a dinner salad. Not Dewey. For him, the inner beauty of food could only be revealed by frying it for all it was worth.

As to the superior quality of the catfish at Bourré there could be no debate. Dewey had heard some talk about how the man who owned the place used a special process to get rid of that muddy flavor that is most times the problem with pond-raised fish. Whatever it was the man did, it sure enough worked.

He stepped into the restaurant, and the four people rose from their chairs. The owner's two sons he recognized, both from the meals he had taken here and the nights they occasionally spent in Dewey's drunk tank.

The woman was an attractive blonde in her midthirties. She looked vaguely familiar. The third man, who was dressed in pants held up by suspenders and a blue-and-white striped shirt, was a complete stranger.

The woman stepped forward. "Thanks for coming, Sheriff. I'm Karen Bradshaw."

"You're the one found your daddy missing, then?"

"And his office ransacked."

Dewey looked at the two sons. "Mark and Luke, right?"

"That's us."

He looked at the fourth person. "And you would be—"

The man held out a business card. "Robert Bruni, lawyer to the family."

Dewey took the card and examined it. He looked up. "You from Houston?"

"I have a few clients in the area. Married a girl from around here."

Dewey tucked the card into his shirt pocket and eyed the lawyer. He turned back to the woman. "So he never made it home last night."

"Plus his car is missing."

Dewey produced a notepad. "Make and model?"

"Lincoln Continental Mark V. Blue."

"Year?"

"'Seventy-eight."

"When's the last time y'all saw or heard from him?"

Mark said, "When we locked up last night, he was in his office, adding up the night's receipts. He liked to do that alone."

Karen described last night's events. Her brothers stood with their arms dangling at their sides while she spoke. They were dressed in jeans and motorcycle T-shirts and athletic shoes and looked like members of a carnival crew waiting for instructions on where to set up a tent. Dewey suspected them of hangovers.

The lawyer crossed his arms over his chest and leaned against the wall. For all his fancy dress he seemed fatigued.

Dewey nodded and took notes. "Then you come over here this morning—"

"I let myself in—"

"Was the door locked?"

"Yes. When I got inside I didn't notice anything unusual until I went to his office and then— Well. Maybe I should just show you."

The kitchen ran most of the length of the building and its walls were lined with sinks and stoves. To the right was a walk-in freezer. In the middle was a large table. From a ceiling rack pans and other cookware hung. It smelled of grease.

Dewey nodded at the freezer. "You checked in there?"

"Yes."

They stopped at the office. It had been turned upside-down.

"Made themselves quite a mess, huh," said Dewey. "Anything missing?"

"There was a safe bolted to the floor next to the desk. Looks like it was pried up and hauled off."

"Your dad keep anything else valuable here?"

"It was his office and pretty much off-limits to us so it's hard to say for sure. I'm guessing mostly he kept papers and correspondence relating to the restaurant business. And to his invention."

"His invention? Oh, you mean the process he uses to make the fish taste better?"

Karen nodded. She seemed on the verge of saying more but stopped at the looks she was getting from the other three men.

"What?" Dewey said.

Mark said, "Daddy is the only one who's allowed to talk about his invention."

Karen said, "It's a control thing. His need to be in control—well, it's a very important part of who he is."

"And," the lawyer said, "in this case, keeping strict control over the information concerning his technology is very wise, in this world where people think nothing of stealing the intellectual property of others. Mr. Bradshaw never discusses his invention with someone unless they have first signed a CA."

"A what?"

"A confidentiality agreement. Pursuant to which the party to whom certain information is disclosed agrees to protect the confidentiality of that information. I have a form of such an agreement with me. If you want to know anything about Mr. Bradshaw's invention, you will need to sign that document first."

This lawyer was beginning to work Dewey's patience, what with his preoccupation with legal niceties in a criminal case that was now under the jurisdiction of the Washington County sheriff's office. "What good would that do, since Mr. Bradshaw is not around to sign on his own behalf?"

"The invention is actually the legal property of Bourré Ventures LLC, a Texas limited liability company, of which Mark and Luke are officers. Either of them could sign and bind the counter-party."

Bind the counter-party. What was it about law school that turned nerds like this with his combed-back hair and fancy suspenders into such annoying pricks? Give a man a law license and right away he feels obliged to clutter his diction with words the length of freight cars.

Dewey said, "Y'all got any reason to think Mr. Bradshaw's invention had anything to do with all this? I mean, if it was so valuable he had to control who knew about it and so forth. Could be the reason his office was pulled apart and the safe boosted was, someone was looking to find out what the man himself was reluctant to discuss."

The three men shook their heads, but Karen just stood there, looking stricken. The sounds of eighteen-wheelers downshifting out on the bypass filled the silence.

Dewey focused on the woman. "You think I'm right, don't you?"

She glanced at her brothers, as though seeking their guidance. Or perhaps looking for signs of some impending threat. "There is something else missing. But not from the office. A piece of equipment from the kitchen. Part of Daddy's invention."

"What's it look like?"

"A white plastic drum with a detachable lid. And a base consisting of two rollers operated by an electric motor encased in a metal shell. You set the drum on the base and engage the motor, and the rollers cause the drum to rotate."

"What does that do?"

"No," said the lawyer. "That question we are not answering. Not without a CA."

Karen looked at Dewey. "That tells you what to look for, right? Is it really necessary to understand what it does?"

Dewey eyed the lawyer. "Maybe I'll get me a court order."

"Try it and see how far you get," said the lawyer.

Karen said, "The point is, whoever did this knew enough to take the equipment as well as the safe. Which means they must have known something about the invention."

"Got any ideas who that might be?"

The two sons just shrugged. Dewey wondered if their apparent lack of interest in this discussion was on account of they had nothing to contribute, or was it the inherent suspicion of law enforcement and authority that he had often encountered in the poor whites of the county? Guys like this were apt to think the income tax was unconstitutional, the Federal Reserve a Jewish cabal, and anyone carrying a badge a blood enemy.

For her part, Karen bit her lower lip. Her eyes cut about. At length she shook her head. "Daddy made vague references to commercializing his invention, but he was always extremely secretive about it. Back to the control thing."

Dewey looked at the lawyer.

"No can do," the man said. "To the extent I know anything, it is covered by the attorney-client privilege. Which only Mr. Bradshaw can waive."

"Don't you think he might want to waive it under the circumstances?"

"That's not a decision I can make for him."

Dewey squinted at the man. "It's almost like you don't care whether this case gets solved or not."

Bruni suddenly appeared exhausted. "Look, Sheriff. I'm bound by the Code of Professional Responsibility. I violate that, I could wind up manning the front door of a Wal-Mart. Mr. Bradshaw would have me lined up against a wall and shot if I say one word to you or anyone else about his invention or the people who might have an interest in it. Now, why don't you stop harassing me and do that Dick Tracy thing you all do."

Dewey grunted. "I have a mobile crime scene unit on its way from Austin for another case. I'll get them to swing by here. Meantime, this restaurant is closed, and no one is allowed in here except law enforcement personnel."

Dewey handed business cards around. "Call me if you think of anything that might be helpful. In the meantime, go see if you can find your father yourselves."

Dewey followed them into the parking lot, where the woman offered to tell their mother the news. Her brothers walked off without responding.

On the way to their vehicles, the lawyer told Mark they had something else to discuss and that he would call him later in the day, but for now he had to get back to the hospital. His client nodded sullenly, and all parted company.

Dewey watched them get into their vehicles and drive off. He stood thinking how the woman knew more than she could say in the censorial presence of the three men. She seemed more moved by concern for the old man whereas the others seemed to be operating out of something else. Fear, maybe.

Dewey went to the trunk of his vehicle to fetch the crime scene tape. Opened the lid and looked inside.

There the tape was, next to the tear gas launcher that weapons sales rep had left with him earlier in the week. The launcher was so badass cool-looking Dewey could hardly stand it. It had a rifle stock on one end and a length of barrel on the other, and in between what looked like an elongated revolver cylinder.

"This is strictly for use in outdoor crowd control," the rep had said. "We strongly advise against using it in confined places. There's been a history of tear gas rounds starting fires if they go off near flammable materials. Like with that Posse Comitatus guy up in Arkansas a few years back, remember? They fired a round through the window of a house, and the whole thing went up in flames."

Dewey hadn't bothered to straighten the man out on how there hadn't been any need for aggressive crowd control in Washington County since the mind of man runneth not to the contrary.

Dewey just said he understood and asked if he could keep the thing and have a couple of rounds so he could test it out.

He damn near said "play with it." Caught himself just in time.

Dewey lifted the launcher out of the trunk and hefted it for a few seconds.

The cool thing about this gig is all the neat shit you get to play with.

He set the launcher back in the trunk and fetched out the crime scene tape.

He went to stringing the tape, whistling the "Aggie War Hymn" while he worked.

He walked the halls of the hospital until he found a nurse pushing a cart, the top of which was loaded with pills in little paper cups.

"How are you today, Ms. Jernigan?"

"Fine, Doctor Anderson."

"Listen, I've just seen Mrs. Spur, and she's doing really well. I think we can take her off the antibiotics now. I'll note that on her chart of course, but I just wanted to make sure you don't dispense at midday. Save these folks some money."

The nurse looked a little uncertain. "You're sure."

"Yes. Very."

"Okay."

"Thanks."

He turned and walked on down the hall and stopped at the sound of his cell phone ringing. He took it from his pocket and studied the display. He held it to his ear.

"Are we all set?"

"All taken care of."

"Guess who's come down with a case of food poisoning. Martha Spur."

"What?"

"She happens to be a patient of mine. In her case, however, I'm afraid the Hippocratic Oath has temporarily been suspended. For a couple of reasons."

"And they would be?"

The doctor looked around. "I'll tell you later."

He ended the call and slipped the phone back in his pocket and stood thinking.

Usually the incubation period is three to five days. In her weakened condition, one, two days at the most. Especially with this strain of bacterium.

The likes of which no one around here has ever seen.

Other than me, that is.

He nodded to himself and continued on his rounds.

16

JEREMIAH HAD JUST FINISHED GETTING DRESSED IN A CLEAN SET OF KHAKIS when his doorbell sounded. He found on his front stoop a heavily bearded man, about Jeremiah's age and weight but a good ten inches shorter, dressed in jeans and a western shirt and a pair of boots with curled-up toes. He had in one hand a large cloth duffel bag. He looked like a dwarf from a fable embarked on some epic journey.

"Help you?"

"You're Mr. Spur?"

"I am."

"I'm Walter Gordon, a microbiologist from the state health department. This place is no picnic to find."

"You seem to've found it well enough. You here to frisk my refrigerator?"

The microbiologist grinned, displaying a mouthful of crooked and off-color teeth. "That's one way to put it. And ask you a question or two."

Jeremiah led him through the house to the kitchen.

The man set down his duffel bag and looked around. "Even if the place weren't as clean as you all keep it, I don't expect the contamination originated in your house. Since it affected multiple households and all."

"I do pasture cattle, so I reckon otherwise it could have been."

The microbiologist raised an eyebrow.

"Doctor down at the hospital told me this bug originates in the gut of cattle." Jeremiah dropped into a chair at the table and leaned back such that the front two legs were off the floor. "This thing apt to go statewide?"

"Multistate, I'd be willing to wager. The bug probably started off in a processing plant, and contaminated product was no doubt shipped to dozens of stores. Although just at the moment all the reported cases are in the Brenham area."

Walter began to remove items from the duffel bag. He set out a box of clear plastic bags and another box that held the sort of gloves that brought to mind one of Jeremiah's least favorite moments of the year. The microbiologist next produced a stack of brown grocery bags.

Walter went for the gloves and pulled on a pair. "These kinds of things happen more often than you'd think. The Centers for Disease Control estimates there are seventy-six million cases annually of food poisoning in this country."

Walter pulled open the door to the freezer compartment. "Y'all don't have a pound of ground beef to your name."

"Martha doesn't much care for it. Wouldn't freezing kill the bacteria anyway?"

The man closed the door. "Nope. Just slows down its growth." He opened the refrigerator. "Here we go."

He closed the door and turned back to the table and took up a black felt-tip pen. He pulled several plastic bags from their box, and each one he marked SPUR. Below that he wrote the date and time.

He opened the refrigerator door once more. "I wish you'd look," he said.

"At what?"

"How organized your wife is. I mean, unless you're the one sets all the bottles of juices and condiments just so, with their labels all facing out."

"No. That'd be her, alright. She's done it all her life."

"You have to admire that kind of attention to detail." The microbiologist reached inside the unit and started pulling out fresh produce wholesale and placing it, packaging and all, in the plastic bags, which he sealed across the top and then set into a paper sack.

Jeremiah said, "Sure is a lot going to waste."

"That's the thing with food poisoning. Between the lost food and lost productivity and health care costs, the annual losses are in the untold billions."

"You'd think someone would take a notion to do somethin' about that."

The man shrugged. "There are some technological fixes around. Irradiation, for one, although people are worried about the side effects from that. They think if they eat irradiated food they'll glow in the dark."

"What about the *E. coli*? Anyone working on getting rid of that?"

"Lots of folks. Just up the road, at A&M, for example, they're trying to come up with a chemical you can add to cattle feed that will neutralize the O157:H7 bug."

The man finished his larder raid and turned toward Jeremiah. "Have you all thrown anything away in the last couple days?"

"Probably. You're welcome to look."

Inside of fifteen minutes the search was completed, and they were back at Jeremiah's kitchen table sipping glasses of iced tea. Walter was making notes as he asked Jeremiah questions like had they eaten out in the last several days and if so where and what was it they ate and had they been to anyone's house for dinner. Except for last night's supper at Bourré, they'd taken all their meals at home.

"That's kindly the point of havin' a kitchen, you see," Jeremiah explained helpfully.

"We got a nice kitchen, too. Gives me a place to deposit the takeout I bring home or the pizza when the man comes to the door with it. Well, I do believe we're about done here." The man took a last swig of tea and got to his feet.

Jeremiah led him to the front door, where the microbiologist turned around. "I'll call you once we have the test results in. Should know something later today or early tomorrow. In the meantime"—he produced two business cards and handed them over—"if you think of anything else that might be helpful, give me a holler."

"I don't need two cards." Jeremiah started to give one back, but the man held up a hand.

"Keep it. You can pass it on to your lawyer."

"What lawyer?"

"The one who'll be contacting you all about suing whoever it is that sold you contaminated food. Believe me, when this outbreak makes the news, they'll be calling."

The man proceeded to his car. He got behind the wheel and backed out of the driveway and disappeared down the road in a cloud of caliche dust.

17

"LOOKS LIKE WE GOT OURSELVES SOME POLICE ACTION." EDMUND SPEAKER eased off the gas the better to watch two deputies approaching a lone black man alongside the road.

His wife, Janet, made no reply. She sat sulled up over this last-minute decision of theirs—no, his, really, and their daughter's—to spend the weekend at their country place up in Burleson County.

Janet Speaker did not care for the Hill, as they called it in their family. There were dust and spiders and the occasional scorpion and dishes to be done by hand and a bed that was no rival for hers back home in Houston.

They had been married too long for Edmund to be oblivious to her pouting, but he figured she'd get over it once the grandkids arrived. That's what gave rise to the trip up here, Melinda calling last night to say Bob wouldn't be back from overseas until Monday and would it be okay if they went up to the Hill so the boys could run around and burn off some of that energy?

Edmund pulled off the highway a few miles northwest of Somerville, and as soon as his truck tires bit into the surface of the caliche road he began to relax. That's why he loved it out here. The isolation and absence of streetlights and traffic noise and the freedom from the short bald-headed boss with hair growing out his ears who always wanted to know, would Ed move his quota of glass this month?

He pulled to a stop at his gate and got out and stretched. In the pasture to his right a rocker arm was working. There had been a modest oil boom here, back in the seventies, and Edmund still got a monthly check.

From the dead oak tree off to his left a flock of doves took wing. Might not be a bad idea to get back down here later with his shotgun.

He bent to unlock the chain, and when he took it in hand it slithered off the gate altogether. He straightened up and looked at it. While the lock held two ends fast there were now two new ends.

He knelt and examined the ground and found the literal missing link. He picked it up and studied what was left. Somebody had taken a bolt cutter to it.

"This doesn't look good." Visions of robbery and vandalism were beginning to work Edmund's imagination.

He pushed the gate open and set the rock in front of it and returned to the pickup. "Someone went and cut the gate chain," he said as he pulled the door closed.

"Why would anyone do such a thing?"

"I can't think of but one reason."

He roared up the hill not even bothering to stop and close the gate.

He parked his truck beside the house and got out. Nothing seemed amiss. He let himself through the gate that fenced off the small yard and proceeded through the screen door onto the porch. On the far end two swings hung from the ceiling on chains. On this end sat a picnic table.

He tried the front door, which was like the kind you would find in a commercial establishment, with a metal frame and a glass front that ran its length. He was a glass man, after all. He had access to such doors. It was locked tight.

He threw the lock and went inside. Nothing seemed to have been disturbed in the slightest. He checked his gun rack and his liquor cabinet. All was as he had last left it.

He went back outside and checked the barn. Everything was secure.

He stood looking out across his land, as if he expected of it an answer to the question of why someone would go to the trouble of taking a bolt cutter to his gate chain and leave the rest of his place unmolested.

18

AS HE WATCHED THE TWO DEPUTIES ADVANCE, HITCHING THEIR GUNBELTS
and working wads of gum in their cheeks, Clyde couldn't help but
wonder if the sheriff meant to sabotage his own investigation. How else
to account for him dispatching Tom and David Powell on this mission?
They were the only brother act in the department, and though they
weren't twins they were alike in being unemployable incompetents whose
very existence was prima facie evidence of inbreeding in the Powell family tree.

They stopped a few feet away and stood with their thumbs hooked in
their gunbelts and looked at Clyde with dim-witted suspicion.

Clyde grinned. "Howdy, fellas."

Tom put two fingers to his mouth and produced a large wad of gum.
He flicked it toward the fenceline. "What you doin' out here by the side
of the road?"

"Well, as you know, I'm in business for myself these days—"

"Uh-huh."

"Clyde Thomas Investigative Services. I work divorce cases, deadbeat
dads, missin' persons, shit like that. I'm out here on a marketing gig."

"Marketing?"

"You know those signs you see alongside the road, 'This Stretch of
Highway Adopted by Such-and-Such a Business'? Sounds all civic-
minded and shit, but it's really just marketin', see. Brings a man's brand
to the attention of the passin' motorist. So, I'm thinkin' about adoptin'
some highway my own self. In fact, I'm thinkin' about adoptin' this
stretch of highway right here." The way he said the last two words, they
sounded like "right cheer." Clyde figured that would help establish his
country bona fides.

David said, "What's that got to do with anything?"

"Well, a man's got to inspect somethin' before he adopts it, now, don't he? Would you adopt somethin' sight unseen?"

"But this stretch of road's got a daddy. I seen a Tubby's Tire and Battery—"

"Yeah, but ol' Tubby might be open to a deal. You don't never know."

Clyde paused a couple beats to let this powerful logic sink in. "Anyway, I seen enough. I got to get on. We'll be seein' you, fellas."

Clyde was halfway to his vehicle when—"Hang on a second, there, citizen."

He tensed and turned around.

They stood right where he had left them. Tom said, "That your Impala?"

"Yeah. That's my Impala."

"Well, in case you ain't noticed, the inspection sticker is up for renewal."

"Hey, man. Thanks. 'Preciate that."

The deputies watched him all the way to the car and turned away just as he got behind the wheel. As he did so he slipped his contraband from his hip pocket and set it in the passenger's bucket. "God *damn!*" he said under his breath.

He forced his eyes to stay on the road until he pulled into his apartment complex. He slid into a parking place and checked the vicinity. No one was about.

Only then did he look at his tiny cargo.

It lay swaddled in gauze like a bloody jewel in a case.

It was a human thumb, apparently a man's. Somebody somewhere was missing one of his opposables.

"What th' fuck am I gonna do with that?"

He knew what Isaac would have him do with it. Isaac would have him lose it down the toilet.

But Clyde was already feeling like he had stepped in it big-time, crossed some line he ought not to have, and the out-and-out destruction of evidence that might be valuable in some criminal investigation was for him a bridge too far.

Yet that just brought him back to the question, what was he gonna *do* with it? Put it in his sock drawer where it would go to festering? Store it in his fridge?

He didn't want the damn thing anywhere near him, truth be told.

One of his neighbors emerged from the front door of the apartment complex and headed Clyde's way. Clyde fetched a sports magazine off the backseat floorboard and used it to cover the appendage. The man got in his car a couple spaces over and started it up and drove off, and with that Clyde made his decision.

He backed up and pulled out of the parking lot.

When he got to the grocery store he parked away from the cars that were clustered near the front door. He adjusted the sports magazine such that there would be no chance the severed thumb could be seen. He walked briskly into the store and to the butcher shop in back. He stood at the display case until a man in a white apron offered his assistance.

"Gimme two pounds of that ground chuck."

"Comin' right up, sir."

While the man attended to weighing and wrapping his purchase, Clyde examined the placement of his video cameras. The area was covered from three angles. Two signs announcing their surveillance were in plain view.

Clyde took his order, wrapped in white butcher paper, and proceeded to checkout, where the same surly clerk from earlier rang up his purchase.

"Any complaints yet?" he asked her.

She shrugged him her indifference and took his cash. She placed his package in a plastic bag and handed it to him without so much as a smile.

Back in his car, Clyde set his package on the floorboard. He needed to move quickly. The small cargo that rested beneath the sports magazine was already bringing an appreciable funk to the car's interior. In another hour his ride was going to reek of putrid thumb, and this was an undesirable consequence.

He drove to the high school parking lot, figuring it would be deserted on a Saturday morning. His package he took from the floorboard. He peeled back the tape and opened up the butcher paper to reveal the ground cow. The sports magazine he returned to the backseat with the flick of a wrist. He grimaced and gently grasped what was lying there in the seat, gauze and all, and pressed it deep into the pile of red meat. He formed the meat back over it.

Once he had wrapped the butcher paper back over the meat and affixed the tape, he set the package back on the passenger's seat. Using his left hand, he opened his glove box and removed some napkins and a small bottle of liquid sanitizer, and this he used to cleanse his right hand of whatever contaminants might have accrued.

A few minutes later he pulled into a parking lot on the north side of town. The sign out front read WASHINGTON COUNTY COLD STORAGE. Signage in the windows of the place offered services in wild game processing. Clyde had never had occasion to patronize an establishment such as this, and it was with some trepidation that he parked and got out, grocery sack in hand. This was the kind of place that was of the rednecks, by the rednecks, and for the rednecks, not for folks like Clyde whose necks were emphatically ebony.

A bell above the door sounded when Clyde entered. The front room was long and narrow and dominated by a counter that sat before doors leading to the back. Atop the counter rested a cash register, and next to that a tall balding white man leaned reading a gun magazine. The man straightened up and set the magazine to one side. "Help you?"

Clyde held up his grocery bag. "Lookin' to rent me some cold storage."

The man eyed Clyde's possession skeptically. He produced a ledger book and opened it to a marked page. He flattened it before him. "Name?"

"Clyde Thomas."

"Clyde Thomas," he said, as he wrote in the ledger book. "Species of game?"

"Do what now?"

"What species? Dove? Quail? Duck? It's too small to be a deer or turkey."

"No, man. It ain't none of those."

"Then what is it? Law says I got to keep a record of what folks store here for inspection by the Texas Parks and Wildlife Department."

It's thumb tartare, you dumb cracker. "It ain't like that. It's hamburger meat."

The man's skeptical look deepened. "What do you want to store that here for?"

"Why do most people trade with you?"

"Not enough room in the freezer at home."

"Well, there you go."

The man held out a hand. "Lemme see that."

Clyde passed the man his grocery sack. He took it and looked at the contents and set it on the counter. He wrote in the ledger book once more. "Hamburger meat," he said. "Two pounds." He shook his head and looked up. "Anything else?"

"That'd be it." Clyde produced his wallet and handed the man a couple fins to seal the deal. He tucked the claim check and receipt in his hip pocket.

Clyde turned to leave the store.

"'Scuse me a second," the man said.

Clyde turned back.

"I know you, don't I? You used to be with the sheriff's department. You gave me a speeding ticket once."

Clyde shrugged. "Don't feel like the Lone Ranger. I was the top producer, like, several years runnin'."

"You heard these rumors been goin' around, about the sheriff?"

"No, man. What rumors?"

"That he can't get his business to stand at attention without he takes one of those little blue pills?"

"You sayin' the man got ED? And, like, the whole town is talkin' about it?"

"I heard it over at the barbershop." The man cast his eyes in the direction of his scalp. "I go there to get my shoes shined."

"Well, if you heard it at the barbershop, the whole town is without a doubt talkin' about it." *Damn, Dewey. You went and made yourself more of a laughingstock than even I thought was possible.*

"Seems to me it's a problem. You know. For the small businessman."

"'Splain that to me."

"If a man is soft there, he's apt to be soft on other things. Like crime."

"So you worried that word will spread through, like, the underworld, and that will increase the risk, your place gets jacked."

"That's what I'm sayin'."

Clyde held up a forefinger. "Have you ever considered the benefits of video surveillance?"

Clyde favored the man with his elevator pitch and left him with a business card and a promise that he would follow up by phone.

Back in his car, Clyde pulled out his cell phone and dialed up Isaac Daniels.

"Yo."

"I done like you asked, man."

"I take it you found somethin'."

"Yeah."

"We cool, then. Just— I don't want to know what it was."

"No, you don't. Look, man. We need to talk."

19

KAREN'S OFFER TO BE THE BEARER OF BAD NEWS TO THEIR MOTHER HAD behind it more than the Good Kid's congenital willingness to deal with all the crap. For she reckoned that if there were anyone in the world who knew her father, who knew his every secret, in whom the man would confide, it would be his wife.

For Patti Bradshaw, it didn't seem to matter that her husband had a personality that on occasion could make Chemical Ali seem like Mr. Rogers. She did her best to love him all the same and adopt the attitude that would be most appreciated by him.

And that attitude was submissive. Undemanding. Expectations so small they could not be detected with the most advanced electron microscope.

Karen came rolling into the yard and slowed, that she not endanger the dogs that emerged at full boil from under the porch. She exited the vehicle and knelt and gave them all some loving and climbed the porch.

She passed through the family room calling her mother's name. She stopped at the kitchen window and saw her mother out back working among the tomato plants, an aging woman in apron and bonnet. She was bent over and having at the earth with a gardening tool. Like a kindly witch out of a fairy tale. Karen swallowed and tears came, and she wondered if this was the life this sweet woman had imagined for herself when she was a little girl.

Karen stepped onto the porch and caught sight of Patti's calico cat, who sat in the sun licking her paws. Karen stood looking across the back of the place, the small vegetable garden off to her right, the barn beyond that.

She never knew what set him off that day, whether it was something one of the boys had done or something a cat had done or some combination. How he felt about it, if he looked back on it at all, she had no way of knowing. She had no idea if he was at all remorseful for anything he'd ever done. The beatings, the deprivation, the abuse.

The three of them had been in the front yard playing catch when Sylvester appeared on the porch with his old .22 rifle in hand and called the boys' names.

She crossed the yard to the little garden. Her mother straightened up and watched her come.

When she saw the look on her mother's face, the combination of fatigue and worry overcame Karen, and she lost all control. She burst into tears and ran the last few steps into her mother's arms, where she stood sobbing.

His face was red as always, and even back then his hair was white, but there was considerably more of it. It looked like a poodle stretched over a balloon. He said to the boys they were to follow him to the barn, and they removed their baseball mitts and laid them up on the porch. So did Karen, but Sylvester told her she was to stay put.

When she regained her composure she turned loose of her mother and pulled a tissue from the pockets of her jeans. "He's sure enough missing, Mama. And someone broke into his office and turned the place upside-down."

"Oh, my. The boys?"

"Haven't seen nor heard from him since last night when they left work."

"But they do know. That he's—"

She left off wiping her eyes and nodded. "They were at the restaurant with me. We called the sheriff, and he came over to start the investigation."

He led them around the house, and she followed at a distance. She stopped at the corner and watched them cross the yard to the barn. Sylvester went inside, and the boys followed.

They walked through the backyard to the porch, where Patti removed her apron and hung it from a wall peg. Once inside Karen dropped into a chair at the kitchen table.

"I'll make us some coffee," her mother said. Typical. Seeking refuge from the crisis of the moment in some small task. She took the glass carafe in hand and filled it with water and poured it into the maker, and into a new filter she spooned fresh coffee from a can of whatever was on sale the last time she went shopping.

Times had been tough for so long for her parents, they had elevated thrift to an art form. Nothing would be purchased but the need be acute, the price comparisons thorough, and the guilt and general agonizing over the matter maximized.

Her daddy liked to say that a quarter looked as big to him as a manhole cover. He had this way of turning his deepest feelings into mildly amusing aphorisms. He spun desperation into one-liners.

While the coffee made, her mother sat at the table and looked out the window at the yard beyond. She had a somewhat confused air about her. As though trying to make sense of the sudden voiding of some iron rule of the world.

Karen covered her mother's hand with one of her own. "We'll find him, Mama."

They hadn't been in there long when Karen heard a flat pop. A few moments' silence. Then another one. Sylvester emerged from the barn alone, rifle in hand. She hid in the bushes and held her breath until she heard the screen door slam.

Then she went running toward the barn.

The coffeemaker gurgled, and Patti got to her feet. She returned with mugs for them both. She set Karen's before her and took her chair.

Karen leaned toward her mother with her elbows resting on her knees. "I need to know who Daddy's been talking to."

"About?"

"His invention."

Her mother sighed. "I don't know that much."

"But you do know something. He would tell you, wouldn't he? He tells you everything, right?"

When she got there she found the two boys on their knees and sobbing. Laid out before them were the bodies of the boys' cats, Spike and Oscar. The smell of cordite hung in the air, mixed with the smell of the hay and the feed in sacks.

She knelt and draped her arms around her brothers' shoulders. "Who shot them?"

Mark said, "Luke and me. Daddy made us."

Her mother managed a small smile. "I remember the day he brought that thing home. He set it on the counter so I could have a good look. I asked him what it was. He said it was a pressurized tumbler. I asked him what it did, and he said he wasn't completely sure. I asked him how much it cost, and he said seventeen hundred dollars. And us barely able to make the mortgage. I told him he'd better find a good use for it."

"Who was he talking to about it, Mama?"

Patti sipped her coffee. "You know what your father needs most in all the world?"

"He's always seemed a little short of ready cash."

The older woman smiled and shook her head slowly. "If even half of what he's told me about his invention is true? We should have retired on the royalties long ago."

"What is it, then?"

"You know already, I expect. It's the need to feel in control. Of everything in his world. Me. You. His invention and what becomes of it. I think he somehow believes, if he can control all these things, then he can get credit for all the good things that happen and assign someone else the blame for the bad. And in this way he thinks he can get the thing he *wants* most in all the world."

"Which would be?"

Patti looked out the window and was a long time in answering. "To be loved."

They sat in silence for a while.

Patti leaned forward with her elbows on the table. "He's had some kind of conversation going on with some people out in California. Produce people. And he's convinced that there is a home use, in the kitchen. But it's like—"

"What, Mama?"

"It's like he hates to go too far with any of this. Maybe because he doesn't trust the people he's talking to. Or isn't sure how to get a deal done."

"Or maybe it's because he can't figure out how to work with people unless he can control them?"

Patti side-glanced her. "I don't know the details of any of this, mind you. Just what I've picked up through small talk, overheard phone conversations. But I think I know where you can learn more."

"Where?"

Patti sat back and looked at her. "When was the last time you were in the barn?"

Karen looked away and swallowed. "I hate that place."

They dug twin graves using shovels taken from the tool rack. It was hard work, and while they were at it buzzards appeared and began circling.

They placed the carcasses in the ground and shoveled the dirt back over them and stood crying.

Finally they turned to walk away.

Karen took Mark by the arm. "Why?"

Her mother got to her feet and headed for the back door. Karen followed close behind, suddenly nervous. They crossed the yard. The cat watched their every step.

The barn door was held fast with a padlock. Her mother grabbed it and spun the dial. It clicked open, and Patti pulled the door to one side.

They stepped inside. It took a moment for their eyes to adjust.

"Good Lord," Karen said underneath her breath.

"He made us!"

"But he must have given you a reason."

Mark stared at her. "He said it would make men of us."

And with that her brothers broke into a run and disappeared around the barn.

20

CLYDE'S ROUTE TO THE DANIELS FAMILY COMPOUND TOOK HIM PAST THE melancholy scenery of small-town Texas. He passed a business establishment devoted in its entirety to the sale of propane. He passed another place of business that had no signage at all other than the one word DONUTS, huge and in fading paint, above the front door.

Just across the town line there was an abandoned filling station that had fallen in on itself, and beyond that what had once been a motor court. A half dozen bungalows painted Pepto-Bismol pink that were today used for what purpose God only knew.

These businesses had depended on the trade of itinerants and were the fallen victims of the bypass. The very word "bypass" seemed to reduce Brenham and its citizenry to a kind of arterial blockage. No one but locals had cause to come this way anymore, and here sat the consequent ruins of lost traffic, while out to the west a whole new economy had been born, catering to the needs of the traveling public. Leaving the arterial blockage to waste away.

This Daniels exercise was beginning to feel like what marketing types call a "branding event." The problem was, the thing might just kick as hard as it shot.

On the one hand, helping the Danielses out would make them a reference account, and a strong one at that. *If you would like an example of a satisfied client, Mr. Suddenly In Trouble and Looking for Help, I can put you in touch with Big Ty Daniels, who is known the world over for his gridiron feats and his toaster oven.*

On the other hand, there was this business of the thumb, and how it came to be propelled out the window of a vehicle driven by Little Ty. That thumb was nothing if not evidence of felonious conduct, and so it could be Clyde stood guilty of obstruction of justice, a beef from which he could come clean only by producing that evidence for the authorities.

In which event his reference account would be lost and gone forever like my darling Clementine.

And if he didn't come clean? His branding event could take the form of an indictment for a third degree felony.

The line Clyde had to walk was worthy of a Cirque du Soleil act.

Clyde pulled his Impala off the highway and rolled to a stop before the wrought-iron gates behind which lived the Daniels clan. Clyde slid his window down and pressed the white button on a speaker box that sat on a pole next to the drive.

"Yes?" squawked a voice.

"Clyde Thomas, here to see Isaac."

There was a buzz and a click, and the gates labored open.

Clyde drove through a line of woods and emerged into a world of opulence. All about lay pastures seeded with grass and tended to such that Tiger Woods and his livelihood sprang to mind. On a ridgeline in the distance horses grazed, as though posed there for some film shoot.

The road crested a hill, and beyond it sat the Daniels compound, three buildings out of all scale to anything this side of a major metropolitan area. The structures had a unifying architectural theme that spoke to Clyde vaguely of French royalty.

The buildings faced onto a circular drive, and in its middle stood a ten-foot tall stone water fountain that gurgled along. On the drive were parked a black limousine and a gray Maserati.

Clyde parked next to the sports car and got out. All three buildings were of pink stucco and white trim and fronted by boxwoods fringed by brightly colored annuals. Everything had been trimmed to a fare-thee-well.

Clyde made for the middle building, and as had always been the case in the past it opened just as his foot hit the front landing, and there stood a white man in a suit and tie. The man somewhat favored that actor who played Hannibal Lecter, and he greeted Clyde by name and showed him into a two-story room lined with bookshelves, some of which were accessible only by mounting a mahogany ladder that leaned against the wall.

Hannibal asked him would he like something to drink. Clyde ordered a Coke.

The butler disappeared, and when he returned he was bearing a silver tray on which rested a Coke poured over ice in a cut crystal glass.

He handed Clyde the drink and a linen napkin, and then the servant bowed his way out and pulled the door closed.

Clyde sipped his drink and looked around. The library was furnished with leather couches and armchairs that rested on Oriental rugs laid over parquet flooring. The walls were loaded with art in heavy frames, landscapes and seascapes, the work of anonymous Europeans who were painting away in their dingy little attics while the Danielses' ancestors were working a cotton patch singing spirituals at the point of a gun.

It was all of a piece, the art and the English butler and the rugs and the books you needed a ladder to reach and the immaculate grounds surrounding the Old Country architectural rip-offs, and it made one statement.

Look here, world. We done arrived. Ain't it some shit?

Except that set back here off Highway 36 in a zip code populated largely by four-legged animals, the Danielses were making their statement mostly to themselves.

The door opened once more, and in walked Isaac, dressed in a suit and tie and carrying a box. "My man," he said.

They did the shake, and Isaac held out the box. "Brought you somethin'."

Clyde drained his Coke and set the glass to one side and examined the box. On it Big Ty was pictured gushing over the product inside to the effect of, why go to the trouble of driving to a coffee shop when you can make your favorite Italian-style caffeinated beverages right in your own home?

"It's a one-cup cappuccino maker," said Isaac. "You put the water in here, and slide in a sealed package of coffee here." He pointed to the image of the device displayed on the outside of the box. "Press that button and in less than a minute? You turned your kitchen into Starbucks while standing there in your underwear."

They took a seat on couches on either side of a coffee table. "Cappuccino, huh. Ain't that a little up market for your all's demographic?"

Isaac smiled and laid his arm across the back of the sofa. "We think we can capitalize on the increasingly popular appeal of the specialty coffee experience, if you know what I'm sayin'. Give the masses access to your highbrow caffeinated drinks."

"How you go about launchin' a product like this?"

"Got to do your market research first. We go to a firm specializes in that. They conduct surveys, focus groups. Then you need a design that's workable."

"You all do that?"

"We know a guy. A guy you gon' meet here before too long, but I'll come back to that. Once we got the specs in hand, then we go to China."

"China, huh."

"It's all made in China, my man. We work with a plastic injection molding firm about two hours north of Hong Kong, in Guangzhou. They do work for Toshiba, Sanyo, you name it. Got a million square feet under one roof where they turn little plastic pellets into rice cookers and coffee machines like that one yonder. Seen it my own self. Biggest problem when you go over there is, they want to wine you and dine you and feed you that shit they eat. Chinese'll eat anything, man."

"Like what?"

"Like fried baby sparrow."

Clyde's eyes narrowed, and he cocked his head. "You bullshittin' me, right?"

"They bring 'em out in a nest made of fried white noodles. They in there like chips in a bowl, beaks and eyes and everything."

"That's fuckin' disgustin'."

"But you got to eat what they offer you 'cause it's rude not to, see." Isaac leaned forward with his elbows resting on his knees. "Once you got the production sourced, then you get down to the all-important stuff."

"Which would be—"

"The infomercial. We work with a couple brothers outta Tampa–St. Pete. They originally from Philly, and they personal style is like, strictly Starsky and Hutch, you know what I'm sayin'? But still they the absolute best in the business. Ever heard of the Ginsu knives?"

"Sure, man."

"That was theirs. And the golf club with the hinge on the shaft. All manner of fitness products, too, like this gizmo, you stand on it and it moves your muscles a hunnerd miles an hour. Shakes the fat right off your ass while you watchin' MTV or listenin' to Fifty Cent.

"They got a patch, you put it on yo' mama's face, it sucks the wrinkles right off. Don't ask me where they go, 'cause I don't know. They just disappear, and in fifteen minutes she looks like her wedding picture. And a portable gas grill, looks like a tiny spaceship, weighs less than ten pounds. Costs thirty-two dollars to make in some Chinese sweatshop and retails for a hundred twenty-nine plus tax, shipping and handling. See if you can't do them margins in your head."

"I hear you, man."

"They workin' on a global network deal, where they shoot the infomercial right there in their own studio with blond spokeswomen fresh off modelin' careers, warranties, like, still good on the silicone implants, and then bounce it off a bird and send it to all the countries in the world in one point five seconds."

"A bird?"

"Satellite, man. It's a helluva bidness, and they could sell shoes to a snake assumin' the snake had cable and a credit card and could communicate through the phoned-in spoken word. Now. Let's talk about the bidness brings you here. I assume you got rid of what you found."

Clyde hesitated. This might all go better if he could bring himself to lie, but that wasn't who he was. "It's in a safe place."

"What's that supposed to mean?"

"It means you don't got to worry 'bout no one else gettin' their hands on it."

"That ain't the same thing as you havin' poured gasoline on it and set a match to it, though, huh?"

Clyde shrugged and looked away. He looked back. "What's goin' on, man?"

"Nothin' you need to know about."

"It involve Little Ty?"

"Look, can I count on you, or what? I need to know I can count on you."

Clyde examined the backs of his hands. "You can count on me."

"Saw your ol' girlfriend this mornin'."

Clyde looked up.

Isaac sat back. "Had to sweet-talk her into cutting Little Ty loose. Y'all still speak?"

Clyde shrugged yet again. "Ain't much call to. She done moved on with her life." That sounded weak to his own ears, so he added, "Reckon we both have."

Isaac dropped his chin and looked at him from under his eyebrows. "What I'm askin' you is, is y'all on speakin' terms?"

"Sure. Why not?"

Isaac got to his feet. "Come on."

"Where we goin'?"

"Want you to say hi to Daddy. Leave the cappuccino maker here. We'll come back for it."

Isaac led Clyde through the entryway with its other and further English landscapes on the walls and grandfather clock ticking in stately fashion and Oriental rugs laid over marble. They proceeded through a kitchen where copperware hung on a rack from the ceiling above an island topped with dark granite.

The yard featured an Olympic-sized swimming pool in which a half dozen brown-skinned children splashed and played. Poolside lounge chairs were occupied by three couples, the women in bikinis that tested Clyde's discipline in respect of his mother's long-ago admonitions of, don't stare, it ain't polite. The men were all lean as bird dogs and wore stylish swim trunks and diamond studs in their ears. A servant with a tray moved among them offering drinks and towels.

The black rich are different from you and me. They got tans.

At the far end stood a wood structure hung with purple cloth. Under it lounged Big Ty Daniels, wearing shorts and a T-shirt from an NBA championship series, smoking a cigar that cost Clyde's light bill. He could have been an entertainment executive taking a break after weeks of frenzied deal-making.

"You remember Clyde Thomas," Isaac said as they walked up.

"My nigger," Big Ty said. He got to his feet, and he and Clyde shook. Ty resumed his lounging. He pointed at Clyde with his cigar hand. "He gon' be able to help us out?"

"He done it already."

Big Ty drew on his cigar and looked at Clyde with evident approval, like a man might look at a prized hound that had earned a blue ribbon in a show. "You got that ol' make-the-startin'-five hustle, huh?"

Clyde shrugged. "Man's got to make a livin'."

"You like Little Ty. And Isaac here. Wanna make somethin' of yo'sef. Not like my other sons and they friends." He waved his cigar in the direction of the loungers. "They want to lay up on they butts, wait for it to be brought to 'em." He looked back at Clyde. "Isaac tell you we workin' on somethin' new?"

"No, sir."

Big Ty gave a nod. "Might could use the help of a man, got some hustle. What you think, Isaac?"

Isaac smiled at Clyde. "I think maybe we need our man on retainer. Say five G's a month."

Clyde wasn't entirely sure what to make of this father-and-son back-and-forth, what project they had in mind, why they felt he could do them five thou a month worth of good with it. What he did know was, that much money would cover his nut like one of Mama's hand-sewed quilts.

Not to mention the reference account value.

Big Ty said, "Sounds about right to me." He jabbed the butt of the cigar Clyde's way. "Why don't you hang around this afternoon? Catch a little time by the pool. We leavin' for the game at four thirty. You can ride with us."

Isaac said, "I'll see if I can find you some swimmin' trunks. You had lunch?"

Clyde allowed he hadn't.

He followed Isaac back to the house.

He could feel the corporate embrace of Ty Daniels Enterprises folding around him.

21

IT WAS MIDAFTERNOON WHEN EDMUND SPEAKER AND HIS GRANDSONS climbed into his pickup and went bouncing across the pasture toward the stock tank. Cows stood footed to their shadows and watched them as they careened along.

"You think the fish will be biting, Grandpa?" said Brad, the eight-year-old.

"I reckon we'll find out soon enough. Now, you all remember what it is we should watch out for when we're down at the tank? Huh?"

"Snakes!" the boys said in unison.

"Just stay back a ways from the tall grass and watch where you step."

Edmund pulled to a stop next to the tank and killed the engine. He got out and went to the truck bed and started laying fishing tackle out on the tailgate. While he was thus engaged, the boys hopped out and ran to the side of the tank, jabbering about the fish they'd surely catch.

Edmund rigged up each grandson by turns with a cane pole and line and bobber and hook baited with a worm. He worked the boys into position on the bank with their lines in the water and then returned to the truck for his spinning rod.

It was still warm, so rather than fish the water along the bank, he figured to work the cooler water in the middle of the tank with a drop shot rig. He affixed a weight to the end of his line and then clipped the plastic worm a few inches above it. He walked off a ways around the bank lest an errant cast catch a young 'un in the head.

He cocked the rod back over his shoulder and then flicked it forward, releasing the catch on the reel just at the right moment. The line went singing off the reel, and the lure traced an arc across the sky, landing with a splash about two-thirds of the way across the tank. He went to the crank on the reel and began to turn it.

When the lure reappeared at bankside, Edmund lifted it from the water, gathered in the slack, and sent it singing once more toward the farther reaches of the tank.

He had been thus engaged for less than half an hour, stopping from time to time to help a grandson refresh his bait or untangle a line, when Edmund's own line snagged up toward the middle of the tank. He tried cranking the reel, but it was caught fast and wouldn't budge.

With both hands he pulled the rod's tip up and over his right shoulder, and the line came grudgingly his way. He reeled in the slack and repeated the motion. He watched as the line drew closer.

At length the end of the line emerged, dragging along with it a red and white plastic cooler. The drop shot rig had managed somehow to wrap itself around the cooler's handle.

"What did you catch, Grandpa?" called one of the boys.

"Looks to be a cooler, of all things."

Edmund laid his spinning rod on the ground and walked to his pickup. He returned with a pry bar that he had stored in a toolbox.

He walked to the edge of the water and reached out and hooked the cooler by the handle with the pry bar and dragged it up onto the bank. The drop shot rig he untangled and laid to one side.

He depressed the button on the side of the cooler and slid open the top.

He hollered and fell backward onto the ground.

When Jeremiah showed up back in Martha's hospital room, he found her engaged in conversation with an attractive young woman in her thirties.

The women left off talking, and the younger woman stood. She had blond hair combed behind her ears and she was wearing a white cloth jacket over her shirt with the hospital insignia on it and a gold nameplate that read BRADSHAW.

"Jeremiah, this is Karen Bradshaw, Sylvester's daughter."

He crossed the room and extended a hand. "You're the one the switchboard told me to expect."

"That's right."

"We was in your daddy's place last night. Before Martha took sick with the *E. coli*."

"I can promise you, she didn't get it there."

"Fact that the other victim didn't take a meal there sort of proves she didn't." He looked at Martha. "State health guy came by and purt' near emptied out the refrigerator."

"He have any idea about the source?"

Jeremiah shrugged. "He packed all the suspects away and headed to Austin to subject them to a laboratory lineup."

A nurse appeared in the doorway, tray in hand. "You ready for your dinner, Mrs. Spur?"

Jeremiah and the pharmacist made way while the nurse situated the rolling table so that Martha could reach her repast. She lifted the cover to reveal a boiled chicken breast, a pile of green beans, and some new potatoes.

Karen said, "Would you mind if I stole your husband for a few minutes?"

Martha took a fork in hand. She looked at the contents of the tray with resignation and then at the pharmacist. "I appear to be doomed to dealing with this disaster-on-a-plate, so please. Go ahead."

Out in the hall, Karen said, "By the way, when did you last see Doc Anderson?"

"This mornin', when I left outta here. Why?"

"He made a note on your wife's chart that I'm not sure about. Having to do with her meds. I wanted to talk to him about it, but I can't seem to find him."

"He was actin' a little off this mornin'. Could be he went home to rest up."

"Could be. He works more than a man his age should."

Karen and Jeremiah proceeded to the cafeteria and got soft drinks, and Jeremiah told her to put her money away and paid for them both. They took a seat on either side of a long table and sipped their beverages like fellow travelers waiting for their flight to be called.

A young mother and her two small children sat across the way. They looked to be killing the afternoon.

One table over from them, an older woman sat with a middle-aged man who appeared to be her son. They sipped coffee and said not a word to one another, as though they were strangers forced to share the same table by overcrowded conditions instead of blood kin.

Some misfortune befell one of the young kids at the first table, and she began to cry. Her mother picked her up in her arms and held the little girl's head to her breast and rocked her. Jeremiah thought how the woman was about the age Elizabeth would have been now, had the cancer not carried her off. Melancholy thoughts such as this, well. He figured he was stuck with them for so long as he drew breath.

Karen placed her glass on the table before her and sat back with her arms folded over her chest. She suddenly seemed as serious as an Amish undertaker.

Jeremiah said, "Okay. So. What seems to be the matter?"

"It's my dad. Ordinarily, after he closes the restaurant on a Friday night? There is only one place he goes. Worldwide. And that's home. But last night he didn't, and no one has seen nor heard from him since. His car is missing, too. And his office appears to have been searched. His floor safe is gone."

She went to the pocket of her lab coat and produced a tissue and dabbed at her eyes. "We're all so afraid something has happened to him."

Jeremiah cleared his throat. "You've told the authorities, then."

"The sheriff was out at the restaurant this morning. You'll forgive me if I'm somewhat underwhelmed by his abilities as a crime fighter."

"Them boys is okay when it comes to pulling over speeders and breakin' up domestic disturbances, but when it comes to honest-to-God crime, it is a sad fact. They don't know c'mere from sic 'em."

"Which is why I was hoping we could get you to help us out."

"I'm not sure I'd be much help. I'm retired, see."

"But you worked missing persons cases, right? Back in the day?"

Jeremiah shrugged. "You make it sound like we're talkin' 'bout the Hoover administration."

"We'd pay you for your time."

"Look, I appreciate it, but—"

"Please, Captain Spur. Just do me one favor. Go check out the barn at my parents' place. Okay?"

"You think he's hidin' in your all's barn?"

Karen leaned in. "You know about my father's invention, right?"

"He showed it to me last night. Some kind of a tumblin' doo-hickey."

"I think it has something to do with his disappearance, this invention of his."

"Think maybe it was some competitor? Somebody who's out there servin' catfish, tastes like mud?"

She shook her head. "There's more to the process than what it does to catfish. Maybe a lot more."

"Like what?"

"Look, when it comes to keeping secrets, Sylvester makes the National Security Agency look like *People* magazine, okay? There was no real documentation of the 'how' of his process other than what he kept in that missing floor safe, and he and my brothers are the only ones who really know how to make it work. Daddy wanted to keep tight control of his trade secrets, see. Part of it is a legitimate fear that someone is going to steal his idea and make a bizillion dollars off it and leave him poor and his genius, such as it is, unappreciated. This means he doesn't talk about it much, not even around family. So all I have to go by is little hints he's dropped along the way."

"Such as—"

"That the process is highly effective on food-borne bacteria."

"Like the *E. coli* that give Martha the drizzlin' you-know-whats?"

She nodded. "I know that must strike you as coincidental."

"It might if I believed in coincidences."

"I'm, we're—the family is uncomfortable sharing information of this nature with someone we can't trust. In the first place, we're not entirely sure whether Sylvester knew what he was talking about. But if he did, and this sort of thing were to leak out, into the public domain, I mean—"

"Which is only too probable if it had something to do with your dad's disappearance, and the sheriff's department goes about the investigation in its usual meat axe fashion. Talkin' to the press and what have you."

"Now you understand our predicament."

"There's somethin' in your dad's barn that feeds these suspicions of yours?"

"That's right."

"Care to elaborate?"

She looked away and then back again. "I'd a lot rather you just went out there and looked for yourself. Drew your own conclusions."

"Well, I'm a little tied down here just now."

"Yes, but your wife has almost fully recovered. They're only keeping her tonight as a precautionary measure."

"Yeah, well. If there's anywhere Murphy's Law can be counted on to be fully engaged, it's in a hospital, you ask me."

Karen leaned forward with her elbows on the table. "What if I kept an eye on her while you're out at my folks' place?"

"You'd look in on her, then?"

"Every hour on the hour."

This would be a more interesting way to spend the evening than watching his wife needlepoint. "Then I reckon all we need do is see if she'll go along with it."

"She will. I talked to her before you arrived. She said she was for anything that got her out of having to watch you sit and fidget."

"I don't know that I'd characterize my watchful concern as fidgetin'."

Karen handed Jeremiah a piece of paper. "Their place is pretty easy to get to." Something across the room caught her eye, and Jeremiah half turned to see what it was.

The lawyer from last night, the one with the little girl who was laid up in ICU, had just entered the cafeteria.

Karen suddenly grabbed Jeremiah's wrist. "Just one more thing."

"Okay."

"I'd appreciate it if you kept this between us."

"I'm not in the habit of talkin' about other people's business."

"Thanks." She let go of his wrist and shot another glance in the lawyer's direction. He was at the counter, filling a tumbler with ice. "Will you call me later?"

"You betchum, Red Rider. Just you don't forget to keep an eye on Mrs. Spur."

She left him sitting there wondering what it was about that lawyer that had jacked her up all of a sudden. Directly the lawyer himself appeared at the table and took the seat recently vacated by the pharmacist.

"Hey, there," he said. "How's your wife coming along?"

"She's about turned the corner, seems like. They're keepin' her one more night for observation, which I think is hospital-speak for 'we hate to see a bed go empty if we can get a another night of revenue from it.' "

The lawyer sighed and seemed to fold in on himself. His shoulders sagged, and his hands hung at his sides. He was a study in worried exhaustion. "Wish I could say my daughter was doing so well."

"Sorry to hear." Jeremiah wanted to ask the man how he knew the Bradshaw woman, but now was clearly not the time to be asking questions of that nature.

"I appreciate that. The doctors say if she can make it through the next couple of days, she has a good chance of—" He stopped and seemed incapable of continuing. He dropped his head and rubbed his eyes with the heels of his hands. When he took them away the tears had started up. "It will be the absolute undoing of Donna—"

"That's your wife?"

He nodded.

"It can be tough on a woman, to lose a daughter. That's somethin' I know a thing or two about."

The lawyer looked a little puzzled. Then he said, "Oh, right. Well, even if little Shelly makes it, they're saying she'll probably have health problems for years to come. And I can tell you one thing for sure."

"Yeah?"

"I have a law license, and I know good and God damn well how to use it. I intend to sue the sorry sons of bitches who did this to us."

"It was more son of a bug than son of a bitch, as I understand it."

"That bug didn't find it's way into my little girl's gut by itself. It was carried there, and I think I know what carried it."

"How could you know that?"

"You were visited by a state health department microbiologist today, right?"

"Yep. Funny-lookin' little bearded guy."

"After he left your place, he went to my in-laws and turned their refrigerator upside-down, same as yours. He told my mother-in-law, he found the same brand of bagged spinach in both places. It was the only food item you and they had in common. He said he'd lay odds the *E. coli* originated in a bag of Happy Valley baby spinach."

"Reckon we'll find out when the test results come back."

The man looked off to one side. When he looked back, his expression was nothing short of murderous. "I'm not waiting that long. I'm filing suit first thing Tuesday morning. Gonna draft the plaintiff's original petition tomorrow, after I've had some sleep. We'll just see how those negligent corporate bastards like their chances in front of a hometown jury. And since I'm filing suit anyway—"

Jeremiah knew what was coming even before the man could get the question out.

"—would you like me to sue on your wife's behalf as well?"

Robert Bruni sat nursing his soft drink after Jeremiah quit the cafeteria. He produced his cell phone and keyed in a number.

"Hello?"

"Hey. It's me. I just saw your sister talking to that retired Texas Ranger. Jeremiah somethin' or other."

"How come, do you think?"

"You tell me."

"She was out at the house today. Mama showed her what was in the barn."

"Seems pretty harmless, I guess."

"Still. I ain't sure I like it."

"Don't get all exercised. There's something else. Something I couldn't tell you this morning with everyone hanging around."

"Okay."

"Isaac Daniels called. They want to meet. Monday."

"Ain't that a little soon?"

"Funny. I sort of thought you were like me, as in not getting any younger."

"Do you really think we should?"

"Doesn't hurt to hear them out. Can you guys make yourselves available?"

"Sure."

"I'll set it up, then."

The lawyer cut the connection and went back to his soft drink.

22

"THIS IS THE PROBLEM YOU'VE GOT, SEE. IT TAKES SEVERAL MILLION dollars to mount a credible campaign in Texas, and that kind of money is mighty hard to come by for a party that hasn't won statewide since 'ninety-four."

Sonya Nichols was sitting on her porch swing with the portable phone at her ear listening to a political consultant based in Austin hold forth in this defeatist fashion.

"I know all about the hammerlock the Republicans have this state in, but don't forget, the shoe was on the other foot twenty-five years ago. So instead of lecturing me about long odds, tell me how we can shorten them."

"Look, it's a chicken-and-egg thing. It takes money to make a credible race, and people will sit on their wallets unless they're confident the race has any chance a-tall."

"Okay, so, how does a person go about building that level of confidence?"

"You got to get yourself known. From the Panhandle to the Valley."

Sonya's eyes drifted to the manila folder that rested on the table before her. "A person would need to get known in the right way, I suppose. As in, for doing justice as part of her civic duty. Not some nakedly ambitious move."

"You got that right. I mean, look what happened to the guy went after the Duke lacrosse players."

"What's all this good advice gonna cost me again?"

"First consultation is free."

"You think I'm done with it after this?"

"I'll send you an engagement letter."

She set the phone aside and took the manila folder in hand. She sat with it on her lap and looked out across her yard at the street where a bunch of neighborhood kids raced their bikes back and forth.

She asked herself, was she just bored? Was that it? Tired of this little life in this little town? Or did she sense there was something more for her out there, if only she had the courage to go chase it?

Did she think she could do the AG's job?

Hell, yeah. She thought she could do the governor's job, for that matter.

But could she get elected to something statewide?

She opened the file folder. Affixed on top with a metal fastener was the report of the Powell brothers, who had returned from the side of the road with a trash bag filled, apparently, with trash. Fast food wrappers, paper cups, old newspapers, nothing incriminating whatsoever.

What interested Sonya, though, was who they found at the scene upon their arrival.

Her old flame, C. Livermore Thomas. Known to most as Clyde and many as "the Judge," since his real first name happened to be Clarence.

The Powells had found Clyde on bended knee studying the ground, and when he stood up it looked to them like he slipped something into his hip pocket. When asked about his presence there he served up what sounded to Sonya like vintage Clyde cock-and-bull, some tall tale about adopting that stretch of road as a marketing ploy.

Sonya knew better. He was out there on a job for the Daniels family. Beating the dullards in the sheriff's department to the punch.

Sonya shook her head and flipped to the next report in the file. The mobile crime scene unit had swept the Hummer and left with what they could find. She would have their full report in the next couple days, but the tech in charge had agreed with her. The substance on the carpet in back sure looked like blood.

She set the file back on the table and folded her arms across her chest and watched the bike races ongoing out on the boulevard.

Ever since her breakup with Clyde, she had been only too happy to give him his distance. He had worn her out with his neediness, his insecurity, his constant taking offense at racial slights often less real than imagined. They hadn't exchanged two dozen words since they parted company, and she was just *fine* with that.

Problem was, when it came to available men in this town, Clyde was just about the entire market. No one else even came close in terms of brains, charm, or sex appeal.

So as a consequence she had poured herself into her career and begun to think of ways to expand her horizons, which in turn had led her to entertain this notion of running for attorney general.

The way she had it figured, the worst that could happen was, she would come to the attention of some big city firm who would make her an offer that would be her ticket right on out of here.

But before even that was possible she would need to mount a credible candidacy.

She reached for the phone again and dialed a number she knew only too well.

An actual business discussion had taken place, but it had been short, and it had been cryptic. Something about some kitchen appliance, the likes of which nobody had ever seen before. The Danielses were going to license the underlying technology and then design and market the machine.

They wanted Clyde to fetch their home appliance specialist from the airport Monday morning, bring him up to Brenham for a meeting. That's all they would say for now. The rest would have to wait till Monday.

After some pool time, he and Isaac had passed the balance of the afternoon in the home theater, a windowless room on the second floor of the main house one entire wall of which was taken up by the largest high-definition television Clyde had ever seen. The walls on either side were hung with photos of Big Ty from back in his playing days.

Clyde and Isaac sat in chairs large enough to accommodate an entire other person; on the arms were buttons by which could be summoned servants bearing soft drinks and snacks. They watched an early-season matchup between powerhouses from the Big Ten and the SEC. It was clear to Clyde from Isaac's emotionally disproportionate reaction to every missed tackle and penalty and turnover that his client had money riding on the outcome.

When they were called downstairs for the trip to Kyle Field Isaac angrily killed the picture by remote. "God *damn* Tommy Tuberville! He got all this talent and not one clue what to do with it. It's like givin' a faggot a key to the Playboy mansion."

He went stomping downstairs with Clyde following behind. They burst through the front door and walked to the limo, which stood idling in the drive. Big Ty was already in the car.

Big Ty pulled the door shut and keyed a switch. "Let's go," he said.

The driver responded, "Yes, sir," and the car eased into motion.

Big Ty looked at Isaac. "How Auburn do?'

"Not well enough to cover the spread."

"What I done told you about that, huh? You keep it up, the sports books take all yo' money." Big Ty looked at Clyde. "You think the Judge here bets college football? No, sir. He too smart for that. Ain't that right, Judge?"

What Clyde thought was, *Great. Nothin' I dig more than bein' put on the spot in a father-son argument.* "Don't know enough about it to bet on it."

Big Ty nodded. "Good thing, too. Gamblin's a sin."

Isaac said, "Where in the Bible it say that?"

"Them Roman soldiers cast lots over Jesus' clothes while he was hangin' there on the cross. You think they wasn't sinners?"

"Fact I'm a sinner and drink iced tea, that don't make drinkin' iced tea a sin. Besides, Joshua cast lots to allocate acreage in the land of milk and honey."

"Look who's a Bible scholar all of a sudden."

"The apostles cast lots to determine Judas's replacement."

Big Ty leaned forward and tapped Isaac on the knee. "Yeah, but they wasn't gamblin' fo' money, see. Gamblin' fo' money is wasteful. You keep it up, the house will take you every time. Wastefulness is a sin. That's, like, the chain of logic here."

"You goin' way overboard with this religious thing, Pops."

"That ain't all. Who is it, owns the gambling casino, huh? It's the white man. The Jew. They just exploitin' you, boy, like they been exploitin' black folks since the dawn of time. How much you into them fo', anyway?"

Isaac folded his arms over his chest and looked out the window at the scenery passing by. "Not more than I can handle."

"Uh-huh. You say that *now.*"

Clyde's cell phone commenced to chirp. He produced it from his pocket and peered at the display. SONYA NICHOLS. He glanced at Isaac, who was reading it alongside him.

Isaac said, "Maybe you better take that."

Clyde flipped the phone open and held it to his ear. "Clyde Thomas."

"Hey. It's Sonya."

"Hey yourself. Been a while."

"How's the private investigator business?"

"Same-store sales is up, year-over-year."

"We need to talk."

"Yeah? 'Bout what?"

"About what happened by the side of the road out on the bypass to-day. I have a report from the Powell brothers that says you were out there, acting strange."

"It ain't against the law to go for a walk in the right-of-way."

"That's what you were doing?"

"It's nobody's business but mine, what I was doing."

"How about I buy you a beer and you can explain to me how your presence at a crime scene is not the business of the Washington County DA."

"No can do. On my way to the Aggies game with some friends of mine."

"That wouldn't be the same crowd I had in my conference room earlier today, now, would it?"

Clyde glanced at Isaac. The man was watching him through narrowed eyelids. Like a cardplayer might watch a dealer he suspected of cold deck-ing. "I said it before and I'll say it again. My business is my business."

"That may be so. You free after the game?"

"I couldn't rightly say."

"What about tomorrow?"

"What about it?"

"Do you have some time to get together or don't you?"

Clyde hesitated. He looked at Isaac. Maybe there was some way to turn this into a positive development, but just at the moment he didn't see how. "How about a cup of coffee at the Big Scoop? Say eleven in the morning?"

"You're on."

The line went dead, and Clyde tucked the phone away just as the limo pulled onto the drive leading to the stadium. The big car motored up to the curb in front of the main entrance and coasted to a stop. Big Ty waited until the driver opened the door, and then he led the way out of the vehicle toward the football field. As each passenger emerged, the driver handed him a sideline pass on a loop of string.

Isaac grabbed Clyde's elbow and pulled him to one side. "Go ahead on, Pops. We catch up with you later."

The older man lifted a hand and kept walking.

Isaac looked at Clyde. "What's she want?"

"Wants to talk, is all."

"She knows you found somethin'."

"She knows squat. Lemme talk to her, find out what she knows and, maybe, like, discourage her from pushing this thing."

Isaac relaxed some. "Okay. You do that. But whatever it is you found out yonder, I want it gone by tonight. We clear?"

"Yeah. We clear."

Isaac stared at Clyde a long moment, and in that moment Clyde worried that Isaac knew he was lying about his intentions. Then the man nodded once. "Let's go." He led the way toward the crush of people pushing through the gate into the stadium. Up ahead, Big Ty towered over the rest of the fans. Now and then he would stop to sign an autograph or shake someone's hand.

Inside the gates the crowd turned right to go up a ramp that led to the seats proper. Big Ty and Isaac and Clyde turned left, and proceeded to an opening in an inner wall where stood two uniformed security guards who waved them through.

They emerged onto a perfectly groomed college football field, seats rising up on all sides, great big scoreboard overhead. The scale of the place made Clyde feel insignificant, like a man standing in an enormous cathedral.

The sun was still high in a cloudless sky, and there was no wind, and the heat trapped in the stadium bowl was stifling.

Isaac took his leave of Clyde and walked over to talk to someone wearing a knit shirt with the Texas A&M logo on it, a man Clyde recognized as the quarterback coach. Big Ty was already over there engaged in conversation, and the two of them stood on the sidelines talking and watching Little Ty, who was taking snaps from under center and firing passes into the hands of receivers who were so far away Clyde had difficulty making out the numbers on their uniforms.

Clyde walked slowly down the sideline so he could think through his call with Sonya. *She suspects somethin'. Maybe even knows somethin'. She wouldn't have called otherwise.*

He wandered toward the bench where young men in maroon and

white ensemble were setting up electrolyte replacement drinks and water and towels and medical supplies. Cables ran this way and that on the ground, and on each end of the bench sat cherrypickers bearing television cameras and their operators, who shot film of the proceedings out on the field. The North Texas Mean Green were working out across the way. They struck Clyde as smaller, slower, whiter, and in general appropriately cast in their roles as sacrificial lambs for Little Ty's season opener in front of the ESPN junkies.

He was beginning to feel the pressure of the position he was in. That thumb didn't find its way to the side of the road by itself, and if it came out of the Daniels Hummer there was a story that went with it that might have career-limiting implications for number 11 back yonder. That was a lot of weight for Clyde to carry.

Then there was the fix Clyde himself was in. How much had the Powell brothers seen? And what other evidence did the DA have? There'd been two other dudes in the car with Little Ty. Could she have gotten one of them to flip?

When th' po-lice took out after us, Little Ty tol' me to chuck that thumb, and I sent it flyin'. Still out there so far as I know.

Fact that it wasn't there didn't necessarily lead to Clyde, though. The Powells might just have overlooked it, little ol' thing like that in all that tall grass. Or something else might have come along and grabbed it. A stray dog, or a grackle maybe.

No, it didn't make any sense to go to panicking. Sonya might *suspect,* but she didn't *know.*

Question was, was he up to lying to her about it?

Better damn well be, 'cause that thumb needs to stay right where it's at for the time bein'. It might look like a severed thumb to ever-one else, but to me, it looks like an ace in the hole.

Then again, maybe there was another way. After all, Sonya didn't know what there was to be found out there by the side of the road. Maybe Clyde should own up to finding *something,* and even produce it. Make it something just harmful enough to throw the dogs off their scent, without hurting Little Ty any.

I know. Somethin' like—

Good God O-Mighty. Look here who's comin'. Talk about timin'.

Let's go find out if what I hear around town is true.

———

Dewey Sharpe had been roaming the sidelines in much the same fashion as Clyde when trouble appeared out of nowhere and tapped him on the shoulder. It took the form of Lamar Jackson, publisher, editor in chief, and main journalist for the *Brenham Gazette*, the birdcage liner that was Brenham's once-a-week newspaper.

"Howdy, Sheriff."

Dewey eyed the man suspiciously. He was all too familiar with the guy's style. He liked to pass himself off as a slack-jawed dolt, asking questions that didn't seem to have much point, until his prey messed up and blurted out something that the entire town would read the following week on the front page, above the fold. Many were the county commissioners and justices of the peace who had been so victimized. "Lamar."

Lamar stood with his hands in his pockets, studying Dewey. "See you got yourself a sideline pass."

"Coach Ballard offered it to me personally."

"Uh-huh."

"What brings you over here? I mean, you all ordinarily run three-day-old wire service reports in your sports section."

"Brenham don't ordinarily have a young man playin' quarterback under the full glare of the national spotlight. After he spent the night in County."

Dewey swallowed. "Where'd you hear—"

"Hell, Dewey. There ain't but one way to get from the front door of the courthouse to a limousine parked at curbside. Musta been three dozen people seen that display this mornin'. Not to mention the busted-up Hummer that sits even still in the parkin' lot. Did you know a mobile crime scene unit went through that thing this afternoon for an entire hour? My phone has been lit up all day with people callin' 'bout this. Would you care to comment in your capacity as sheriff of Washington County? Give you a chance to practice for when the big city papers and sports nets start callin', soon as they pick up my copyrighted exclusive."

Dewey's eyes cut about. Way downfield, Big Ty stood watching Little Ty take practice snaps, but his other son, Isaac, had turned and was looking Dewey's way. Just a few yards this direction stood Coach Ballard, his play chart held at his side. He, too, was showing interest in Dewey's conversation with the journalist.

I don't handle this the right way, I've seen the last of sideline passes. Hell, they might come after my season tickets.

"I can't give you no on-the-record comment."

" 'A high-placed source in the sheriff's department—' "

"Not even that. 'A source familiar with the case who requests ano-nymity—' "

"Okay."

" 'Reports that no charges are expected to be filed other than operat-ing a motor vehicle in excess of the legal speed limit.' "

"That's it? What about the crime unit?"

"We still off the record?"

"Yeah."

"Ordered up by the DA. Out of an excess of caution."

"Some might say an excess of ambition."

"I don't think she's made no secret of her desire to improve her life, career-wise."

"Uh-huh. I'm workin' on another piece of investigative journalism I think maybe you could help me with. One of strictly local interest."

"What would that be?"

"Do you suffer from erectile dysfunction, Sheriff?"

"*What?*"

"That's the story that's makin' the rounds."

It was all Dewey could do to contain his horror. "How's that any-body's business but mine?"

"That don't sound much like a denial, Sheriff."

"But we are talkin' here about somethin' that is entirely *private.*"

"You're a duly elected public official. The public has a right to know, are any of its law enforcement personnel experiencing health problems."

"But even if it were true, and I'm not sayin' it is, mind you, it ain't job-related."

"I wouldn't go so far as to say that, Sheriff. Testosterone is how the west was won. If it hadn't been for that, there wouldn't be no Kyle Field nor Bryan–College Station nor Brenham neither one. Be nothin' around here but a bunch of Comanches cookin' buffalo meat on open fires in front of teepees and scalpin' one another for sport."

"You're kidding, right? Tell me you're kidding."

"Seems to me, if you're settin' around preoccupied with your loss of manhood, we're at high risk of seein' an outbreak of lawlessness at any time."

"I am not believin' this."

"Would you be willin' to release your medical records to the public?"

"The answer to that is not just no, it is hell no."

"What if I sued for 'em under the Open Records Act?"

"I'd fight you till hell freezes over, and then I'd fight you on the ice."

Lamar shrugged. "Of course, I might could see my way clear to sit on this story if I thought you could help me with the bigger one. About how come Little Ty spent the night in the clink and there's yet to be an offense report filed of record."

Dewey leaned in. "That there is blackmail, Lamar."

"I prefer to think of it as an exercise of rights guaranteed us under the First Amendment. You smoke it over and get back to me. Tomorrow wouldn't be none too soon."

Dewey turned and stormed off, not entirely sure where to go. All he wanted was to be away from this pestilential man with his nosey parker damn questions and congenital need to pry into things that don't concern him.

The players had quit the field, and the Aggie Band struck up the fight song at the far end zone and began marching into place. It was ungodly loud, and Dewey was of a sudden in no mood for it.

Dewey had never before been so thoroughly caught between the devil and the deep blue sea. Either he fed Lamar what there was to be fed on Little Ty or he saw his nether region issues get such a public airing his mother could read about them, for crying out loud.

Maybe he should hold a press conference and—

"Dewey! Yo, Dewey!"

The band music was so loud the sheriff could barely hear his name being called from not more than fifteen feet away. He looked and yonder stood his former deputy, Clyde Thomas.

What was he doing here? Did they let just anybody on the sidelines?

Clyde closed the distance and held out a hand. They shook just as the band left off playing and a man's voice echoed around the stadium over the public address system.

"Been a long time, man."

"Yeah, it has."

"You look a little distracted."

"Yeah, sorry. Got a lot on my mind. Cases to work. You know how it is."

"Yeah, well, good luck with that, okay? Say, mind if I ask you a question?"

Oh, no. Good God. Please don't tell me—

Clyde leaned in and dropped his voice. "I was doin' some business in town today and somebody said to me that, um, what's the best way to say this? That yo' pencil was a little short of lead."

Oh for the love—

"Well?" said his former employee.

"You know what Kingfish would say?"

"Kingfish? You mean, from *Amos 'n Andy*?"

"That's the one."

"Sheriff, that was a racist show. Only point of it was to poke fun at black folks."

"He'd say, 'I resent the allegation and I resent the alligator.' "

As Dewey stalked off, the band out on the football field struck up the theme music from *Patton*. It was so military and so male it was hard for him not to take it as a form of mockery.

"Wait, Sheriff! Wait! Didn't mean to offend you, man!" Clyde hustled up and caught Dewey by the elbow. "What you rushin' off for? I need to ask you somethin'."

Dewey pulled free. "You done asked your damn fool question."

"It wasn't like that. I was just wonderin' if what I'd heard was true, you know. 'Case you know where a man like me could score some of that stuff you takin'."

Dewey stared hard at Clyde, trying to see, was the man carrying him high or not.

There was not one thing about Clyde that did not drip of concerned sincerity.

"Why, hell, Clyde," Dewey said. "A man's gotta have a prescription. You can't buy it over the counter or nothin'."

Dewey charged off, leaving Clyde staring after him.

23

THEY PULLED OUT OF CALDWELL HEADED SOUTH, BURLESON COUNTY sheriff Mike Seawright leading the way in his cruiser followed by two EMTs in an ambulance. Just before they got to the county line, the sheriff pulled his cruiser onto a dirt road that led past a couple of modest wood frame houses with attendant outbuildings and vehicles parked about, to a gate that stood propped open by a rock.

The sheriff drove through the gate and onto the pasture and followed tracks made previously by other vehicles. He topped a rise and looked at the scene below. Several men stood around a stock tank.

Deputy Ben Oppermann's cruiser was parked just this side of the tank behind a pickup that had attached to it a gooseneck trailer. A backhoe had been unloaded and stood in readiness.

The sheriff parked and got out and joined the group of men, followed close behind by the two EMTs in their white coats. In addition to Ben there was a backhoe operator and a sidekick of his who was wearing waders up to his chest. Finally there was the landowner, who introduced himself as Edmund Speaker from Houston, Texas.

Downwind of them sat a red and white plastic cooler.

"That's it over yonder, then."

Ben nodded. "I opened it just enough to confirm. It's sure enough got a piece of a arm in it. Although it is peculiar lookin' as hell, I must say. It's like it's been bleached out and all but drained of blood. You ought to have yourself a look, Sheriff."

"I'll pass." The sheriff motioned to the EMTs. "Fetch that damn thing to the ambulance."

The sheriff turned his attention to the stock tank. "Only one way to know for sure if there's more Cracker Jack surprises lyin' out yonder, and that's drain the dadgum thing." The sheriff looked at Speaker. "You sure you're okay with that, sir?"

"Hell, Sheriff, I'm more than okay with it if it means we can avoid a repeat of this episode. Hard enough to get my family to spend time up here as it is, without body parts in coolers showin' up in my tank."

The sheriff turned to the backhoe operator. "Where you want to make your cut?"

The man motioned off to the right. "Over yonder where the water'll run off into that draw."

"Let's get on with it, then."

The man climbed aboard and fired up the machine and shifted it into reverse, and it made a great beeping sound. He drove a ways and then reversed direction and chugged toward the tank.

The backhoe climbed the bank and turned parallel to the water's edge, and there it stopped. The driver activated the claw, and it reached out, slowly, prehistoric-looking, and bit into the ground. The dirt it collected it deposited on the other side of the cut.

By the third cut the water began to stream over the breach. The operator dug up another couple claws full of mud, and then he reached for the gearshift and drove back down the bank.

Inside of thirty minutes the tank was but a few acres of mud on top of which were at least a dozen red and white plastic coolers along with numerous flapping fish. The coolers had started to become visible when the tank was down to just a couple feet of water, rising from the ground like plants germinating from seeds as studied with the aid of time-lapse photography.

The sheriff motioned at the man in waders. "Fetch 'em to shore, and the EMTs'll take it from there."

"Sure thang, Sheriff."

He began laboring through the mud to the field of coolers. Each step involved steadying himself on one leg as he wrenched the other free of the muck and brought it forward. Like a dreamer caught in a nightmare.

It was all but dark before the coolers were collected and in the back of the ambulance. The EMTs took off, bound for Austin and the Department of Public Safety crime lab.

Once the ambulance had disappeared over the hill the sheriff said to the backhoe operator, "Go ahead and mend it back, I reckon."

The man mounted his machine and proceeded to do as instructed.

The man in waders said, "Anybody care for some fish?"

Sheriff Seawright said, "I don't believe."

"They just gonna go to waste."

"Bring me a couple," said Speaker. "I'll fry 'em up for dinner."

"Mind if I hep myself to a few?"

"Take as many as you'd like."

The man in the waders headed back onto the mud field. He stopped a few yards in and turned back toward the bank. "Hey! They's somethin' else here!"

"What?"

The man in waders bent down and began to tug at something that seemed part of the very earth. He dropped his backside and raised his head in the manner of a weight lifter having at a clean-and-jerk. "Looks for all the world like a safe."

"A safe?"

In response the man grunted hugely and rose to a standing position cradling a metallic box in his arms. He staggered through the muck until he had cleared it and dropped his plunder with a thud on the bank. Sheriff Seawright and Speaker walked over to get a better look. The sheriff nudged it with the toe of his boot.

It was indeed a safe, with a combination lock operated by a dial set into the front door. The sheriff looked at Speaker, who shrugged in response.

The sheriff looked once more at the safe. "Signs and wonders," he said. "Get you to carry this thing to my cruiser for me, Wendell?"

Jeremiah rolled his pickup into Bradshaw's yard and killed the engine. The house had the look about it of a do-it-yourself project that had slipped its leash. It was in need of paint and three solid days of hedge trimming and grass clipping.

A couple of dogs emerged from under the porch and stood looking at him with their tails going. The sun had dropped lower in the sky, and the shadows had grown longer. Parked in the yard were a pickup and a couple of sedans. Jeremiah exited his truck and made for the front door.

The dogs went to sniffing at his pants leg and jumping up for attention. He spoke to them of their better qualities and scratched their heads in passing and gained the front porch. The screen door was closed, but the hardwood door behind it stood open, and light shone

down a hallway that had rugs on the floor and framed family photographs on the walls. Jeremiah knocked, and the screen door rattled on
its hinges.

A young man appeared from down the hall. "May I help you, sir?"

"Lookin' for Mrs. Bradshaw."

"May I tell her why?"

"Tell her my name is Jeremiah Spur—"

"Oh. The Texas Ranger." The young man opened the door and extended a hand. "Will Mappelbeck. I'm her nephew. You must be here
about Mr. Bradshaw."

The hall led to a kitchen that was a sort of shrine to Formica and appliances from yesteryear. Jeremiah hadn't seen anything like the refrigerator since he'd had his granddaddy's similar model hauled off after the
old man died in the sixties. On the stove, which itself belonged in some
museum of frontier cooking devices, there sat a pot from which the smell
of chicken and dumplings issued. Having had nothing but corn flakes to
eat the day long, Jeremiah's stomach instantly went to growling.

At a breakfast table sat a woman he recognized as Patti Bradshaw,
talking to a man he didn't know. The man got to his feet and walked
over offering a hand.

"This is Jeremiah Spur," said Will.

"I'm Jimmy Mappelbeck. Patti's brother." Jimmy was about Jeremiah's age, with a weak chin and a protruding stomach and thin arms. He
wore faded khakis and a short-sleeve shirt that buttoned down the
front. He looked like an actor playing a barber in a sitcom set in rural
America.

Jeremiah shook the man's hand and doffed his hat. He nodded at
Patti, who bore a worried look. "Karen come to see me about Sylvester.
I take it he ain't been heard from."

She shook her head. Her chin went to quivering, and she looked
away.

"Well." Jeremiah waved his hat vaguely in the direction of the back of
the place. "She wanted to know, would I take a look in your all's barn."

The woman nodded.

"Anything we can do to help?" asked Jimmy.

"No. Y'all go ahead on with what you were doin'."

"Wasn't doin' much. Just settin' here, keepin' Patti company."

Jeremiah set his hat on his head and squared it. He nodded to them each in turn and made for the back door. As he stepped through, a calico cat that was sitting on the porch tensed and looked his direction. Its tail switched back and forth.

The barn was a two-story affair painted the traditional red and white. A gravel drive led to a door that rode on tracks. A lock had been placed on the door, but the combination had been worked, and it hung loose. He lifted out the lock and took hold of the handle and hauled the door open.

He stood blinking in the gloom and looked around for a light switch. He found one set into a wall to his left and threw it, and what was revealed by the floodlights overhead was something the likes of which he would not have thought possible.

There was no sign that the place had ever been used in pursuit of agriculture. Instead, the barn had been converted into a laboratory. The flooring was white tile interspersed with drains. There were benches on which sat beakers and fancy-looking equipment, and there were sinks and stainless steel hoses along the far wall and what appeared to be a series of refrigeration units.

Jeremiah made for the refrigerators and pulled one open. In it was a collection of plastic bags similar to those the microbiologist from Austin had used for the collection of samples. Inside the bags were what appeared to be all manner of food items, each grouped on its own separate shelf. One shelf contained chicken wings, another fish fillets, a third baby carrots, a fourth some manner of leafy greens. Each plastic bag had a date and other markings on it in black.

Another shelf was devoted entirely to the storage of petri dishes.

Jeremiah closed the door and looked around. Lined up on the lab bench were two tumbling gizmos like he had seen the previous night at the restaurant and two other contraptions that looked like a Crock-Pot sitting on a base.

Jeremiah walked to a desk that sat butted up against a wall. He picked up a photo in a frame. Three men in fishing gear. Sylvester, Doc Anderson, and the brother-in-law Jimmy, the one Jeremiah had just met.

He set it back down and reached for a sheet of paper that had been tacked to a bulletin board. It was an invoice for the legal services of one Robert Bruni. "That would explain it," he muttered.

He tacked it back up and reached for another item posted there.

"What the hell do you think you're doin'?"

Jeremiah looked up to see one of Sylvester's sons standing there with his fists clenched by his sides. Hard for Jeremiah to tell the two of them apart sometimes, but this seemed to be the older one. Mark was his name, wasn't it?

Jeremiah set the paper he'd been reading down on the desk. "I'm Jeremiah Spur. Maybe you've heard of me."

"I don't care who you are. You got no right to be here."

"Actually, I'm here at your sister's request."

"Karen asked you to come poke around in here?"

"She's worried about your all's dad. He is still missin', right?"

"This is Daddy's special place. Ain't no one else allowed in here."

Jeremiah hesitated. Here was a man clearly in his twenties but who spoke about his father in a way that seemed more appropriate to a person half his age. "It don't matter to you that somethin' in here might tell us what become of him?"

"Mister, nothin' matters to me, 'cept makin' sure he don't find out one of us let you in this place."

Jeremiah shrugged and glanced once more at the paper he had been holding, the better to fix its contents in his head. "Reckon I better leave, then."

He stopped when he got within arm's reach of Mark. "Before I go. Mind if I ask you a question?"

Mark regarded him sullenly. Like a man who had been drug from a deep sleep to answer the doorbell only to find a political activist there. "I got nothin' to say to you."

"I'll take that as a yes. My question is, what are you afraid of? Is it your old man? Or is it that someone will find out what become of him?"

The punch was telegraphed from somewhere near the county line. Jeremiah stepped to one side and grabbed the young man's forearm with his left hand and jerked it down and brought his right elbow up and crashed it against Mark's temple. The man's eyes lost focus and his knees buckled and he hit the ground.

Jeremiah walked back to the desk. He took up the item that had attracted his attention and folded it into squares and stuck it in his hip pocket.

He was behind the wheel of his truck and about to start the engine when there appeared at his window a beautiful black woman who was maybe twenty years of age. She was dressed in tight jeans and a T-shirt. She had a harried look about her, as if on the run from something. "Excuse me," she said. "Do you happen to know if Mr. Sylvester's around?" Her eyes cut about.

"I don't believe he is."

She bit her lower lip and looked away. "Damn," she said softly.

"Is there somethin' wrong?"

She looked back at Jeremiah. She seemed on the verge of tears. "We didn't get our ingredients today like he promised. We don't get those ingredients, my mama gonna go back to the way she was, sure as the world. Then—" she shook her head.

She turned to walk off.

Jeremiah stepped out of the truck. "Hold up a second."

She turned back.

"I'm lookin' for Sylvester, too."

She shook her head. "I don't know where he's at. That much ought to be plain."

"Seems nobody does. Man has up and disappeared."

"Well, if you find him you tell him the Bensons are hurtin' for ingredients."

"We both need to find him, then, right? Maybe we could help one another."

"You a customer, too?"

"His daughter asked me to help find him."

"Why she ask you that?"

"I used to be in law enforcement. I was a Texas Ranger."

She planted a fist on her hip. "Ain't that a baseball team?"

"Well, yeah, but—"

She held up a hand and smiled. She had the natural beauty young women have, which shows all the more when you see them happy. A smile is all the makeup a truly beautiful woman needs. "I jus' messin' with you, sugar. I know what a Texas Ranger is."

"I'd like to know what these ingredients are you're talkin' about. Might help me figger out where to look for the man."

"This ain't somethin' I'm at liberty to discuss."

"But you want to find him, don't you?"

"It ain't a matter of want to. I got to."

"Then what have you got to lose? Come on. Get in the truck."

She hesitated and then walked back and got in the passenger side. Jeremiah got behind the wheel and engaged the transmission and backed up and turned around. He held out a paw. "Jeremiah Spur."

"Your people give you a Bible name, huh. So did mine." She took his hand. "Salome Benson."

"Ain't that the woman—"

"Yeah. Served up John the Baptist's head on a tray like it was a pig in a blanket."

"Well. Pleased to meet you." He headed for the highway.

"We need to stop and pick up my ride. I parked just up the way. Out of sight. Mr. Bradshaw don't care for us to come around here."

"Fine. Then can we go somewhere and talk?"

"You can follow me to Mama's, and we can talk there."

Doc Anderson walked into his sixty-five-hundred-square-foot house in Country Club Estates and proceeded directly into the kitchen. It was a lot of house for a man who'd lived alone his entire adult life, but he liked it that he had plenty of room to rattle around in. Besides, what else was a man going to do with his money in this town?

He set his bag down on the kitchen table and opened it. Before he could reach inside it his cell phone set up. He took it out of his sport jacket and examined the display.

HOSPITAL PHARMACY.

He punched a button and sent the call to voice mail. He figured it was Karen Bradshaw, calling to question him about some of the instructions he'd left this afternoon concerning the dispensing of various medicines, on Martha Spur's chart and that of a few other patients. He knew his orders would be at odds with standard protocol in every case.

Karen Bradshaw would know that, too, and that's why she'd be calling.

She must be about convinced by now, I'm starting to lose it some. The thought made him grin.

He reached into his satchel and collected a clear plastic bag that contained a number of syringes, each of which had a cap over the needle. He turned to his left and opened his refrigerator door and leaned down and opened the vegetable crisper drawer. He deposited the plastic bag in the drawer and then shoved it home and closed the door.

His cell phone sounded once more, and after checking the display he decided this was a call he had better take. "What's up?"

"I think we may have a small problem."

24

ISAAC DANIELS PACED THE AGGIES SIDELINE, UNABLE TO SHAKE HIS
troubles.

Wasn't how the game was going that had him bottomed. Just five
minutes into the second quarter, the Ags had all but salted it away. Little Ty had accounted for all three of their touchdowns, two by air and
one by land. The rushing touchdown was one of those things of beauty
he seemed to pull off with no apparent effort. Little Ty had taken the
ball from center and dropped back and saw a field before him, looked
like a mall parking lot on Christmas morning. Off he went, highlight
reeling it all the way to the end zone, where he struck the Heisman pose
for the folks out in TV-land.

No, Isaac's problems lay with the lights on the scoreboard and the
display on his BlackBerry, both of which were showing him scores from
other games that were as grim as a minibar stocked by a Muslim. He was
gonna be out a couple G's unless he ran the table in the Pac-10.

On top of his bad betting day, there'd been all this pregame drama,
that tub-o'-lard sheriff talking to the local newspaperman, hisself nothin'
but a dumb cracker, and then his boy Clyde buttonholing the sheriff, the
two of them looking all intense and involved in their conversation.

It had to be about Little Ty, right? What else would have them two
huddled up, talkin' like old pals that had just bumped into one another
at the dry cleaners?

He might feel better about all this if Clyde had done like he was told,
and gotten rid of whatever it is he found out there in the roadside
weeds. But so far the man had not done so, had all but gone out of his
way to make sure Isaac knew it.

As though to threaten him in some way.

Could he trust Clyde not to shake him down?

Isaac wasn't sure. Suddenly he was sorry he hadn't reached out to the dude more in the past, made him a part of the Daniels inner circle. Bought that old loyalty like you'd buy a bottle of ketchup.

He hadn't been sure what to make of it when Clyde came up to him and said he needed to leave early. Asked was it okay if the driver took him back to the Daniels place so he could get his car.

"What you sayin', dog? Don't you want to stay, watch the game?"

Clyde had looked away. "Got somethin' I need to do. Tonight. It just come up."

"You was over there talkin' to that sorry excuse for a sheriff. He give you an assignment I need to know about?"

Clyde looked him in the eye. "It ain't like that."

"Gettin' all defensive on me."

"You the one wants to be kept in the dark. I'm just doin' like you asked."

Isaac flipped a wrist by way of dismissal. "Go on, then. But I want a report tomorrow. After you and your girlfriend have your all's heart-to-heart."

"I'll call you."

"See that you do."

Isaac had watched Clyde disappear up the tunnel, less sure what to make of the man than ever.

At the half the Ags had stretched their lead to thirty-one, and the Mean Green looked completely gassed. Isaac was making book mentally on how many snaps Little Ty would take in the second half when his BlackBerry chimed. The display said UNKNOWN NUMBER. He held the thing to his ear. He liked everything about the device except how it felt when he used it for a phone. It was like talking into a Pop-Tart.

"Isaac Daniels speaking."

"Your brother's big on taking risks, ain't he?"

"Excuse me?"

"Like that third down pass he threw into double coverage. Pass like that is a cornerback's dream if the quarterback don't spot it."

"Who is this?"

"Friend of Little Ty's."

"How come you don't say who you are, then?"

"I'm his friend, not yours."

"How'd you get my cell phone number?"

"I loaned your brother somethin' last evenin', before he decided to join the NASCAR circuit. I'm a little curious what's become of that item."

"What makes you think I know?"

"He told me you're the fixer in your family. Every family has one, you know. Usually it's a woman. This thing I give him to hold. You know what it is, right?"

"No. And I'd rather not know."

"Suit yourself. I just need to rest easy that it's not gonna show up somewhere it shouldn't. Like in the cops' hands."

Isaac was running through a mental list of Little Ty's friends and acquaintances, trying to place this strange voice on the phone. He was coming up empty. Lately there had been some elliptical references to someone Little Ty was in touch with about a matter bearing on the family business and brand, but no specifics.

Had to be this guy, and now here he was wanting to know things Isaac couldn't—

Wait. What does a smart gambler do but hedge his bets?

"You ever heard of a former deputy sheriff, name of Clyde Thomas?"

"Maybe I have and maybe I haven't."

"Well, you might want to figure out how to meet him."

"On account of how come?"

"You'll pardon me if I don't go into a lot of detail, but the item in question? The one you say you loaned my little brother? It's him that has it."

The line went dead without so much as a good-bye.

Clyde mounted the front steps of a modest but well-kept single-story residence over in the black folks' part of town. It was just past full dark, and the neighborhood was empty. No kids playing in the yards, no traffic on the streets, no noise. Everybody inside, tuned to the game.

Brought home to Clyde once more the power this one season, this one player, had over folks. It had united the town like nothing he had ever seen. Everybody pulling in the same direction, wanting the same thing, didn't matter, really, what church you went to or what your politics were or anything else. If in this area code anywhere could be found a group of people for whom football had little meaning, a sect of Hare Krishnas maybe, he had no doubt but that tonight they would still all be huddled around the high-def in their saffron robes thumping their bongos in time with the "Aggie War Hymn."

He knocked and stood waiting with his hands clasped behind his back.

The door swung open, and there stood Bernice Frazier in housedress and shawl with her gray hair pinned up and her reading half-eyes perched on the end of her nose. "Clyde Thomas. As I live and breathe. You get in this house this instant."

Clyde stepped over the threshold into 1951. The Frazier place seemed to have been designed for a remake of *Pollyanna*, with lace doilies and lamps made of cut crystal glass and china dogs sitting on the floor with patient looks painted on their faces.

Clyde kissed the houselady on the cheek. "You lookin' mighty fine, Mrs. Frazier."

Her smile grew the warmer. "Liver pills and clean livin'." She nodded toward the rear of the house. "He don't approve of them pills. But I don't let him tell me how it is."

She led him through the house until they came to a book-lined study in which sat a gray-haired black man dressed in khakis and a cotton shirt, watching a television set. He got to his feet and extended a hand although he could barely take his eyes from the screen. "Come in here and have a sit. We'll visit when halftime comes."

Clyde dropped into an armchair that was a twin of his host's and accepted Bernice's offer of a soft drink and turned his attention to the television. Aggies had the ball on their own forty-five. Graphic at the top of the screen told the story. A little more than two minutes left in the half, score of twenty-eight to zip, third down, three to go. Little Ty had the offense in shotgun formation.

"Looks like they fixin' to throw the ball, huh," said Clyde.

"You can't never tell with that boy at the helm."

Little Ty lifted his left leg and planted it back as before, and the center hiked the ball. The blocks held, and the running back picked up an outside linebacker blitz. Clyde counted in his head. One-Mississippi, two-Mississippi, three-

Little Ty tucked the ball and ran off right tackle. The safeties chased the runner out of bounds fifteen yards downfield.

Dr. Frazier clapped his hands together. "Damn, he has some fine moves. Mother," he called into the next room. "You ought to get in here and see this." The lenses of his spectacles reflected back the television screen.

"Got dishes need doin'," came the reply.

"Dishes can wait. It can all wait." He grinned at Clyde and clapped him on the knee. "Ain't that right? This is *the* year."

"That's what I know."

"Long as number 'leven yonder stays healthy, our boys goin' all the way. I delivered him, you know. Born at two thirty in the mornin'. Soon as I had him in my hands I knew I was holdin' somethin' special."

The half ended with the Ags comfortably ahead. Doc Frazier and Clyde sat back, and the old man muted the sound. "Don't expect we'll see Ty much in the second half."

"Not with Arkansas comin' up next week."

Doc Frazier clapped Clyde on the knee again. "Good to see you, son. What brings you around here of a Saturday night?"

"I need to ask a small favor." Clyde leaned in and spoke briefly of his request.

The doctor took his glasses off his head and wiped them with his shirt and placed them back. "You let the commercials they show during the golf get to you, Judge?"

"It ain't like that."

"It's okay if it is. Ain't no stigma."

"I ain't plannin' to take 'em. Not me nor no one else."

"Then why should I cut you the 'scrip?"

"Because it can be helpful in a case I'm workin' on." Clyde sat back. "Now, that's all I can say. Rest is strictly on a need-to-know basis."

"Need to know, huh. Need to know."

"I understand, this all seems real cloak-and-dagger. But I promise you, man. I got nothin' but the best of intentions."

"Well," the doctor said. "It's not like it's a controlled substance." He walked to his desk and fetched a pad. He came back and dropped into his chair and sat scribbling and then tore off the top page. "Here."

Clyde got to his feet. "Any idea where I can get this filled?"

"Only one place open tonight. Pharmacy over at the hospital."

"I really appreciate this, man."

The doctor showed him out the door, and Clyde was barely off the front porch when he noticed a vehicle he recognized parked behind his own.

25

JEREMIAH DROVE WITH ONE HAND, AND WITH THE OTHER HE PULLED from his khakis the item he had taken out of Sylvester Bradshaw's laboratory.

It was three sheets of paper stapled together. On each page was a table, data arranged in columns and rows.

Columns headed DATE, PATHOGEN, PROCESS TIME, CONTROL, SAMPLE, LOG REDUCTION.

The rows were labeled with the names of food items. CHICKEN. BEEF. CATFISH. CARROTS. LETTUCE.

He laid the paper down on the seat next to him and drove on.

He followed Salome to a quiet residential street in that part of town where lived most of Brenham's African American folks. She pulled into the drive of a single-story structure with cedar shake siding. He slid to the curb in front. They met on the walk and proceeded to the front door together.

Salome pushed through the front door without knocking. "Mama! Yo, Mama!"

A slender woman of about fifty materialized through a door leading to the back. She had her hair up in a kerchief and was wiping her hands on a dish towel. "Hush up that hollerin', girl. Who's that?" She jerked a chin Jeremiah's way.

"This is Mr. Spur." Salome glanced at Jeremiah. "This here is Mama," she said unnecessarily.

Jeremiah touched the brim of his Stetson. "Mrs. Benson."

"What'd you bring him here for?"

"He wants to know why we lookin' for Mr. Bradshaw."

"What business is that of his?"

"He's doin' likewise."

"At his daughter's request," said Jeremiah.

"We ain't s'posed to be talkin' about none of this."

"We goin' out to the back porch, Mama. Bring them pictures."

"Somethin' has got to be did about you, girl."

"Just bring 'em, Mama."

Salome led Jeremiah into the kitchen. "You want somethin' to drink?"

"Water would be good."

She opened the freezer door and filled a glass with ice. Jeremiah stood looking around. The kitchen was well kept and lit with the slanting light of the vanishing sun. In one corner sat a table on which rested a machine like the one Sylvester had demonstrated for him the night before. "That's Sylvester's device."

Salome handed him his water glass. "You just pretend you never saw it. Better for us if you do."

On the porch, they took seats in cane-bottom rocking chairs. The small backyard was planted in pansies, and baskets of begonias hung from an oak tree beyond which sat a utility shed.

Jeremiah sipped his water. "Quiet in this part of town."

"Ever-body inside, watchin' the football."

The door opened, and out walked Mrs. Benson carrying a photo album. She handed it to her daughter and turned around to head back in.

"You welcome to stay, Mama."

The woman shook her head. "Nuh-uh. I'll not be a party to it."

"Suit yourself."

Salome opened the photo album and turned a couple pages. "Here. This is a good one." She came over and set the photo album in Jeremiah's lap. "This was taken 'bout two years ago."

She planted a forefinger on a picture showing her in a different hairstyle standing next to a woman who must have weighed two hundred fifty pounds. "Who's that big ol' gal you're with?"

"That's Mama."

"Do what now?"

"Uh-huh. If she'd been lighter than air we'd've painted 'Goodyear' on her side and flew her over sports events."

"There sure ain't as much of her now as there used to be." Jeremiah turned more pages in the album. In all the pictures Mrs. Benson was fully double her current size.

"Back then, she was in terrible health, too. Type two diabetes, heart problems, all that weight on her. All on account of her diet."

"Which consisted of—"

"She was the mayor of Fast Food City. Like, for life. Them golden arches was just a big ol' magnet for her, three, four times a day. Burgers, fries, chicken wings. Whatever fatty thing they was available to eat."

"What was it, made her change her ways?"

"We was in Bourré one night, and Mr. Sylvester came and sat at our table—"

"Sylvester Bradshaw?"

She cocked her head to one side and looked at Jeremiah. "I know what you thinkin'. You thinkin' the man has a race thing. It ain't really that, see. It's more like a class thing. Since he been longtime poor himself, he relates to the likes of us. The man just be real careful how much of that side of hisself he shows. Like that night we was in there. Place was about to close, and it was only us was left."

"So he felt comfortable sittin' down for a visit. No witnesses."

"He tol' us he'd been watchin' us come in for some time and had got to wonderin', how was Mama's health? And we said, you know, she had the type two and the heart and the blood pressure, and he said would we be interested in tryin', like, an experiment to see, would it make her feel better?

"We asked the man what he had in mind, and he said he'd be around the next day to 'splain it to us if we'd tell him where we live.

"Next day, here he comes with his gizmo and a whole sack full of groceries. Chicken and catfish and vegetables. He had us sit in the kitchen and watch while he mixed the ingredients and put in the food and tumbled it all in his machine. Then he cooked it up. But he didn't fry it. No, sir. The meat was baked and grilled, and the vegetables he served raw, and it was the best food we ever ate. Better than fast food even.

"We asked him, what made it taste so good? And he said he couldn't much talk about it, but it had somethin' to do with how his invention returned the food to its original state of freshness, made it taste like the vegetables was straight out of the garden and the chicken killed here back of the house, 'stead of bein' full of germs and chemicals like everything is by the time it makes its way down seventeen hundred miles of interstate highway to a grocery store or restaurant."

"When did all this happen?"

"Summer a year ago. Since then, Mama ain't had the first Big Mac or bucket of extra crispy. She does her own shoppin' and cookin', and she lost all that weight and feels better and more energetic, and her blood sugar levels is down where they belong."

"Just because Sylvester's invention made her food taste fresher?"

"You ever tasted really fresh food, Mr. Spur?"

"I did, back when I was a boy and we grew everything our own selves."

"We talkin' a while back, then."

"I've been around since the earth cooled."

"You had dinner?"

"No."

Without a word she got up and went into the house. Jeremiah sat thinking about what he had heard. If Sylvester's invention could make people want to eat food that was good for them and thereby improve their health and energy levels, then it seemed to him the thing had enormous commercial potential.

Not to mention, it represented a meaningful threat to the bottom line of any number of businesses that were dependent on poor dietary practices being widespread among the population. Fast food franchises principal among them.

When the back door flew open again, Salome walked out carrying a tray on which sat not the head of a prophet but a plate of food and a glass of iced tea. "Here. See for yourself."

Dinner consisted of a fish fillet that had been baked and sprinkled with herbs, broccoli, a side salad. Just the kind of meal that here lately he had been force-fed at home.

He thanked her and took the fork in hand and took a bite of fish.

He chewed.

"Damn. This is better even than fried. This is Sylvester's fish?"

"Uh-huh."

He took a bite of vegetable. He set the fork down and looked at his hostess. "This beats all I ever had."

"You feelin' me now, huh?"

Jeremiah tucked back into supper. "Sylvester's process takes what out of the food again?"

"He calls 'em impurities. Anything God didn't mean to put there, that got picked up along the way in the process of mass packagin' and distribution. That's on account of the food business itself, see. It ain't principally 'bout feedin' folks, accordin' to him, but 'bout makin' money."

"You think you all were the only such experiment Sylvester conducted, or were there others?"

"Mr. Sylvester, he never said. All he said was, we was not allowed to talk about any of this to anybody or he'd come get his machine from us. But there was another man come by this summer, a man Mr. Sylvester sent 'round. He allowed as how they was maybe a dozen of us."

"What was this other man's name?"

"He never said, but I think he might have been a doctor of some kind."

"What makes you say that?"

"On account of he give Mama a free physical. Blood work and everthing. Said he was workin' on some kinda study."

"Can you describe him?"

"Older white gentleman. White hair. Real nice bedside manner."
Tres Anderson.

Jeremiah set the tray to one side. "You said somethin' over at Sylvester's about some kind of ingredients?"

"For the process. It ain't just the machine, see. It's what you put in it to make it work. Mr. Sylvester, he usually make the delivery himself, first day of the month. He don't show up, we start to get antsy around here."

Jeremiah recalled Sylvester saying something about some kind of acid. "Any idea what those ingredients might be?"

The woman shook her head. "We wasn't allowed to know."

"Well." Jeremiah got to his feet. "I best better get high and behind it."

She rose as well and led him to the front door of the place.

"I appreciate the meal and the information."

"You find Mr. Sylvester, you tell him we need our month's supply."

"You bet." Jeremiah started down the front steps. He stopped and turned around. "Just one more question."

"Okay."

"You all wouldn't by any chance know the Ty Daniels family, would you?"

The woman grinned. "This here is Brenham, Mr. Spur. All the black folks know one another. Fact is, the Danielses go to our church."

"Figgered as much."

He turned and walked to his pickup and got under the wheel. He pulled away from the curb and drove to the end of the block and was about to take a left when he saw a familiar vehicle parked on the street a few doors down.

Huh. Twice in one day.

26

AT HALFTIME DEWEY MADE HIS WAY BACK INSIDE THE STADIUM PROPER.
He found a spot against the inner wall where he could stand without
being jostled and dialed his cell phone and held it to one ear and stopped
the other ear with a finger.

The DA answered on the first ring.

"Hope I'm not disturbing nothin'," he said.

"I'm doing what single women in Brenham do on Saturday night.
Inhaling and exhaling and waiting for Monday to be here."

Dewey cleared his throat. "Just checkin' to see if there's anything
new on the Little Ty matter. He's having a helluva game tonight."

"Which is relevant how?"

Dewey shrugged. "Just thought you'd like to know."

"If I wanted to know I'd have the television on, wouldn't I?"

God. She can be such a bitch.

She said, "The crime scene techs say they'll have a report to me early
next week. Meanwhile, I am sitting down with my old friend Clyde
Thomas tomorrow morning to find out what he was doing out by the
side of the road when those moronic Powell brothers showed up to conduct their so-called search."

"Clyde Thomas? Hell, I just saw him this evening. Here at the game.
I think he must have come with the Daniels family."

"Why would you think that?"

"He had a sideline pass. They don't hand those out to just anybody.
Plus I saw him talkin' to that other Daniels boy, the one who came to
the meeting."

"I figured as much. He'd better have some good answers for me tomorrow."

They said their good-byes, and Dewey cut the connection. He would like to think the taxpayers of Washington County appreciated his work-ing his fanny off here on a Saturday evening when he should be relax-ing and enjoying the game, but like as not they'd never learn about the earnest strivings of their diligent sheriff.

What they were more likely to learn about him, if Lamar Jackson had his way, was a good deal more personal and embarrassing.

Dewey sighed and looked around for a men's room. He needed to bleed his traitorous lizard before the second half kicked off.

The vehicle pulled off the street into the parking lot and nosed into a space. The driver killed the engine. He double-checked the page he'd ripped from the telephone directory. This had to be the right place. Problem was, the telephone listing did not include an apartment num-ber, and there must be a good fifty units here, maybe more.

He took a brown paper sack in hand and stepped from the vehicle and proceeded to the sidewalk. He followed it around to the front of the apartment complex, which was marked by an arch that led to an inner courtyard with a swimming pool and what looked to be a clubhouse. Lights set atop poles illuminated the common area. A lone young man stood at a grill turning steaks and drinking a beer from a green glass bottle.

"Excuse me. I got a delivery here for a Clyde Thomas, lives at this address. You wouldn't happen to know which apartment is his, would you?"

"Sorry, friend. I'm new here myself. You might check the mailboxes over by the clubhouse. Residents' names are all displayed there."

The man grinned and nodded. "Much obliged."

He found the mailbox for C. Thomas. Unit 121. He set out wander-ing until he found a door with those numbers affixed. He stood listen-ing. No sound from inside. He looked around to make sure no one was watching. He pressed the doorbell button and stepped quickly around the corner of the building. The door stayed closed.

He returned once more and examined the door. It was held fast by a dead bolt. It could be overcome only by sheer force, and that would at-tract entirely too much attention.

Nothing to be done but wait.

He found a bench where he could watch the apartment without being noticeable himself. Took a seat and set the paper bag at his feet. He sat with his legs crossed listening to the various country music tunes played by the jukebox in his head.

At that moment, Clyde was approaching the driver's side of the pickup that sat parked behind his Impala. Jeremiah raised a hand in greeting.

Clyde laid a hand on the door. "Second time in one day."

"Small towns favor chance encounters."

"Could make a man begin to wonder if he was bein' followed."

"What's to be gained by following you?"

"Not much of nothin'."

"Drive a grammarian crazy to live in these parts, I imagine."

"Do what now?"

Jeremiah grinned. "You got a minute? Want to bounce somethin' off you."

Clyde shrugged. "Fire away, man."

"You know that restaurant out on the bypass? Catfish joint called Bourré?"

"I know the place. I don't eat there, though."

"Why not? Their fish is pretty fair."

"Man that runs the place is a racist. That's why not."

"How do you know that?"

Clyde shrugged again. "It's common knowledge, he don't make black folks feel welcome."

"Well, this guy—his name is Sylvester Bradshaw, by the way—he went missing last night."

Clyde's thoughts turned immediately to his roadside find. "Is that a fact?"

"Yep. Seems he might have been snatched. Whoever it was snatched him also turned his office upside-down and carried his floor safe off."

"What's that got to do with me?"

"I'm comin' to that. His daughter asked me to look into findin' him, but since it's been almost a day I'd be surprised if he turns up alive."

"I'm guessin' you have a theory about what happened to the man."

"Workin' on one, has to do with a thing he invented. You might call it a process. You put food through it and it comes out tasting better and it's better for you, too. This is a process a person can use right in their own kitchen. Doesn't take special training of any kind, just a tumbling device and some ingredients."

"Still not seein' that ol' Clyde connection, my man."

"Last night I was standing around up at Emergency, after they brought Little Ty and them in, talkin' to Bobby Crowner, when I overheard the Daniels kid say somethin' about the family finances maybe bein' sorta puny. Then earlier today, I ran into you out by the side of the road, apparently lookin' around in just the spot where Bobby saw those boys chuck somethin' while he was tryin' to pull 'em over."

Clyde started to say something, but Jeremiah held up a finger.

"You know the Bensons, live just down the street yonder?"

"I know Salome some."

"Seen her mother lately?"

"Not that I recollect. Where is this goin', man?"

"I was out at Sylvester's this evenin', and Salome showed up, huntin' Sylvester and a supply of the ingredients that are used in this process of his. Seems the Bensons have been testin' Sylvester's process for some months now. As a consequence of which it has totally converted them away from fast food and onto healthy eatin'. Changed the mama's whole life around."

"Good for her."

"So. Here's what I'm wonderin'. Suppose word about this miraculous invention of Sylvester's made its way to the ears of the Daniels family, who would be interested, maybe, in expanding their kitchen appliance business out of toasters. And suppose they approached Sylvester about some kind of business proposition and further suppose that he received them none too kindly, which would be typical of him. Do you reckon the Danielses might be in need of a new source of cash flow so much that they would lay their hands on Sylvester's process, not to mention his person, in a felonious manner?"

"How would I know?"

"You were sent to that roadside by somebody with an interest in what got tossed from that Hummer last night. That just about had to have been a Daniels. And if by chance them boys were carrying somethin' in that Hummer that tied them to Sylvester's disappearance, well. That would explain why they lit a shuck when Deputy Crowner tried to pull them over."

Clyde shook his head. "Sorry, man. Can't help you. Don't know nothin' about any of this."

Jeremiah turned the key in the ignition without taking his eyes off Clyde. "Well, just thought I'd ask. You take care now, you hear?"

Clyde took a step back. "Yeah, man. You, too."

He watched the Ranger's pickup out of sight, and then he got in his Impala and started it up. He drove a few blocks and then pulled over to the curb to think.

The old Ranger had furnished him a plausible explanation for the source of the thumb and Little Ty's involvement with it, and that cast matters into a new and more troubling light. Not that there could ever be an innocent explanation for a severed thumb by the side of the road, but there could have been an explanation that didn't implicate the Danielses.

Now he was hard-pressed to imagine any other.

It wasn't a woman's thumb he'd stumbled across out there in the weeds. It was a dude's, an old white dude's. That much was clear.

Everything else was the stuff of speculation, starting with this catfish restaurant fool and what might have become of him.

Who would have thought the old guy behind the counter at that catfish place was capable of inventing something that would attract the attention of the mighty Daniels family? Assuming Jeremiah wasn't mistaken in this theorizing of his.

If the man *was* right, what duty did Clyde now owe the Danielses? Was there some kind of privilege that bound him to silence, as would be the case if he were their lawyer?

Then there was the question of his own legal exposure—he hadn't told anyone what he had found out there, so how could it be tied to him in any way?

He didn't see how it could.

Still, it left him feeling ill-at-ease. Concealing evidence, accessory after the fact—these were concepts that were apt to interfere with a man's sleep and digestion.

If that meat locker wasn't closed for the rest of the weekend he'd be inclined to go fetch his package of hamburger and drive to the Brazos River and chuck it as far as he could downstream. Probably what he should have done with the thumb in the first place.

But that option would not be available to him until Tuesday morning.

"Maybe it's just as well. Gimme time to think all this through like a rational human being instead of a man who's trippin' over the position he finds hisself in."

He pulled down on the tree and drove on.

27

KAREN BRADSHAW WAS AT HER POST, FILLING LITTLE PAPER CUPS WITH pills for the following morning's patient rounds and trying to decide if she needed to talk to hospital administration about Dr. Anderson.

When she had first stopped by Martha Spur's room that afternoon, she had reviewed the patient's chart and was surprised to find that Tres had stopped her antibiotics. Karen knew full well, the proper course of treatment for *E. coli* included ten days solid of antibiotics, lest the infection return.

She had gone in search of the doctor, but he was nowhere to be found. His cell phone rolled to voice mail.

It seemed little short of malpractice to her, and it made her wonder, was he getting too old to be treating patients? It wasn't the first time Doc Anderson had stumbled here of late. There had been a half dozen occasions since the beginning of the year when Karen had had cause to question his judgment and methods.

Maybe it was time to speak to hospital administration.

Such was her state of mind when in walked Jeremiah Spur. She set her task to one side and went around the counter to shake his hand.

She tensed slightly at the thought of what might have caused him to seek her out. She swallowed and forced a smile. "Hey. I was just about to go check on your wife again. How's she feeling?"

"Like she can think of better places to spend the night."

"She is doing so well, I'm sure they'll discharge her tomorrow." She bit back her concern about Doc Anderson and the meds.

"Best better not be standin' between her and outta here when they do."

He adjusted his Stetson and leaned on the counter. She looked into a pair of eyes that were as blue as any she'd ever seen. There was nothing to be read there.

"I went to your folks' like you asked. That's some setup in the barn."

"It's a microbiological research laboratory with all the trimmings is what it is."

"Your dad a scientist in some former life?"

"Just a poor but honest restaurant owner. Emphasis on 'poor.'"

"I'm guessin' all that gear comes none too cheaply."

"I have no idea where he got the money for it all."

Jeremiah looked away, and then he looked down at the floor. "He's not come into some kind of inheritance that you know of."

"None."

He looked back up. "Been no oil wells drilled on his land."

"The restaurant is it. Mama's been buying day-old bread for as long as I can remember."

"Some folks do that 'cause it's all they know how to do. You can't escape your antecedents. I take it your mother didn't volunteer an explanation for the setup in the barn."

The pharmacist shook her head. "She said all he told her was, he intended to do his own research, since he was the only one he could trust completely. Told her to stay away from the barn. Which she mostly did. Except nights when she was sure he'd be tied up at the restaurant and wouldn't catch her slipping out to the barn to have a look inside."

"She see anybody else hanging around out there? Like Tres Anderson, for example?"

Karen swallowed. "Yes, as a matter of fact. How did you know?"

"Tell you in a minute. First, take a look at this." He handed her some pages that he pulled from his pocket.

She unfolded them and looked them over. "These are lab test results. Showing reductions in microbial loads as a result of some kind of process."

"Your dad's?"

"I guess. Wow. They're pretty compelling. Some of these show close to one hundred percent reductions." She held up the pages. "Mind if I make a copy?"

"Go ahead."

Upon returning from the copier, she gave Jeremiah's set back to him. He tucked them away.

"I also found an invoice from a lawyer, name of Bruni. You probably know this already, but his little girl is also an *E. coli* victim. That's how come him and me met. He was awfully reluctant to talk about his clients. And then, this morning, he went off somewhere because of a client emergency, accordin' to his wife."

"He was at the restaurant when we met with the sheriff. The boys called him."

"The look you gave him in the cafeteria this afternoon—I'd say you're probably not running for president of his fan club."

"He strikes me as a bit . . . reptilian."

"I think they start growin' scales while they're in law school. What's Robert Bruni do for y'all?"

"I honestly don't know. You'd have to ask him. Or my father."

"I doubt Bruni would tell me, although I aim to ask just the same. Seems a little odd, the two of us meetin', both of us with kin took sick with the same food poisoning. But that don't by any means exhaust all the oddness in this deal."

"No, I suppose not."

"One of your brothers caught me in your dad's barn, by the way, and had a mind to run me off. Took a swing at me in the bargain, but that fracas didn't turn out quite like he hoped it would. He might could use your services come morning.'"

Karen's hand went to her throat. "Captain Spur, I am so sorry. I think it's the stress of Daddy's disappearance."

Jeremiah shrugged. "It's sure enough the stress of somethin'. You said your brothers and your dad are close?"

"They work together a lot. He can be hard on them, but they know, deep down inside, he loves them."

"Question is, do they love him?"

"Look, I know they're pretty rough-and-tumble, the boys are, and Daddy and they have had their issues in the past, but they're fine now."

"What do you mean by 'issues'?"

"He was real tough on them when they were coming up. Spare the rod and all that. I suppose that had as much to do with his own childhood as anything. His father made Pap Finn look like Dr. Phil."

"What about more recently? While they were workin' together?"

Karen sighed. "Well. My father learned his management style as a drill sergeant in the Air Force. I'm grateful Bourré has never come to the attention of Amnesty International."

"And yet—"

She shook her head. "No way they could have had a hand in Daddy's disappearance."

"Uh-huh." Jeremiah looked away. He seemed to be contemplating a poster on the wall that illustrated the steps required to administer CPR. Then he looked back. "Another thing I noticed. Your dad had a picture in a frame on his desk. Him and Doc Anderson. That's how come it occurred to me he might know about your dad's lab."

"They've known each other since forever. Daddy sometimes picks Doc's brain about what he calls the 'deep science' behind his process. Doc is as close to a microbiologist as Daddy has access to."

"There's one more thing. When I was out at your parents' house, I was approached by a young black woman who was huntin' your dad. Somethin' about needin' ingredients for the process."

Karen's eyes widened. "What?"

"Seems your dad had gotten this woman's mama to use the process in her kitchen. Idea was to help her with some health problems by improving her diet. Your dad was usin' these people like human lab rats. I take it this all comes as news to you."

"Totally."

"Well. I'll say one thing for your dad's invention. Those people sure love it. Matter of fact, her mama had lost considerable weight. Made me wonder whether that could have brought your dad's invention to the attention of anyone else."

"Such as?"

"Our local toaster millionaire. Big Ty Daniels. You wouldn't know whether they've shown any interest in talkin' to your dad about this thing, would you?"

Karen shook her head again. "I'm sorry. I have stayed out of the business and—"

Jeremiah held up a hand. "Fair enough. You reckon you could get one of your brothers to restock the ingredients supply for that young woman I met this evening?"

"I could always ask."

Jeremiah produced a notepad and pen and wrote down a name and address and tore the page off. He handed it to the pharmacist, and she tucked it away.

He turned and walked to the door. When he got there he stopped and turned back. "I don't reckon it's too likely your brothers would sit still to be questioned by me, is it?"

She shook her head. "I can't see that happening."

"Didn't think so. I bet you could get 'em to talk to you, though."

He opened the door and went through it before she could frame a reply.

Ten minutes later she was sitting on a stool at the counter reading an article in a technical journal about the growing resistance of pathogenic bacteria to anti-infectives when the door opened and a good-looking black man with a shaved head walked into the room. She set the magazine to one side and got to her feet. "May I help you?"

"Got a prescription needs fillin'."

He handed her the paper, and she glanced at it. There were any number of things she could have said, but her training as a professional supplied her with filters that stood in the way of every one of them. "This will just take a minute."

"Much obliged."

She went back among the stacks of pharmaceuticals and found the big jar of blue pills and returned to the counter to measure them out. She was weary after her short night last night and ready for the day to end. It seemed unreal to her, this business with her father.

Maybe life would seem more back to normal after a good night's sleep.

Or maybe this *was* the new normal.

She placed the pill bottle into a white paper bag and went around to the front of the counter and punched the keys on the cash machine. The young man had been studying the CPR poster on the wall. He turned away and reached for his wallet.

"Do you have any questions for the pharmacist?" she asked her customer.

"Just one."

She looked at the man, who was watching her intently. "Okay."

"What does the pharmacist's husband think about her workin' this late of a Saturday?"

"I meant about your prescription."

"I got no questions about that."

She pointed to a touch pad on the counter where he could make a record of that fact. He took the stylus in hand and touched the screen and looked up. "I don't believe we've met."

The man held out a hand. "Clyde Thomas. And you would be?"

Karen shook his hand. "Karen Bradshaw."

His eyebrows shot up. "You know, there's a man, name of Sylvester Bradshaw—"

"He's my father."

"Small towns."

"Beg your pardon?"

"I ran into Jeremiah Spur this evening. He said something about helpin' you with a matter related to your dad. Don't worry," Clyde added quickly. "He wasn't bein' indiscreet or nothin'. He thought I might have some useful knowledge. I'm a licensed investigator, used to be a deputy sheriff in this town, so I, you know. Hear things."

Karen looked at her customer coolly. "Well? Have you heard anything useful?"

Clyde shrugged. "Not really, but I tol' him I'd keep my ears open while I'm makin' the rounds. You got any late-breakin' developments?"

"Unfortunately, no."

Clyde seemed on the verge of saying something else, then apparently thought better of it. He said good-bye and walked out the door, leaving her to lock up.

She closed the door and threw the dead bolt and stood looking at her image reflected in the glass pane in the upper half of the door. She could see the fatigue in her eyes, the worry.

She could use a little fun, some kind of distraction from this daily grind, this incessant anxiety over job and family, the birthright of the Good Kid that never let her be.

Karen still needed to figure out what to do about Doc Anderson's course of treatment for Martha Spur. As tired as she was, though, that would have to wait for tomorrow.

She sighed and headed to the parking lot.

The small town thing was beginning to wear Clyde's patience. What had Captain Spur called them? *Chance encounters.*

I been chance encountered till the world looks level.

When the pharmacist said she was Sylvester Bradshaw's daughter, his first instinct was to drop her hand and back slowly out of the room. As though he had stumbled into a bank lobby while an armed robbery was in progress.

Clyde wheeled the Impala into the parking lot of his apartment complex and slid it into a space. He stepped onto the tarmac and proceeded into the common area, his shadow cutting across the light that lay pooled along the way from the lamps above. He paused before the mailbox and retrieved its contents, its flyers and solicitations and dun notices. The folks who reached out to him by mail fell into two categories, generally speaking. Those who wished to have him in their debt, and those who had gotten that wish, very often to their dismay.

Maybe between the Danielses and the video business I'll finally be able to afford this ongoing leeching by utility companies and insurance providers that passes for my "lifestyle."

Upon arriving at the door to his apartment, he clutched the mail to his stomach with one hand and selected out the key with the other and slotted it. He put his shoulder to the door and pushed it open and was slammed from behind with such force it sent him sprawling into his apartment, mail flying in all directions.

"Th' fuck?"

The door closed with a bang, and he pushed himself into a sitting position and looked up at the man who stood holding a gun on him. He was a seriously big human being, north of two hundred fifty pounds. His face was concealed by a ski mask.

"Yo, man. What kinda fool home-invades a five-hundred-dollar-a-month apartment? You ought to take that shit over to the Boulevard, where the money's at."

"Shut up and tell me where it is."

"Where's what, man?"

"You know good and God damn well what. What the Danielses sent you to the side of the road to retrieve today."

"Where'd you hear about that?"

"You don't really expect me to answer that question, do you?"

"Well, you outta luck, 'cause I ain't got it."

"Where's it at?"

"Probably in Fort Bend County."

"Do what?"

"I chucked it in the Brazos River. It's bound to have floated a few dozen miles downstream by now."

"Get your ass up and sit it in that chair yonder." The intruder pointed out the one he had in mind with a flick of his gun hand. Clyde noticed as he got to his feet, the man had a brown grocery sack in his other hand.

Clyde walked to the chair and turned it so he could sit.

The gunman walked around behind him. "Put your feet up on the table and your hands behind your back."

Clyde did as told. "You jus' wastin' yo' time, man."

"You stay like that until I say you can move."

"Yeah, yeah."

The man grabbed both his hands in a big paw and squeezed.

"Ow! Hey, easy does it."

What followed was the sound of tape being torn loose from a roll. The man used it to wrap Clyde's wrists.

"This place is a dump," the guy said.

Clyde looked around. Dirty dishes in the sink, running gear tossed in one corner, empty soda can resting on some sports magazines in the tiny sitting area. "I wasn't expectin' no company."

The man came around to where Clyde could see him with the roll of duct tape in hand. He went to work on Clyde's feet, taping the ankles together. He had tucked his piece in the waistband of his jeans.

Clyde studied the man while he went about his taping operation.

This dude seems familiar somehow. I think maybe he's local.

Once the man had Clyde trussed up he walked back behind him, and when he reappeared he had his brown grocery sack in hand once more. He set it down and reached inside and produced a pair of surgical gloves and pulled them on. He proceeded to the kitchen, where he opened the freezer compartment of the refrigerator. He stood there looking inside. Condensation billowed out and floated up before it disappeared.

He closed that door and opened the one to the refrigerator. After a few seconds he slammed it and turned toward Clyde.

"Half a six-pack of Dr Pepper and some stale bananas? That's it?"

"I ain't much into meal preparation."

The intruder began opening cabinet doors and drawers at random to the sound of cutlery and serving implements rattling.

Meanwhile Clyde was beginning to regard his predicament in a somewhat different light.

Ain't but one way this guy could know I was on the case for the Danielses today.

That changes ever-thing.

Makes it all simpler, in a way.

And with that, the plan fell into place.

"Yo," he said.

The guy left off his rummaging and turned toward Clyde.

"What you lookin' for? It ain't here, okay? But it's in a safe place. Where no one but me can find it."

"Yeah? Where would that be?"

"Free up my hands and I'll tell you."

"I'm not sure I trust this."

"What am I gonna do? Try to get the drop on you with my feet taped together? Flap my arms and fly out the window?"

The man hesitated. Then he pawed through a couple drawers until he produced a steak knife. He took his gun in his right hand and the steak knife in his left and swung around behind Clyde, giving him a wide berth, as though working his way around an aroused rattlesnake.

He fell to sawing at the tape. The force pulled Clyde's arms back and down, and it felt like his shoulders might detach from their sockets. "Easy, man."

The guy pulled the tape free and said, "There."

Clyde brought his hands around and rubbed first one wrist, then other. The guy stood before Clyde with the pistol pointed at his head.

Clyde said, "I got somethin' in my hip pocket I want to show you."

"Fine. Just do it in super-slow motion."

"No problem." With utmost deliberation, Clyde hiked himself up on his left haunch and reached into his right hip pocket. He extracted a folded yellow receipt, and without unfolding it he handed it to the gunman.

The man unfolded the receipt. He nodded. "Cold storage. Smart."

"It's all yours, baby. All you got to go do is ask for it come Tuesday."

Despite the ski mask, Clyde could tell the guy was grinning. He tucked the gun into his waistband once more. "You stay just like that until you done counted to a hundred."

"Whatever you say, man."

The man took his grocery bag and disappeared through the door.

28

THE SOUND OF BIRDS SINGING IN THE LIGUSTRUM OUTSIDE HIS BEDROOM window brought him to just before dawn. He sat up and swung his feet to the side of the bed. Stood and stretched and padded to the kitchen to cut on the coffeepot. The answering machine sat in one corner, message light blinking. It had been in that condition when he got home last night, but he'd been too tired to listen to the thing play.

Odds were, it wasn't for him anyway. Calls for him on the home phone occurred with roughly the same frequency as manned lunar landings.

Directly he was dressed and headed out the back door with a steaming mug of black in hand. Jake met him on the porch and in anticipation of his master's intentions reversed direction and bounded toward the pickup. Jeremiah let the tailgate down, and the big black Lab took the truck bed in one leap and stood looking at Jeremiah.

Jeremiah closed the tailgate and scratched behind the dog's ears. "Wish everybody was as easy to please as you."

He got in the cab and inserted the key. The engine roared to life.

The truck rumbled over the cattle guard through the back gate, and he followed the dirt road that traced the perimeter of the field. The clouds to the east were bloodred. That meant it would rain later. It meant that nine times out of ten in his experience.

He drove his pastures and studied his herd, looking for signs of disease or injury. In this country, cattle and wealth were synonymous, and a man no more discussed the size of his herd than he did the balance in his bank account. If someone, some unenlightened but well-meaning stranger, asked how many cattle he ran, he would ignore the question or change the subject.

It wasn't a matter to be discussed outside the family.

And this morning it was thoughts of family that had him preoccupied as he drove his ranch. Martha was fond of quoting some Russian about families. How the happy ones were all happy in the same way but the unhappy ones were all different in their unhappiness. Thinking about the Bradshaw family, he could sure see the truth in that.

Jeremiah couldn't say of his own knowledge what kind of husband and father Sylvester was, but he had a notion. A notion Karen had largely confirmed last night.

He could not shake the feeling that the House of Bradshaw contained within it the key to Sylvester's disappearance and almost certain death. By now the trail would have gone colder than frog piss, and there wouldn't be much to do but wait around until a body surfaced, which it would, sooner or later. Then it'd be up to the law to deal with it.

Jeremiah would ask Doc Anderson a few questions when he saw him this morning, and then he figured his part in this would be done. Besides, he didn't need any more excuses to avoid the hospital.

Martha was coming home today. Cheered him up just to think on it.

He clicked on the radio and studied his land. It had been an uncommonly wet summer, and all about the pastures were green instead of bare and brown as usually they were come early September. On the radio they were giving the sports scores, with special attention being paid to the performance last night of Little Ty Daniels, who led the Aggies to a 56–7 pasting of the North Texas Mean Green. He was off to the fast start all had been expecting.

His cattle watched him pass from where they stood. They looked fat and healthy. He would have a good year if beef prices held up.

At length he pulled back behind the house and killed the engine. He let the tailgate down, and Jake hit the ground with a grunt and trotted off to relieve himself against a fence post.

Jeremiah went inside and poured himself another cup of coffee and found a pad and a pen and went to the answering machine.

There were two messages, and both were for him.

The second was a call he had just missed, from that state microbiologist. The man allowed that the source of Martha's food poisoning was the bag of baby spinach he'd found. "It was fairly hot," the man said. "*E. coli* contamination was detected to the tune of several hundred thousand CFUs per gram."

The man went on to say that the state would be considering whether to ask the FDA to issue a recall of any product with the same lot number. He apologized for calling so early on a Sunday but said that the results had just come in and he assumed Jeremiah would want to know about them.

All of that was of some interest to Jeremiah, but of greater interest was the first message on the machine.

It was Clyde Thomas.

Karen pulled her car up into the front yard of the converted hunting cabin and killed the engine. She watched the place for signs of life. There was none, nor was there a sound to be heard.

She knew they had to be home, for their pickup was in the yard. Besides, where else would they be at eight thirty of a Sunday morning?

Certainly not church. They all three well knew that their irreligious ways drove their devout father slightly insane, and that was reason enough to quit the church the moment they were at liberty to. It was a small skirmish in their guerrilla war, this showing their backs to God and in so doing giving the finger to the man who would be God to them.

The cabin sat in a clearing that was surrounded by a natural wall of mesquite and post oak. It could not be seen from the road, nor was any other house in sight. Even though Brenham had grown in this direction through the years, that growth had not yet reached this far.

Karen had some idea what to expect if she carried through with her plan and knocked on yonder door. She would be greeted, if that was the right word, by a sullen and hungover young man who had been roused from sleep and who would be in no mood for the questions she had at the ready for him.

This entire mission was in all likelihood a waste of time.

Still, from the moment Jeremiah Spur put the idea in her head, it had worked her imagination something fierce.

Had her father finally paid the price for all the things he'd done over the years? For that afternoon out at the barn, which was simply one of the starkest examples of his bizarre and abusive behavior? For the way he'd bullied and ridiculed and bossed and tormented his boys?

The way he'd treated their sainted mother?

She mounted the steps of the cabin and squared her shoulders and knocked. No one responded, no one called out, no foot fell.

She walked off the porch and stood in the yard looking around.

That's when she first heard voices.

She followed them to the back of the house. There sat an outbuilding, what looked to be a large single-story garage and workroom that sat perpendicular to the cabin. It was of more recent construction. The side facing to her left was dominated by two large overhead doors, the kind common to garages. Set into the wall facing her was a regular door with a pane of glass in the top half. Through it she could see a light.

It was from this building that the voices were issuing, and they were her brothers'. They were having to shout to be heard over the roar of an air compressor.

She closed the distance and peeked through the window in the door.

Mark and Luke were dressed in their white restaurant aprons, and they stood before a stainless steel machine that was perhaps three feet tall. It consisted of a drum with a box behind it and rested on a base likewise made of stainless steel.

The air compressor cut off, and in its place came a rhythmic *hiss-thunk* every five seconds or so and also her brothers' conversation, which she could now make out.

Luke said, "I just don't want to be taken advantage of, is all."

"That's the kind of thinkin' that has kept this family poor these many years."

"So what? You make a bad deal, it could cost you forever. Ain't that right?"

"The poorhouse is beginnin' to feel like forever to me. We ain't got a pot to piss in nor a window to throw it out of. I'm tired of livin' like that."

"So am I. But you got to weigh the risks."

"The lawyer will see to it that we get a fair shake."

"There's another one that worries me."

"You have to trust somebody. Him you can trust."

"How the fuck would you know?"

Mark shrugged by way of reply.

The *hiss-thunk* noise ceased, and there was a long high-pitched sound like that of air escaping from a balloon. The brothers turned toward the device and threw a couple latches and swung the lid up. Luke reached inside and pulled out a stainless steel basket that came up dripping fluid.

He carried the basket to a sink that stood against a wall, and he set it on the sideboard to drain.

The Good Kid believed in nothing so much as the Golden Rule, and this spying on her blood kin was making her increasingly uncomfortable. Besides, there was no way to be sure what was going on here without a direct conversation. Still, she hesitated.

Knock on the door or just walk in on them?

Luke said, "We're runnin' low on Baggies."

"They's some more in the house."

As Mark turned toward the door, Karen stepped back, fear tightening her throat.

Out stepped her brother, who stopped and looked at her. "What are you doin' here?" He had a bruise on his face that she imagined he owed to Jeremiah Spur.

She took a deep breath. "Mr. Spur said I should talk to you guys about what you know that maybe could explain Daddy's disappearance."

You could say Mark scowled, but that was the way he always looked. He was never not scowling. It was his trademark, what the price tag on the hat was to Minnie Pearl. Karen imagined he scowled in his sleep.

"We don't know nothin'. Same as you. We don't appreciate you invitin' some stranger into it, neither. This here is family."

"I asked him to help because I have no confidence in the sheriff's—"

"He'll turn up. Wait and see if he don't."

"Can we just the three of us talk about what might have happened Friday night?"

"I done told you. I ain't got no idea."

"What about Luke?"

"Him neither."

"I'd like him to speak for himself."

She took a step toward the door, but he blocked her way. She stepped back.

"What?"

"He's busy. Processin' fish for when the restaurant opens again."

"So that's your plan for dealing with this. Just go back to slinging plates of catfish at people."

"We're gonna open up and we're gonna—"

He stopped. As if rethinking what he was about to say.

"You're gonna what?"

He just stood there.

"Tell me what you were about to say."

"Luke wouldn't care for it if I did."

"What's going on, Mark?"

"I got to get some Baggies."

He headed to the cabin.

She ran after him and grabbed him by the arm.

He turned toward her. He glanced at the outbuilding and looked back at her once more. "They's some people, showin' some interest in the process. Daddy didn't want to have nothin' to do with 'em, but Luke and I— We think we ought to at least hear what they have to say."

"Even though Daddy would disapprove."

"Makes no sense not to hear 'em out, see. You hear 'em out and you don't like what they got to say? You can tell 'em to pound sand."

"'Pound sand?'"

"That's how the lawyer put it."

"Who? Bruni?"

"He said it wasn't a bad idea to talk to these folks."

"Why don't you just say their names? Who are you planning to talk to, Mark?"

He hesitated. Then he turned his back and proceeded toward the cabin.

She stood where she was. "Who are they, Mark?"

Without turning around he said, "Don't come around here no more without you call first."

"Did you know Daddy had given equipment and ingredients to people with health problems, to see if it would help them?"

He turned around and looked at her. "Bullshit."

"It's not bullshit. I know it's true."

"He ain't got the money to be givin' away—"

"He doesn't have the money for that setup in the barn, either."

"That's different."

"Different how?"

"He told us he got a grant for research."

"A grant? Who in the world would give him a grant?"

"He said he got it from the gummint."

"That is completely insane."

Her brother shrugged. "That's what he said."

He looked like he might be about to say something else, but he didn't. Instead he turned back to the cabin.

She said, "Some of the people who've been using the process are running low on ingredients. Is there any way—"

He just kept walking.

"I'd like to know, can we get them some ingredients?" She practically shouted it.

He disappeared into the cabin, and she stood there trying to decide what to do.

When she could think of no other purpose to be served by her presence there, she headed back to her car.

She got behind the wheel and sat wondering who it was her brothers were talking to about the process, and where they had gotten the equipment she had watched them operate. It looked like the prototype machines she had seen in her father's barn-turned-laboratory only it was much, much bigger. Big enough to process forty, fifty pounds of product. She wondered where they had found the money to have the thing designed and built. Couldn't have been cheap.

Maybe from their father, who obviously had tapped some source of funding. She didn't for one second believe it was a government grant. She couldn't see the government coming across with major dollars for a man like her dad, who had to his credit many a starred and boxed entry in the Annals of Whackjobbery.

For that matter, she couldn't imagine Sylvester applying for a government grant. Fact of the matter was, he hated the government and he hated politicians.

Where else, though, could he have found the money to build a laboratory and finance equipment like she had seen out back? Had he secretly raised money from a venture capitalist?

She shook her head. Even that was simply beyond imagining.

She left her brothers' place with more questions than she had when she arrived.

In his mind's eye he could see her all too clearly, had a life-sized mental image of Martha, dressed to the nines, sitting in that chair in her room, tapping her foot, ready to be sprung from the grip of the health care system.

So when Jeremiah arrived at the hospital he went looking for Doc Anderson everywhere but his wife's room.

He found the man in the cafeteria, drinking a glass of juice while leafing through a news magazine.

Jeremiah fetched a cup of black from the bar and made straight for the table. Upon his approach the doctor closed the magazine and pushed it to one side. The two men shook hands and settled into chairs.

Jeremiah set his hat on the table and scratched at his scalp-line. "So, how is the good doctor this fair mornin'?"

"Couldn't be doin' better if I had good sense. You?"

"Still kickin', not raisin' much dust. You an orange juice man in the mornings, huh?"

"Best thing in the world for swallowin' down pills. You get to be my age, you got to swallow a mess of pills every day."

"I hear that. Martha ready to go home?"

"You obviously haven't been by her room, where she is at this very minute gunning her engine."

"That's what I figgered. I have somethin' I need to visit with you about first."

"What would that be?"

"Sylvester Bradshaw. He's gone missin'."

The doctor sipped his coffee and set it back down. "I hadn't heard. We should have T-shirts printed up. 'Your town called. Their curmudgeon is missing.' I assume he'll make his way back here at some point."

Jeremiah shrugged. "Hard to say. 'Pears that on Friday night someone snatched him from his restaurant and turned his office upside-down in the bargain. Ain't been seen nor heard from since."

"What do you figger? Robbery?"

"Maybe. Or industrial espionage."

The older man's eyebrows levitated. "In Brenham? When you hear hoofbeats, think horses, not zebras."

"Beg your pardon?"

The man smiled. "It's an old doctors' saying. Don't go looking for exotic explanations for ordinary symptoms. A case of sniffles and a cough is more than likely a cold, not the bubonic plague. Hard for me to imagine that Sylvester dropped out of sight on account of anything as fancy-pants as industrial espionage. Not in this town."

Jeremiah leaned in. He set his elbows on the table and dropped his voice. "But you do know somethin' about this process of his, right? His daughter said Sylvester liked to pick your brain about what she called the deep science."

Anderson got that knowing smile doctors get, the one that says they've seen more and know more than we mere mortals and they have the skills and experience to spare you from the bony embrace of the Grim Reaper if only you'll summon the basic smarts to call their office and make an appointment. Assuming, of course, you have major medical.

"Well, Brother Spur," he drawled, "Sylvester has sought my counsel a few times about the properties of his device and what it might be doing by way of microbial intervention. Our friend Sylvester is a lot of things, but a man well versed in the lysis of pathogenic bacteria is not exactly one of them."

Jeremiah took a few moments to parse this eruption of polysyllabic jargon. He recognized it for what it was from similar interviews over the course of his long career. An attempt to confuse the uninitiated by resort to language not far removed from its Greek and Latin roots. Surprised him some, his old friend Tres trying that gambit.

"Lysis would be—"

"Destruction of microorganisms by virtue of some breaking of the cellular membrane. This is the upshot of what Sylvester's process does to pathogenic bacteria."

"I don't reckon you could maybe dumb all this down for me. Pretend you were talkin' to a fifth grader."

The doctor smiled. "I hate to insult your intelligence."

"Maybe I should walk out and come back in again."

"Jeremiah, old friend—"

"Just tell me what the process does in words of one syllable."

"Sylvester's device exerts a combination of mechanical and chemical forces on bacterial cells. The mechanical force is a result of a change in the atmospheric pressure in the device. The chemical force comes from the fact that the device is half filled with a solution consisting of water and an organic acid. In combination these two factors work to weaken and finally rupture the cellular membrane. Whereupon the bacterial organism goes poof."

"You helped Sylvester figger this out?"

"And run the tests necessary to prove it."

"That's what that lab in his barn is all about, then."

This seemed to take Doc Anderson off guard. "How'd you know about that?"

"Was out there yesterday afternoon. Quite a setup."

"Yeah, it is. I actually helped Sylvester design it and select the right equipment."

"You got any idea where he got the money for all that?"

The doctor shrugged. "I would no more ask him that than I'd ask you how many head of cattle you're running."

"I expect that's right. So, about these tests. How do they work exactly?"

"It's pretty standard scientific methodology. You take a food product. Say, a head of lettuce. You cut it in half. Put one half through the process. The other half you leave as is. We put the test product and the control through a wash and collect the rinse from the wash in a petri dish and add a plate-count medium that reveals the presence of microorganisms. We compare the two samples immediately after processing and then at set intervals, say, one day, three days, five days."

"And these tests told you all what?"

"Sylvester's process eliminates over ninety-nine percent of food-borne bacteria. It makes food safer and extends its shelf life, too, since bacteria are a primary cause of oxidative decay."

"There you go again."

"They cause food to spoil. One potential commercial application of the process is to extend the shelf life of perishable food products."

Jeremiah sipped his coffee. "And it works on *E. coli*, you say."

"It's even more lethal on that bad bug than it is on spoilage bacteria."

"To know that, wouldn't you all have to test specifically for that strain of bacteria?"

"Indeed. A friend of mine in the beef research department over at A&M, a microbiologist named Clark, supplied us with some of the bug for use in testing."

"When did you all run these tests?"

Tres shrugged once more. "I dunno. Maybe a year ago now. I forget exactly. Anymore it seems like I have a raging case of CRS disease."

"CRS?"

"Can't remember shit. About a lot of things."

Something was beginning to work the margins of Jeremiah's mind. Just what it was, he couldn't yet say. He'd need to think on it some.

"Sounds to me like Sylvester could have sold this thing for money enough to burn a wet mule and sat on his porch for the rest of his days. Wonder why he didn't."

"You mean, aside from the fact that, not knowing the first thing about marketing and salesmanship, he couldn't sell dollar bills at half price?"

"I reckon that would be reason enough."

"Yeah, well." Tres looked off into the distance. He seemed to be weighing his words with some care. Then he looked Jeremiah in the eye. "Since he came up with the idea, Sylvester has had his heart set— set, mind you—on building a business around it, and he has worked and sacrificed to make that happen like no man I ever knew. The problem is, he sees himself as running that business, controlling it personally, with his two sons as members of his senior management team."

"That don't seem all that far-fetched. It is his invention, after all."

Doc nodded. "It is. But before it can achieve its potential as a commercial application, you have to convince people to give it a chance. Now, who is more likely to persuade a potential customer into taking a risk on a new technology—a somewhat, shall we say, eccentric restaurant owner from some rural nowhere who's got no formal training in the food business and whose credibility in that industry roughly approximates that of Bozo the Clown, or an actual professional manager with years of relevant business experience on his résumé and valuable contacts in his address book?"

"I see your point."

"I've been trying to get Sylvester to bring on professional management for years, but he wasn't having any. The frustrating thing about Sylvester is, he'd rather fail his way than succeed someone else's."

Jeremiah consulted his watch. "I best better get high and behind it."

He got to his feet, and the doctor did likewise.

As they left the cafeteria, Jeremiah said, "So, tell me. What do you think has become of Sylvester?"

"You mean, assuming he hasn't just wandered off somewhere for reasons sufficient to him only to turn back up in another day or two?"

"Yeah. Assuming that. What's your gut tell you?"

The doctor stopped and dropped his head. Stood there thinking. When he looked up, he said, "People like to talk about the power big oil companies have. Or big drug companies or HMOs or the insurance industry. Big and powerful as they are, none of them touches every American's life on average three times a day, every day a week. When you take the food industry as a whole, starting with the big corporate growers and processors right down to your local grocery store or fast food joint, it is as big and powerful as you can imagine. Sylvester's process threatens a lot of people in that business. As long as no one took him seriously, it didn't much matter. It could just be, someone in that big ol' industry decided to take Sylvester seriously for once and that the said someone did what people naturally do."

"Which would be?"

"They got rid of Sylvester so as to protect themselves."

Jeremiah fixed the doctor with a look that made the man grin.

"I know," Tres said. "You're thinking, that's the zebra hypothesis."

"Could be."

"And that the horse hypothesis is, he was done in by one of the several thousand people in this county that he has offended in some way with his crankiness."

"That seems more probable."

Martha was so happy to be going home she apparently elected to pass on any sharp comment about how long it took Jeremiah to come collect her. She sat on the passenger side of the pickup with her purse in her lap and listened while Jeremiah filled her in on his doings since yesterday afternoon.

"So," she said. "What do you think has become of Sylvester?"

"I think he's more than likely buried in some pasture somewhere. If it were otherwise, I expect someone would've heard from him by now."

"Who do you like as the killer?"

Jeremiah studied the passing scenery. Pastureland for the most part in which cattle either stood or were bedded down. Rain clouds were building in the northwest.

"There's a story from back in the frontier days, about an old boy who was hauled before a judge and accused of horse theft. After the judge heard the evidence, he sentenced the defendant to be hung. The defense lawyer jumped up and objected.

" 'But Your Honor,' said the lawyer. 'In the case before this one, the defendant was convicted of murder, and you only give him five years in the penitentiary. How come you to sentence my client to be hung?'

"The judge said, 'Counsel, I've known many a man that needed killin', but I never knew of a horse that needed stealin'.' "

"I'm not sure I follow you."

"I don't think it would be hard to compile a list of people who thought Sylvester needed killin'. Some of those folks even stood to gain by it."

"You mean in terms of the money to be made off his process."

"That's just exactly what I mean."

"Why do you care?"

Jeremiah shrugged. "Would like to see some justice done, for the daughter in particular. She seems genuinely to love her dad, warts and all."

"What about the two sons?"

Jeremiah worked his jaw. "About them, let's just say I've got my substantial doubts."

"You really think they—"

"I think money does funny things to people, is all. Plus, it sounds to me like the three of them had some amount of trouble gettin' along."

They were quiet for a while. Then he said, "I also find it right peculiar, the timing of all this. Sylvester goin' missin' the very weekend you take sick from an illness his process could have prevented."

"You could just chalk that up to coincidence."

"Not after what I've seen in this life."

"Where's the connection, then?"

"Don't know just yet. Need to think on it some. Main thing is, though, you're better. And I'm grateful for that. I don't care for it when you don't feel well."

She laid her left hand over his right, which was resting on the steering wheel. "The other good news is, sounds like the little Bruni girl is gonna make it. They're sayin' she turned the corner last night."

"Good to hear. Excuse me."

She turned loose of his hand, and he reached into his shirt pocket and produced his cell phone, which had gone to ringing.

"This is Spur."

"It's Karen Bradshaw. I wanted you to know, I talked to my brother Mark."

"What did they allow?"

"He swears they don't have any more idea what's become of Daddy than I do."

"Do you believe 'em?"

Hesitation. Then, "Yes. I honestly do. Plus, I just can't conceive of it."

"That's that, then, I reckon."

"I also asked them where in the world he could have gotten the money for that lab. They say he told them he was the recipient of a grant."

"From who?"

"They didn't know any of the details."

"You sound skeptical."

"Captain Spur, I have done a fair amount of government-funded research. The grant process requires months of effort, and unless the granting agency is convinced you've got the right training and background, you can pretty much forget it. Plus, there's something else."

"Okay."

"I saw the boys working with a new piece of machinery. Very modern design, highly automated, made of 316L stainless steel, I'd be willing to bet. In order to stand up to the acidity of the solution over time."

"News to you they had this machine, then."

"Daddy's talked about building it for years. It was his idea for making his process a hundred times more effective. It's to the tumbler what the PC is to the hand calculator. It would have taken real money to design and build this thing. In the tens of thousands of dollars."

"Money your dad didn't have."

"But somehow managed to lay his hands on. I've got an idea where."

Jeremiah wheeled into his driveway and pulled around back and killed the engine. "Let's hear it." He got out to fetch Martha's things from the back of the pickup.

He heard the low roll of thunder in the distance. It sounded and then faded away. It was a sound that stirred something in his blood, something no less felt for his inability to describe it, something felt by all men who have in common that they work land.

The pharmacist had hesitated before she responded. "I'm not a finance person myself, so this is a bit of a stretch for me, but, as I understand it, venture capital works like this."

Martha swept past him and unlocked the door since his hands were full.

"An investor makes capital available to another person who has a good idea or invention that the two of them think can make money with further development. In exchange for which the investor gets some ownership interest in any resulting business and perhaps some say over how that business is run."

Jeremiah walked into the bedroom and set Martha's bag on the bed and turned back toward the family room. "You think your dad made a deal with such an investor."

"It's the only thing that makes any sense."

"Then why wouldn't he just say that?"

"Probably because there was something about the deal that he didn't want to own up to. The amount of ownership the venture capitalist got, maybe. Or the amount of control. Besides, there was the pride thing. Sylvester is nothing if not proud about what he thinks of as his invention. His business."

Jeremiah dropped into a chair in the family room and checked his watch. No sooner had he gotten here than he needed to leave again. "I sure enough saw that with my own eyes Friday night."

"Thing of it is, though, once you take someone else's money to develop a business, it's not yours anymore. It's yours and his. And that would have led to a fundamental difference between Sylvester and anybody who invested with him. Because that person would have soon learned, there is one thing in this world you don't do with Sylvester Bradshaw, and that is try to tell him what to do."

Jeremiah could think of other complications that would attend such an arrangement, but these he decided to keep mum about for the time being. "Who you reckon this venture capital provider could be?"

"I just can't imagine Sylvester taking money from anyone he didn't know pretty well. Which more than likely means someone local, who has plenty of money to invest in a highly speculative venture."

"Now we're gettin' somewheres."

Martha emerged from the kitchen and took a seat on the couch. She folded her hands in her lap and sat looking at him.

"There's one more thing. Mark let slip that they've scheduled a meeting with someone who has an interest in commercializing the process."

"I don't reckon he named any names."

"No. That he did not do."

Martha was still sitting there, just studying him, and he realized he needed to bring this conversation to a close. "This has give me plenty to cogitate over, but at the moment I need to get high and behind it. Maybe we ought to talk again later today."

"Alright. I'll give you a holler."

"You do that." Jeremiah cut the connection and slipped the cell phone into the pocket of his work shirt. "So," he said to Martha, "nice to be home?"

Martha stood up and proceeded to do something she had not done in many a year.

She planted herself in Jeremiah's lap.

He leaned back and looked at her. "Somethin' I can help you with?"

"You can, number one, stop paying attention to young women whom you've done favors for while your aging wife was laid up sick and, number two, pay some attention to said aging wife."

"I can't deny you're agin'—"

"Watch it, buster."

"We both are. But you're still the purtiest thang in five counties." Jeremiah drawled out the words, giving them a little extra country emphasis. "And if you think I ain't ever bit as in love with you as the day we tied the dadgum knot, then—"

She put a finger to his lips and laid her head on his shoulder. "I know you love me, dear. You show me every day."

"Is that a fact?"

"Yes."

They were quiet for a while, and then she sat up and looked at him. "Well," she said, "I show you I love you, too. Like, I don't make you watch *Dancing with the Stars* with me because I figure you'd hate it."

"You really think you could make me watch that show?"

"I think I might."

"You and whose army?"

She smiled and took one of his shirt buttons between her fingers and started playing with it. "You know, I feel so much better today, and it's so nice to be home. It has me feeling a bit—" She looked into his eyes and smiled. "Frisky."

Jeremiah stole a glance at the wall clock and stifled a groan. "Would it be at all possible for you to hold that thought?"

29

SONYA STEPPED OUT OF HER BMW AND LOOKED AROUND THE PARKING lot. There was Clyde's Impala, plus another sedan that had seen its better day, a veritable Bondo display it was, and a pickup truck. Surprised her to find that much traffic here, this hour of a Sunday morning. Who was partial to ice cream at such a time of day?

The sky to the northwest had been growing darker and the sound of thunder drawing closer. Sonya opened the back door and fetched out her briefcase and umbrella. She had her hair pulled back in a ponytail and was wearing a shirt that buttoned down the front with the tail out over her jeans. She wore hoop earrings and a touch of makeup, and she looked like a regular on an HBO original production of *Sex and the Country*.

She entered the ice cream parlor and looked about. Clyde was seated in a booth off to the left and lifted a hand in greeting. He managed a smile. She nodded him back an authoritative nod, intending to establish the tone from jump ball. Beyond him sat a man, an old rancher from what she could tell, with his back to the door, his shoulders hunched, perhaps over coffee. He could have been any of fifty ranchers she saw every week, driving into town in their trucks loaded with hay or feed or agricultural implements.

She walked to the counter to place her order, and there she was met by an older, heavyset black woman wearing a blue gingham apron. She brought to mind Hattie McDaniel playing Mammy in *Gone with the Wind*.

The black woman studied her from under hooded eyelids. "Hep you?"

"I'll have a cup of coffee."

The woman poured the coffee into a heavy porcelain mug and set it down in front of Sonya, who dug out two dollars and handed them over. She took the mug in hand and juggled it and briefcase and umbrella on her way to Clyde's booth.

"Don't you want yo' change, sugar?"

"Keep it."

Sonya slid into the booth opposite Clyde.

"I must say. You lookin' mighty fine, Ms. District Attorney."

"Thank you. You look . . . you look good, too." Even as she said it, she realized she didn't feel a thing for this man anymore. It was almost like their relationship had been between him and somebody else. "How you been?"

Clyde shrugged. "Life ain't as much fun as when we was hooked up. I miss that. 'Too soon old and too late smart,' my mama always said. You?"

"Just trying to give the taxpayers their money's worth."

"I hear tell you lookin' to juke this burg for Austin."

It was Sonya's turn to shrug. "There's been some talk about me making a run at statewide office." She sipped her coffee and set down the mug and squared her shoulders. Her signal that she had timed out on small talk. "Okay, so. You gonna come clean with me about what you found out by the side of the road yesterday? Or are you gonna stick with this adopt-a-highway nonsense?"

In response, Clyde produced a plastic ziplock bag and dropped it on the table. It contained about two dozen blue pills, each in the form of a diamond.

Sonya looked at the bag. She looked at Clyde. "What the hell is that?"

"What you think it is?"

"This is what you found on the side of the road?"

Clyde looked out toward the parking lot and grinned. He looked back at Sonya. "What if I told you that young people today are into this stuff for various reasons, having to do mostly with them likin' to experiment and what have you? And them boys had this on 'em the other evenin' and got rid of it on account of not havin' a prescription?"

Sonya sipped her coffee. "It's a lifestyle drug. Not a controlled substance. It's not against the law to possess it."

"Yeah, but them boys wouldn't necessarily know that, right?"

"I'm not buying it, Clyde."

He grinned again and palmed the bag off the table. "Didn't know whether you would or not. Thought it might be worth a shot anyway. Till I got to thinkin' how easy it would be for you to check around, see who might have been buyin' this stuff in the last twenty-four hours. That and some other developments, like, forced me to reconsider."

"Look, Clyde. This is serious business. Is there any way we could cut to the actual chase?"

Clyde leaned forward on his elbows. "Okay—but first, we got to have a deal."

"What kind of deal?"

"A deal where I give you what you want, which is a lot more than you got now, plus a context. A theory. You see, I found somethin' on the side of the road, alright, but that don't mean it came out of the Daniels vehicle. It's the theory I'm gon' give you that's as important as what I found."

"And in return, you get?"

"I get to walk away clean."

Sonya frowned. "I can't help you with the Danielses."

"I'm not talkin' about that. I got other fish to fry with them, so to speak."

Sonya paused to think. "Concealing evidence is serious crime, Clyde. How can I know what you have to offer is heavy enough?"

"Any reasonable person would say it is. I just need you to promise to be reasonable. Take a professional approach. Not use this as an occasion to settle any old scores, if you get my meaning."

"I ought to slap the hell out of you."

"That is what I would refer to as an unprofessional approach."

"Just to be clear, this is in the nature of a plea bargain. Were I representing you, I'd advise you to put your proffer of evidence in writing and likewise my agreement to forbear and make the one contingent on the other."

Clyde grinned. "I don't need a legal document. I got me a witness." Clyde swiveled his head. "Captain Spur?"

The old rancher in the other booth slid out and got to his feet, and there stood Jeremiah Spur, whom Sonya knew from previous dealings of one kind or another. He walked over and spoke Sonya's name, and they shook hands. He slid into the booth next to Clyde.

"So," Clyde said to Sonya. "Here's how it breaks down. Isaac Daniels called me yesterday mornin', said he'd like for me to go out to this particular patch of right-of-way, see what there was to find that did not appear to belong."

"He did not say what to look for?"

"No, he did not."

"Okay."

"So I go out there and I'm lookin' around and I'm not findin' nothin', and up rolls the Cap'n here. Come to find out, he was up at the 'mergency room Friday night, when they brought Little Ty and them in and so had heard 'bout the chase."

Jeremiah said, "About the litterin' citation, too. That's what put me in mind that maybe Clyde was out there cleanin' up after some mess of Little Ty and them's. I told him, he'd best better not fool with evidence in an ongoing criminal investigation."

"I knew better myse'f, truth be tol'. Some folks just hard to say no to. Your millionaires and what have you. They tuned to the Yes Channel, like to hear it all day long. So, anyway, the Cap'n leaves out of there, and I'm about to pack it in when somethin' catches my eye. Piece of bloody gauze lyin' there on the ground. I bend down to get a closer look, and nestled in that nasty ol' thing was a thumb."

Sonya was taking notes, and at this announcement she looked up. "A thumb?"

"That appeared to have been forcibly separated from its owner, which from the looks of it would have been an older white person, most likely male."

"Where is the thumb now?"

"We'll get to that. Cap'n Spur here thinks he might know whose thumb it was and how it came to be travelin' at a high rate of speed in a Hummer driven by a future NFL number one draft pick."

"Maybe yes and maybe no," said Jeremiah.

Sonya said, "Maybe you know whose thumb it is and maybe you don't?"

Jeremiah shook his head. "I mean maybe Little Ty makes it to the NFL draft, and then again maybe he gets to spend his prime football-playin' years stampin' out license plates. On account of I think I can stitch all this together and tie it right back to the Danielses, and it starts with the disappearance two nights ago of a man by the name of Sylvester Bradshaw."

Sonya had returned to her scribbling. "And he would be?"

"Owner of a catfish restaurant out this way called Bourré. You know it?"

"Heard of it. Never personally been there."

"You don't care for catfish?"

She looked up. "I have bottom-feeders for breakfast, but only metaphorically. I take it you think the thumb in question was once affixed to this Bradshaw's hand."

"That's right. Although you'll want to call all the hospitals in the area to see if they've treated any nine-fingered people in the last forty-eight hours."

"And if they haven't—"

"Then we're back to my theory, which starts with Bradshaw bein' more than just a restaurant owner. He had developed some kind of process for use on food products that renders them bacteria free."

"How does this process work?"

"It uses some kind of pressurized device. You put the food in it and then treat it with a citric acid wash."

Sonya looked up and frowned. "This is for real? I mean, he's got test data to show what this process does?"

"Apparently so. He had even gone so far as to pass his process along to certain folks for use in their homes on a trial basis, and them that was usin' it experienced an improvement in their diets and their overall health."

"And your interest in all this was—"

"Bradshaw's daughter come to me yesterday for help in figgerin' out what happened to the man. Her faith in local law enforcement is somewhat lackin'."

"Ah, yes. The Washington County Sheriff's Department, land of the misfit toys. They couldn't find a missing person if he was sitting in their reception area playing a harmonica for a dancing dog." Sonya glanced outside. The trees that bordered the parking lot bent and twisted in the wind and then righted themselves. Wouldn't be long before the rain came on. "But look. If this man Bradshaw had invented such a beneficial and powerful technology, what was he doing running a restaurant in rural Texas? Why wasn't he cruising the Mediterranean in a yacht the size of an aircraft carrier?"

Jeremiah leaned back. "The man couldn't get out of his own way. Part of it was pure cussedness, apparently, with which he was amply supplied, but part of it was, he had this peculiar need to be right about ever' dadgum thing. And while the man wasn't always right, he was never in doubt."

Clyde said, "That ain't to say no one was interested in gettin' they hands on the man's process."

Sonya said, "I'm guessing this is where the Daniels connection comes in."

"The Cap'n here, he figgers they heard tell of this invention from one of the experimental users, some of which were my people. And the both of us think the Daniels family might be under some financial pressure, what with their toaster about run its course and no new Daniels-branded blockbuster consumer product in the pipeline. Plus, I think Isaac may be into the sports books out in Vegas for some serious dollars."

Jeremiah said, "I overheard Little Ty in the emergency room, talkin' 'bout how their money had a way of vanishin' on 'em. And Sylvester's sons told his daughter this mornin' that someone has approached them about a deal for the invention—"

"Meanwhile, Isaac done tol' me, he wants me available tomorrow for when their home appliance marketing genius comes to town. To attend a new product meeting. On Labor Day, no less."

Sonya tapped the top of the table with her ballpoint pen. "Why would Bradshaw have to be gotten rid of?"

Jeremiah shrugged. "Like I said, the man felt like ever-thing had to be his to control. Plus, could be he had some"—he paused and glanced at Clyde—"some racial biases that were hard to set to one side."

"So, you guys think the Danielses did away with him so that they could deal with his more reasonable successor?"

Jeremiah said, "Could be. Or it could be somebody in his family got tired of him standin' between them and that yacht."

"Like who?"

"Like his sons, maybe."

"Whoa."

"The daughter made it sound like they had a rocky relationship with the old man. It explains the thumb, too. Before the Danielses went to the trouble of openin' discussions with the sons, they'd want to know the old man was gone for good, see."

Clyde said, "Check this out. I had a visitor last night, at my apartment. Big ol' boy wearin' a ski mask and totin' a wheelgun, had a accent, made him sound more country than an Arkansas pig herder. He was lookin' for the thumb."

"How'd he know you had it?"

"The only one way he could know this would be from one of the Danielses."

"Ah."

"He tied me up and started tossin' my place until I stopped him."

"How'd you do that?"

"Told him it wasn't there. Told him where he could find it."

"Which would be where?"

Clyde glanced at Jeremiah and sat back. Jeremiah leaned in and said, "Look, so far, all this is just so much guesswork and speculation, right? We don't know whose thumb Clyde found out by the side of the road. Even if it was Sylvester's, that don't mean the Daniels boy and his friends threw it from their vehicle. So about all we can do at this point is sit back and wait for Sylvester's body to turn up."

Sonya thought about the bloodstain on the floor of the Hummer, but she held her piece. "Okay. So, what's your point?"

"My point is, we are well served by showin' a little patience and seein' how this thing develops. Clyde here is on the inside with the Danielses and can monitor that situation. I can do a little more diggin' myself. Could be there are more angles to this thing than we're aware of at present. But the ace in the hole is the thumb."

Clyde leaned in and started talking. When he was done explaining what he had in mind, Sonya sat thinking for a few moments. At length she said, "It might work."

"Point is, it don't cost a thing to try."

"How fast can all this come together?"

"I can have what we need rigged up before the day is out."

And with that the sky finally cut loose and it began to rain, sheets of it coming down so that you couldn't see to the other side of the bypass. They sat watching it.

Jeremiah said, "I knew it was gonna come a toad strangler the moment I saw that red sky this mornin'."

Clyde looked at Sonya. "We good now?"

She hesitated, then nodded. "You hold up your end of this thing and we'll be good enough. But look. Don't ever put me to this choice again, okay?"

Jeremiah slid out of the booth so Clyde could make his exit.

Clyde eased out and stood. He nodded at Sonya and headed to the front door. Then he turned around. "You got any need for this?" He showed Jeremiah his bag full of blue pills.

Jeremiah worked his jaw. "You better get a move on before I take a notion to pull your arms and legs off."

Clyde grinned and once more made for the door.

Sonya and Jeremiah heard the front door open, and it let in the sound of the rain, pouring off the roof and rattling the hoods of the cars. Then the sound subsided, and they watched Clyde hustle to his car and get inside and drive off.

Sonya pushed her empty coffee mug to one side. "I'm glad you're available to continue consulting on this thing. I could use the help."

"Let me give you a couple of phone numbers."

He gave her his home and cell, and she wrote them down on her pad.

"In the meantime," he said, "there's this lawyer, represents the Bradshaw family. He knows more than he's letting on. I aim to go see what I can jar loose from him."

"He's a local lawyer, then?"

"Based in Houston but has clients up this way. Name of Bruni. Robert Bruni."

Sonya made a note of this and set down her pen. "Let me know what you stir up."

"Yes, ma'am, I most certainly will."

Jeremiah pushed out of the booth and stood looking at the rain. He seemed for a moment like he was about to say something. Then he turned and held out his hand. "Good to see you again."

Once he had driven off she started packing her things away. The professional thing to do was call Dewey and tell him what she had learned, but that she could do from the office.

After Jeremiah left Martha spent a few minutes just wandering around the yard, admiring how the pansies brightened her flower bed, enjoying the fresh air. Listening to it thunder in the distance. Glad just to be shed of that hospital bed.

At length she got to thinking about things that needed doing, but to prolong her reverie she started by watering her pot plants and relieving them of dead leaves with a pair of gardening shears.

When that diversion gave out she turned to household chores. Took stock of the laundry situation. One more day in that hospital bed and it would have been approaching a critical phase.

Next she examined the contents of the refrigerator. It was mostly bare shelves, thanks to the guy from the state health department.

She sat at the kitchen table making notes about what to get down at Postelwaite's. The list grew long. As she wrote, she began to feel a little queasy. Not as bad as last Friday night, but still. Her stomach didn't feel entirely right.

She set her pencil down and made for the bedroom.

Martha figured all she needed to do was get off her feet for a bit.

30

JEREMIAH FOUND THE MAN HE WAS LOOKING FOR IN THE WAITING AREA on the hospital's fourth floor. The lawyer sat hunched forward over a laptop. He wore a dress shirt with the tail out over jeans and loafers with no socks. He looked like a man who'd spent the night on a couch after a fight with his wife.

Next to the laptop a legal pad rested. Next to that, a white legal-sized envelope, label side down, and a foam cup about half full of coffee. A collection of rapidly aging magazines had been moved to the floor, where they sat stacked one atop the other.

The room was otherwise empty.

Robert Bruni looked up as Jeremiah took a seat in a chair to one side. "Ah, good," the lawyer said, as he reached for the foam cup. "Just in time. What's your wife's first name again?"

"Martha."

"Oh, yeah." The man bent once more to the laptop. He worked the keys with an efficiency worthy of the pole position in the steno pool.

"I hear tell your little girl is on the mend."

The lawyer didn't respond immediately. He pounded away at the laptop and then raised his eyes and did something with one hand and sat back with his coffee. He propped one loafer on the table and looked at Jeremiah. "Seems we dodged a bullet. We'll have to wait and see whether she has any longer-term health consequences."

"Your wife in there, lookin' after her?"

"Donna decided to go to her parents' for a shower and a decent meal. She'll be back after a while."

"When do you all get to take your daughter home?"

The man shrugged. "Midweek, maybe. Which is fine. We need to stay in town through Tuesday so I can file this." He gestured at the laptop.

"That's your pleading, then?"

"Our pleading."

"That's right. Which would make you my lawyer."

"Yep."

"That means you can't tell anybody anything I tell you. Not even another client. Even if it involves that other client. Ain't that right?"

The lawyer sipped his coffee. "What are you driving at?"

Jeremiah leaned forward with his elbows on his knees. "I have come by certain information that you should know but that you should keep in confidence. Which is, one of your other clients is nowhere to be found and has been missing since Friday evenin'."

The lawyer kept sipping his coffee.

Jeremiah pressed on. "Now his sons are shaping up to take a business meeting about a certain secret process the old man invented. A business meeting their father would in all likelihood tell them to whoa up on, since if it were to go anywhere it could lead to him losin' control of matters to people he don't trust. Now, if you think about it, the father's disappearance makes a meeting, and maybe a business deal, *possible* that otherwise would be *impossible*, and since the sons clearly have their reasons for wanting to move forward with meeting and business deal alike, well—" He sat back. "I expect that's math you can do for yourself."

Jeremiah watched for what reaction this might fetch. He looked for a small eruption of moisture at the hairline, a slight trembling of the coffee cup, a shifting in place, a cutting about of eyes.

But whatever guilty knowledge the man might possess, he was right disciplined about his reaction. He seemed to be thinking, alright, but he did not seem to be under any particular stress. No sweat, no shakes, no shiftiness.

At length he said, "What else do you know?"

"I ain't at liberty to say."

"Why do you care?"

Jeremiah sat back and crossed his legs. "A member of the family asked me to see what I could find out, and now, based on what I've been able to dig up over the last day or so, the DA has invited me to pitch in. She's on this thing like it had missed a payment."

The lawyer looked away for a few moments. Then he looked back. "Maybe that's a good thing. Her inviting you in like that."

"It is, huh."

"You know," the man said, as he set his cup down, "I googled you."

"You did what to me?"

"Put your name through a search engine and pulled up what there was to be found on the Internet. You were no slouch, in your day."

"My career ain't really the topic at hand."

"I guess not." The young lawyer leaned back and laced his fingers behind his head. "Look, I can't really discuss this with you, okay? There are rules—"

"I know all about your rules. Just now finished recitin' 'em to you."

"Fine. But know this. Those boys, I mean the Bradshaw boys, would not do one thing to harm their father. Not one. They idolize that man even though he treats them like crap. So, with all due respect, I'd suggest you go bark up some other tree."

"It's kindly a big forest where Sylvester is concerned, ain't it?"

"He doesn't suffer fools gladly and is blunt and unapologetic about that fact."

Jeremiah uncrossed his legs and leaned forward once more. "So, who do *you* reckon might've kicked him off the bus?"

"Funny you should ask." He nodded toward his laptop. "It so happens that the one business organization that would have the most to gain if Sylvester Bradshaw were out of the picture is the very defendant in our shared lawsuit."

"The spinach people?"

"Here's the deal, okay? Bagged salads cost about three dollars, retail, and there are roughly a billion of them sold in this country every year. That's a big business, and the produce companies make more money off that business than any of their other businesses, and do you know why?"

"I dunno. I guess because they charge more for stuff in a bag."

"Precisely. All these bags are labeled 'ready to eat.' Creating the impression that the time-pressed consumer need only buy it, open the bag, dump the stuff in a bowl, pour on the dressing, and she's done. No need to waste time chopping or, more importantly, rinsing the salad. It was in fact just such a practice that led my little girl right to death's door, and gave your wife a very rough night indeed. Actually, cut produce is much more vulnerable to bacterial contamination to begin with, and once it's closed up in a bag, the conditions are perfect for the little bugs to start reproducing themselves."

"Wouldn't Sylvester's process help these folks produce a safer product?"

"Bingo. And they well know this. Sylvester has tested their product with and without his process and sent them the results. The processed product was all but bacteria free. The unprocessed product—well, if you'd seen the test results, you'd have a hard time eating bagged salads again."

"And still you let your little girl eat it."

"I was out at a client dinner or I would have intervened. Honestly, though, I thought my wife knew better."

"Why didn't the salad people try to make some kind of deal with Sylvester?"

"They wanted to, but he wouldn't even discuss it with them."

"Why?"

The lawyer shrugged. "They'd honked him off somehow. Believe me, it wasn't hard to do. Sylvester can get honked off for life because you carry your spare change in your left pocket instead of your right. Still, he kept testing their product and sending them the results, as a way of reminding them he knew what they were up to. It's actually a good thing for us that he did."

"How's that?"

"They'll have a thick file of Sylvester's tests we can make them turn over during discovery. It will prove they knew that if they changed their methods of production, they could have produced a safer product. That will establish legal liability. Then it's just a matter of showing damages."

"I reckon I can see how that would make them none too happy with your client."

"Maybe even to the point where they took corrective action, right?"

"Maybe, but how does any of that explain the meeting the sons are fixin' to take? Remember, I know who it's with and I know why they want to meet, and it's got nothin' to do with bagged salads."

"Oh, it has everything to do with bagged salads."

"How's that?"

The lawyer leaned forward, too. "Put yourself in the shoes of the salad guys. You sell a filthy product and you know it. However, even if you could make a deal to license Sylvester's technology, which you've got to believe is highly unlikely given his ways, for you to change your production line to incorporate that technology would cost millions upon millions of dollars. Yet you know, to a moral certainty, that every year, some number of people will get sick, and some percentage of that number will

actually die, from eating what you sold them. This exposes you to continuing legal liability and damages your brand. How do you square the
circle of not having to incur the costs to produce a safe product, yet not
poisoning your customers?"

"I got it. By havin' folks clean up the salad themselves, before they
eat it."

"The home application of Sylvester's technology, were it to become
used on a widespread basis, solves the salad guys' problem for them. As
a public relations matter, they can say, 'Look, we produce our product
in full accordance with all applicable governmental safety regulations,
but if you're worried about bacterial contamination of the food supply,
by all means, use the process in your home.'"

Somewhere a doctor was being paged. Then another. A hospital is a
place that often seems to be talking to itself, like a mental defective in a
bus station. "How would we go about testing out this theory of yours?"

The lawyer took up the white envelope. He held it in his hands and
looked at Jeremiah. "It is a not uncommon tactic, in matters that are on
the verge of going to litigation, for the plaintiff to provide defense counsel with an advance copy of the petition, as a way of getting settlement
negotiations started. If the other side recognizes its culpability and makes
a fair offer, money and time can be saved."

He gestured at the laptop before him. "When my wife returns, I'll
go find a connection to the Internet, do a bit of research, find a printer,
and produce a hard copy. For presentation to the other side. If you'd
like, you can make the delivery and in the course of so doing, direct
your questions to the one man who is sure to know about it, if it was
indeed the Pricks of Produce who spirited Sylvester off."

"They got themselves a local lawyer, do they?"

In response, Bruni handed Jeremiah the white envelope. He turned
it over in his hands and looked at the address label.

"Shithouse mouse," he muttered.

After he left the ice cream parlor Clyde's mood fell off the cliff it had
been perched on since the moment he had reached consciousness this
morning. It was a bad mood he'd felt coming on for hours, and he felt
fully entitled to wallow in it.

He pulled into the parking lot at the self-storage place and rolled to a stop beside the keypad that controlled the gate. He keyed in a number and watched the gate slide laboriously open.

The inclement weather took part of the blame for his mood. As did his sleepless night, most of which had been devoted to a wrestling match with his conscience.

He knew he had every right to come clean with Sonya and Jeremiah, and there wasn't any reason for his conscience to be in an uproar about it. Isaac had bitched out on him pure and simple, for that was the only explanation for last night's events.

Yeah, he had every right.

Didn't mean he had to feel good about it, though.

He had been hired to do a job, after all, part of which was, get rid of what he found out there in the right-of-way. Not just find it. Make it go bye-bye.

He hadn't, and that had been at least partly for his own selfish reasons. Which left him in the position he was in where he felt like he had no choice but to turn on the Danielses and their seductive affluence, if for no other reason than to save himself from some kind of criminal liability.

The implications of that decision were yet to play themselves out, but if life had taught him anything it was that what flows from a man's choices are rarely obvious to him at the time he makes them.

He pulled into a parking space and stepped out into the rain. He made for the storage unit, the doors of which slid open with an electric hiss. Inside the air-conditioning was running, and after the heat and humidity of the outdoors it felt cold on his skin.

He walked a hall lined on both sides with metal garage doors.

He reached his unit and twisted the dial on the lock until it opened. He took the handle of the door in hand and jerked it up with a measure of vehemence, as though it bore some responsibility for his black humor. It sailed up on its rails with a rattle made all the greater by the complete absence of anything in that space to muffle the sound. He stood squinting at the boxes stacked there in his dimly lit five-by-ten, feeling slightly ridiculous about acting all badass with an overhead door.

He separated four cardboard boxes from the collection in his storage unit and set them in the hallway outside. Closed and locked the door.

One by one he carried the boxes back to his ride and set them in the trunk. All the while reminding himself of that old-timey pop song his mama had so often recited.

Accentuate the positive.

Eliminate the negative.

Leave ol' Mr. In Between to his own devices.

As he pulled out of the parking lot with his load of gear, his cell phone fell to chirping. He plucked it off his belt and eyed the display. SONYA NICHOLS.

He flipped it open. "Hey."

"Hey yourself. I was able to reach the guy."

"That was blazin'."

"Just took a couple of calls."

"He up for it?"

"Yeah. Once he heard it was free. And got over his annoyance at having his Sunday disturbed. Said he'd head on over there."

"So I should, what?"

"Go on over and wait for him, I suppose."

"On my way." Clyde paused. "We're square, right?"

"Yeah. We're square. Look, you did the right thing. There may be times when you won't feel like it, but you did."

"Oh, sure. Always a good idea for a man to drop his best client in the grease."

"There are more important things than money."

"Maybe, but a man's gotta eat."

Clyde steered the vehicle through the little bit of traffic there was out this morning. The rain had about stopped. He was the one who broke the silence. "Say, you wouldn't want to get dinner or somethin'. For old times' sake?"

"Actually, I was thinking we ought to get together."

"You were?" Clyde's hopes began to elevate.

"Yeah. If I file for attorney general, I'm gonna need all the help I can get. Wanna pick your brain about how to work the African American vote."

Well, that ain't what I got in mind, but it ain't nothin'. "Fair enough. You the one with the busy schedule. Just let me know when and where."

They said their good-byes, and Clyde proceeded through town until he arrived at the cold storage place.

It took the better part of an hour, but at length a vehicle pulled into the parking lot, a yellow Volkswagen Bug with a faded GORE-LIEBERMAN sticker on the back glass. From it stepped a little man of about forty wearing pink-tinted sunglasses despite the overcast and who had curls permed tightly to his scalp. He wore a Hawaiian shirt over shorts and a pair of flip-flops. He looked vaguely like Richard Simmons on holiday.

He walked Clyde's way, worrying a ring of keys as he went. His stride brought to mind a lady of privilege chasing after a poodle. Clyde stepped out to meet the man, who found the key he wanted just as he arrived at Clyde's car. He offered up a shake, with his hand bent at a forty-five-degree angle to the wrist.

"So. You must be Mr. Thomas. I'm Nick Lockhart, Brenham's very own thimble full of fabulous."

Clyde did what he could to hide his incredulity. He took the man's hand briefly and dropped it. "This your place of business?"

Lockhart cocked his head to one side. "Why? Does that surprise you?"

Clyde's eyes traveled to the front of the establishment, with its hand-lettered graphics concerning the going rate and variety of options for the processing of wild animal carcasses. Everything about it, right down to the dirt dauber nests that had collected under the eaves, bespoke of good ol' boy, redneck, masculinity. "You don't seem the meat locker type, is all."

Lockhart planted a fist on his hip and pivoted slightly Clyde's way. "What type do I seem to you, then?" He said it with a look on his face and a tone of voice as coy as a debutante's. Clyde fleetingly wished he could call on the protection of the Fellowship of the Wedding Ring.

"I don't know," was all he could manage.

"You don't know. Well. In fact, I do own this place. Along with my brother." He turned and sashayed toward the front door. "We inherited it from dear old Dad," he said over his left shoulder, "when the lung cancer carried him off. He left it to us boys *per stirpes*, in the words of the probate lawyer."

Lockhart slotted the key. "Stir-peas. Isn't that a delicious word? Latin for something or other, I suppose, but it brings to mind images of dear old Mum, standing at the stove, wooden spoon in hand, working away at a simmering pot of black-eyeds."

He threw the door open and went to a wall switch and cut on the lights.

Clyde followed him in. "This shouldn't take very long."

"I'll just sit over here out of the way."

As Clyde fetched the boxes inside, Lockhart sat cross-legged on a stool and attended to his fingernails with an emery board.

Once Clyde had his gear unloaded and unboxed he looked around. "Okay if I set it in that corner yonder?"

Lockhart looked at the corner at which Clyde was pointing and shrugged.

"Gonna need to drill a couple holes to mount it."

Lockhart folded his hands in his lap and studied the flip-flop that hung loosely from the toes of his topmost foot. "Shouldn't we consult a feng shui expert first?"

"Do what now?"

The man grinned. "Only kidding. By all means." He flopped a hand toward the corner in question.

It was against the possibility that he might be called on to do so himself that Clyde had watched closely while the tech set up the video surveillance system at the grocery store. This one here would be a single-camera operation, and that would make it a sight easier. He mounted the camera and strung the cable above the gypsum ceiling tiles and pulled it through into the small office in back.

The proprietor sat watching with his right leg crossed over his left and his right foot kicking up and down. The flip-flop hung from his toes as an ape might hang from a vine.

Clyde plugged the cable into a computer and set a monitor on top of the box and connected everything up to a wall socket. He threw all the switches and peered at the monitor. The camera in the front room picked up the customer service counter and everything within a five-foot radius of it.

It was perfect.

He stuck his head through the door. "Mr. Lockhart?"

"Coming!"

The proprietor joined him in the back room, and Clyde led the man through the system's operation.

"So the hard drive stores all the images from the camera?"

"Yep."

"*Très* high tech!"

"We'll come in once a month and back the hard drive up to a disc and free up space for more recording."

"I assume you'll want me to post one of those cute little signs that tells one and all Big Brother is watching? That they are the very apple of our eye in the sky?"

Clyde hesitated. "Yeah. Eventually, but not for a couple days. Look, can I get a look at your log or whatever you call it? The thing where you sign folks in who want to store their shit here?"

"We have not been reduced to shit storage as of yet, but sure."

Lockhart returned to the front of the store and reached beneath the counter. He produced the book aforesaid and handed it to Clyde, who opened it to the last page.

"Okay. Here is the entry from when I come in here and left a package."

Lockhart looked at the page. "'One two-pound package of ground beef.'"

"Now, the DA and me, we interested in knowing about it whenever anyone shows up with the claim slip for this item."

"But isn't it your ground beef?"

"It is."

"Then won't you be the one who claims it?"

"That claim slip was taken from me by force last night in a robbery."

"Somebody robbed you to get the ground beef you stored here?"

Clyde cleared his throat. "Look. It's a long story, okay? Which don't touch you or your business topside nor bottom except that we want to know about it when somebody asks for that package."

The man shrugged. "Okay."

"Good. Here's my card. I've printed the DA's phone number on the back, see?"

Lockhart inspected Clyde's card and nodded.

"Good. We appreciate your cooperation."

Clyde collected his empty boxes and carried them back to his car. He slid behind the wheel, his foul mood from earlier a thing of the past.

Funny how being productive can do that for a man.

Martha Spur jerked awake to the sound of the phone ringing. She had no idea how long she had been asleep, but her nap had not been a very restful one. Full of the kind of frantic dreams that visit one who's beset by a fever. She had begun to sweat lightly.

She sat up and reached for the handset, thinking she still felt a bit off. "Hello?"

"How you getting along, young lady? Just called to see if you're doing okay." It was Doc Anderson.

She brushed a gray curl out of her eyes. "That's awfully kind of you."

"I'm sorry. Did I wake you? You sound as though you were asleep."

"Oh. Well. I just closed my eyes for a few minutes. Still feeling a little strange. A little feverish and—"

"And what?"

"Gassy, I guess I'd say. To be honest."

"Not to worry. Totally to be expected after the couple of days you've had. Got some Pepcid around the house? Some Advil?"

"Sure. Of course."

"Just take them for the next day or two. Follow the instructions on the bottle. And call me if you're not feeling totally well by Wednesday, okay?"

"Okay. Thanks for checking in, Tres."

Martha hung up the phone and stretched out once more on the bed. It was a source of comfort to know she would need a little more time to recover, before she felt her old self.

Nice of Doc Anderson to call and lay her fears to rest.

31

COME MOST SUNDAY MORNINGS IT WAS EXPECTED OF DEWEY SHARPE THAT he set aside everything that came naturally and try to be a Christian for a couple hours. Generally this meant taking his place with his too tall, too skinny, and too talkative wife in his accustomed pew at the First Baptist and sitting as still as he knew how for an hour.

On the Sunday before Labor Day of that year, though, it meant specifically showing up at the lake with a barbecue trailer worthy of our Lord and Savior. For the deacons had deemed that the summer's passing be marked with an old-fashioned revival service followed by a barbecue lunch. This meant someone had to lay his hands on a barbecue trailer equipped to feed brisket, links, and ribs to the flock, since Brenham was no Holy Land hillside and loaves and fishes would fall well wide of the culinary mark.

Had Jesus been a Texan instead of inconveniently and somewhat confusingly Jewish, he would have worked his famous miracle on beef and pork products.

Dewey had volunteered to get ahold of a barbecue trailer on account of his card playing and golfing pal, Les Adams, had the best barbecue trailer in the entire area code. It was, in fact, Les's prize possession. Made of stainless steel, it had a huge cooking box and a smoker, and it rode like a luxury automobile on Monroe shock absorbers and Goodyear tires when Les pulled it behind his Ford F-150 to his barbecue cook-offs.

"Not a chance," Les had said.

"All I want to do is borrow your barbecue trailer."

"No."

"Why not?"

"I'm worried you'll mess it up."

"It's a barbecue trailer, for cryin' out loud. How in the world could I mess it up?"

"You'll figger out a way. Trouble follows you around like no man I ever knew."

"I'll be very careful. I swear. I'll pick it up the morning of the barbecue and bring it straight back when we're done. We're only talkin' a few hours here."

Les worked his jaw while he thought. "You ain't give me one reason to agree to this, you know. There's nothin' in it for me but risk."

"And a star in your crown on Judgment Day."

"I'd a lot rather have a few future speedin' tickets dismissed."

"I could probably see my way clear to makin' a couple go away."

"A couple? I was thinkin' more like, ten."

"Ten! Oh, c'mon. I'll go three."

"I won't take less than eight."

They dickered in this fashion for a spell, finally agreeing on five speeding tickets or one DWI, at Les's election, to be exercised within a year.

The morning of the actual barbecue God saw fit to ruin with a howling rainstorm about halfway through the children's sermon. Dewey had arrived early and parked the barbecue trailer off to one side and unhooked it from his truck and was all set to fire up the grill once services had concluded. He stood next to it as though it were a Nubian king and he a warrior tasked with protecting it from harm.

The congregation had taken up seats facing northwest, and so they could actually watch the rain bearing down on them across the lake for some minutes before it got there. Where it fell the water surface looked as though it bore upon it an unseen horde of water-walking varmints running full tilt.

So the decision was made to take a literal rain check and remove themselves back to the church. They would still have the barbecue, they'd just have it indoors.

The rain arrived just as people were making for their cars, and Dewey was left to hook the barbecue trailer back up to his pickup by his lonesome and follow the congregation back to town. This he did while it was raining harder than a cow pissing on a flat rock.

When he got behind the wheel of his pickup he was wet and miserable. He cranked the engine and made for the highway.

He had reached cruising speed and was watching the houses and pastures go by, checking now and then the status of the barbecue trailer rocking away in the rearview, when his cell phone set up. He fetched it off the console and looked at the display.

SONYA NICHOLS.

He flipped open the mouthpiece. "This is Sheriff Sharpe."

"Sorry to bother you on a Sunday morning."

"No problem."

"There's something we need to discuss. I understand you're working a case involving a missing restaurant owner named Sylvester Bradshaw."

"That's right."

"Well, some things have come to light that lead me to think his disappearance may relate in some way to that business involving Ty Daniels Friday night."

"You don't say."

She explained how Clyde Thomas had been dispatched by Isaac Daniels to the side of the road and how Clyde had found a severed thumb there, which in turn led to last night's assault at Clyde's apartment. How this man Bradshaw was apparently the inventor of a technology of which the Danielses could reasonably be thought to be covetous for its revenue generation potential. How all that could help explain Little Ty running from the deputy instead of just pulling over and taking the speeding ticket.

"Now," Sonya said. "Here's where you come in. You remember that stain on the back floorboard carpeting? The one that looked like blood?"

Dewey rounded a curve onto a straight stretch of road that ran downhill for perhaps a mile until it curved again back east once more.

"Yeah. Was it blood?"

A car rounded the curve up ahead in the oncoming lane. It was an older sedan with rusted spots and a coat hanger for a radio antenna. Immediately, the driver swerved out of his lane and into Dewey's and then back again. He looked like a June bug trying to shake off a hungry duck. Dewey thought he could hear a horn blowing.

"I don't know yet. Might find out as early as today. If it was, we'll need some of Sylvester's DNA to test to see if there's a match."

Dewey was trying to puzzle out what was going on with the bizarre driving behavior up ahead—*reckon the guy could be drunk?*—when he felt a presence off his left shoulder. He glanced out the window.

There, in the left lane, rolled the barbecue trailer. It looked like it was of a mind to pass him by.

"Okay," he said into the phone, his eyes wide with horror.

"I want you to go to the man's house and collect something we can use. Hair off a comb. Anything. Bring it to the office and round me up a deputy to take it to the DPS crime lab up in Austin."

Dewey fought to keep the panic from his voice. "I can do that." He eased off the accelerator for lack of a better idea, and the barbecue trailer went thundering by, its stainless steel body shiny even though the clouds obscured the sun. It rolled on as if exhilarated by its own freedom.

"Can you get to it this morning?"

The driver of the oncoming car apparently had concluded that the road was not the place to be. He quit it for the right-of-way, pulling his vehicle off into the grass and parking it at a right angle to the road.

"I'll head over to the Bradshaw place as soon as I can," Dewey said.

"Are you okay? You sound a little stressed out."

Dewey could barely breathe, and he was helpless to do aught but watch as the barbecue trailer made for the junker car as if it were laser guided. The occupants of its target burst out of it and went running. They were dark-headed people. From this distance Dewey judged them to be Asian.

"No, I'm fine," he said in a voice that was pitched a full octave higher than usual. "I'll call you when I'm headed your way with the evidence."

He closed the mouthpiece and slowed to a full stop.

He looked on helplessly as the barbecue trailer bore down on the sedan with a seeming vengeance. It did not deviate from its path. It was like a harpoon that had been launched at a whale.

Dewey was still a good quarter mile away when the barbecue trailer slammed into the car's left rear quarter panel with a great bang. The impact lifted both vehicles off the ground slightly, then they crashed back down to earth once more.

The next instant the sedan exploded into flames.

32

JEREMIAH PULLED HIS PICKUP INTO THE DRIVEWAY OF GEORGE BARNETT'S ranch house and killed the engine. He took up the white envelope and stepped out of the truck.

As he approached the front porch he couldn't help but draw comparisons between George's spread and his own. George's house looked like some movie director's idea of ranch living, with wraparound porches and two stories of white trim over gray clapboard atop which sat dormers indicating a third floor. The land was marked by white rail fencing. The place had an air of rustic regality, so unlike Jeremiah's humble home, the one-story ranch house with air-conditioning units protruding from the windows.

Fact of the matter was, George could live off his law practice and didn't need the hard work and aggravation of raising beef cattle. He kept horses instead.

Jeremiah mounted the porch steps and knocked on the front door.

Directly it opened inward and there stood George, wearing little reading glasses perched on his nose and holding a newspaper. He had on a golf shirt and slacks. George's large nose and smallish eyes gave him a vaguely feral look.

"What are you doin' here?" he said.

"I need a minute of your time, if you can spare it."

"What about?"

"It's a business matter. Maybe we should discuss it inside so your central air won't all leak away."

"Come on in, then." George turned and left Jeremiah to let himself in.

They entered a family room with an arched ceiling and an array of furniture and knickknacks chosen apparently for their ability to convey the impression of a tasteful western lifestyle. As one might find pictured in a magazine spread of some real estate mogul's Montana ranch. George took a seat on a couch covered in an elaborate needlework pattern, at right angles to which sat a matching chair. Before the couch was a coffee table on which rested a Remington bronze of a cowboy breaking a bronco. On the wall above the couch hung a painting of an old-timey cattle drive.

It was all so carefully thought out and obviously expensive that it made Jeremiah's ass hurt.

He took a seat in the armchair and picked up part of the Sunday paper that lay strewn about. "The *New York Times*, huh."

"I like to keep up with what's going on in the world outside of Brenham."

Jeremiah squinted at the paper. "There's a world outside of Brenham that's worth keepin' up with?"

"Please. Spare me the reverse snobbery. I'm not buyin' it from you."

Jeremiah scanned an article. "You read this, about the painter?"

"Haven't gotten to the Arts section yet."

"He says his art is all about makin' fun of God. What do you make of that?"

George shrugged. "God pretty much always has the last laugh, seems to me."

Jeremiah set the paper aside. "Here."

George took the envelope Jeremiah proffered and pulled from it the legal pleading. He glanced at the first page and then flipped to the last. He snorted.

"Robert Bruni." George shot Jeremiah a look that said mischief was being perpetrated on somebody, and it wasn't George. "So, you're a party to this thing?"

"Read on."

"I do believe I will."

George flipped back to the first page and commenced. There are cardplayers and there are cardplayers, and Jeremiah knew George to be a cardplayer from old. He would profit not in the slightest by sitting there studying George's facial expression.

He got to his feet and walked to a window and looked. The land sloped gently down to a tank next to which sat a gazebo. Off to the right, the horse barn. Corral of white rail fencing. Beyond the tank and the barn, the land sloped back up and crested at a hill where a copse of mes-quite stood.

Behind him there was silence except for the occasional turning of a page.

At length George said, "Sorry Martha took sick."

Jeremiah turned around. George was sitting leaned forward on the couch. He was twirling his reading glasses in his right hand. The plead-ing rested on the coffee table before him.

"Thanks."

"She gonna be okay?"

"Went home this mornin'."

"Give her my regards."

Jeremiah nodded.

"This," George said, indicating the legal document, "is complete bullshit."

"My lawyer doesn't seem to think so."

George grinned. "Your lawyer. We'll come back to him in a bit. Let me tell you why this is complete crap. For openers, food poisoning at-tributable to produce does not happen in a onesy, twosy way. It happens across multiple states, with hundreds of victims. This illness cannot have been caused by my client producing an unclean product."

"The state microbiologist tied the bug back to your all's bagged spin-ach."

"I said it cannot have been caused by my client, not that it couldn't have its source in a bag of our spinach."

"How can you be so sure?"

George reached down and picked up a device about the size of a coaster. It had a screen and keys like you might find on a typewriter built for a tiny person. "All outside counsel receive e-mail bulletins from Happy Valley's general counsel the instant an outbreak of food-borne illness occurs anywhere in the country. I have received no such e-mail on my little handheld device here."

"Maybe it's early days yet."

George shook his head. "I don't think so. The way food gets distrib-uted in this country, a place like Brenham is at the end of the line. Bagged spinach out of the same lot that got delivered here last week would have gotten delivered to major population centers fully a week or so earlier.

The DCs are located much closer to cities so as to minimize transportation costs."

"DCs?"

"Distribution centers, where perishable products are shipped in bulk by producers for redistribution to restaurants and retail grocery stores. No, if we had shipped a load of hot spinach, there'd be word of it already and the FDA would be involved." He held up his little e-mail device. "There's been nary a peep."

"How you reckon the bacteria got in your all's spinach bag, then?"

"I dunno. Coulda been product tampering. Like what happened with Tylenol a few years back. You remember."

"Who would do such a thing?"

"Hey. What are you askin' me for? You were the famous Texas Ranger, the one who had the uncanny insight into the sick and twisted criminal mind."

"Maybe we'll just let 'em sort all this out down at the courthouse."

George just shrugged. "Fine. Sue us all you want. Just a big waste of time and money, you ask me. Filing a lawsuit is like shade in the summertime. Brings a modicum of relief to the afflicted but doesn't solve the basic problem."

Jeremiah sat down in the armchair once more. "Mind if I ask you a different but related question?"

"If you want."

"You got any idea what has become of Sylvester Bradshaw?"

George draped one arm along the back of the couch and crossed his right leg over his left. "It's Sunday afternoon. He's probably sittin' home, pullin' the wings off flies."

"You're not a big fan of his, I take it."

"A meeting of the entire membership of the Sylvester Bradshaw Fan Club could easily be convened in a phone booth."

"He went missin' from his place of business Friday night."

"Maybe he was accepted into the Federal Asshole Protection Program."

"I saw you in there that evenin', with Joe Bob Cole, by the way."

"So what? The place has the best catfish in captivity. Occasionally I indulge my weakness for fried food there. Doesn't mean I keep tabs on the man who runs the joint."

"The family has asked me to try to figure out why he didn't come home Friday night. Not only is he gone but his office was turned upside-down and his safe hauled away. In that safe were documents containing valuable trade secrets about a certain process he had invented and was thinkin' about bringin' to market. A process that eliminates bacteria from produce, among other things. 'Course, you knew that already."

"I did, did I?"

"He sent you a bunch of tests for you to send along to your lettuce client. Folks who cannot have been too happy about his persistent tendency to cast doubt on the safety of their products. Preachin' is one thing, but meddlin' can get a man killed, I expect."

George cocked his head. "If I didn't know better, I'd think you were implyin' that my client had somethin' to do with that old fool disappearin'."

"Go to the head of the class."

George leaned forward with his elbows on his knees. "Look, there's somethin' you need to understand. We'd've been more than happy to sit down with Sylvester and talk with him about his process. Made him that very offer on numerous occasions. But he wasn't havin' any, okay? Apparently, early on, he took offense at the way one of the company's less than subtle QA people treated him, and that was that. All he wanted to do after that was send us his little lab tests, like we were supposed to get all nervous about it and do like he wanted."

"Which was?"

"Fire the QA guy who watered him off to begin with. Which Happy Valley wasn't ever gonna do. Besides, there was never any chance the company would license Sylvester's technology, even if it turned out that it worked."

"Why not? Wouldn't that be better than sellin' a product that makes people sick?"

George shrugged and leaned back. "Look, the company could use Sylvester's process or any one of the ten thousand other processes that have been pitched to them and it still wouldn't solve the problem. Not completely, anyway. All it would do is increase the cost of bagged salads to the consumer. Which in turn would undercut demand."

"Uh-huh. With Happy Valley's bottom line sufferin' in the bargain."

"The point is, the company produces bagged salads by the millions upon millions every year, and only a tiny percentage of those cause anybody to get sick."

"Last time I heard such an argument made, it was in defense of automobile gas tanks that had a tendency to explode on impact."

"This is not even remotely comparable to exploding gas tanks, which all would agree tend to be not the kind of thing you walk away from. Most folks that get food poisoning recover fully."

Jeremiah worked his jaw. "And the ones that don't? What about them? Just a cost of doin' business, like you said?"

"It's like this, okay? We are talkin' about a global business that employs tens of thousands of people, the stock of which trades on the New York Stock Exchange, the production methods of which are under the daily regulation of the Food and Drug Administration. Happy Valley Produce is not the Mafia. They abide by applicable government safety regulations in producing the best product they know how at a price that makes it affordable to people of even modest means. The damn few who are so unlucky as to get sick are welcome to sue and recover their damages, and many of them do."

"Like sittin' in the shade in the summertime, though, right? Doesn't solve the basic problem."

George threw up his hands. "There *is* no solution to this problem, okay? None, nada, zip, zero, zilch. Bacteria are in the food supply. Period, full stop, triple exclamation point. Nothin' can be done about it. End of story."

"You're forgettin' that Sylvester Bradshaw had come up with a way to get bacteria out of the food supply. But because he was some nobody from the middle of nowhere, your big corporate client couldn't believe he really had somethin' that worked. Right? He was just an annoyance, but a dangerous one, on account of he stuffed your all's filing cabinets full of proof that you all were sellin' a dangerous product."

George leaned forward once more. "I can suggest an alternative theory. One that's a good deal more plausible than the one you're peddlin'."

"Go ahead on."

"You know your lawyer's a solo practitioner, right? Not with a firm?"

"What's that got to do with anything?"

"Did you know he once was with a big firm? Out of law school?"

"He said somethin' about that. Said he left to escape the politics of the place."

"That's what he told you. Not that they ran his ass off. For breach of firm policies having to do with making undisclosed investments in his clients' businesses."

Jeremiah shrugged. "First I heard of that."

"That's a rather significant no-no at your larger law firms these days. Owning equity in a client. Too many conflicts. Malpractice carriers generally won't allow it. It's an even bigger deal if a man owns equity in his clients and doesn't tell firm management about it. That gets to things like character and judgment."

Jeremiah sat back and looked at the painting of the cattle drive hanging on the wall. "You think Bruni has an interest in Sylvester's business?"

"Wouldn't surprise me if he did."

Jeremiah asked the question, even though he knew the answer already. "How is that a motive for getting rid of Sylvester?"

"That business is goin' nowhere with Sylvester runnin' it. The man doesn't have the business sense God gave a horny toad. If I had money up with the man, I'd despair of ever seeing anything out of it so long as he was runnin' the show."

"There's one problem with your theory, George, and that's that Bruni spent all Friday night in the emergency room, same as me."

George shook his head. "Sorry. His alibi doesn't extend to anybody he might have subcontracted the actual job out to. A man like Robert Bruni is unlikely to get involved in the physical stuff himself."

"Still seems a stretch to me." Jeremiah stood to leave. "I think your guys have more of a motive, and more means."

George just looked up and shrugged.

"You'll be hearing from Bruni in the next day or two. He's gonna want to talk about whether you all are up for settlin' before you have to deal with the publicity that would attend an actual filing."

"I'll take it up with my client come Tuesday."

Jeremiah headed to the door and out it into the front yard.

Before he got to his truck, he heard George saying his name. "Yeah?"

George was leaning against a column with his hands in his pockets. "You heard the latest about our sorry excuse for a sheriff?"

"Can't say as I have."

"He's got ED. Has to take those stiffening pills. Whole town's talkin' about it. I've had friends call me from as far away as Houston to carry me high about it."

"Well."

George looked off into the distance. "Helluva thing, to have to defend a sheriff who's got that particular problem. Got me to thinkin' the other day. About how we might be better off if there was a man in that job who wouldn't be a constant source of embarrassment. An actual law enforcement professional. That somethin' you might could see yourself doin', maybe?"

"Me? As sheriff?"

"You'd be the perfect candidate."

"I don't know, George."

"Give it some thought, okay?"

Jeremiah turned and lifted a hand in farewell. He got under the wheel of his pickup and cranked the engine and headed back the way he came, his mind turning over all that he had heard.

33

VOLUNTEER FIRE RESPONDED TO HIS CALL WITH REASONABLE PROMPTNESS. Once they had the fire out they separated barbecue trailer from sedan. They helped Dewey hook the scorched remains of his borrowed responsibility to his trailer hitch.

The tires had survived the conflagration, so the thing rolled well enough. It was a sight to see, though, like some bombed shell of a building left behind by infantry as they advanced on the enemy capital.

Dewey returned home with the trailer in tow and parked it out of sight behind his house. He knew if he was still there when his wife got home from church he would be subjected to a cross-examination that he was in no mood for, so he changed into his uniform and went back outside and got into his cruiser and headed for the hospital.

"It's enough to make a preacher cuss," he said out loud, in reference to his cascading misfortunes. "A blue streak."

The incident report would be filed by Volunteer Fire and become a matter of public record. To the rampant local speculation about the chemical assistance his nether regions required would now be added discussion of his incompetence with a simple trailer hitch and the spectacular consequences that resulted.

"Great. Just great."

He pulled into the hospital parking lot and slid into a space near the front door. He sat there, thinking his melancholy thoughts.

His cell phone rang, and he looked at the display.

LES ADAMS, it read.

He sighed and punched the key that sent the call to voice mail. He'd deal with Les later, when he was in a better frame of mind.

That part of his brain that wasn't feeling sorry for himself was beginning to think twice about asking Sylvester Bradshaw's daughter for a sample of the man's DNA. Seemed like an awkward thing to do. You don't commonly need the DNA for someone unless there is good reason to believe they've assumed room temperature. Asking for it might lead her to put to him questions for which he had no answers.

He slipped the transmission into reverse.

Ten minutes later, he pulled the cruiser into the lot at Bradshaw's restaurant. It had remained closed through the weekend, crime scene tape strung across the front door. The forensics unit had come by yesterday afternoon as requested and dusted the place for prints and looked for trace evidence, some of which they had collected and carried back to Austin for analysis. They'd left word it was safe for Dewey to do any other nosing around the premises he thought might be called for.

He ducked under the tape and let himself inside. With the shades pulled and the sun over on the other side of the building, the front room was about as gloomy as Dewey's mood. The air smelled of old grease.

He walked into the kitchen. A humming issued from the refrigerator. A faucet dripped. He could hear the sounds of traffic moving out on the bypass behind him. Beyond that, nothing. The light was better thanks to the windows along the back wall.

Dewey pushed the door to the office open. The place was in the same state of uproar it had been in when he first saw it yesterday. He suffered a pang of guilt, this time from not having had the dedication to hang around and do proper detective work when he was here the first time.

Maybe if he were more committed to his duties as a public servant, people wouldn't be so prone to engage in humiliating chatter about him behind his back.

He'd be the sheriff who gets it done, not the sheriff who can't get it up.

He stepped among the papers that had been strewn about and dropped into the chair. On top of the desk sat a ten-key adding machine and a legal pad on which were notes scrawled in blue ink. Some kind of list of things to do, near as Dewey could figure.

He used a pocket handkerchief to open the desk drawer. Some loose change, pencils, business cards, a little flashlight. Binder clips.

He closed that drawer and opened the one next to it and hit pay dirt. A comb lay there, a single white hair still in its teeth. "Bingo." He took comb and hair alike and placed them in a Baggie he pulled from his pocket and sealed it and wrote on the outside of the Baggie the date and time in black marker.

He set that to one side and opened another desk drawer that held files, some of which appeared to have been removed and were now among the papers scattered around the room.

Not completely sure what he was looking for, he thumbed through the files until he came across one labeled OPERATING AGREEMENT. This he removed and opened on the desk.

It contained a legal document, perhaps two dozen pages typed single space. The top of the first page read:

Operating Agreement
of
Bourré Ventures LLC

In the first section of the document numerous capitalized terms were assigned definitions. It then proceeded through sections and subsections that described the business and the ownership interests of the Members. Next came pages of technical tax language.

In the governance section, Sylvester Bradshaw was designated "Managing Member," and in the event of his death or resignation, his son Mark was his chosen successor. After that came all the provisions that prevented a transfer by a Member of his or her Interest. Reading this was transporting Dewey back to the business law class he'd taken in college.

Dewey read it all the way through to the end and then returned the document to the file folder and sifted through the remaining files but found nothing of interest. Just receipts from dealings with various vendors. Some tax forms and employment records in the service of generating which trees had been slaughtered wholesale.

He started to push the drawer home, but then he stopped. Something about the drawer. It didn't seem deep enough for the bay that held it. He pulled it out a bit farther.

There, behind the files, was a panel that slid into grooves on either side of the drawer. It looked like the back of the drawer, but it wasn't. Between it and the real back of the drawer was one more file, slid into a space not much thicker than the file itself.

Dewey plucked it out and laid it faceup on the desk. The tab read CONVERTIBLE DEBT. Dewey pulled from it two more legal documents.

The top document was styled PROMISSORY NOTE. Dewey read the legalese. Something called Pebble Beach Investors LLC had made fully five hundred thousand dollars available to Bourré Ventures LLC, at an interest rate equal to prime plus two.

"That's a buncha money," Dewey said aloud.

The rest of the agreement was a standard form of promissory note given to evidence an obligation for repayment in a commercial transaction.

Dewey set that aside and examined the other document. It was entitled CONVERSION AGREEMENT, and it went on at some length. Dewey had to read it twice before he had the gist of it. This document extended to Pebble Beach Ventures the right to exchange Bourré Ventures' promissory note for a 50 percent interest in Bourré Ventures. The debt would in effect be forgiven, and the creditor, Pebble Beach, would as a result own one-half of the debtor, Bourré.

This option could be exercised any time after the death of one Sylvester Bradshaw.

However, that was not the most interesting thing to Dewey.

No, the most interesting thing was who had signed this agreement on behalf of Pebble Beach. "Looky yonder, Andy."

Robert Bruni.

He stood up and collected his two file folders and the plastic bag with the comb in it and walked into the kitchen. He paused there and looked around. All was as it had been yesterday.

He opened a door set into the wall. It led to a large pantry where the dry goods and nonperishables were kept. Bags of flour, containers of shortening, great tubs of ketchup, and other condiments on shelves that ran the length of the space. Salt, pepper, sugar, artificial sweetener, paper goods. Everything organized and arranged just so.

The top shelves were dominated by sacks with printing too small for him to read. He stepped up on a stool and peered at the labels. Citric acid and salt. Pounds and pounds of the stuff.

He climbed back down and quit the pantry and was about to leave the kitchen when a shadow moved across the room and he froze. Something was outside the window, moving with great deliberation. Dewey placed his hand on the butt of his pistol and eased slowly to the back wall.

He parted one of the sheers that covered the window and peered out. The back of the restaurant had a paved area and a ramp for taking deliveries and beyond that a Dumpster. Past the Dumpster a stand of trees marked the property line.

Everywhere in the area this side of the trees, on the pavement and the ramp and prowling the Dumpster lid, were cats of every kind and color. They sat looking about or licking their paws or stretching or running their backs along the Dumpster corner.

He shuddered and let the sheer fall. Something about all those cats out there made his blood run cold. He supposed he could understand their affinity for a commercial enterprise that served fish-based meals, but still. It had about it the feel of ill omen. He turned away from the window and took up his file and his Baggie and headed for the safety of his cruiser.

He took the two-way mike in hand. "Dispatch, this is Sheriff Sharpe."

"Come in, Sheriff."

"Who we got on duty today, Darlene?"

"Bobby, 'Nando, and the Powell boys."

"Okay. Have one of those Powells meet me at the courthouse. In the DA's office. I got somethin' needs fetchin' up to Austin this afternoon."

"That's a roger, Sheriff."

Dewey killed the connection and keyed the engine to life.

When he was done at the meat locker, Clyde headed to the Dairy Queen for a later than usual lunch. He sat in a booth by his lonesome and tucked into his repast and tried to decide how to handle his telephone call to Isaac Daniels, a call he'd rather not make. The man had specifically asked him to call, though, and he needed to do what he could to stay on Isaac's good side.

Not to call might raise all kinds of suspicions.

This was a new role for Clyde, pretending to work for somebody when instead he was, like, working for the other side. Like a Cold War double agent.

Except those guys prowled the streets of great European cities and had wiener schnitzel for lunch. Wasn't no Cold War superspy double agent who ever chowed down on a chicken fried steak sandwich at the

DQ off Main Street. That was the forlorn fate reserved to small-town private-dick double agents.

He looked around at the other diners. He was the only person of color in here.

The rest of 'em, bunch of fat white women and men with mullets and kids with T-shirts featuring cartoon characters—hell, they looked like they had stopped in here on their way to a high school reunion in Dogpatch, USA. Add their IQs together and square that sum and what you got would be like a really strong batting average.

He focused back on his lunch. Tried to put himself in Isaac's position.

The man was likely to have his doubts about Clyde's loyalty and reliability, and Clyde had to do everything possible not to feed them. He had to act completely normal.

The question was, should he let on about the visit he had last night from Mr. Armed Ski Mask Person?

Probably not. Isaac was so into deniability that even if it had been him that sent the man around to rough Clyde up, he'd never own up to it.

Clyde consumed the last of the fries and gathered up his leavings and slid out of the booth. He dropped the trash in a can and walked outside. Plucked his cell phone from his belt and found Isaac's number in the address book.

One ring on the other end, then, "Yo."

"It's Clyde."

"I was expectin' you to call like an hour ago."

"Had another client I needed to attend to."

"Workin' on the Sabbath, then, huh."

"You the one wants me to work Labor Day."

"We'll come to that. Tell me how it went with you and yo' bitch."

"She ain't no bitch o' mine."

"You tell her what you found out by the side of the road?"

"Told her and gave it to her both."

"What?"

"Bag of about two dozen blue pills, for use in the woodification of reluctant peckers. Tol' her I couldn't trace it back to Little Ty, but my guess was, them boys was tryin' it out fo' fun and didn't want to get caught at it."

Laughter on the other end of the line. "You really do that, dawg?"

"Had to improvise some, but yeah."

"She bought that shit?"

"Maybe. I think so."

"You done earned yo'self a substantial stipend, you know what I'm sayin'?"

"Want me to tell you how to make out the check?"

"Tomorrow. When you come up here. First thing in the morning, though, you got to go down to Intercontinental, pick up the most famous home appliance guru of all time. Man name of Knut Riesmeier."

"How I know what he look like?"

"You'll know. He's Austrian."

Clyde couldn't resist the temptation to bust Isaac's chops. "He look like a kangaroo, then."

"Not Australia, fool. Austria. It be, like, a suburb of Germany."

Clyde held the phone to his ear with his shoulder and pulled out a pad and pen. "Gimme the flight details."

He wrote as Isaac talked and then tucked his pad and pen away. "If his flight's on time, we'll be at your all's place by ten at the latest."

"See you then."

Sonya closed the file and looked out the window. Her forefinger tapped the desktop lightly. "I think maybe we ought to give Captain Spur a call."

Dewey said, "Sure."

She punched her phone, and a dial tone filled the room. She consulted a pad and keyed in a phone number. They sat listening to the phone ring on the other end.

Click. "This is Spur."

"It's Sonya and Dewey. Hope you don't mind if we have you on the speakerphone."

"Nope."

"Dewey here just came in with some legal papers he found in a search of a desk out at Bourré, and we thought we'd pass this along so you could be thinking about it, too."

She described the operating agreement and convertible debt documents.

"Five hundred thousand dollars, huh?" said Jeremiah. "That would explain where Bradshaw got the money to outfit his barn with a full-blown microbiology lab. And his lawyer signed the papers on behalf of ever-who these Pebble Beach people are."

"What did he need a microbiology lab for?"

"Run tests on the effectiveness of his invention against bacteria. Apparently he liked to test produce in particular, and then send those tests along to the produce people. For no better reason than to get their goat."

"How do you know this?"

Jeremiah took them through his conversations earlier in the day with Robert Bruni and George Barnett.

Sonya said, "Did he test anybody else's produce, or just Happy Valley's?"

"Happy Valley is the only name that's come up."

Sonya thought for a moment. "I think I know who might be behind Pebble Beach Investors, then. You know what Pebble Beach is, right?"

"Golf course out in California?"

"On the Monterey Peninsula. Guess what famous American writer is most closely associated with that part of the world?"

"I could guess until the cows came home and it wouldn't—"

"John Steinbeck."

"You think he's the one put the five hundred thousand dollars in?"

"He's been dead for years. I only bring him up because in *East of Eden*, he wrote of a fictional incident in which his character Adam Trask tried to ship produce grown in the Salinas Valley back east, iced down in boxcars. The trip took longer than expected and the ice melted, and by the time the boxcars got to New York the lettuce had spoiled."

"Sylvester's process could've prolonged the shelf life of that lettuce."

"The point is, Adam Trask was like a lot of failed entrepreneurs. He wasn't wrong, he was just early. Today, most of the nation's leafy greens come from the Salinas Valley, thanks to a half dozen large growers and packers, most with household names, and the Salinas Valley is just east of Eden—that is, it sits just east of the Monterey Peninsula. Home of Pebble Beach."

"I guess I still don't see—"

Sonya leaned into the speakerphone as if she were too far removed from it to be understood well. "What I am positing is this. These produce growers? They are in an intensively competitive, not to mention commodity based, business. If one of them thought it could get a meaningful edge over the others, it would jump at the chance, right? Give it a shot at increasing its market share in a business where your lettuce leaf is pretty much identical to my lettuce leaf."

"I reckon."

"Okay. Suppose one of Happy Valley's competitors got wind of Bradshaw's invention, through industry gossip or whatever, and approached him with a proposition. 'We'll fund your research in exchange for an ownership interest in your technology and your promise not to train your guns on our products.' That would give the competing company the pole position as respects the technology at the same time it took their products out of Bradshaw's line of fire."

"How come you to know so much about the produce business anyway?"

Sonya grinned. "I did my senior thesis on Steinbeck, specifically *East of Eden*. Even spent a week in the Salinas Valley and the Monterey area doing research."

"Okay, well, aside from all this bein' rank speculation based on the name of this outfit what put the money in—"

"Can you think of a better explanation for that name?"

There was a pause on the other end of the line. "What I was gonna say is, your theory might explain how Sylvester come up with his money, but it don't account for what got him dead."

Sonya looked up at Dewey and grinned. "Yeah, it does."

"How's that?"

"The debt can't be converted to equity until Sylvester shrugs off this mortal coil. Maybe the lettuce boys were tired of waiting for that timely coronary and decided to take matters into their own hands."

"Could be, I reckon."

"You know what I'd like to know?"

"What would that be?"

"I'd like to know how Robert Bruni came to be Sylvester Bradshaw's lawyer in the first place. You think the daughter could tell us that?"

"I owe her a call anyway. I'd be happy to ask."

They said their good-byes, and Sonya cut the connection. She sat back in her chair and looked at Dewey. "I think it's time we pulled out all the stops on this one."

Dewey sat forward with his elbows on his knees. "What you got in mind?"

"Getting Judge Simmons to issue warrants to search Sylvester Bradshaw's home and place of business. Get his telephone records, bank statements, the whole megillah. Give me until tomorrow and I'll have the affidavit ready for you to sign."

"Sounds good to me."

Dewey got to his feet and squared his Stetson on his head.

As he walked out of the room, his cell phone chirped. He looked at the display.

LES ADAMS.

He sent the call to voice mail and headed for the parking lot.

Jeremiah dropped the cell phone into his shirt pocket and sat watching the sunlight diminish across his land and the shadows augment.

The rain had cooled things off some, and they had the doors and windows open so as to take some of the pressure off their electric bill. Through the screen Jeremiah could hear the radio playing that song again.

> *Lord give me the grace*
> *'Fore we meet face to face*
> *Without so much as a sigh*
> *My fate in Your hands*
> *To accept like a man*
> *Where armadillos go to die*

Jeremiah thought, *That damn song is inescapable. It's like it's ever-where a man goes. Don't folks get tired of it at some point?*

When he got back home, he found the radio on and Martha laid up in bed with her eyes closed and a wet washcloth across her forehead. He sat on the bed next to her and took her hand.

She opened her eyes.

"You ain't goin' backwards on us, are you?"

"No," she said. "I don't think so. I talked to Doc Anderson, and he said I'd be a couple of days feelin' totally right."

"Okay. Can I get you anything?"

"No, thanks. Once my head settles down, I'll get up and make us some supper."

She had shooed him out of the room, and a few minutes later she was up and puttering around the kitchen. He offered to help, but she waved him away.

Now he sat staring out at his land. There just happened to be an armadillo working the fenceline over near the water tank, hunting grubs. This particular armadillo did not seem in the market for a place to die just at the moment. Above armadillo and tank and fence his windmill was framed against the sky, turning slowly.

Sonya's lettuce business conspiracy theory, which seemed to have been triggered by the name of this group that lent Sylvester money, struck him as pretty far-fetched, and mostly a product of her college thesis about this Steinbeck fellow.

To Jeremiah's way of thinking, you didn't have to go clear out to California to explain all this. The theory that was beginning to grow on him didn't require a man to leave this county right here.

When you hear hoofbeats, look for horses, not zebras.

From his shirt pocket he took his cell phone. He opened his notepad to the page where he had Karen Bradshaw's number and dialed it.

"This is Karen."

"It's Spur. Want to catch you up on the events of the day. Been right active for a Sunday. I got to warn you, though. Some of this might not be easy to listen to."

"Okay."

He began by describing his morning meeting with Clyde Thomas.

"Clyde Thomas?" she said. "Young black man, shaved head, maybe six-three?"

"I take it you all have met."

"He came by the hospital pharmacy last night looking to buy— looking to have a prescription filled."

"I know. For Viagra. He was gonna use it as a throwdown."

"A *what?*"

Jeremiah took her through the entire conversation with Clyde and then the rest of the events of the day—their meeting with Sonya, his discussion with Doc Anderson, Dewey's discovery at the restaurant, Jeremiah's meeting with George Barnett. The call with the DA and the sheriff.

At his mention of the severed thumb she inhaled sharply and said something unintelligible.

When he was done she was quiet for a while.

At length she said, "So you think the Daniels family is somehow in-volved. That they had Daddy's thumb in their possession and that they are the ones the boys are planning to meet with."

"Yep."

"I take it you don't think some big produce grower is behind all this."

"I got my doubts. Let me ask you this. How'd your daddy come to be Bruni's client in the first place?"

"In all honesty, I couldn't say. I wasn't that—"

"Involved in the business. Yeah, I know. What about your brothers? Think they might know?"

"They might."

"Check with them when you get a minute, okay?"

"Sure."

Jeremiah hesitated. "I'm afraid this ain't lookin' all that positive in terms of—"

"Look, I appreciate everything you've done."

"Don't mention it."

"There's one more thing I think you should know." Hesitation. Then, "My father has worked my brothers night and day for years now for so little pay it's—well, it's shameful. Even so, they have been there for him without hesitation or complaint, always doing like he asked, and while part of it is they're good sons, there's more to it than that."

"What else?"

"He's told them for years now that his invention is a gold mine and it will make them millions upon millions of dollars someday. If they knew he'd basically sold half the business for five hundred thousand dollars to someone else, well—"

"They'd be none too happy."

"In fact, they'd feel cheated and they'd be mad about it, and they'd have every right to be. Do you understand what I'm saying to you?"

"Yessum. I read you loud and clear."

They said their good-byes, and Jeremiah tucked his cell phone away. He heaved himself out of his rocker and headed inside to wash up for dinner.

Karen stared at the phone. She knew this conversation was better had in person but she didn't have it in her to go out to the depressing little cabin in the woods yet again. Being around her brothers was sometimes too much like being around her father. The wall-to-wall surliness, the impression they cultivated that they were, endlessly, aggrieved.

What a way to live life.

She lifted the handset and dialed the number.

"Hello?"

"Mark, it's Karen."

"Hey. Heard anything about Daddy?"

"Still nothing to report. Although I think Captain Spur may be closing in on what may have happened."

"Okay."

"He wanted to know how Robert Bruni came to be Daddy's lawyer."

"What makes you think we'd know anything about that?"

"I guess because you and Luke are, you know. So intimately involved in Bourré."

"Well, what difference does it make how the man came to represent us?"

Karen suddenly felt like he was sparring with her. Why be so evasive if he knew the answer? Did he know and was simply reluctant to say? Or did he not know and was reluctant to own up to that—because it would be yet another example of how their father had worked the boys like field hands but rarely treated them like partners or colleagues.

"Look, Mark. Can you help the man out, or can't you?"

Now she knew she had made a mistake by not taking this up with her brother in person. She would so like to see the look on his face right now, as this silence in the conversation stretched on and on.

"Are you still there?"

"I think maybe he started comin' to the restaurant and met Daddy there. That's how come the two of them to hit it off."

"He always showed up alone?"

"Not always. Sometimes he had someone with him."

"Who?"

"Doc Anderson. I think maybe they knew one another somehow. For all I know, it was Tres introduced the two of 'em. Tres probably figgered Daddy needed somebody to look after the legal side of things."

"Okay, thanks. That helps." She paused.

"That it for now?"

"Just one more thing. Did Daddy ever say anything to you all about a five-hundred-thousand-dollar loan that could be, umm, I don't know the exact word for it but, exchanged, maybe, for half the business."

At first her brother made no reply.

Then he said, "I got to go."

The phone went dead.

Dewey made his way down the hall to his office and let himself in through the front door. He waved at Darlene, who was in the dispatch booth in the back, attacking her nails with an emery board. "Everything under control?"

She set her emery board aside. "It is down here in Washington. They got themselves a situation up in Burleson, though."

"What's that?"

"Sheriff Seawright and them fished a buncha body parts out of a tank yesterday afternoon. They was packed away in little picnic coolers."

"Good Lord."

"Uh-huh. That's serious crime for little ol' Burleson."

"Thanks, Darlene."

Dewey hustled back to his office. He picked up the phone and speed-dialed the Burleson Sheriff. They patched him through to Seawright's cell phone.

"This is Seawright."

"Mike, it's Dewey Sharpe."

"Hello, Dewey. How's life in the Birthplace of Texas?"

Dewey winced. Ever since the county commissioners had seen fit to place those fancy stone markers at the county line so designating the county where the Texas Declaration of Independence was signed, he'd been hearing about it from his colleagues in the area. He tried to chalk it up to jealousy, but still.

"I hear tell y'all found body parts in a tank yesterday evenin'."

"Yep. That and a safe, of all things."

"A safe? You mean like a person would lock away valuables in?"

"Hell, Dewey, what else could I mean?"

Dewey could barely contain himself. "I think," he said, "I might know who the vic is. I assume you all sent the remains to Austin?"

"SOP for us. Who you think it is?"

"Man by the name of Sylvester Bradshaw. Runs a restaurant over on the bypass. Place called Bourré."

"I know that joint. Great catfish. Listen, Dewey. We didn't find no head, and even if we had, the state of decomposition—well, it's not even that."

"What?"

"I didn't look at the body my own self, you understand, but the med techs did, and they said it wasn't like nothin' they'd ever seen before. Was like all the blood had been sucked from the body parts. They was kindly white and limp lookin'."

"That's pretty rough."

"Yeah. And in the absence of a head and dental work and what have you, it's gonna take a DNA analysis to ID the guy."

"Which Austin is all set up to do. I sent them a sample of Bradshaw's DNA just this afternoon."

"Good timin'. Since it's our body and therefore our case, they may get back to us afore they get back to you all. Soon as we hear somethin', we'll let you know."

"'Preciate that."

When the call was done, Dewey went charging down the hall to Sonya's office, to tell her the latest.

Felt to him like his luck was on the mend for sure.

34

ISAAC HAD TOLD THE TRUTH OF IT. THE MAN STOOD OUT LIKE A PIG AT A piano recital.

He wore his gray hair long and was dressed in a cream suit that hung on him oddly. His coat rode back on his shoulders as though he were unsure whether to shrug it on completely. The buttons on his shirt, his belt buckle, his pants zipper—they did not form a uniform line, as Clyde had been taught they should. Instead they were a study in misaligned European insouciance.

He was jabbering in some foreign language and barely nodded at Clyde, who stood at Arrivals holding a sign with the man's name penciled on it. He walked up and handed his briefcase to Clyde without so much as a pause in his phone call, and then he followed Clyde to the parking garage.

They were cruising northwest on Highway 290 before Riesmeier finished his phone call and started yet another.

"Good morning, darling. It's Knut. . . . No, I am calling you from Texas. Here to see the Daniels people. . . . Yes, I know. But what can be done?"

Riesmeier put his phone away just as they hit the bridge over the Brazos. Clyde glanced in the rearview mirror. "First time in Texas?"

The Austrian sat looking at the passing scenery. "No. I have been here, a few times before."

"Yeah? What do you think?"

"I want to see an armadillo," said Reismeier.

"They plenty of them out there. They just don't care to show themselves much."

"I wonder if they truly exist, these armadillos. One hears about them, but one never sees them."

"They real enough."

It was coming up on ten o'clock when Clyde rolled to a stop at the Daniels place. He walked around to get the door for his passenger, thinking the while how driving for rich assholes could get tedious even at his hourly rate.

The man stepped out just as the front door opened and Isaac emerged, wearing a pinstriped double-breasted suit and a bright purple tie.

Isaac and the Austrian embraced and turned to go into the house.

"How's your father, then?"

"He's good, man. Be joinin' us after a while, I expect."

"Excellent."

Isaac led them to the kitchen, a fancy place of black granite countertops and cherry cabinets into which Clyde's one-bedroom apartment would have fit with ease. In the middle of the room stood an island above which hung a copper pot rack festooned with a variety of expensive-looking cooking utensils and accessories. Two top-of-the-line Big Ty toaster ovens sat on the counter. Presiding over this space was a big white man wearing a chef's hat and an apron.

In anticipation of their arrival, plates of raw meats and vegetables had been tastefully arranged on the island. Clyde would not have been surprised had Martha Stewart herself come bursting from the pantry.

The main attraction and indeed the very reason for this Labor Day get-together also sat on the island in all its unwieldy glory. It consisted of two parts, a plastic drum with a removable lid, and a metal device, an eight-inch by four-inch box that was attached to one end of an inch-high, foot-long tray, and also to two metal tubes that ran the length of the tray. Isaac swept one hand toward the device.

"Here it is, my man. We managed to get our hands on one over the weekend."

Riesmeier squinted at it. "This is perhaps the ugliest thing I have ever seen in my life. It is uglier even than my first wife."

"Yeah, it's butt ugly, all right. That's why we need you." Isaac nodded at the chef, who began to run tap water into the drum.

"This," Isaac said, as he picked up a Baggie of what looked to be sugar, "is the most common of everyday substances, what the FDA calls 'generally regarded as safe.'"

"Meaning, your regulatory approvals—"

"Don't need any. Sweet, huh?"

Riesmeier took the Baggie and examined it. He read the label attached. "Maybe ten cents a bag to produce, including packaging and transportation, if one buys in bulk."

"Make 'em for a dime, sell 'em for a dollar. This is where the real margin is, see. It's like razors and razor blades. You practically give away the razor"—he laid his hand on the machine—"and make your money on the refills."

"This would be a better business model than the toaster."

"That's what I'm talkin' about."

The chef finished running water into the drum and stirred in the contents of the Baggie with a wooden spoon. Next he added half of each food item that was laid out on the counter.

"We doin' half of everything, and leavin' the rest out, so we'll, like, have a processed piece and a control piece to compare it to, see," Isaac said.

The chef placed the lid on top of the drum and hooked an air hose up to the valve on the lid. Somewhere in the distance an air compressor began to labor.

Isaac said, "We changing the internal pressure now."

When he was finished the chef closed the valve and removed the hose. He set the drum on the metal tubes and flicked a switch on the attached box. The drum began to turn. They could see the food inside, riding up out of the solution and then falling back in.

The chef let the device run for a few minutes during the course of which Isaac explained that the food was being cleansed of all bacteria as well as any residual antibiotics and pesticides and what have you. "So it be safer to eat and it last longer in the fridge."

Riesmeier said, "How is this possible?"

"Bacteria is what causes food to go bad, see."

Riesmeier favored Isaac with a look of pure skepticism.

Isaac grinned. "I been doin' my homework, man. Got me a microbiology consultant, on retainer."

Half an hour later, they were done. The chef had retrieved all the food items from the tumbler and laid them out for inspection. Then he cooked the chicken and fish, both the processed and unprocessed pieces, seasoning them very lightly, and let the men taste them along with the fresh vegetables. Riesmeier chewed his food and looked thoughtful.

"The fish," he said. "It is much sweeter and juicier. The chicken as well."

As the chef began clearing everything away, Riemeier said, "Let us go to the study so we can talk."

That's where they found Big Ty, dressed in a silk shirt open halfway down, matching slacks, and sandals. He had a chain around his neck from which hung a gold 87, his uniform number back in his playing days.

Big Ty got to his feet to hug the Austrian. "My man. How you been?"

"Fine, a few alimony payments aside. You?"

"Jes revelin' in it. Friends, family. How the good Lord doth provide. Please." Big Ty swept a hand in the direction of the furniture. "Take a load off."

Once they were seated, Riesmeier leaned forward and looked at Isaac. "I see several issues," he said. "Major issues."

He was up while it was still full dark, gathering his clothes and boots from the closet as quietly as he could so he'd not wake Martha, who was snoring softly. He'd slept well himself, but he knew she'd been in and out of the bathroom a few times during the night. Better to let her sleep in.

He carried his apparel into the family room and dressed and went into the kitchen to cut the coffeemaker on. When the black was ready, he poured himself a mug and took his cell phone from the kitchen counter and made for the back porch.

Jake got up from his dog nest and stretched himself and came over to have his head scratched. Jeremiah bent over to accommodate him and then stood upright and leaned against a porch column and sipped his coffee and watched the day accruing. He listened to the mourning doves call and tried to think of any way his life could be better than it was and he came up short.

This was a fact he reckoned George Barnett had no understanding of.

Yet Jeremiah couldn't completely shake loose from the man's suggestion of yesterday.

For if he were being honest with himself, Jeremiah would have to admit, he missed the action that went with active duty law enforcement. The paycheck was not without its appeal, of course, and there was that sense of mattering somehow, of putting his skills and experience to use so as to make a contribution.

He tossed the rest of his coffee into the yard and took the mug back inside. When he came back out he was wearing his Stetson and had his key ring in his hand.

Directly he was bouncing across his pasture, dog in back along with the gear he'd need for his morning chores. Only then did he fetch his cell phone from his shirt pocket and key it to life. He had voice mail from yesterday evening.

It was Karen Bradshaw, saying she'd spoken to her brother and they weren't sure how Bruni came to be their daddy's lawyer. He just started showing up around the restaurant a year or so ago. Could be he had some kind of a relationship with Doc Anderson or it could be the two of them met through Bradshaw.

Jeremiah deleted the message and tucked the phone away.

Or it could be the brothers know more than they're sayin'.

Now wouldn't be a bad time to be toting a sheriff's tin, and with it the power to make those Bradshaw boys answer him a few questions.

He pulled to a stop in his back pasture and surveyed the task before him. He had taken a chain saw to some two dozen mesquite trees and post oaks and hauled the debris over to one corner. Now he needed to see to the stumps.

The rain they'd been getting ought to make this easier than it would otherwise be.

He slipped the transmission into park and got out. He let the tailgate down, and Jake hit the ground in one jump and went trotting off toward the brush pile.

"You keep an eye out for snakes," he told his dog.

Jake was too intent on his business to pay this advice any mind. He proceeded right up to the brush pile as though he had made his mind up to do this some time back, and when he arrived there he lifted a leg and made water with a vengeance.

Jeremiah pulled a shovel and a hatchet from the bed of the pickup and went to work on the area around a stump. It took him a half hour and all the cuss words he could think of before he got a goodly portion of the stump exposed. The sun was up and the humidity had come on, and Jeremiah was sweating like two lustful monkeys in a pepper patch on the Fourth of July.

He went back to his pickup and returned with a length of chain, which he wrapped around the stump. The other end of the chain he attached to a hook on the underside of his bumper.

He got behind the wheel and slipped the transmission into drive. He turned and looked through the back glass and fed the engine gas. The chain stretched tight against the stump and halted his forward movement. He pressed the accelerator a little harder and felt the stump beginning to give. A few more ounces of pressure on the accelerator and—

His cell phone rang. Without taking his eyes off the stump, he fetched it from his shirt pocket and held it to his ear.

"This is Spur."

"Good morning, Captain Spur. It's Sonya."

Jeremiah watched the stump pull completely free. He faced forward and steered the pickup in the direction of the brush pile. "What can I do you for?"

"I just got off the phone with the DPS crime lab. They found blood in the Daniels Hummer. Thanks to a DNA sample we got to them yesterday, they have identified it as that of Sylvester Bradshaw."

Jeremiah parked next to the brush pile. "Reckon we know who that thumb belongs to, then."

"Yeah, but it's still pretty circumstantial, especially in the absence of a body, or at least DNA analysis of the thumb. I'm not sure it amounts to probable cause."

"Maybe we should get it out of cold storage and send it to Austin."

"That's what I'm thinking, too. In the meantime, I'd like to conduct a couple of interviews. Starting with Little Ty."

"He won't tell you nothin'. They'll lawyer him up to a fare-thee-well."

"Probably."

"I got a better idea."

"Okay."

"Let's talk to them two rascals who were with him that night. I bet they got less access to lawyers. Maybe they'll roll over on Little Ty, and then you'll have all the PC you can say grace over."

"That's a great idea. Is there any chance I could get you to lend a hand?"

Jeremiah looked over his field of stumps. He really ought to stay right where he was until this pasture was clear.

"Wouldn't miss it for the world," he said.

When he got back to the house, he went straight into the bedroom to change. The bed was empty and the door to the bathroom closed.

He rummaged in his closet for a clean shirt and swapped his work boots out for a pair to go to town in.

Martha emerged from the bathroom, bent slightly at the waist and shuffling her feet.

"Uh-oh," he said.

She raised a hand. "I'm fine, really. Had some cramping earlier, but it's much better now."

He eyed her. "Maybe we should call Tres."

She shook her head. "If it comes back, I'll call him." She sat on the bed and looked at his feet. "You're goin' to town."

"Not if you'd rather I didn't."

She stood and shrugged on her robe. "Nonsense. I'll be fine."

"You're sure?"

"Of course. Now go on, and if I need you, I'll call you."

Jeremiah kissed her on the cheek, and with that he set his doubts to one side and headed for the back door.

That's right, thought Isaac. *You dig it and you know it.*

Isaac knew the Austrian had two stock reactions to any new product idea.

Reaction One: It's shit. Why did you waste my time showing it to me, you fool?

Reaction Two: It is a good start on an idea, but it needs my touch, my genius, my complete understanding of the American consumer and what she will *buy,* before it can be brought to market. Stand back, while I work my magic.

That was the reaction Isaac was reading in Riesmeier. He could barely contain his excitement. He leaned forward.

"What issues?"

"There is the ugliness factor, which is substantial, but the most fundamental problem is the positioning. Permit me to illustrate with an example. A few years ago, in this country, approximately one hundred children died each year by electrocution, when hair dryers were accidentally dropped into their bathwater. These deaths were all the more tragic since there was a five-dollar item that could be attached to the hair dryer plug that would cut the power as soon as the dryer hit the water. It was available everywhere, but no one would buy it. This is because, people will not pay for safety." He illustrated their indifference with an exaggerated shrug.

"Why?"

"No one thinks bad things will happen to them. Bad things happen only to the other person. Consider the seat belt. Detroit has been installing them for years, and yet no one used them. They came into usage only when it became legally required."

"So therefore—"

The Austrian crossed one leg over the other. "We must not market this device as a home safety product. It would be of interest solely to the health-conscious and foodies."

"And yet—"

The Austrian held up an index finger. "Most people will pay for something that saves them money. Show the consumer how you can extend her buying dollar and she will gladly purchase and use your product."

"Makes sense."

"This is how the thing must be marketed. As a shelf-life extender. It must be redesigned to be made smaller and smarter looking, and it must be made to operate faster and completely silently. Who owns the technology?"

Isaac said, "Some local folks. They ain't all that sophisticated. Should be no problem to license it from them on the cheap."

"But they think it is valuable, no?"

"Like I said. Their generation the first to enjoy the benefits of indoor plumbing."

Riesmeier uncrossed his legs and leaned forward. "The value add will be in machine design and marketing. The infomercial is key. Your father"—he nodded toward Big Ty—"he is the perfect product spokesman. 'Why let good food go to waste? Use Big Ty's tumbler and start reaping the savings.'"

Big Ty said, "I be expectin' my usual five percent off the top."

"A legitimate marketing cost, but this product will not support heavy royalties for the technology. A few cents per unit at most. The inventors must be made to understand that. If not, we will reverse engineer the process and do it without them."

Isaac said, "Better to pay 'em a little and avoid the risk of litigation, though, huh?"

"Will they understand? That this is the best we can do?"

Isaac glanced at his father and then Clyde and then back at Riesmeier. "They might not've a week ago. I b'lieve they will now, though."

"When can we talk to them?"

Isaac smiled. "One o'clock today soon enough?"

Clyde had felt Isaac's eyes on him all morning, like he was being checked for signs of something. He wasn't entirely sure what. Some treachery, some lack of dedication to the Daniels family cause, even though he'd been up early to fetch this Euro-trash fool in the ill-fitting suit and the stringy hair from the big airport down in Houston.

There was something else coming off Isaac, too. Some new condescending vibe. Like the man knew all about what went down in Clyde's apartment Saturday night, and he's all of a sudden, like, *I own you, motherfucker.*

Clyde had maintained his poker face as best he could. Avoided eye contact. Spent time in the prolonged study of his own boots.

When Isaac announced that there was a further meeting on this matter at one o'clock, Clyde made his move.

He got to his feet. "'Scuse me," he said to the group. "Gotta visit the men's."

Isaac dismissed him with a wrist flick.

Once there, Clyde hit the switch on the exhaust fan and pulled out his cell phone.

When Jeremiah walked into Sonya's office, she was reading a law book and making notes on a legal pad. She sat back and stretched her arms over her head.

Jeremiah dropped into a chair. "Taxpayer's gettin' his money's worth out of you."

"Divide my salary by the hours I work and you get less than minimum wage."

Jeremiah removed his Stetson and laid it on her desk. "The way I hear it, you might be lookin' to upgrade your professional status. Maybe run for statewide office."

She shrugged. "It's crossed my mind."

"I can see how this town might could get tedious for a young person. Fits an old dog like me just about perfect, though."

"Funny you should mention that. George Barnett called me last night. Wanted to know what I thought about you taking Dewey's job."

Jeremiah worked his jaw. "Ol' George still thinks he runs ever damn thing."

"This county is growing like Topsy, and the crime rate is starting to reflect it. People would sleep a good deal better at night if they had a more seasoned hand in the sheriff's office."

Jeremiah leaned forward and tapped a couple of file folders that lay on the DA's desk. "These the jackets?"

"Nothing on this Mario character other than a few moving violations. XT? He's another matter."

Jeremiah took the folders in hand and leaned back. He opened the first one and glanced at it and set it back on the desk. "Probably sings in the church choir. Makes you wonder what he was doin' in that car."

"Could be he got trapped in orbit around the supernova known as Little Ty."

"Prob'ly." The other file he set to studying. "Xavier Thomas, aka Bullet X, aka X Dawg. The likes of these generally don't have an abundance of life expectancy."

"Just being out as late as he was, much less traveling in a speeding car? Smoking weed? If there's such a thing as a parole violation spree, he was on one."

Jeremiah set the file back on the desk. "Dewey around to lend a hand?"

"Yeah. He's waiting on his own call from forensics."

"'Bout what?"

Sonya passed along the report about the body parts and safe found in the Burleson County stock tank.

Jeremiah grunted and looked out the window. A flock of grackles was taking up noisy residence in the oak trees on the lawn.

"Them birds is nothin' but a nuisance," he said. "They crap on everything in sight, and they're ugly to boot."

Before Sonya could reply, Jeremiah's cell phone rang. He pressed it against his ear. "This is Spur."

"Yo. It's me. I'm hidin' in a toilet at the Danielses place. Can you hear me, man?"

"Sounds like you're in a wind tunnel or somethin'."

"That's just the fart fan. Listen, the Danielses is plannin' to sit down with the Bradshaw boys at one. Gon' try to license the technology from those cedar choppers for a song. Hell, not even a song. More like a tune hummed off key. Which they'd be in no position to do if the ol' man was still around with his cranky-ass stingy ways."

"Sounds kindly like motive for gettin' the ol' man out of the way."

"That's why I'm callin' you, man."

The line went dead, and Jeremiah relayed the conversation to Sonya. She said, "The Bradshaw boys are awash in motive, too. Past and present."

"It's hard to imagine two sons carvin' their daddy up into pieces."

"Which may be just why they did it. To make the killing look so heinous it calls into question mere patricide. Or maybe they just hated him that much."

"That's not the way their sister tells it."

"But how well did she know the two of them? Really?"

"They were blood kin."

"Which often leads to profound blind spots." She thought for a few moments. "You think the Bradshaw boys and the Danielses could have been partnered up on this thing?"

"If they were, they about to have their first partnership fallin'-out. Sounds like the Danielses aim to take advantage of their superior bargaining position."

There was a knock, and the door opened. A young man stuck his head in. "They're both here. Mario is in the big conference room, and XT is in the little one on the south side."

Jeremiah nodded. "Go get the sheriff, would you?"

Dewey showed up inside of five minutes.

Jeremiah said, "Heard anything from Austin?"

Dewey shook his head. "They said it'd be later today."

"You got time to help with this pending interrogation?"

"Sure."

"These boys ain't under arrest, so there's nothin' keepin' 'em here if they decide to go. Plus this one, calls himself XT? He'll know to dummy up."

"So, what would you suggest?"

Jeremiah sketched out his idea, and when he was done nods made their rounds.

Mario was sitting at the conference table when the three of them walked in and took their seats. He had a diamond stud in his left ear and was attired in a red T-shirt bearing the image of a basketball player in mid-dunk. He wore workout shorts that hung to his knees.

By previous agreement, Jeremiah did the talking. He set the two file folders on the table before him and introduced himself. "I'm a retired Texas Ranger. You know what a Texas Ranger is, son?"

"Badass state cop," the kid said.

"Nowadays I help folks out with problems, such as the family of the man whose thumb you all pitched out the window of Little Ty's Hummer the other night."

The kid looked away. "I don't know what you talkin' 'bout."

"Yeah you do. Now here's the deal. You give us Little Ty and that other kid, and I might be able to talk your PO into goin' easy on you. Maybe keep you from havin' to go back to juvenile correction. You go back for this and no tellin' how long it'll be before you breathe free air again."

The kid sat there staring, with his mouth hanging open.

"I ain't gonna ask again. Either give me Little Ty and this Mario kid, or back to Gatesville you go."

"I ain't never been to Gatesville!"

Jeremiah reached for a file folder and opened it. He looked up. "You ain't Xavier Thomas?"

"Naw, man."

"Son of a gun. Sorry 'bout that." He grinned and got to his feet. "I'll be back here directly. Dewey, you want to keep our guest here company while Sonya and I go down the hall?"

"Sure, Captain Spur."

He and Sonya walked out of the room.

"You think that'll work?" Sonya whispered.

"Has ever time I tried it before."

They found XT slouched in a chair in the south conference room. He, too, was clad in shorts, although his were of the walking-around variety, and a short-sleeve cotton shirt. He had a trace of beard that ran along his jawline and a round face and half-lidded eyes. He looked like the business manager for a rap star.

Jeremiah and Sonya sat in chairs across the table from him. Jeremiah made a show of opening and studying his file. He waited for the kid to speak.

"They a reason," XT said, "you all carried me up here on Labor Day?"

Jeremiah set the file down. "You from around here, Xavier?"

"Naw, man. I grew up in Houston."

"But you live here now."

"Yeah. Go to Blinn."

Blinn was the local junior college. "Your field of study would be—"

"Computers."

"Good future in that, I expect."

"Who the fuck are you anyway, man?"

"Jeremiah Spur. Retired Texas Ranger. This here is Sonya Nichols. She's the DA and the one who'll be chargin' you with parole violation. I hope your fall tuition is refundable."

XT grunted. "I ain't done shit, man."

"That's not how the State of Texas sees it. 'Course, you might could do yourself some good if you was to 'splain us how you all ended up with somebody's thumb."

XT crossed his arms over his chest. "I want a lawyer."

"What do you want with a lawyer?"

"I know my rights."

Jeremiah looked at Sonya. "Is he under arrest?"

"Not yet."

He looked back at XT. "You're not under arrest. You can walk out of here at any time. We just thought you might want a chance to make things better for yourself. So you won't miss school on account of being locked up for serial parole violations."

XT sneered and got to his feet. "Like the Danielses gonna let that happen, man. They gon' look out for XT, 'cause they know XT gon' look out for them."

Jeremiah shrugged. "We'll be seein' you."

Sonya got to her feet. "I'll show you out."

She led him out the door and down the hall away from the conference room where they had left Mario.

Jeremiah found Dewey standing in the hall outside the other conference room.

"How's our boy Mario doin'?"

"He's twitchin' like he's got poison ivy on his pecker."

"Wait here."

Jeremiah went in and sat down. Mario's T-shirt was dark under the armpits, and moisture had appeared at his hairline. He was studying his hands and swallowing.

Jeremiah crossed his arms. "So. Your buddy XT. Has his heart set on learnin' all about computers, seems like."

Mario looked up. "Look, man. I can't do no jail, okay? It would break my mama's heart."

"Okay. But I need you to say more than what you've said."

"You promise if I tell you, I don't have to go to jail?"

"I'm a private citizen. No authority to bind the state. What I do know is this. It'll go a lot better for you if you talk."

Mario looked away. He sat swallowing. He seemed to be weighing his choices. Without looking back, he said, "We was just out drivin' around, like we do. Little Ty was all hyped about the season startin', said he needed to blow off some steam. Then after midnight he gets this call on his cell. I don't know who from, and he didn't say. He just turned down the music and had this convo, see."

"Convo?"

"Conversation. 'Bout meetin' up with some dude. So we drove around till it was time for Little Ty to make his meetin'."

"He say what the meetin' was about?"

"He was, like, very vague on the subject. Somethin' to do with his pops's business. Although how that could have been—" He stopped and sat looking at his hands.

"Go on."

He looked up. "'Long about one thirty, Little Ty took us down some back road, south of town. Place where trees was growin' right up 'side the road. Over it even. Was so dark, man, you couldn't see nothin' but what the headlights showed you. We went back there and he killed the high beams, and we just sat there listening to music and smokin' this really fine tea XT had brought along. That's the hook between Little Ty and XT. He's like the go-to man for that shit.

"'Long about two, another vehicle come up behind us. Couldn't see on account of the man had his high beams on."

"What kind of vehicle?"

"Pickup of some kind. The man stops, and Little Ty tells us to stay where we at. Then he gets out. When he comes back he's holdin', like, a sandwich bag and laughin'. At first I thought he'd scored us some more weed, but then he held it up under the dome light and I seen what was in the Baggie. Fuckin' thumb, all bloody and shit. Little Ty said it was a souvenir and he was gonna take it home, show it to his brother. Called him on the phone while we was sittin' there, left him a voice mail about it.

"XT went to whoopin' from the backseat and asked could he see it, and so Little Ty passed it back. Damn if that boy didn't take it out he was so wasted. Dropped it on the flo', where it rolled around at his feet in the damn dark. Then while we was drivin' down the highway, that cop come out the bushes, emergency lights and siren all goin'. Little Ty tol' XT to get rid of that nasty fuckin' thumb, and XT, he like rolled down his window and sent it sailin'. Little Ty hit the accelerator, and we was maybe about to pull free of the man when we hit that curve and over we went. Scared the shit outta me."

They sat quietly. They could hear the grackles outside, fussing at one another as they moved mindlessly from branch to branch, tree to tree.

Sonya came in and took a seat. Jeremiah repeated the gist of Mario's story and then turned to Mario. "You never saw the driver of the other vehicle."

"We didn't head back to the highway until after the man had turned his own ride around and took off. I 'spect he tol' Little Ty it needed to be that way."

"You sure there was just one person in that truck?"

"I don't know, man. Coulda been more than one. Like I said, he had his high beams on."

Jeremiah glanced at Sonya. She was jotting down notes and chewing her bottom lip. She looked across the table at Mario, who sat with his shoulders slumped.

She said, "Can you hang around for a bit? I'd like to get this down in writing, have you look it over and sign it."

Mario looked away. "I feel like shit."

"Can we get you something? Soft drink maybe?"

When he looked back, a tear was working its way down his cheek. "It ain't like that. I feel like shit that I done dimed out Little Ty. XT I don't give a damn about. But Little Ty—he's my man."

Sonya looked at Jeremiah, who just shrugged. This business of re-morse setting in after one guy had given up another—he'd seen it so often it barely registered.

She looked back at Mario. "Give yourself a break. You did the right thing."

He sniffed but made no reply.

Jeremiah and Sonya got to their feet. She said, "I'll be back with the written statement for you to review as soon as possible, okay? Then you can get out of here."

As they walked to Sonya's office, Jeremiah said, "I think we ought to pay a call on the Daniels family a little after one o'clock, since the Brad-shaw boys will be there, too. Just to see what we can stir up."

"Works for me."

"Why don't you invite the sheriff to join us. We can go in his cruiser. Make it seem more official."

Sonya glanced at her watch. "See you around one, then."

Jeremiah headed downstairs and out into the sunshine. His pickup was parked close enough to the trees to have become a target. Just one more thing to add to his list. It wouldn't do to be driving around town in a pickup bespeckled with grackle crap. He had just enough time to get it washed and get back here.

He was behind the wheel and had turned the key in the ignition al-ready when the idea occurred to him.

Maybe we ought to invite one more player to this afternoon's event.

The car wash would have to wait. He pointed the pickup toward the county hospital.

Later in the morning the cramps started up again, only more frequently and painfully. They bent her over double and brought tears to her eyes.

After that she was beset by the runs, just like Friday night but with-out the blood.

She was alone and scared, and she didn't think it was supposed to be this way.

On a break from the bathroom she looked up Dr. Anderson's phone number and called him. She got his service and left word.

She was about to call Jeremiah when the phone rang.

"Hello?"

"Martha, it's Tres. I just got your message. I take it you're not doin' well."

"I'm in a lot of pain and the diarrhea is back and—"

"Just try to relax. I'm on my way over."

"Oh, Tres, I hate to—"

"Don't be silly. I insist."

She watched out the front window until she saw his Prius pull into the drive. When he gained the front door she was waiting for him, bent slightly at the waist, trying to control her bodily functions.

He led her back to the bathroom and waited while she endured the next episode. Then the doctor helped her to bed and opened his black bag and went about checking her vital signs.

When he was done, he packed his thermometer and blood pressure cuff away and produced a syringe and a vial. "You seem to have relapsed a bit," he said, and he stuck the needle into the vial and drew fluid into the syringe.

He set the vial to one side and flicked the syringe with his middle finger and then depressed the plunger until a bead of fluid appeared at the tip of the needle. He set about swabbing her inner arm with a cotton ball loaded with alcohol.

Martha said, "Do I need to go back to the hospital, do you think?"

"Oh, no. I shouldn't think so."

He inserted the needle into her flesh and depressed the plunger fully and removed the needle and covered the entry wound with the cotton ball. "Hold that there, would you, Martha?"

He tucked the syringe back into his bag and looked at her. "That was a shot of antibiotics combined with a mild sedative. The former ought to knock out the bug, and the latter ought to knock you out so your system can get some rest. Where's Jeremiah?"

"Went to town. Not sure why."

"Well. You just close your eyes and see if you can rest. I've got his cell phone number. I'll call him and tell him to come home and take care of you, okay?"

"Okay. Thanks, Tres."

He sat by her side until he could tell from her breathing she was asleep.

He reached over and lifted the telephone receiver off its hook and laid it on the bedside table. Then he stood and took up his bag.

He walked through the house into the kitchen and stopped before the refrigerator. He set his bag on the kitchen table and opened the re-frigerator door. He paused for a minute and then made his selection. He took out a bottle of orange juice and set it on the table next to his bag.

He reached inside for a plastic bag containing a number of syringes with caps covering their needles. He removed a syringe and emptied its contents into the mouth of the orange juice bottle.

He placed the bottle back in the refrigerator and closed the door.

35

DEWEY WALKED BACK INTO HIS OFFICE AND SAW DISPATCH WAVING AT HIM from her cubicle.

"What is it?"

"Lamar Jackson needs you to call him *ándele pronto*. He said you'd know why."

Dewey groaned. He trudged back to his office and closed the door and dialed up the newspaper. The woman who answered said Lamar was expecting his call.

"Hello, Sheriff."

"Lamar."

"You got anything for me? I'm up against my deadline here."

"Look, Lamar. I'm workin' this Daniels thing along with the DA and a number of others. There's nothin' to pass along to the press just yet. Can't you give me another week? I mean, c'mon. There's a lot at stake here."

"I couldn't agree more. A whole lot at stake. 'Specially for you."

"Lamar, when we're ready to talk to the press, you'll be the first—"

"Maybe you better go check your fax machine, before someone else does."

Dewey hung up with a sigh. He heaved himself out of his chair and hustled to the communications room. Immediately the fax machine hummed to life.

It wasn't but a three-paragraph story. Quoted anonymous sources to the effect that the sheriff had sought medical help for a condition related to his sexual performance.

"Sexual performance? What the hell? They went and made it sound even worse than it is. God damn son of a bitch."

There was a quote from some doctor discussing certain side effects of the pharmaceuticals commonly used in the treatment of Dewey's condition and leaving open the question whether they could impact his ability to discharge his duties.

"Lamar, you sorry sack of shit. I'm gonna kill you and tell God you died."

He wadded the page up and tossed it into the wastebasket. Then he retrieved it and smoothed it out and fed it into the shredder.

Jeremiah found Karen working away at a computer terminal. When he walked into the pharmacy she looked up and then swiveled her chair and got to her feet. Worry clouded her features.

"I can't believe you're here with good news."

Jeremiah leaned forward with both elbows on the counter. "Just the sight of me is like the Jewish telegram, huh?"

"How's that?"

"It said, 'Start worrying, details to follow.' "

This fetched a weak smile. "So, what are the details?"

Jeremiah reviewed the day's events, including the pending meeting of the Bradshaw boys with the Danielses, and what they'd learned from Mario. She appeared to be struggling with what she was hearing, about the trace evidence in the Hummer that matched her father's DNA, and the thumb in the sandwich bag. She seemed on the verge of tears.

"He's really gone, then."

Jeremiah said, "I know it kindly looks that way, but let's not give up just yet."

She dropped her head and shook it slowly. "I'm so afraid."

"Of what?"

"That the boys were involved somehow."

"That's one possibility."

"One possibility? Can you imagine another one?"

"Sure I can."

She sniffed and looked up. Her face was wet with tears. "Yeah, but they were the last ones with him. And it's not like they were without their reasons. And, and—they're meeting with the Danielses this very day, as if they already know for sure he's gone. I mean, how else can you explain it?"

"Don't go jumping to no conclusions, okay? Look. We're of a mind to pay a call on the Danielses this afternoon while your brothers are there. Just to see what kind of reaction we get. Maybe we'll learn more. You want to come along?"

She sniffed. "You really think I should?"

Jeremiah nodded.

"Okay. I guess."

"Be at the courthouse at one o'clock, then."

"Yes, sir."

He turned to go.

"By the way," said Karen. "How's Martha doing?"

"Not as well as either one of us would like, I'm sorry to say. She was runnin' a fever yesterday and had cramps this morning."

Karen's expression changed from worried to stricken. "Oh, my God. That's not good."

"What? She ought to be totally on the mend now? Doc Anderson told her it could be a couple of days—"

"There's something you need to know," she interrupted. "Something I had completely forgotten about until just now."

She told him of her concerns that Tres's age was beginning to affect his abilities, and how he had taken Martha off antibiotics way too soon, in Karen's estimation. Jeremiah listened, working his jaw throughout.

"I'm so sorry I didn't mention this to you before."

"Forget about it. It ain't like you had nothin' else on your mind." He took his cell phone out of his shirt pocket and keyed in his home number, then cut the connection. "The line's busy." He looked down and then back up. "You sure enough worried about her relapsing?"

"I wish I could say otherwise."

"I better pass up on this Daniels thing and go tend to her, then. Can you tell the others when you get to the courthouse?"

"Sure."

He headed out of the pharmacy, all but running.

Over sandwiches they reviewed financial projections that gave an indication of the profit potential of the tumbler business. The ramp-up in sales volume over time for machine and ingredients both, price points, possible accessories and line extensions. Assumptions about manufacturing costs, marketing dollars. Retailer discounts, stocking fees, costs of

performing on product warranties. Big Ty's celebrity endorsement royalty and the royalty to be paid to the Bradshaws for the license of their
technology.

This last item caught Clyde's attention. "Outta all this money, you
ain't payin' much for the actual license."

"Didn't you hear Knut? There ain't a lot of margin in this thing to
start with. Can't be strippin' more out just because these fools stumbled
onto the idea. That's like rewardin' luck, when it's hard work and investment needs to be rewarded."

Clyde wanted to say it took the Bradshaws substantial hard work and
investment to bring the process to where it was today, but he kept mum.

Riesmeier and Isaac spent time mapping out the critical path for the
launch. The press release at 12:01 in the morning, preferably on a Tuesday
in the fall, when product was ready to ship. In advance of the Christmas
season. The calls to the media. Infomercial placement, which markets,
what time slots. Use of free media to the extent possible, starting at the
bottom of the food chain with local television coverage, working their
way up to the *Today* show and maybe, with a little luck, the total Holy
Grail of marketing, Oprah's "Favorite Things" show.

Isaac said, "Oh, man. If we could only get placed on *that*."

Riesmeier said, "I know a couple of the producers, and she is into the
healthy living thing. I think we send around a prototype and get them to
test it. This is a very unique product, and that should work to our advantage."

Around twelve thirty, Clyde's cell phone went to vibrating. He took
it out and looked at the display. Text message from Sonya that read:
Expect party crashers soon. We can pin the thumb on Ty.

He texted back: *OK*. Clipped the phone back to his belt and looked
around. No one seemed to be paying him any mind.

As it grew closer to the time for the meeting, Isaac said, "What we
need to do is, be respectful of what they have created, but disabuse 'em
of any notion it's worth all that much money, unless we can bring a
product to market. Okay?"

Clyde and Riesmeier nodded their agreement.

"So I'll be, like, leadin' the discussion. Knut, speak up, you got anything to add."

Knut set down his coffee cup. He ran a hand through his hair so as to
get it out of his face. "It's your show."

Clyde figured the reason they had included him in all this was to further Isaac's desire to keep him a "warm and fuzzy" as opposed to a "cold and prickly." He'd been more than happy to play along, since it was part of his undercover gig.

Everybody playing everybody else to get an advantage. That's what life's all about, right? Whether you're talking about the marriage bed, the church social, the business meeting, or the prison yard. People look out mostly for themselves and what they want. There's a billion Donald Trumps for every Mother Teresa.

The Bradshaws arrived at straight up one o'clock. The butler showed them into the study where the introductions were made. They had with them their lawyer, Robert Bruni, who handed cards to Isaac and Knut and Clyde.

Bruni was wearing a charcoal gray suit with a red tie and a white shirt. The two Bradshaws were in jeans and golf shirts with the word BOURRÉ embroidered on the left breast. They looked like clean-shaven versions of the Cro-Magnon men from that automobile insurance ad campaign.

The butler returned with a tray of soft drinks from which everyone helped themselves as they talked college football and the weather. Clyde studied the two Bradshaws. Whatever nerves they were feeling they did a good job of hiding behind a screen of impenetrable sullenness.

They sat in chairs and on couches arranged around the coffee table. Isaac said, "Thanks for comin' in. Wanted you all to meet Knut here and talk some about commercializin' yo' daddy's invention."

Mark said, "But you don't know nothin' about it."

Isaac said, "We know more than you think we do."

"How can that be?"

Bruni shot Mark a look and leaned in. He said, "So, you think it may have promise for home adaptation?"

Clyde's cell phone fell to vibrating. He looked at the display. Text message from Sonya: *Five minutes.*

Riesmeier cleared his throat. "Not in its current form. It requires redesign to achieve ease of use. It must be small and inexpensive. Two hundred fifty dollars at most, the outer limit of what someone will gladly pay for a wedding gift. Also, positioning is key. Even though it improves the taste of food, people will not buy it for this purpose."

Bruni said, "Maybe you should try tasting food after it's been processed before you reach that conclusion."

"I did. This morning. We had a demonstration here."

The two Bradshaws sat back and looked at one another. They seemed on the verge of panic. Bruni glanced at them and then said, "How can you have—"

Isaac raised a hand. "We know y'all want to keep this thing a secret, okay? And we ain't tol' no one else. But we know how it's done. There's certain people usin' it already, right? Some of 'em are friends of ours, here in town. Folks that go to our church. Like that."

The two Bradshaws looked more and more confused.

Bruni said, "How do you see us working together?"

"We want a license from you. Pay you a set amount per unit of equipment and ingredients sold. Now I got to warn you, this gon' be a thin margin, on account of what Knut said about holding down the price point and all. We got manufacturing and marketing costs to consider."

"I assume you've got some economic projections done already?"

"They rough, but yeah. Looks like we can't afford to pay more than ten cents a unit by way of license fees. Twelve cents at most."

Mark Bradshaw exploded, "That's bullshit! Without the process, you've got nothin' to sell to start with!"

Bruni raised a hand in a gesture that said, *Easy, now. Let me handle this.*

Mark looked at him. "But they're tryin' to *steal* it."

Luke said, "Sounds to me like it's done been stole."

Bruni said, "Hang on, hang on." He turned toward Isaac. "We obviously think that's a little on the light side."

"We happy to show y'all how the numbers work."

"Maybe that would be a good idea."

Mark said, "This is bullshit. I think we should get the hell out of here, okay?"

"You all are here now. Let us just show you what we got before you bounce." Isaac got to his feet and started to walk toward a desk where sat a stack of papers but stopped when the butler appeared at the door. "What is it?"

"May I see you for a second?"

Clyde's phone vibrated. He looked at the display.

We're at the door. See if you can maneuver the Bradshaw boys out here.

He attached the phone back to his belt and sat thinking. How the hell was he supposed to do that? And why?

Meanwhile, Isaac had disappeared into the foyer.

Riesmeier produced a cell phone and got to his feet and walked a few yards off.

Clyde thought furiously.

Then he had an idea.

Dewey pulled the cruiser up to the squawk box and rolled down the window. He punched the button and sat waiting for the response.

"May I help you?" a voice said.

"This is Sheriff Sharpe. I've got District Attorney Sonya Nichols and a couple of other people with me. We'd like to speak to someone in the Daniels family about the incident involving Little Ty this past Friday night."

"Do you have an appointment?" the voice said.

"Maybe you didn't hear me right. I'm the sheriff. I'm here with the DA. We want to speak with the Daniels family."

"I need to ask someone—"

"Look. If you don't open this gate right now, I'll be back in an hour with a search warrant and half a dozen deputies. I promise you, your bosses will like that a whole lot less than if you just let us in."

From the passenger's seat, Sonya said, "Tell that idiot I'm about to call the judge and he doesn't want me to—"

At that moment, the gate began to swing open.

"That's better," said Sonya.

Sonya glanced back at Karen Bradshaw, who sat staring out the window.

"You sure you're up for this?" Sonya said.

Karen nodded but said nothing.

Dewey followed the drive up to the house and parked alongside a pickup.

"That's my brother's," Karen said.

Sonya said, "I'm gonna text Clyde now."

They exited the cruiser and walked up to the porch. Dewey rang the bell and stood there with his thumbs hooked into his belt.

The door swung open and revealed an older white man dressed in a charcoal gray suit. He said, "I'll let Isaac know you're here."

He closed the door. They stood there, looking at the house and the carefully tended grounds, like tourists awaiting admission to the ancestral home of a Founding Father.

The land speed record Jeremiah set early last Saturday morning between his ranch and the hospital didn't stand three days. In the course of breaking it that Monday afternoon, he kept continuously speed-dialing his house.

Each time, all he got was the taunting buzz of the busy signal.

He roared up his driveway and skidded to a stop. He leapt from the cab and flew through the yard gate, all but colliding with Jake in the process.

He burst through the back door, calling Martha's name. At the bedroom door he stopped and caught his breath.

She was in bed, eyes closed. Next to her head the phone was off the hook.

He hustled to her side and sat on the bed. The telephone receiver he picked up and replaced.

He laid a palm across his wife's forehead. Seemed to him like she might be running a fever. She did not stir under his touch. Her breathing was quick and shallow.

He leaned in close. "Martha?" he whispered.

Nothing.

He decided it would be a mistake to panic. Maybe the thing to do was let her sleep and see how she was doing once she got her nap out.

This might all go a sight better with a cup of black.

He tiptoed from the room and went to the kitchen. There was the better part of a cup left in the machine from the morning's pot, but he thought a fresh brew in order.

He opened the refrigerator, which was where they kept the coffee. Was about to take it from its place on the shelf in the door when something caught his eye.

That ain't right.

Then he heard Martha cry out, and he shoved the door to and went running back to the bedroom.

36

CLYDE PRODUCED ROBERT BRUNI'S BUSINESS CARD AND BEGAN TAPPING the man's mobile number into the TO field of a new text message on his cell phone.

The Sheriff and the DA are at the front door. You might want to take your clients and get out of here. Clyde.

He hit the SEND key and waited. Instantly a beep was heard on the lawyer's person. The man reached inside his coat pocket and produced a BlackBerry. He stared at it and then looked at Clyde, who nodded once, slowly.

Clyde glanced at Riesmeier, who was engrossed in a cell phone conversation of his own. He was paying no attention to the proceedings over by the coffee table.

The lawyer leaned toward Clyde. "What are they doing here?" he whispered.

Clyde shrugged and looked away.

The lawyer sat thinking. Then he looked at his clients. "I'm not sure there's much to be gained by sitting here. Let's take their numbers and study them on our own. Then we can put together a list of questions and get back to them. How's that sound?"

"Sounds good to me."

"Me, too."

Bruni helped himself to copies of the financial projections laid out on the desk. His clients followed him out the door.

As they disappeared, Clyde heard voices being raised toward the front of the house.

When next the door was opened it was by a younger black man dressed in a business suit. Dewey and Sonya recognized him as Isaac Daniels.

"Somethin' I can do for y'all?" he said.

Dewey squared his shoulders. "We are here to discuss certain information that has come to light concerning the events of this past Friday night. If we could just come in for a few—"

"No."

"Excuse me?"

"You heard me. You can't come in. We more than happy to hear you out, okay? But this ain't the time nor the place, and I am gonna want to have a lawyer present."

"Just give us a few minutes of your—"

"*I done tol' you, no, okay?* I'll find out when our lawyers are available and I'll call you and we'll set somethin' up—"

The door opened wider, and through it came Robert Bruni and the two Bradshaw boys. Bruni looked quickly at the delegation assembled on the front steps and turned to shake Isaac's hand. "We helped ourselves to copies of your numbers. We'll look them over and get back to you."

Sonya glanced at Karen. She was staring at her brothers. She seemed about to cry once more.

Bruni nodded at Jeremiah and headed to the driveway. The brothers would have followed but for Karen grabbing Mark by the arm as he tried to pass.

"What do you think you're doing?" She said it barely above a whisper.

Mark looked at her like a man might look at a stranger who had solicited him for spare change. "Let go of me."

"Tell me what you know about Daddy. Tell me! You know, don't you?"

"I done tol' you I don't know nothin'! Let go of my arm!" Mark jerked himself loose, and he and his brother continued on toward their pickup.

Karen watched them go, tears working her cheeks. They reached the pickup and got in without a word. They and their lawyer drove away in their separate vehicles.

Meantime the door to the house had closed and Isaac had disappeared inside.

Sonya said to Dewey, "I guess that's that."

They were on their way back to Dewey's cruiser when his cell phone rang. He held it to his ear. "Sheriff Sharpe speaking. . . . Yes. . . . Okay, can you fax it to the office? . . . Sure. . . . And what would that be? . . . Citric acid, huh? Alright. Thanks."

Dewey cleared his throat and looked at Karen. "I'm afraid I've got some terrible news."

As bad as it had been Friday night, this bid fair to be worse. Martha's pain was such that she couldn't speak. Could barely move. She lay on the bed gritting her teeth and moaning.

Jeremiah located her houserobe and draped it around her. "We need to get you to the hospital. Now."

"I don't know that I can walk."

"Well, if I can't carry the likes of you, then I'm a Japanese aviator."

He gathered her up in his arms as a groom might his bride, the better to carry her over a threshold. In this fashion he carried her to the truck and set her in the passenger seat. She half lay there, moaning and gasping.

He got behind the wheel and cranked the engine.

He wanted to know what the phone was doing off the hook, but that question would have to keep.

He took out his cell phone as he drove and got Information to connect him to the hospital. The switchboard patched him through to the emergency room, and he told the nurse on duty they were on their way, and why.

Fifteen minutes later Jeremiah carried his wife into the emergency room.

The admitting nurse got to her feet immediately and showed them to an examining table in back. The ER doctor and a nurse materialized before Jeremiah could lay his burden down.

"You go wait out front," said the doctor, a middle-aged man Jeremiah had never seen before. The doctor patted him on the shoulder. "I'll be out to speak with you directly."

Jeremiah started to argue that he'd much rather stay put here, but the doctor gave him a look that said he'd get nowhere with his protest.

In short order he dropped onto the same couch where he'd spent Friday night. He looked around at the other poor souls there, some who sat watching a soap opera on the one television set, others at their magazines. He had hoped he was shed of this place for good. Now here he was again.

The admitting nurse took to the chair behind her desk and looked his way. "Would you like for me to see if I can find Doc Anderson?"

Jeremiah hesitated. "I'd as lief you didn't."

She looked a little surprised. "Okay."

Jeremiah crossed his arms and sat worrying.

At the courthouse, Karen said her tearful good-byes and drove off, headed to see her mother, carrying the tragic news that Sylvester Bradshaw's dismembered remains had been found in a collection of plastic picnic coolers at the bottom of a Burleson County stock tank.

On the ride back to the courthouse, Sonya had been in touch with Clyde once more by text message, and he had kept her apprised of his plan to leave the Daniels place as soon as he could without provoking raised eyebrows. Indeed, he rolled up at the courthouse curbside in his Impala shortly after Karen Bradshaw's departure.

They gathered in a conference room to discuss what next to do. Sonya briefed Clyde on the scene in front of the Daniels house, and Clyde described his day there. Dewey passed around copies of the report from the DPS crime lab, which they sat studying.

Clyde was the first to speak. "Shee-ut. Wonder what Cap'n Spur would think of this."

Dewey said, "Now that you mention it, maybe we should give him a call. See how his wife is getting along."

In response, Sonya leaned forward and keyed the speakerphone to life. The room filled with the sound of the dial tone. She consulted her legal pad and dialed in a number.

"This is Spur."

"Captain Spur, it's Sonya. I have Clyde and Dewey with me."

"Hey."

"How's your wife feeling?"

"Pretty poorly. We're down at Emergency. Doctor's taking a look at her now."

"I'm so sorry. We'll just talk to you later."

"Hell, let's talk now if you all got somethin'. Beats sittin' here in this waitin' room with my teeth in my mouth."

Sonya told him of all that had happened, finishing with a summary of the lab report. When she was done, there was silence on the phone.

Then Jeremiah said, "So the remains had been largely drained of body fluids, and they contained trace amounts of citric acid."

Dewey said, "As though they had been washed in a citric acid solution before they were packed away in those coolers."

"Sylvester's process uses citric acid, and them boys of his were experts at it."

Clyde said, "So were the Danielses, man. They'd picked up on it somehow themselves."

"Yeah, but there's the question of equipment. All the Danielses had was that tumbler you saw, right?"

"So far as I know."

"The Bradshaw boys had access to somethin' else, a machine capable of processin' greater volumes. Karen saw it when she was out there yesterday. I expect it would've taken equipment a good deal bigger than that tumbler to do ol' Sylvester."

"Hard to imagine sons would do their daddy that way."

"Yeah, well. In my experience, people have an almost unlimited capacity for surprise. What do you think, counselor? You got PC for a search warrant? 'Cause if we're right about all this, should be trace evidence all over the Bradshaw boys' place."

Sonya said, "It's a lock. I'll have the affidavit ready for Dewey to swear to inside of an hour."

Dewey said, "When you think we should serve it on 'em?"

"Early tomorrow mornin'. Just before sunup. That'd be my guess. Best time to catch 'em unawares. Here comes the doctor. I got to git."

With that the phone went dead.

The doctor walked Jeremiah's way, studying something on a clipboard. He looked up just in time to offer his hand. "Bryan Little," he said.

"Jeremiah Spur."

"You'll be happy to know, we have your wife reasonably stable. She's on an IV to get her rehydrated and something for the pain. It says here she was released just yesterday after treatment for *E. coli* poisoning. She was under the care of Doc Anderson, right?"

"Yep."

"I must say, I'm a little puzzled why he discontinued her antibiotics, but I'm sure he had his reasons. Anyway, he'll be around to see her sometime this afternoon."

"If it's all the same to you, I'd rather you stayed on her case till we're done."

The doctor cleared his throat. "That would be a little—I dunno. Unusual, I guess. Mind if I ask why?"

"The fact that we're back up here today and she's relapsed—"

"You're assuming it's a relapse."

"Well, ain't it? The symptoms are the by-God same."

The doctor shrugged. "We won't know for sure until we get her lab tests back."

"Well. I'd rather you kept her on as a patient."

"Sure. Happy to."

Later that evening, Martha was asleep in her hospital bed and Jeremiah had dozed off in a chair beside her when a hand on his shoulder brought him to. He looked up to see Karen Bradshaw standing there. She motioned for them to go out in the hallway.

Jeremiah eased the door shut behind him and turned toward her. "I heard about your pa. Can't tell you how sorry I am."

"To be honest, I don't think it's really sunk in yet, that he's gone. It has with Mama, though. The boys and I spent the evening with her. She's a wreck."

"I reckon so."

"We finally got her to sleep, and the boys went back to their place. I just couldn't stand to stay in that house any longer. Decided to come up here and make the pharmacy ready for me to be gone for a couple of days. Funeral arrangements and so forth. I see they admitted your wife again. How's she doing?"

"I dunno. She seems sicker than last time. If that's even possible. Dr. Little was in a little while ago. Said it looks like the *E. coli* again, but it ain't necessarily a relapse. Said he's not sure but what it's a different strain of bug from the first time."

"He has her on some heavy-duty meds, that's for sure. With orders that she's to stay sedated."

"Let me ask you somethin'."

"Okay."

"What are the odds of one person contracting two separate cases of
E. coli inside of a week?"

"Not very great."

"Figured as much. Somethin' ain't right here, but I'm damned if I
know what."

They stood in silence for a few moments.

Jeremiah said, "There's somethin' else you should know. The sheriff
is shapin' up to serve a search warrant on your brothers at first light.
The crime lab found traces of citric acid in your daddy."

"I know. They told me. And I told the boys tonight, and asked them
how they thought that could be. They didn't have what you'd call a
very good answer."

"No one is sayin' they did anything. Not at this point, at least. The
sheriff just wants to search the place."

"Mark told me he thinks the two of them are probably the prime
suspects. If the sheriff shows up at their front door, they'll know they
are. No tellin' what they might do." She bit her lip and looked away.

"You're worried there might be trouble."

"If they feel like their backs are against the wall—"

"It's how their daddy'd respond, I expect. You can't escape your antecedents."

They were quiet for a few moments.

"I best better warn Dewey, then, I reckon."

"That's another thing. Between the sheriff's ham-handedness and
the boys' unpredictability—" Of a sudden she seized Jeremiah's forearm. "Is there any way Dewey would let you ride along tomorrow
morning?"

Jeremiah shrugged. "Don't see what good that would do."

"I don't— I'd just feel better about it if you were there. To keep
things under control."

"Umm. I'm a little tied up. You know." He jerked a thumb toward
Martha's room.

"If you'll do this for me, I'll come sit with her while you're gone.
Gladly."

"I don't know. I—"

"Please, Captain Spur. I promise I'll stay with her every second. I can be of more help to her anyway. As a trained medical professional. You know."

Jeremiah worked his jaw. "I reckon I see your point. Alright. Let me call Dewey and make sure he's okay with it."

She exhaled. "Thank you. So much."

They sat in their little cabin, passing a bottle of Jim Beam back and forth until it was drained and then breaking the seal on a second one and having at it in similar fashion. With the single-minded purpose of men who have run out of options.

Luke was the first to speak. "They're comin' after us for sure, ain't they?"

"I expect. Wouldn't you if you was them, after what that lab report said?"

"But we ain't got nothin' to be afraid of, right? Innocent until proven guilty. Ain't that the way it is?"

"It is for the rich man. Last time I checked, we wasn't rich."

They drank some more in silence.

Mark said, "Thing about cops is, they get paid to find someone to point the finger at. Once they decide it's you, they don't stop until you're behind bars. In this case, they think they got scientific evidence to go by. Maybe even our own sister's word. And that old Ranger's. Shouldn't have taken a swing at the man, I suppose."

"Maybe we should make a run for it."

"Fuck that."

"Well, I don't know that I care to stand around and just let the law do us any way it damn well pleases. Which is sorta how it's beginnin' to feel to me."

"I got me an idea what we ought to do."

"What would that be?"

Mark handed the whiskey bottle to his brother and staggered from the room. When he returned he had a .30 caliber deer rifle in each hand. He leaned them up against the couch, where his brother sat drinking and watching him.

Then he left to get the shotguns and the pistols.

37

IN HIS DREAM HE WAS IN AN AIRPLANE THAT WAS ON ITS ASCENT, CLIMBING higher and higher, leaving the cloud cover far behind. Then he wasn't in the airplane anymore. He was by himself, way up in all that sky, so high he could see the curvature of the earth and beyond that the indigo vault, and nothing.

When he came to he saw that Martha was awake, too. She was staring at a chair in the corner of the room, and the look she gave it was such that Jeremiah turned to see what might be there.

"Do you see her?" Martha whispered.

"Who, sweetheart?"

"It's my grandmother Cecil, wearing that flowered housedress she always wore. Right there." She lifted a hand and pointed at the corner, where there was naught but a chair so far as Jeremiah could tell.

He got up and wet a washcloth and put it to his wife's forehead. "I think maybe you ought to think about gettin' a little more rest. You've had a time of it."

She kept on staring for some minutes, but after a while her eyelids began to droop and she once more drifted off. She was still asleep when Karen Bradshaw walked into the room at five o'clock.

When he got back to the ranch it was still full dark and the moon was hanging just above the horizon. He fed the dog, who whined pitifully from the moment Jeremiah stepped into the yard until the feed hit the bowl.

Jeremiah proceeded into the kitchen to fix some coffee. Opened the refrigerator to get the Folger's and stopped when he saw it once more.

"I wish you'd look," the state health department guy had said.

"At what?"

"How organized your wife is. I mean, unless you're the one sets all the bottles of juices and condiments just so, where their labels are facing out."

"No. That'd be her, alright. She's done it all her life."

There sat a bottle of orange juice. Turned so that you couldn't see the label.

Jeremiah fetched out the coffee and got it started. He walked back to his bedroom and switched the light on. Went to the bedside table and lifted the phone.

Punched REDIAL.

It rang once. A second time.

"You have reached the voice mail for Dr. Tres Anderson—"

He hung up the phone.

Ten minutes later he emerged from his bedroom, showered and wearing a fresh change of clothes. He unlocked his gun cabinet and opened the bottom drawer. Fetched out his SIG SAUER and a box of rounds and his handcuffs. Dropped the cuffs into his hip pocket. Loaded the SIG and a spare clip and strapped it on.

Back in the kitchen he took two dish towels from a drawer.

He reached inside the refrigerator and, using the towels so as not to touch it, removed the bottle of orange juice. He tightened the lid firmly and found a paper sack and set it inside and folded over the top.

Directly he was out of the house and headed for his pickup, paper sack in one hand, mug of black in the other.

Dawn was still a good hour off when Dewey arrived at the courthouse, but even so the weekly issue of the *Brenham Gazette* beat him there. The paperboy had leaned it against the courthouse door.

There was a light on inside the entryway, and it shone through the glass door and illuminated the front page. It was there, above the fold.

"Jesus H. Christ on a cast-iron crutch," he muttered.

He walked through the door and tossed the paper against the wall and headed upstairs.

He found them in the bullpen in his office, Jeremiah Spur and the two Powell twins, munching in silence on a box of kolaches and sipping coffee from foam cups. They looked like a Bible study group trying to get awake enough to discuss a chapter from First Samuel. Laid out next to the box of kolaches was the search warrant itself.

Dewey was more than happy to accept Jeremiah's offer of last night, to pitch in on this jackpot out at the Bradshaw boys' place. The way his luck had been running here lately, he felt like he needed every edge he could get.

When Dewey entered, everybody howdied him, and Jeremiah gestured in the direction of the pastries. "Brought us some breakfast."

Dewey tried to set his fury at the weekly paper to one side. He selected a kolache at random and bit into it. Ranchero. His gut would burst into flames well before lunchtime. Thanks to the mood he was in, he couldn't have cared less. "What do you reckon?" he said to Jeremiah. "Think they'll give us trouble?"

"They seem of a kind not to take well to the intrusion of armed law enforcement before the coffee's done finished makin'."

Dewey took another bite and chewed. It was like eating hot sauce straight from the jar. He could feel it going to work on the lining of his stomach. "You carrying?"

Jeremiah swept his sport coat aside to reveal the SIG riding on his hip.

Dewey held a knuckle to his chest and belched mildly. "That oughta do it. You want to ride with me?"

"I'll just follow you in my pickup."

Dewey took the search warrant in hand and tossed what was left of his kolache in a wastebasket. "That damn thing was hotter than the hinges of hell," he said.

On their way to the parking lot Dewey found he could not contain himself. "There's a article about me in the morning *Gazette*."

"I never read that thing. Never anything in it but cake recipes and death notices."

"Don't you want to know what's goin' on around town?"

"If I want to know what's goin' on around town, I go get a haircut. My barber has forgotten more about what's going on in this town— Hellfire, Dewey." Jeremiah turned and looked at the sheriff. "Was that you?"

"It was that damned ranchero kolache. They make me fart like a bloated mule."

The ride out to the Bradshaws' took fifteen minutes. Dewey had the lead, with his deputies in their cruiser behind him and Jeremiah bringing up the rear.

Dewey pulled off the highway and up the two parallel ruts that served as a driveway. He parked in the yard next to a pickup. The Powells pulled up next to him. The doors of both vehicles opened, and the men stepped out. The Powells were carrying sawed-off shotguns and wearing Kevlar vests.

Jeremiah had parked out on the highway right-of-way. He came walking up the driveway as Dewey went to the back of his cruiser.

Dewey opened his trunk and fetched out a Kevlar vest and shrugged it on. He whispered, "Sorry I ain't got a spare."

Jeremiah just shrugged. He saw little need for whispering given the racket the sheriff and them had made coming into the yard. The element of surprise would have been better served by them all parking out on the highway. Still, he kept his voice low. "I've always been of a mind that when your number is up, ain't no amount of Kevlar can do you much good."

"Even so. Why don't you bring up the rear?"

"I think maybe somebody ought to take the back door. Just in case they put up a fight and get a notion to try to flank us."

"It's all yours."

Jeremiah walked toward the corner of the house and eased around the side.

Dewey looked at the Powells. He'd like his job a sight better if the county had the funds to employ deputies who had more sense than these two here, but here they were, and they had a job to do. That his deputies were eat up with the dumb-ass was no excuse for not doing it.

The morning sun was just beginning to lighten the eastern sky.

Time to get on with, I reckon. Maybe if I can make a big-time collar in this Bradshaw business, people will not focus on the deficiencies relative to my johnson, the fact of which is now front-page news.

"Let's go," he said.

He led the way onto the porch. He positioned himself just to the left of the front door and motioned for the Powells to take up their stations on the right. He leaned against the doorjamb and knocked hard.

"This is the Washington County sheriff," he barked. "We got a warrant to search this place. Open up."

He stood listening and was raising his hand to knock once more when he got his answer.

Jeremiah eased around the side of the house, watching the windows as he went. He reached the backyard, grateful that so far they seemed to have escaped notice. There wasn't a sound to be heard.

He stood off to one side, where he had a clear view of the back door, but where he couldn't be easily spotted by anyone exiting through it.

This business of being up before dawn, approaching the residence of some murder suspect, warrant to be served—it had been a while since Jeremiah had seen live action of this kind.

Fact of the matter was, he missed it. He was having fun, and he felt alive in ways he hadn't since the day he retired. He'd even been all but able to put from his mind the plight of his poor wife, laid up in the hospital like she was.

He heard Dewey announcing himself in a loud Voice of Authority.

The next thing he heard was the sound of a shotgun discharging.

He turned and ran back down the driveway.

By the time he got back to the front yard the gunfire had become general.

The shotgun blew a hole the size of a bowling ball through the front door. Dewey and the Powells reacted as would anyone. They quit the porch in one leap over the boxwoods and made for the cover of the cruisers.

Gunfire issued from the front windows of the house, and slugs kicked up dirt and slammed into the automobiles. Dewey and David made it to safety, but Tom gave a cry and crumpled to the ground. Dewey went to his stomach and looked at Tom from under his cruiser. The deputy lay motionless, with his face turned the other way. A red stain was spreading on the back of his right leg, just above the knee.

Dewey tried to think what to do. His bookshelf full of management treatises wasn't of much use in this situation. *The Seven Habits of Highly Effective People* came up a habit or two short. His cheese had been well and truly moved, but to reclaim it could get him dead.

The gunfire had subsided.

Dewey looked under the car again, to see how Tom was doing. He was conscious and was trying to crawl to safety on his elbows. Dewey worried how long the man would have before that leg wound bled him to death.

He pulled his cell phone off his belt and dialed 911.

"Sheriff's Department. Please state the nature of your emergency."

"Becky, it's Dewey."

He tried to keep the excitement from his voice. He knew these calls were taped and could end up being played on television. It was important to appear in control. Especially in light of what the morning paper contained.

That thought gave rise to another one that began to bug him.

"Hey, Sheriff. What can I do you for?"

"Me and the Powells are trying to serve a search warrant at eleven seven ten Old Caldwell Road and have come under fire. Tom Powell took one in the leg. I need you all to send out an ambulance."

"What about backup? You need backup, Sheriff?"

This is where that thought came in, the one that had started bugging him.

He needed backup, sure as the world.

He would be damned if he would request it, though. What with that article about his underperforming manhood on the front page of the paper, he needed to do something heroic to offset that. He needed to show the people of this county that what mattered was not the lead in a man's pencil, but the starch in his spine.

Dewey needed a big fat *W* to erase this pesky *L* from his forehead.

He thought about the contents of the trunk of his cruiser.

All the backup he needed was in there.

Jeremiah appeared from the other side of the pickup, moving low to the ground. He came scrambling Dewey's way.

"Naw," he said, in a voice as Gary Cooper cool as he could muster, "I shouldn't've let 'em get the drop on us, but all we need do is get Tom looked after and we can take it from there. We got this sitchy-ation under control."

"Roger that. Ambulance is on its way."

He put the phone away as Jeremiah arrived. Dewey ducked his head and checked on Tom. The deputy had just about elbowed his way clear.

"Keep on comin', Tom. Ambulance is on the way."

Jeremiah said, "Backup comin,' too?"

"Who said anything about backup?"

Jeremiah worked his jaw. "Look, Dewey, this here is your rodeo. I just think it might not be a bad idea to call in the cavalry and then wait these boys out."

Dewey glared at the old Ranger. "You think I ain't got the chops to get this done? Huh?"

"Easy there, big fellow. I'm just outlinin' another option for you is all."

"I'll play this the way I goddamn well please."

"Fine, fine. Like I said. Your rodeo."

While the two of them had been going at it, Tom had managed to elbow his way around to the back of the cruiser, where he lay in a state of exhaustion.

"Let me have a look at your leg," Jeremiah said. He bent over and examined the deputy's thigh. "It don't look much worse than a scratch."

"Hurts like a sumbitch though. God damn," the man said through gritted teeth.

"Ambulance'll be here directly."

It had gotten uncommonly quiet. Jeremiah could just hear the ambulance siren in the distance. He looked at Dewey.

"You thought at all about callin' 'em and tryin' to talk 'em out?"

Dewey was fumbling with a ring of keys. "The time for talk ended when they started shooting Washington County peace officers. Now they're fixin' to find out we don't take kindly to that around here."

"I think you've watched too many Clint Eastwood movies."

"Very funny."

"Just what is it you got planned?"

Dewey grinned. He slotted a key into the trunk of his cruiser. The trunk lid bounced up a fraction of an inch. Dewey pushed it all the way open with the heel of his hand.

This action provoked more firing from the house. Rifle slugs slammed into the trunk lid. The men ducked their heads and waited for the barrage to end. At length it wore itself out and all was silent.

Jeremiah looked up. "Your trunk lid ain't gonna keep the rain out no more."

"Just one more reason to make these peckerwoods pay big-time."

"Whatever you say, Clint. Although I can't imagine Clint sayin' 'peckerwoods.'" Jeremiah turned toward their wounded comrade. "How you doin', Tom?"

The man said something unintelligible and groaned.

"A few stitches and you'll be good as new."

Dewey had about half his body in the trunk by now, keeping it low as he could, out of the line of fire. When he slithered back out, he had a launcher in one hand and a couple of tear gas grenades in the other.

Jeremiah said, "Where the hell did you get the riot gun?"

"It's on loan from a dealer."

"Good thing he wasn't peddlin' Sidewinder missiles, I reckon."

"What's that supposed to mean?"

"Look, Sheriff. We got these boys boxed in. We don't need to go to any extremes."

Dewey wasn't paying him any mind. He was turning the launcher over in his hands and looking at it like an aborigine might look at a golf club. "I saw the guy load this thing, but I'll be damned if I—"

Jeremiah said. "Gimme that."

"You familiar with this model?"

"You know what they say." Jeremiah took the launcher in hand and flipped a lever to open the breach. He slipped the two rounds into the magazine and closed it back up. He handed it back to Dewey. "One riot gun, one Ranger."

Dewey turned back toward the Bradshaw house. The targets mainly on offer were the two windows that looked out on the yard, either side of the door.

Dewey scooted on his butt toward the end of the bumper, the better to have an angle for his shot.

"Hang on a second," said Jeremiah.

Dewey turned back toward the man. "What?"

"We ought to get David to cover the back door, in case they make their exit thataway."

"Good idea."

"And before you light 'em up with the tear gas, I think maybe we ought to get his brother out to the highway, so the ambulance can fetch him to the hospital."

Dewey's eyes narrowed. "You're not playin' for time, are you?"

"No, Clint. I'm just tryin' to think this dadgum thing through."

"Fine. Go ahead, but let's hurry up, okay?"

Jeremiah worked his way over to where David Powell was hunkered down behind the other prowl car and told him what to do. David nodded and set his shotgun on the ground and moved to where his brother lay prone. Jeremiah followed.

They helped Tom to his feet, and the three of them moved as fast as they could toward the highway. Jeremiah and David half carried the wounded man. This action provoked more firing from the house.

Before long everything was set. Jeremiah had rejoined Dewey behind the cruiser, and David had made his way up the driveway to Jeremiah's former position, where he could keep an eye on the back door.

Dewey gave a quick nod to Jeremiah and began edging once more toward the side of the car. He used the bumper as a rest and shouldered the launcher.

He aimed at the window on the right and pulled the trigger.

A *whump* issued from the launcher followed by the sound of glass shattering.

"Bull's-eye," Dewey muttered.

He aimed and fired the second round. The occupants resumed their rifle fire. Those slugs that missed the cruiser went hissing overhead into the woods.

Dewey turned and scooted back to where Jeremiah waited, watching the front door of the cabin through the back glass of the cruiser. The firing subsided.

"Shouldn't be long now," Dewey said.

"I'll go check on David."

Jeremiah crab-walked around to the side of the pickup. David was at his post, watching the back door. He looked Jeremiah's way and gave a shrug.

Jeremiah turned and went back the way he came. "Nothin' goin' on back yonder."

A minute or two elapsed, and Dewey said, "I'm beginning to wonder—" Then he stopped and wrinkled his nose. "Is that tear gas?"

"Nope. Plain ol' smoke."

It was just then that they heard it for the first time. Crackling noises coming from inside the cabin. The sounds of a fire building.

"Oh, shit," Dewey said.

He crawled to the door of his cruiser and jerked it open. Reached in and took the two-way in hand. "Dispatch, this is Sheriff Sharpe. I'm going to need you to send the fire department out to this location. We got ourselves kindly an emergency here."

By the time he got back to Jeremiah's position, flames were coming through the window he'd shot out with the tear gas canister.

38

JEREMIAH SAID, "SHITHOUSE MOUSE."

Dewey looked at Jeremiah. "Think we ought to do anything?"

"Hell, yeah, we ought to do somethin'. You got a damn bullhorn?"

"Sure. In the trunk yonder."

Jeremiah unstrapped his SIG and laid it on the ground.

"What are you gonna do?"

Jeremiah got to his feet and reached in the trunk. He took the bull-horn in hand and thumbed it on. "Mark! Luke! It's Jeremiah Spur! I'm unarmed, and I'm comin' your way!"

"Are you crazy?"

Jeremiah proceeded up the front walk. He could smell the tear gas now. It began to work his nose and eyes. He took his handkerchief from his pocket and covered his nose.

The fire seemed confined to the rooms on the right side of the house. He got to the front porch and stopped.

He hollered into the bullhorn, "Listen to me. Y'all need to come out of there before you burn plumb up! Ain't nobody gonna shoot you, now! You have my word on it! So come on out! But leave your weapons behind!"

He stopped to listen. Wasn't even sure they could hear him above the fire.

Then all of a sudden the front door flew open, and they came stumbling out, coughing.

Jeremiah dropped the bullhorn and helped the two men down off the porch. They got to the front yard and sank to their knees, coughing violently.

Behind them the fire kept building until the entire house was ablaze.

278 | JAMES HIME

By the time the fire truck roared into the yard, the Bradshaw boys had been frisked and handcuffed and placed in the back of the Powells' cruiser. The firemen hit the ground and rolled out their hoses and began training streams of water on the conflagration.

The cruiser pulled out of the yard, headed down to County with David at the wheel. On his way he passed the ambulance, parked by the side of the road. His brother sat in back and watched while a medical technician worked on his wounded leg.

Dewey and Jeremiah stood watching Volunteer Fire work to get the fire under control.

Dewey said, "Feel sorta bad, I burned down their house."

"Yeah, well. They started it, what with shootin' at us like they did."

"I reckon this clears up ol' Sylvester's killin', huh? Hard to think his own sons done him that way. Killed him and then chopped him up like he was a side of beef. But nothin' says 'I'm guilty' like openin' up with your weaponry on somebody who's tryin' to serve you with a search warrant, ain't that right?"

Jeremiah worked his jaw. "I expect."

In another hour, it was about over. The firemen hosed down the rubble where the house had once been. Meanwhile a mobile DPS crime scene unit had rolled up. Dewey had called Austin the previous evening and asked them to send one around in anticipation of needing forensic help.

The crime scene techs had gone back behind the house to give the outbuilding a once-over. Directly they came around the side of the house carrying plastic evidence bags, and after they set them in the back of their vehicle they joined Jeremiah and Dewey.

Their names were Pickens and Stillwell. They were in their midthirties and full of piss and vinegar. Jeremiah could remember what that felt like, but just barely.

Pickens said, "We worked the barn over with luminol, and it lit up like Vegas."

Stillwell added, "Was a damn slaughterhouse of some kind."

Jeremiah said, "Human blood?"

Pickens said, "That we won't know until we can run some tests." He nodded toward the charred rubble. "This looks like a day at the beach."

"Well," said Jeremiah. "I'd love to hang around here and jaw with you all, but I got to get on." He turned to Pickens. "You got a second?"

"Sure."

"Come with me."

Jeremiah led the man to his pickup and opened the driver's side door. He produced a paper sack and handed it to the tech. "Need you to run an analysis on this."

The tech took the sack and looked at it. "What is it?"

"Bottle of orange juice."

"What am I lookin' for?"

"Test the contents for pathogenic bacteria. *E. coli*, in particular. Dust the thing for prints, too."

"I'm sorry. Who are you again?"

"Jeremiah Spur. I used to be—"

"No. That's okay. I recognize you now."

"Do this first thing when you all get back, okay? As in, before anything else."

"Sure. How do I reach you?"

They exchanged telephone numbers and parted company.

Jeremiah got behind the wheel of his pickup. He was bone tired and feeling out of sorts, now that the adrenaline had stopped flowing.

Part of it was, the whole Bradshaw mess was eating at him.

Dewey was right, of course.

The logical assumption to make was that innocent men do not set their hands to gunning down lawmen who are simply trying to do their duty. That seemed a pretty eloquent confession of culpability, what those boys had done.

And Lord knows they had motive a-plenty. Revenge for how their old man had treated them going back to when they were kids. Control of his invention. Who knew what all else.

Still. It sorted oddly with some of the other evidence. Such as their years of loyal service in the business. The fact that by all accounts they truly loved the man.

Families could get complicated. Jeremiah well knew this.

Maybe the answer was as simple as that.

He took his cell phone off the console. He powered it on. Once it got its bearings, the display told him he had three voice mail messages. He listened to them one by one. They were all from Clyde Thomas, and they were all variations on the same theme.

Shortly after that cold storage place opened at eight o'clock this morning, someone showed up and claimed the package of ground beef containing Sylvester Bradshaw's thumb.

Jeremiah wheeled into Washington County Cold Storage and slid into a space next to Clyde's Impala. He got out and walked inside. The counter was manned by a tall white man with a bald head who could not have looked more surly were he doing time in Huntsville.

"Hep you?" he mumbled.

"Lookin' for a friend of mine, Clyde Thomas."

"Through that door yonder and down the hall."

Jeremiah found Clyde seated at a desk, studying a computer monitor. Perched on the edge of the desk was a man with tightly curled hair and earrings in both ears and a funny way of holding himself, dressed in overalls that had been cut into shorts. He introduced himself as Nick Lockhart.

"I follow an alternative lifestyle," the man said, without the slightest provocation and even less need. He batted his eyes at Jeremiah as though they weren't focusing like they should.

"Pleased to meet you. Could you maybe give us a second?"

"Sure." The man got to his feet with a little hop. "Take all the time you need. Just don't take any of the office supplies."

Nick went flitting out the door. Jeremiah pulled the door to. "My Elizabeth swung that way, bless her heart. But I mean God Almighty."

"Tell me about it. He's been hittin' on me ever since I got here. Look at this."

Jeremiah walked behind the desk and leaned in to see. Pictured on the computer monitor was a grainy black-and-white image of the very customer receiving area through which he had just passed. In the lower right-hand corner of the screen was displayed in white numbers the date and time the image was recorded.

"What the heck am I lookin' at?"

"Let me back it up a second."

Clyde clicked the mouse, and a man walked backward away from the counter and out of the shop. Clyde executed another mouse click, and the man reentered.

"It's not the best angle in the world, unfortunately," Clyde said.

"Maybe not, but if that ain't Joe Bob Cole—"

"Yep."

"Ain't it common knowledge that he and the Bradshaw boys didn't get along?"

"Uh-huh. I broke up more than one fight between 'em myself, back when I was with the sheriff's office. Where you reckon he fits in?"

Jeremiah worked his jaw. "I'm a sumbitch if I know. Any way I can get a copy of that so I could play it for someone?"

"All I gotta do is burn it to a DVD. Take about five minutes."

"Let's get on with it, then."

Clyde loaded a disk into the computer. "Who you plannin' to show it to?"

"George Barnett. Joe Bob's been his project since Hector was a pup."

Clyde executed some on-screen maneuvers. Then he sat back. "Won't be long now."

"This here is a pretty slick setup."

"I'm glad it worked like it should, you know what I'm sayin'?"

"Impresses me no end. I never did understand computers worth a damn."

"I'm just learnin' myself when it comes to video surveillance. If I hadn't watched the techs do the installation down at Postelwaite's, I'd've been up a creek."

Clyde leaned forward and collected the DVD from the computer and slipped it into a paper envelope and handed it to Jeremiah.

Not long after Jeremiah left, Dewey commenced to wonder what purpose was served by his continued presence. He was tired and depressed, and that ranchero kolache from earlier was banging on the lower intestinal door.

He asked the crime scene techs if they needed him for anything else.

"I think we got it under control, Sheriff."

"Well, I'm like the monkey who was screwin' the skunk."

"Do what now?"

"I've enjoyed about as much of this as I can tolerate."

"We'll finish up here and fax you the report."

Dewey opened the door to his shot-up cruiser and stopped. In the driver's seat was a scattering of glass fragments. He pulled out his wallet and used it to scrape the shards off the seat onto the floorboard and out the door. When he could seat himself without fear of injury he got behind the wheel.

The vehicle brought to mind nothing so much as that scene in *Bonnie and Clyde* where the two of them buy the farm and their transportation gets shot up practically beyond recognition.

He turned the key in the ignition. Sure enough the engine turned over. The next problem was the windshield, which was spiderwebbed. Dewey went to work on it with his nightstick, clearing an area big enough for him to see through. It would be noisy, but he could drive.

He backed up, turned around, and headed to town. The drivers he passed stared and pointed.

His cell phone rang, and he took it in hand. The display read GEORGE BARNETT.

Hellfire and damnation. Just what I need. Bet he's callin' about that damn newspaper story.

He held the phone to his ear. "This is Sheriff Sharpe," he hollered.

A woman said, "Please hold for Mr. Barnett."

Came as no surprise that George felt he was above placing his own calls. When it came to aloofness and the high-handed treatment of his fellow man, George was a sixth degree black belt.

Nor did he waste his breath on pleasantries when he got on the line. "Dewey, I need you to come by my office. Right now." Dewey had to strain to hear the man.

"George, maybe you've forgotten, but you ain't the DA anymore, and you can't tell me what to do. You don't run this county."

"Would you like to rephrase that in the form of a wager? Where the hell are you anyway? What's with all the noise?"

"Look, I've had an awful morning, okay? Been in a live ammo fracas, and I need to go write it up."

"Fracas? What kind of fracas?"

"Went to serve a search warrant on the Bradshaw brothers, and they responded with gunfire. Hell, you ought to see my cruiser. It's more holes than car."

"How'd it end?"

"Their damn house caught afire and burned up. They're in custody."

"Huh. And hard on the heels of the old man meeting his demise."

"You heard about that, huh?"

"It's one of the things I need to talk to you about. I wonder who that leaves in charge of the business. The wife, maybe?"

"Hell, George, how would I know?"

"I reckon I ought to call that little shit Robert Bruni and ask. Maybe there'll finally be somebody involved who's got some business sense."

"Look, I got to get back to the office and file a report and I been out there all mornin' and I need to hit the head somethin' fierce and—"

"God damn it, Dewey. It's not like this law office isn't a part of the civilized world. We got a commode, and you're welcome to it. So you can either shag your ass over here right now or start figuring out who besides me is going to chair the finance committee of your reelection campaign."

Dewey groaned. "I'll get there quick as I can."

Ten minutes later Dewey pulled his cruiser to the curb in front of a two-story building facing on the town square. Given the absence of windows, he made no effort to lock the thing. He hurried into the building and up the stairs.

He disappeared into the men's room and reappeared a while later, feeling a measure of pity for any poor soul who happened to wander in there now.

He walked through the door that said GEORGE BARNETT, ATTORNEY AT LAW and into an area commanded by a receptionist Dewey recognized from back when George was protecting the peace and dignity of the state from his corner pocket at the courthouse.

"Howdy, Elaine."

"Go right on in."

Dewey pushed into George's office, which was nearly a replica of the one he had as DA, complete with a Wall of Honor on which were displayed photographs of George and every politician of note that had ever visited or needed anything from Washington County, from presidents down to state representatives. Also hanging there was George's taxidermy collection, featuring all manner of wildlife that he had personally dispatched.

George himself was standing at the window looking down at the street, smoking a cigar. The office smelled like the inside of a chimney.

He gestured with his cigar hand at the street below. "Damn if you're not driving the world's first ever fishnet automobile."

Dewey joined him. A crowd had gathered around his cruiser. People were taking pictures of it with their cell phones. A couple of kids had put their eyes to bullet holes as if there might be something inside to be peeped at.

"They really did a number on it."

George gestured at a guest chair. "Make yourself at home."

Dewey sat and propped his elbows on the armrests and steepled his fingers. George took to his chair and leaned back and rested his hand-tooled smooth ostrich skin boots on the desk, one crossed over the other, and puffed on his stogie. "So, you like the Bradshaw boys for what happened to their daddy?"

"I can't imagine they'd've started shootin' if they was clean."

George tapped ash into a tray cut from an artillery shell. He stuck the cigar between his teeth. "Maybe that makes the part of this meeting that has to do with Sylvester moot, then, but I'll go ahead and say my piece anyway. Spur came around to see me Sunday. He seemed to be suggesting I or one of my clients might have had a hand in what became of Sylvester. I just wanted to make sure we're clear on that between us. I ain't got any Negroes in the woodpile where that's concerned."

"George!"

The man grinned. "You gettin' all politically correct on us, Dewey?"

"Nobody says things like that no more!"

"I don't know why, to be honest with you. After all, I did use the polite form of the noun."

Dewey shook his head at the futility of such a discussion with a person of George's background and personality. "Okay. So now I know your woodpile is free of any Sylvester issues. That's not the only reason you wanted to see me, though, huh?"

George blew more smoke and tapped more ash. "This item in the morning paper. You might think you're the only one affected, Dewey, but I assure you, you're not."

Dewey shifted in his seat. "Wasn't anybody's pecker written about but mine."

"I'm afraid it ain't that simple. You've hauled off and exposed everyone who lives in this county to ridicule for having an incumbent sheriff who's lacking an essential male characteristic. Which would be testosterone adequate to permit him to be a man in the one way that's maybe the most important."

"Well. It ain't like I did it on purpose."

"Doesn't matter. The minty fresh Colgate cannot be coaxed back into the tube."

"I've heard that the Japanese say, after ninety days, no one remembers."

"This look like Tokyo to you, Dewey? This here is Brenham, Texas. People remember everything forever, right down to how many zits you had in the picture you took for the high school annual your sophomore year. No one is going to forget all the phone calls they're getting from their friends and kinfolks over in Waller County, or up in Burleson. Hell, I got an earful about it from my cousin this morning, and he lives way the hell over in Gonzales."

"That's damn near to San Antonio! How'd they hear about it over that way?"

"The Internet, Dewey. Apparently you got picked up by some kind of blog or somethin' and news about your erectile issues is on the verge of going national."

Dewey hung his head in despair. "Great day in the mornin'."

"We'll need to give this some careful thought, Dewey."

Dewey looked up. "We who? You and me?"

"Me and some of the other people in town who make the reputation of the Birthplace of Texas their very serious business."

They heard voices coming from the reception area. The door flew open and in walked Jeremiah Spur, followed by the receptionist, who was protesting that he couldn't do what he had just in fact done.

George called the receptionist off with a wave of his hand.

She stopped where she was. "I'm so sorry, Mr. Barnett."

"It's all right, Elaine. Just pull the door to, would you please?"

Once the door was closed, Jeremiah said, "You told me you didn't have anything to do with what became of Sylvester Bradshaw."

"That's right, and I just finished telling Dewey here the exact same thing."

Jeremiah was holding a square of paper. "You got a computer that'll play a DVD?"

"Sure."

"Load this up and take a look."

George dropped his feet to the floor and took the paper from Jeremiah. He slid the DVD into the computer that rested at his feet. He opened the file, and it played on the computer monitor that sat atop the credenza.

It revealed a video of Joe Bob Cole entering a business establishment and standing at a counter and then turning around and leaving.

George swiveled around and looked to the Ranger for an explanation.

Jeremiah pointed at the monitor. "That video was shot this morning over at Washington County Cold Storage, where Joe Bob laid claim to a package of frozen hamburger meat inside of which was buried the thumb of Sylvester Bradshaw."

George glanced at the computer monitor as though he would have it play the video again, and then he looked back at Jeremiah. "How in the world—"

"That's not important, George. What's important is, what did you and Joe Bob have to do with the murder of Sylvester Bradshaw?"

Dewey could see George was none too happy with either the question or the way it had been posed. "Speaking for myself, not one damn thing. I can't speak for Joe Bob."

"Bullshit, George. He doesn't scratch his ass unless you tell him where it itches."

George held up a hand. "Okay, wait a minute. There was one thing—this was months ago, now. He heard me pissin' and moanin' about how Sylvester was stiff-arming our every effort to engage him in some kind of discussion about his invention, and in response he offered to approach Doc Anderson on Happy Valley's behalf. He thought maybe we could get to Sylvester through Tres since the two of them were close."

Jeremiah thought for a few moments. "Well? Did he?"

"I don't know. The subject never come up again."

"Where do you reckon I could find Joe Bob?"

"It's a Tuesday. The office or the golf course one, I expect."

"Thanks." For the first time he seemed to take notice of Dewey. "You headed to the courthouse this morning?"

Dewey nodded. "Soon as George and I are done here."

"Why don't you show that DVD to the DA? She might could think of somethin' useful to do with it."

"Okay."

With that, Jeremiah walked back out the door.

39

JEREMIAH KEYED HIS PICKUP ENGINE TO LIFE, ENGAGED THE TRANSMIS-
sion, and set out. He took the highway out of town headed east, toward
the country club. He arrived at a subdivision of larger homes on well-
tended lots that sat behind gates on which hung a sign reading COUNTRY
CLUB ESTATES. The streets themselves were named after famous golf
courses. Augusta Drive, Shinnecock Lane, Winged Foot This, Colonial
That. Not being a golfer, Jeremiah was familiar with these names mostly
as words spoken by sportscasters in segments he had to suffer through
until they got to the team sports.

He drove until he found the street he was looking for.

Pebble Beach Drive.

He drove on until he pulled to the curb in front of a two-story stone
and brick affair with a gabled roof, flower beds bright with annuals.
The lawn had been mowed of late.

The mailbox read:

FRANK ANDERSON III, M.D.
6631 PEBBLE BEACH DRIVE

Jeremiah looked at the mailbox and he looked at the house.

Pebble Beach Drive.

Pebble Beach Investors.

Jeremiah took his cell phone in hand and fished in the pocket of his
shirt for a business card. He found it and dialed the office number for the
state microbiologist who'd been at his house on Saturday. Then he slipped
the transmission into drive and rolled away from Doc Anderson's house.

"Walter Gordon," the man said.

"Howdy. Jeremiah Spur here."

"Hello, Mr. Spur. How's your wife coming along?"

"She's took sick again."

"Yikes. Sorry to hear that."

"Got a question for you."

"Fire away."

"You said that these food poisoning outbreaks tend to affect large areas, right?"

"Usually we see hundreds of cases across a dozen or so states."

"Okay. Now, what about this outbreak that made Martha sick? Seein' that same thing happenin' elsewhere, are you?"

"You know, it's funny you should ask. We haven't had a single report of a similar case outside of your town. The whole thing seems to have been confined to that one store in Brenham. Why that would be, I have no idea."

Bet I do. "Okay. Thanks."

He cut the connection and sat thinking.

Today was Tuesday. The day of the week Martha, creature of habit that she was, went to the grocery store. Every Tuesday for thirty-plus years, she had been doing this.

His cell phone set up, and he looked at the display.

Damn.

He held it to his ear. "You hear about your brothers?" he said into it.

"I heard," said Karen Bradshaw. "I heard they also might be dead if it weren't for you. But that's not why I'm calling."

"Why, then?"

"To tell you, you better get over here. As fast as you can."

"She in her same room?"

"No. Come to ICU."

He cut the connection and fed the engine gas. He figured to be at the hospital in under five minutes.

Meantime, he had another call to make.

For want of any better way to spend his time, Clyde Thomas decided to pay a visit to Postelwaite's grocery store, to see how the test of his video surveillance system was holding up. His cell phone rang before he was halfway there.

He took it from his belt and glanced at the display. Held it to his ear. "Yo."

"You took off outta here yesterday like a scalded dog," said Isaac Daniels.

"Had someplace I needed to be, man."

"We had things to discuss with Knut that didn't involve you, so it worked out."

"You hear about what went down out at the Bradshaw boys' this mornin'?"

"Yeah. It's headline news on all the channels."

"Guess that's apt to slow down the licensing discussions, huh?"

"That happens when the counter-parties has their asses arrested. But that's okay. We were plannin' to back off a bit anyway. Seems your ol' girlfriend wants a session with Little Ty this afternoon. The lawyers are, like, negotiatin' the terms right now. Until all that noise is behind us, we gonna focus away from the Bradshaw thing."

"Makes sense, I reckon."

"So, anyway. Knut's flight back east leaves at three today. Can you be here by one to fetch him down yonder?"

Clyde rolled into the grocery store parking lot and slid into a space. He shifted the transmission into park and cleared his throat. "I'm afraid that won't be possible."

"What's that supposed to mean?"

"It means I'm tied up this afternoon, man. Get yourself another driver." Clyde almost said "boy," but he stopped himself in time.

In fact, he was a little surprised to hear these words coming out of his mouth riding a tone of voice with a slight edge. At the same time, it felt good. He'd been pushed around and taken for granted by the Danielses long enough. Time to find something to do that didn't have a tendency to remind him how long before he'd be dead.

"Fine," Isaac said, his own tone of voice conveying how he felt. "Just don't come around here, beggin' me to put your sorry ass to work."

The line went dead before Clyde could respond. "Okay, I won't," he said out loud as he clipped the phone back to his belt.

Inside the store he took a seat at the command station he had set up in the back room and fell to checking the computer monitors, hard drive, and camera angles. He was almost done when his phone rang again. This time, it was Captain Spur.

"What's up, man?"

"How long you had your video gear in Postelwaite's?"

"About two weeks."

"Got the produce section under surveillance, do you?"

"Got the whole store on film. Why?"

"Can you go back and check the tapes from produce prior to last Wednesday? I think maybe somebody contaminated the bagged spinach and that's how come Martha to take sick."

"You think it might have been Joe Bob?"

"Maybe. Or Tres Anderson."

"Doc Anderson? Are you kiddin' me?"

"I take it you know him."

"Yeah. Used to see him up at Emergency back when I was with the sheriff's office. Seemed like the nicest man God ever made."

"I thought so, too. Not sure what to think anymore. Can you do like I asked?"

"Sure. I'm actually up there now. Might take a few hours."

"Thanks. Call me if you come across anything interesting."

The line went dead. Clyde put the phone back on his belt and went to work.

Sonya Nichols hung up the phone just as Dewey walked into her office. She folded her hands on her desk as he dropped into a chair.

The walls were hung with modern art, and on her desk an orchid sat in a vase. Family photographs adorned the bookshelves together with a small collection of seashells and other artifacts. Dewey had never submitted himself to the indignities of psychological counseling, but he could imagine the proceedings taking place in an office such as this were he ever to do so.

"You're having quite the day, Sheriff."

He turned his head and looked out the window. "It's like those Southwest Airlines ads where somebody does something completely stupid and embarrassing and the voice-over says, 'Ever wanna get away?'"

"This too shall pass."

"Why do we keep relearning the same lessons in life? That's what I'd like to know. Like, for example, Mr. Ranchero Kolache is not our friend. My gut has been in an uproar all damn day on account of my dadgum breakfast, and it's given me a case of—"

"Is there anything I can say to persuade you to choose with greater care the information you share with me?"

Dewey seemed not to hear. He sat looking out the window at the birds in the trees. "I think the day God made the grackle, his mind was elsewhere."

Sonya gestured at the phone. "It might interest you to know, I was just talking to the Danielses' lawyer. He's agreed to bring Little Ty in this afternoon to make a statement if we'll share whatever evidence we have with them. Which we're really not obligated to do at this point, but I see no reason not to. He says he's been through everything with his client and is convinced there's no chargeable offense here."

"What about the thumb?"

"What are we going to charge him with? Possession of stolen property? It's not like he's the one who cut it off."

Dewey looked at her. "Doesn't sound like the Dragon Lady I know."

"It's called prosecutorial discretion. I have the power to exercise it as I see fit."

"Uh-huh."

"Don't get all cynical on me."

Dewey sighed. "I guess I ought to be happy. He'll play out the season and maybe lead the Ags to the national championship."

"Looks that way." Sonya nodded in the direction of the DVD Dewey had in his hand. "Whatcha got there?"

In response, Dewey handed it across the desk. "Video evidence of who might have took Sylvester Bradshaw's thumb."

Sonya turned around and popped the DVD into her computer. It opened onto the screen, and she watched it. Then backed it up and watched it again.

"I'll be damned," she said.

Joe Bob Cole pulled off of Highway 290 onto the frontage road just south of the Washington County line. He was at the wheel of the same pickup he'd used to carry the picnic coolers up to that tank in Burleson County early Saturday morning. On the seat next to him rested a package wrapped in white butcher paper.

Time to have shed of this thumb problem once and for all. God *damn* but it would never do to have random incriminating body parts bouncing all over Creation.

Body parts. Ugh.

Made Joe Bob about half sick to his stomach to think back on last Friday night. All that damn blood. The whine of the saw as it cut bone.

He wouldn't have thought the man capable of that kind of butchery, but that was before all this.

Ever since Tres had come to him with this scheme of his for getting rid of Sylvester Bradshaw and taking control of his technology, it seemed like the man had just grown harder and colder and less feeling by the day. Or maybe that's who he'd always been, deep down inside, and he'd mastered the skill of presenting the world a false front. Some people could do that, Joe Bob knew.

Maybe if a man sees enough weakness and disease and pain and suffering in people, enough whining about fate and how it's done you dirty thanks to your cancer or your heart problems or your gout, he starts to hold all of humanity in low esteem. Like the disease he cures them of is their fault, something that could have been avoided if only they were somehow *better.*

As to the purity of the doctor's motives in this caper, Joe Bob had his own big-time doubts, despite how the man portrayed it.

Yeah, he had heard all Tres's big talk about how he wanted to make the process available for the good of humanity, how he was tired of seeing Sylvester Bradshaw's ego, his need for control, his cussedness, stand in the way.

For his part, Joe Bob couldn't help but wonder, was there more to it than that? Had Doc Anderson grown so tired of Sylvester's tendency to piss people off for the sheer pleasure of it, his perennial surliness, that he just decided the planet would be a better place without the man?

That came as close to anything to explaining why it was ol' Doc took the Skil saw to Sylvester with such relish that night, in the shed back of the Bradshaw boys' cabin, Hippocratic Oath be damned. He'd put on rubber gloves and rubber apron and clear plastic mask and just gone to town.

He'd said at the time that putting Sylvester's body parts through his own process would be the best way to eliminate any evidence that could trace back to the two of them. Sounded good in theory. The practice of it like to made Joe Bob sick up.

Joe Bob had to wonder whether Doc didn't enjoy dismembering Sylvester just a bit more than he should have. He'd even laughed and said it was more fun than surgery since it didn't matter if he cut something the wrong way.

Those trailer trash Bradshaws were never the wiser, thanks to the sedative the doc had administered to their dead-to-the-world drunk asses upon their arrival with Sylvester's body in the bed of Joe Bob's pickup, covered up with a tarp. Doc had simply walked into the house and injected them with dope, pretty as you please.

Doc had said the medical examination of Sylvester's remains would turn up residues of citric acid in the tissue and that would tie the Bradshaw boys to the murder, along with the trace evidence he and Joe Bob left in the shed.

The one slipup was the thumb Little Ty just had to have as proof that Sylvester would not return from wherever he'd gone and once again resume his lifelong role of skunk at the garden party. Even that could be pinned on the Bradshaws, probably.

Joe Bob pulled to the side of the road just before he reached his destination, a bridge over the Brazos River. He took the package off the seat and stepped out of the pickup.

He walked the short distance to the bridge and stood looking around.

Then he dropped the package over the side and watched it sink out of sight in the brown water.

Jeremiah found Dr. Little and Karen Bradshaw waiting for him outside the door to Martha's room in ICU. Their worry was evident on their faces.

The doctor spoke first. "I'm sorry to have to tell you this, but your wife has taken a serious turn. About an hour ago her fever shot up and she went into convulsions. She does not seem to be responding at all to the course of treatment. If anything—" He stopped.

Karen said, "The truth is, we don't know what we're dealing with here. If it were the O157:H7 bug, it should be under control by now. This is some other strain. One we're not sure how to treat."

"If she doesn't improve," said Dr. Little, "we could be looking at re-nal failure soon. Maybe worse."

Jeremiah worked his jaw. "She awake?"

"She was a few minutes ago."

"Okay if I go in there?"

"Sure."

He let himself in and eased to his wife's side. The room was crammed with tubes and machines and the other mystifying implements and ac-coutrements of modern medicine.

He leaned in and kissed Martha on the cheek. "How you doin', sweetheart?"

She looked at him. He could see the fever at work in her eyes. "I want to ask you to do me a favor," she said in a voice that was but a whisper.

He took her hand in his and leaned in. "What's that, dear?"

"Actually." She closed her eyes for a moment and swallowed hard and opened them again. "It's more like two favors."

"Let's hear 'em."

"I want us to be buried next to one another."

"Hush, now. You don't need to be talkin' like that."

She swallowed again. "Be still and hear me out. All Rangers can apply to be buried with their wives in the state cemetery in Austin. Right?"

He nodded. He suddenly could not trust himself to speak.

"That's where I want you to bury me. That's where I'll wait for you."

"Martha, I—"

She stopped him with a weak wave of her hand. "The other thing is, when I'm gone, I want you to find someone new to share your life with, and I don't want you to feel badly about it."

"I wish you'd stop—"

"I mean it, Jeremiah. You have been a wonderful husband, and I love you with all my heart, but I hate to think on you alone. Men don't do well alone. So you promise me, okay? And I'm fine with it if she's bur-ied next to you, but I want to be on your left. That's where I've slept for better than thirty years, and I'm claiming that for myself."

Jeremiah swallowed and squeezed her hand and tried to think what to say. He worked his jaws and blinked his eyes, and finally he responded how he'd more or less always responded to her. How men in love have responded to their women since time immemorial.

"Yes, ma'am," he said.

It took Clyde three solid hours to find what he was looking for.

According to the date on the screen, it happened just before closing time, a week ago yesterday. Doc Anderson appeared on-screen from the bottom, as though doing his regular produce shopping. He was pushing a cart before him.

He stopped and tested the avocados for firmness. Bagged a couple and set them in the cart. Moved onto the tomatoes. Selected a package of them.

Stopped in front of the counter where the bagged spinach was on display. As though just now noticing it. Pushed his cart to one side and stood with his stomach practically pressed against the counter. Apparently oblivious to the video camera that was capturing his every move.

From almost any other angle, he would seem merely to be reading the nutritional label, but what the camera had recorded was the doctor taking a hypodermic syringe from his coat and carefully inoculating a half dozen packages of spinach. He tossed a clean package of spinach into his basket and moved out of the shot.

"Son of a bitch," Clyde said.

He backed up the file and slipped a DVD into the computer.

Clyde reached for his cell phone and dialed up Jeremiah Spur.

It rang once. Twice.

Damn. Gonna get voice mail for sure.

Martha had nodded off, and when next she awoke she was afflicted with cramps so severe that Jeremiah called for the nurses and then left the room while they tended to her.

He stood out in the hallway listening to the sounds of pain from within and tried to be tough-minded. He didn't care for the worries and concerns that were growing in his head, the fear that had set up in his insides.

He wouldn't let himself think about it. About what such a deprivation as he now feared would mean for him and his life.

He'd been married to this woman for so long.

His cell phone had rung a couple times while he was sitting with her,
but he had ignored it. Now he took it from his pocket and looked at the
display.

Two calls, one from Clyde Thomas, and one from a number he
didn't recognize.

He called Clyde back.

"Where you at, man?"

"Over at the hospital. Martha's faring poorly."

"Damn. Sorry to hear."

"How are things on your end?"

"Found what you thought I'd find, in the video archives at Postelwaite's. I got Doc Anderson on film, slippin' a hypodermic needle to
packages of bagged spinach. The good doctor infected the greens, man,
and we got him doin' it."

"Good job." Jeremiah worked his jaw. "You make a copy?"

"Damn straight."

"Take it to the sheriff. Tell him to look at it and then sit on it and that
I'll be in touch."

"Got it."

Jeremiah cut the connection and called the other number.

"Ace Pickens."

"This is Jeremiah Spur, returning your call."

"Oh, terrific. Just wanted to let you know. We analyzed that orange
juice like you asked."

"Yeah?"

"Damn, it was nasty. Full of *E. coli*. Not just any kind, either. Was a
particular strain known to produce what doctors call extended-spectrum
beta-lactamases. That means they are highly resistant to antibiotics and
extremely difficult to treat."

Jeremiah looked up and saw Dr. Little walking his way.

He said into the phone, "If you don't mind, I'm gonna put someone
on the line, a doctor, and I want you to tell him just what you told me."

Jeremiah walked up and handed the phone to Dr. Little. "This is a
DPS crime scene tech, callin' about an analysis I asked him to do of a
bottle of orange juice that came out of my refrigerator at home."

The doctor held the phone to his ear. "This is Dr. Little."

As he listened to what the caller had to say, the doctor's eyes grew wide.

That entire night, he never left her side. He sat and held her hand and mopped her brow and studied her face and wondered would she make it to the following morning.

Dr. Little had hung up from talking to Pickens and immediately ordered that some new treatment protocol be followed. They'd changed her medicine and taken various steps of a medical nature that were alien to Jeremiah and well beyond his kin.

All he knew to do was sit and wait and hold his wife's hand.

So that is what he did.

About an hour before dawn he walked out of the hospital and climbed into his pickup truck.

40

THE ALARM CLOCK NEXT TO TRES ANDERSON'S BED WENT OFF AT SIX o'clock that morning. He sat up and stretched and went into the bathroom to see to his person, humming a hymn as he splashed water into his eyes.

He came out shrugging on a robe and yawning. Stuck his feet into some bedroom slippers and padded into the kitchen.

He went to the refrigerator and fetched out a bottle of orange juice. He poured himself a glass and set the bottle back inside. He swallowed his blood pressure medication and a few other pills, taking large gulps of juice with each pill.

He went back to the refrigerator and opened the freezer compartment to pull out a bagel for breakfast, and when he closed the door he jumped slightly, for standing there in his kitchen holding an automatic pistol on him was Jeremiah Spur.

"What in the world— What are you doing here? Why are you pointing that gun at me?"

"I came here to watch you die."

Jeremiah pulled a pair of handcuffs from his hip pocket and crossed the room. He hooked the doctor up to his refrigerator door and stepped back. He holstered his weapon.

"Watch me die?"

Jeremiah dropped into a chair at the breakfast table and kicked another chair in Tres's direction. "Here. Might as well be comfortable while you're waiting for the *E. coli* to go to work."

The doctor sat down. "What *E. coli*?"

Jeremiah nodded toward the juice glass. "It was in the juice you just drank. You see, I swapped what was in my refrigerator for what was in yours. I expect you know what that means."

"I don't know what you're talkin' about."

"Sure you do. When Martha started feelin' poorly on Monday she called you. You come over and tampered with my orange juice and somehow infected her with more bacteria. Which saw her back into the hospital before the day was out."

"You can't prove that."

"I took a sample from the orange juice bottle and gave it to the DPS crime lab up in Austin. They found the *E. coli*."

"That doesn't have anything to do with me."

"Yeah, it does. You see, they also lifted your fingerprints off the bottle. They know they're yours, because every doctor in the state is fingerprinted by the Texas Medical Board as a matter of course, to weed out the ones hiding their convictions. It was just a matter of running a check against those records."

The doctor sagged a little in his chair.

"Oh, and we also got you on film shooting up bagged spinach at Postelwaite's. Guess you didn't know the man had recently installed video surveillance."

"I never did any such thing."

"Fine. Be that way. We'll just sit here while those bugs go to work on your insides. Or—"

"Yeah?"

"Or I could call the sheriff to come lock your ass up and get you some medical attention. Before your kidneys start to give out."

The doctor cleared his throat. "Well. Why don't you?"

"I might. First I want to know why you chopped up Sylvester Bradshaw. You and Joe Bob Cole. And what possessed you to poison my wife with a damned bacteria."

The doctor snorted, and his eyes grew cold. "The first one is easy. Sylvester Bradshaw needed to be dispensed with. He was single-handedly preventing the triumph of man over disease. Not to mention, running a company that I was half owner of into the ground before my very eyes."

Jeremiah leaned his chair back and set his elbow on the breakfast table. "It always comes down to money, don't it?"

"Not to mention, the man always has been a greedy, insufferable fool. I mean since the day he was hatched."

"You can't escape your antecedents. Where's Joe Bob fit in?"

"At my age, I needed someone to help me in dealing with Sylvester, and Joe Bob Cole was only too happy to oblige, in return for a promise of part of the profits from the technology, once it's in widespread use. It would have all gone just fine if you had stayed out of it, old friend."

"Just too bad Martha ended up buying one of those bags of spinach, huh?"

"That does indeed seem to be what has brought us here today."

"And you spiked the spinach because—"

"To create grounds for a lawsuit against Happy Valley, of course. Which would force them to deal with us on the technology, as a consequence. However, when I saw Martha in the hospital on Saturday morning, I realized her case was so mild that it was unlikely to lead to any meaningful liability. So I decided to raise the stakes a bit. I had a rather more lethal strain of bacteria in Sylvester's lab, and I used that to contaminate Martha's water glass at the hospital."

"That would have been only too easy to do, I reckon."

"The fact that by then Karen Bradshaw had called you, undoubtedly to ask you to help find her missing father—well, I thought there might be an added benefit. That a deathly ill wife might be enough to distract you from making any real effort toward finding out what happened to Sylvester. Seems I underestimated you."

"I reckon."

"I was also a trifle concerned that if someone dug deep enough they would realize that Martha had fallen victim to two different strains of the pathogen instead of one, and only one strain would be found in the spinach, of course. So I decided to load up your orange juice as a way of explaining where the second strain originated. How did you know about that, by the way?"

"You left the bottle such that the label wasn't turned out. Martha ain't done that in her life. I knew as soon as I saw it, it had been tampered with."

"It seems I've gone and drunk my own poison, then." The doctor chuckled and ran a hand through his white hair. "So. Are you really going to sit there and watch for the entire three-day incubation period? I'm afraid we'll run short of things to talk about."

Jeremiah looked away and worked his jaw. When he looked back, he said, "Reckon it'd be less painful for both of us if I just went ahead and blew your brains out, huh? Save us both some time and aggravation."

"That's not what I meant—"

Jeremiah let the front two legs of the chair down and got to his feet. He walked over to where the doctor sat.

He took his pistol from its holster and placed the muzzle against the man's temple and cocked the hammer.

He could see the man trembling where he sat.

"On second thought," Jeremiah said, "you ain't worth the powder it would take to blow you to hell."

He took the gun from the man's head and let the hammer down and walked slowly from the room.

"Wait!" called the doctor. "Jeremiah! Wait!"

Dewey Sharpe stood at the foot of Tres Anderson's driveway and watched Jeremiah walk out the front door of the house and come striding his way.

When he reached Dewey's position, Jeremiah stopped and stood looking at the horizon to the east. It was just past sunup.

"Red sunrise again," Jeremiah said. "Gonna rain later."

"I expect."

Jeremiah unbuttoned his shirt pocket and fetched out a microcassette recorder. He dropped it into the palm of Dewey's hand. "It's all there. You all can go get Joe Bob now."

"Many thanks."

Jeremiah turned on his heel and headed to where he'd parked his pickup by the side of the road.

Dewey hollered after him. "What about Doc Anderson?"

Jeremiah turned around. "What about him?"

"Should I take him in?"

Jeremiah looked toward the house, and then he looked back at Dewey. "Give him a couple hours to sit there and think about it. He ain't goin' nowheres. Then you can run his sorry ass in."

He turned and proceeded toward his pickup.

"Thanks," Dewey hollered.

Jeremiah raised a hand in response and kept going.

41

TWO DAYS LATER, SYLVESTER BRADSHAW WAS LAID TO REST IN A CERE-
mony conducted at the Free Will Baptist Church followed by a reception at Bourré. It was better attended than most people would have
figured, given Sylvester's dyspeptic ways. Although it could be some of
the folks showed up just to make sure the man was well and truly dead.

His two sons were there. They had been let out on bail so they could
join the others in attendance. Robert Bruni was already working on a
deal that would see them plead to a resisting arrest charge. This would
have them doing six months in County plus making restitution for the
automobiles and deputy they'd shot up.

The thing that most surprised the Bradshaws was the two dozen or
so mourners from Brenham's black community who came to pay their
respects to the man who had shared with them the technology that had
improved the health of their loved ones. They sat in a couple rows to
themselves and cried and said "Amen" from time to time.

Even Big Ty Daniels put in an appearance, wearing a three-piece suit
that was the most expensive ensemble by far in the place. At the reception, he took Bruni aside and told him he'd still be interested in pursuing a licensing arrangement for the technology, once the estate was
probated and someone could act on behalf of the heirs.

Karen stood watching her father's lawyer talk to the town's biggest
celebrity, just wishing it was all over so she could go home. She couldn't
remember the last time she'd been so tired, after the late nights with her
mother and at the hospital. She felt like she could sleep for a month.

She saw the sheriff making his way toward her through the crowd.
He carried his hat in his hand and he had about him a hangdog look,
and she figured she could guess what was coming.

He stopped at her side and cleared his throat. "I just wanted to say,

I'm sorry about your pa. And about what become of your brothers' house and all."

She looked him over and decided she was too sorrowful and weary to make anyone else's life any more miserable than it already was. "No one thinks you meant to set that house on fire, Sheriff. Least of all me."

"I appreciate your understanding."

"Besides, the boys should have known better than to start shooting at you all. That's just the kind of hostile attitude that served Daddy so poorly through his life. So I guess they came by it honest."

"I reckon."

She sighed and looked around the restaurant. "I just wish I knew what to do with this place."

The sheriff looked at her in surprise. "Beg your pardon?"

"The restaurant. The technology business. With the boys in all likelihood going to jail for months, I'm stuck trying to figure this out on my own. I'm not trained in business matters, Sheriff. I'm a pharmacist. I don't know anything about building or running a profit-making enterprise."

"Well, maybe I could help."

Karen gave him a sharp look.

"No, seriously. My college degree was in accounting, and I took a boatload of business courses. Plus I've read every management bestseller that's ever been written. I'd be proud to talk to you about instituting inventory control systems, hiring practices, what have you. I took an entire semester in entrepreneurship, too. Bet I could help you figure out what to do with your all's technology."

"But don't you have a job?"

Dewey glanced in the direction of George Barnett, who was having a three-way conversation with Big Ty and Bruni. "I'm actually thinkin' about runnin' for county judge next term. Ol' Lee Ellison is gonna retire, and some of the local powers that be—well, they've suggested that might be a good move for my political career. That's not really a full-time job these days, so, you know . . ."

Karen shrugged. "Let me think on it, and I'll get back to you."

"Okay. Fair enough. Plenty of time for that. And, listen. I am truly sorry for your loss and how all this ended up."

Jeremiah Spur was likewise in attendance. He was talking with Sonya Nichols about her plans to have Joe Bob Cole and Tres Anderson arraigned the following day when Congressman Albright came up and stole her away to talk to her about her statewide ambitions, which seemed to be gathering momentum by the hour. Jeremiah stood awkwardly by until George Barnett walked up and laid a hand on his shoulder.

"I can't believe Joe Bob got himself all tangled up in this damned Sylvester business."

"I know y'all was close, George, but I had to do what I had to do."

"I hear you."

"No bad blood?"

"What would the point of bad blood be?"

"I reckon you're right."

"Dewey's probably not gonna stand for reelection, by the way. Has his eye on the county judge's seat."

"I heard Lee was retirin'."

"County's gonna need a new sheriff, old friend."

Jeremiah looked at George. "I'll study on it. I just don't aim to study on it today. Got more important things on my mind."

"I understand. I surely do."

They shook hands, and George walked off, leaving Jeremiah to his own thoughts.

Directly Clyde Thomas strolled over and stood, sipping from a glass of ice tea.

"How's the video surveillance business lookin' these days?" Jeremiah said.

Clyde shrugged. "Hard to tell what the reaction is gonna be in these parts to bein' filmed when you go about your daily life. Big test is Postelwaite's. He's supposed to let me know, end of the week."

"Good luck."

"Thanks, man."

"You ever think about goin' back to law enforcement for a livin'?"

"I dunno. I might could get tempted. Word is, you givin' that some thought yourself."

"I guess I miss it some. I did love it all those years. A thing can only be what it is. You know?"

"So they say." Clyde stuck out his hand. "Let me know where you end up with that."

They shook, and Clyde wandered off.

Jeremiah stayed until there were just a few mourners left, and then he got in his pickup and drove toward town.

He clicked on the radio, and the opening chords to a song issued from it.

> *There's a place that I love*
> *It's like Heaven above*
> *Especially if you are a guy*
> *A wide spot in the road*
> *You can lay down your load*
> *Where armadillos go to die*

He listened to the lyrics all the way through. He hadn't realized how mournful it could sound, this song about the armadillos going someplace to die.

He didn't much feel like being all mournful and melancholy today, even though he had just been to a funeral. No, indeed, he did not.

The weatherman had promised them it was done raining for now and they had a stretch of fair weather ahead. That would give him a chance to catch up on his sorely neglected chores around the ranch.

Day after tomorrow, the Ags would tee it up against the Arkansas Razorbacks, in the Ozarks. That would be a game worth watching. The Hogs might could stay in the game till halftime. Especially in their home stadium.

Jeremiah was already looking forward to reading the Sunday newspapers, lingering over the postgame interviews in which the opposing coaches would sound as though they had had their wits stole in the service of trying to stop Little Ty.

In a few weeks' time the late summer heat would abate and winter would set in.

The next song the DJ spun up was more to his liking.

"Right in Time," by Lucinda Williams.

He hummed along up until he pulled into a parking space at the hospital and killed the engine.

He was whistling it when he walked through the door, and immediately he saw Martha, waiting in her wheelchair, nurse in attendance.

His bride's hair all done, makeup in place. Flowers in her lap. Smiling.

Pretty as a picture.

He doffed his Stetson and smiled right back.

"You ready to go home?"